Books by JEROME WEIDMAN

NOVELS

I Can Get It for You Wholesale
What's in It for Me?
I'll Never Go There Anymore
The Lights Around the Shore
Too Early to Tell
The Price Is Right
The Hand of the Hunter
Give Me Your Love
The Third Angel
Your Daughter Iris
The Enemy Camp
Before You Go
The Sound of Bow Bells
Word of Mouth
Other People's Money
The Center of the Action
The Temple

THE BENNY KRAMER SEQUENCE

Fourth Street East
Last Respects
Tiffany Street

SHORT STORIES
The Horse That Could Whistle "Dixie"
The Captain's Tiger
A Dime a Throw
Nine Stories
My Father Sits in the Dark
The Death of Dickie Draper

ESSAYS AND TRAVEL
Letter of Credit
Traveler's Cheque
Back Talk
A Somerset Maugham Sampler

PLAYS
Fiorello!
Tenderloin
I Can Get It for You Wholesale
Asterisk: A Comedy of Terrors
Ivory Tower (with James Yaffe)

THE TEMPLE

a novel by

Jerome Weidman

SIMON AND SCHUSTER

New York

DESIGNED BY EVE METZ
MANUFACTURED IN THE UNITED STATES OF AMERICA

2 3 4 5 6 7 8 9 10

LIBRARY OF CONGRESS CATALOGING IN PUBLICATION DATA
WEIDMAN, JEROME
THE TEMPLE.

I. TITLE
PZ3.W4257Te   [PS3545.E449]   813'.5'2   75-19212
ISBN 0-671-22100-0

FOR
ELIZABETH ANN AND BENNY

All day long, and all night through,
One thing only must I do:
Cool my pride, and quench my blood,
Lest I perish in the flood.

Countee Cullen

PART I

1

"You're young and you're young and you're young," his father had once said. "Then one day you look in the mirror, and you realize you're not young any more."

Looking into his bathroom mirror, Dave Dehn realized his father had been right again. This pleased Dave. The old man had never been wrong. Or so Dave liked to believe. Today, on his sixtieth birthday, Dave was not only pleased. He wished the old man were alive. He would have enjoyed Dave's pleasure.

The phone buzzed. Dave put down his razor. He crossed to the small table beside the bathtub. Twenty-eight years ago, when Dave had acquired the land and set the project in motion, the architect had sketched the tub into the drawing he made for what was to be Dave's private suite on the third floor.

"Yes, Fanny," he said.

Dave didn't have to ask who was calling. Not on this phone. It was sure to be Fanny.

"First," Fanny said, "happy birthday."

She had come to work for him while the compound was still under construction. In 1947 Fanny had been what she herself described as no chicken. The staff Social Security records in the office downstairs were more specific. They indicated that in 1947 Fanny had been forty-three years old. That meant that today, when her boss was touching the sixty mark, Fanny Mintz was at least seventy, possibly seventy-one. Nobody, Dave felt, would know it from her voice. She still sounded like Jimmy Cagney laying it on the line.

"Thanks," Dave said. "And second?"

"You know a girl named Renata Bazeloff?"

"Nobody is named Renata Bazeloff," Dave said.

"D.D., please," Fanny said. "This is important."

Dave did not doubt it. His bathroom phone did not go through the big switchboard downstairs. Only three people had the unlisted number. Of these three, only two used it the way Dave insisted it be used. His partner, Sid Singer. And his Gray Eminence, Fanny Mintz. When either one called him in the bathroom, Dave knew it was important.

"How important?" he said.

"You tell me first if you know anybody named Renata Bazeloff," Fanny said.

Dave turned with the phone. He looked out at Long Island Sound, across to Sea Cliff and Glen Cove. He never tired of the view. On his first day in Beechwood, the view had moved his heart. It told him he had come to the right place. Now, after twenty-eight years, Dave no longer had to be told. But every morning he still turned to the Sound as every morning he turned to his vial of Aldomet tablets. Both kept him going.

"Bazeloff," Dave said. "Wait. A few years ago? When we had that trouble with the Lessing Rosenwald bunch? Wasn't there a guy with that name on the committee they sent up here from Philadelphia to see me?"

"There was," Fanny said. "And this Renata Bazeloff is his daughter."

The average secretary would have given him that fact before she went on with her message. Fanny Mintz was not the average secretary. She had devoted almost twenty-eight years of her life to David Dehn. She expected him to live up to the devotion. By forcing him to think, getting him to

14

dredge up the name, she had brought his sharp mind to the cutting edge needed for handling the problem, whatever the problem was. Fanny did not coddle him. She merely loved him. To get the best out of her, Fanny forced him to cooperate. He always did. Dave did not love her. His feelings for Fanny Mintz went deeper than love. He respected her.

"Mordecai Bazeloff," Dave said into the phone. It was coming back to him. "Mordecai J.?"

"That's right," Fanny said. "J. for Judah."

She was pleased with him. Her voice had not changed. Cagney was still rapping out the drill. But Dave could tell. He had passed another of the innumerable tests she was continually setting up for him. And because Fanny Mintz was pleased with him, Dave was pleased with himself. The day was starting the way a man's sixtieth birthday should start.

"The way I remember this joker," Dave said, "he was a horse's ass of rather large proportions. Why is he suddenly important on my sixtieth birthday?"

"Not him," Fanny said. "It's his daughter who is important. Renata Bazeloff."

"Why?" Dave said.

"You know that new magazine the A.O.J.C. started last year?" Fanny said. "*Mitzvah?*"

"Of course I know it," Dave said irritably. "I never forget my larger sources of heartburn. These God-damn fools will do me in before my high blood pressure does. Christ, when will they wake up to the fact that this is America, not Lithuania? Even those smart alecks on the American Jewish Committee have enough sense to call their lousy magazine *Commentary*. In the U. S. of A. in 1974, who goes around calling a magazine *Mitzvah?*"

"The American Orthodox Jewish Congress," Fanny said. "Short for your heartburn, long for A.O.J.C. And what they call their magazine has nothing to do with why Renata Bazeloff is important. She's important because she's on the staff of *Mitzvah* and she's been trying to get you for more than a week. I've held her off with the usual series of fibs, but I can't do it much longer, and she just called me again."

Dave glanced at the watch he had unstrapped from his wrist. He had set it on the table when he started to shave. The watch showed ten minutes to seven.

"Where are you?" he said into the phone.

"Where would I be at ten minutes to seven in the morning?" Fanny said.

The question was rhetorical, just as his had been stupid. They both knew where Fanny Mintz was at ten minutes to seven in the morning. In her house down the road on Saul Street. The house in which Fanny Mintz had spent almost every minute of the past twenty-seven years. Except for the hours from eight in the morning to eight at night. Those she spent, seven days a week, in the room outside Mr. Dehn's office on the ground floor of the big stone building from which he was now talking to her on the phone. It overlooked the approach to Turkey Hill Road. The structure dominated the surrounding area like a benevolent fortress.

At ten minutes to seven on this morning of Mr. Dehn's sixtieth birthday, therefore, Fanny Mintz was where she always was and always had been at this hour of every other morning since his thirty-third birthday. Ministering to the phones and other office equipment with which she had converted the Mintz dining room into an extension of the room on the ground floor of the stone house on the hill. In that room she watched over the life of Dave Dehn with as much dedication as she had once devoted to the lives of her parents. It was more than love. It was a matter of survival. He held the key to her mortality.

"I'm sorry, Fanny," Dave said into his bathroom phone. "What I meant by my dopey question, you said this Renata Bazeloff, you said she just called you?"

"She did," Fanny Mintz said. "And I said she's been calling for a week."

"What I meant was, how the hell did she get your home number?"

"I don't know," Fanny said. "And please, D.D., don't ask me why I didn't ask her."

"Okay," Dave said, "I won't ask you. Just tell me what she said when you did ask her."

"She said it was none of my business," Fanny said. "The important thing was she'd known how to reach me, Miss Bazeloff told me, and she wanted me to tell you she wanted to see you."

"She sounds like an arrogant little punk," Dave said.

"I've never seen her," Fanny said. "Just been talking to her on the phone for a week. But when they talk to you like that on the phone, newspaper people, these writers for magazines, those people, it's usually because they've got you over a barrel, or they think they have. That's why I feel this is important, D.D."

"What barrel has Miss Bazeloff got me over?" Dave said.

"She didn't say," Fanny said. "In fact, all week she hasn't used those words. Over a barrel is my phrase. All she's been saying, she keeps saying she wants to see you, and it's important."

"Important to her?" Dave said. "Or to me?"

"D.D., please stop being funny," Fanny said. "Miss Bazeloff says she wants to see you, and it's important."

"I'm listening," Dave said.

"First," Fanny said. "To you *Mitzvah* may stink. The public likes it. They're only ten months old, and already they're over a hundred thousand copies per issue ahead of A.J.C.'s *Commentary*. They've captured an audience, and it's growing. They've got clout, D.D. Publications with clout, when they come knocking at your door, it seems smart to let them in."

"Okay," Dave said. "Two."

"Two," Fanny said. "They seem to have connections. Getting my unlisted number here on Saul Street, that you don't do by looking in the Westchester phone book."

"How do you do it?" Dave said.

"By using connections," Fanny said. "When she first called,

the Secretary of State was testifying before the Senate Foreign Relations Committee on the Near East, and he quoted a long section from the lead editorial in last month's *Mitzvah*."

"So to get your unlisted phone number up here in Beechwood," Dave said, "the connections this Miss Bazeloff used, you think they could be Washington stuff?"

"I think it's safe to assume they are," Fanny said.

All at once, so did Dave. He had suddenly realized Fanny was laying in each word with great care. As though every syllable were a stitch in a delicate piece of needle point.

"What's your number three?" he said.

"Have you read any recent issues of *Mitzvah*?" Fanny said.

"I told you I can't stand the damn thing," Dave said.

"My stomach is not as delicate as yours," Fanny said. "We're on their freebie list, so whenever you throw your copy in the wastebasket, I've been fishing it out and taking it home, and you want to hear something funny, D.D.?"

"It's about time," Dave said.

"If Ma and Pa were alive," Fanny said, "I think they would love this magazine."

"For God's sake, why?" Dave said.

"*Mitzvah* is something new in Jewish magazines," Fanny said. "What *Mitzvah* is peddling is sensationalism. It's the old self-righteous act. If we Jews want the world to respect us, we Jews must clean our own house. And boy, D.D., are these slobs cleaning it. What the reader of *Mitzvah* gets is juicy articles on embezzlers named Pincus. Fraudulent stock issues floated by rabbis. Doctors appointed to head up big hospitals supported by U.J.A. and it turns out years ago they ran abortion rings. Jewish movie starlets who last year were call girls in Las Vegas."

"Fanny, you're kidding."

"Not by much, D.D. It's a pretty ruthless rag. I don't think it's a good idea not to see their reporter. It might give them an opportunity to think you've got something to hide."

There was a pause. Dave allowed it to go on. He wanted to give Fanny an opportunity to examine her last words and then modify them. She always did. It was one of her favorite tactics. Having jolted him into an awareness of something unpleasant that Dave had been refusing to face, she would back off with an "Of course, you understand, D.D., that I didn't actually mean—"

But Fanny Mintz never said anything she did not actually mean. Not to Dave Dehn. Having accomplished her purpose, however, Fanny always saved his face by backing away from what she had said. She knew that having been alerted, Dave would do the right thing.

This time she did not take the opportunity he provided with the pause. So Dave knew what she wanted him to do.

"Okay, Fanny," he said, "I'll see the little bitch. Fix a date for some time next week."

"Miss Bazeloff said she's tired of being stalled. She's got to see you today."

"Fanny, for God's sake," Dave said. "Today is my birthday. The whole damn town of Beechwood has got celebration things fixed up."

"Miss Bazeloff knows that," Fanny said. "She said it was important to see you before the festivities start."

"Where?" Dave said.

"She's staying with friends in Greenwich," Fanny said. "She can be here in twenty minutes. She says she wants to see the place."

Dave made a conscious effort. He pulled the conversation back into his control.

"No," he said. "I don't want her here."

It was his place. He had made it. Nobody was going to stain it.

"Where, then?" Fanny said.

"Tell her to meet me for lunch at the City Club," Dave said. "Twelve-thirty."

"All right," Fanny said.

Pause.

Then: "D.D.?"

"Yes?" Dave said.

"Remember that first day?" Fanny said. "Back in 1947? When the whole thing was just a bunch of stakes in the ground? With pieces of clothesline tied between them? The day you drove me up here to show me the place? The day you gave me the job?"

The uneasiness that had invaded Dave's gut began to ease away. She sounded like Jimmy Cagney again. He was going to be all right.

"Of course I remember," Dave said. He and Fanny. They were both too old to forget. "What about it?"

"Something you said to me," Fanny said. "Something your father once told you. When you were a kid. About when you're going to build something, how you should do it? Remember your telling me?"

Dave Dehn could do better than that. He could hear his father's voice telling it to him.

PART II

PART II

2

"Never buy an old city," his father had said. "It's cheaper to build a new one."

Dave Dehn's father never managed to put his hands on so much as the price of a pup tent, much less a city. But he did own an original mind. It ranged. It was the only legacy the old man had left his son. The unwritten bequest had paid off handsomely. Dave had never lost money by following his father's approach to the way most human beings work out their destinies.

"Don't die early," the old man once said. "It makes people think you were ashamed to live."

But the old man had broken his own rule. Cancer. Dave's father had died while Dave was still overseas. Two years later, however, on the rear seat of the Carey Cadillac that was carrying him up to Westchester, it occurred to Dave that he was still following the flights of his father's sensible fancies. This cheered Dave about his mission for the day.

He had racked up almost thirty-two years of ramshackle living. In that time, when it came to their ability to arouse his admiration, most people Dave encountered had turned in spotty performances. Not Dave's father. He remained the only man Dave Dehn had ever been able to respect without qualification.

"We anywhere within striking distance?" he said to the driver.

The driver looked up into the mirror over the windshield. "About twenty minutes, I'd say, sir. If we've got the address right."

Dave enjoyed the "we." It implied that the driver was not an unwitting hired hand laid on for the day, but Dave's partner in a long-range enterprise of which this automobile ride was a ground-breaking step.

"We've got it right," Dave said.

Dave could not have got it wrong. Because Sid Singer had written it out for him. Sid was not only Dave's lawyer and partner. He was also Dave's slave. Shortly after they made it over the Remagen bridge, Dave had saved Sid's life. No heroism involved. Just instinct. For a Jewish boy born in Albany, Sid had possessed an uncanny talent for guiding Sherman tanks into a Gentile invention: the land mine. Dave, who had been born in the same place, possessed a nose for avoiding them.

"Turn left off the Merritt at 28?" the driver said. "Then across on Longmeadow to the big green-and-white Beechwood sign?"

Dave looked at the typed slip of paper Sid had given him.

"That's right," he said.

Once you kept him out of a land mine, Dave had found Sid Singer as dependable as Lindbergh had found *The Spirit of St. Louis*.

"Then I'd say about another ten minutes," the driver said. "Maybe fifteen. If we don't get screwed up by these little country side roads."

Dave did not count that as a major worry.

"It won't matter," he said. "The people I'm heading for have nothing to do except sit there and wait for me."

In a business deal that was the best position to be in. For you, of course. Not them.

"Here's the Beechwood sign," the driver said.

He eased the big black Cadillac off into an "Exit" curve marked "Ramp Speed 20 M.P.H." The last time Dave Dehn had seen a similar sign, it had peeled him off one of Hitler's prize autobahns leading to Bremerhaven. Where the U.S.S. *San Antonio* was waiting to take him and approximately 8,000 other crusaders home from the Great Crusade. Dave remembered two things. No, three.

One, the ramp speed had been marked in kilometers. Two, the U.S. Army temp sign with white masking-tape arrows pointing the way to the U.S.S. *San Antonio* had read "Abfahrt 1400." And three, with his bare hands, if nothing more efficient was available, Dave Dehn had wanted to kill every fucking German on the face of God's green earth.

Except that to Dave Dehn the earth no longer looked green. And he no longer believed in God. When he left Germany, he had been three weeks short of his thirty-first birthday. It is not a good age at which to come to atheism.

"This one is marked Main Street," Dave said. "It says here to stay on it till we hit Turkey Hill Road."

The car turned into a street that could have been painted by Thomas Hart Benton. The Cadillac moved smoothly past Bohack's. The Beechwood Art Movie Theatre. The Dress Box. The In-At-10-Out-At-4 Dry Cleaners. Eckerd's Drugs. The Burger 'N' Shake House. And the First Beechwood Bank and Trust.

It was all clean and neat and Gentile.

"Turkey Hill Road," the driver said, turning left, and they were out of the clean, neat, Gentile landscape. They were in Winslow Homer land. The knot in Dave's gut eased away.

It was land he had never before seen, but it was land Dave knew he wanted to own. It took you in.

The road had not been made by a contractor. It had been cut by cows coming home to be milked. The uneven blacktop on which the Cadillac bumped along was an afterthought.

The road made Dave feel better about what he was coming here for.

He knew his father would have liked Turkey Hill Road. The roads the old man had known were parts of comic-strip towns named Minsk or Pinsk and, later, Albany. But the old man would have dug Turkey Hill Road. You could feel the presence of the people who had waited for those cows to come home and be milked. People without much money. People like Dave's father. With minds that ranged. In good directions. Dave's lingering doubts disappeared. He was absolutely certain he was coming to this place for the right reason.

"There's the mailbox with the red tin flag," the driver said.

He touched the brake. The car eased up to the battered gray metal cylinder nailed on top of a four-foot length of even grayer sapling.

Sapling?

Probably. It was not thick enough to be a tree trunk. But it had obviously once been on its way to becoming a tree trunk. Before somebody had cut it down and pounded it into the ground to make it serve as the support for a mailbox.

In this small, foolish confusion about how to identify a piece of gray, weatherbeaten tree trunk, Dave sensed something of the problems he was heading into.

How was he to know what to call these damn things? When he was a kid in Albany it would have been a good chunk of wood to find in an empty lot. Wood to drag back to Westerlo Street for the Election Night fire. Now it was what?

"You say Biaggi?" the driver said.

Dave looked out at the mailbox, where the driver had brought the car to a stop. It said Biaggi. So did the slip of paper Sid Singer had prepared.

"This is it," Dave said.

It looked like a house put together by somebody who had never heard of architects. Not exactly a shack, but it was obvious that that was how it had started. A shack to which things had been added. Not a structure. A house. The way mud huts in the Congo are houses. Put together because human beings needed shelter.

One of the human beings came out the door and down to the Cadillac.

"Which one of you is Mr. Dehn?" she said.

The driver looked startled. Dave just looked. It was quite a sight. To his knowledge nothing more feminine had thus far been invented. Dave doubted that it ever would be. It occurred to him that even the Manhattan Project, which had put the nuclear warhead into the language, would not be able to put to more advantage roughly one hundred and ten pounds of female flesh. Dave found himself staring at: a pair of robin's-egg blue pedal pushers and a man's white T-shirt. No shoes.

"I'm Mr. Dehn," Dave said. "This joker up front is my hired driver for the day. You and I will get along better if you don't get me mixed up with him, Miss Biaggi."

She gave Dave the sort of look he had spent almost four years learning to get from peering through the sights of a Garand rifle. It is a point of view you don't acquire on Westerlo Street in Albany.

"Sorry about the mix-up," she said. "We don't get to see many Cadillacs on Turkey Hill Road."

She opened the back door of the car and pulled it wide.

"When I do see a Cadillac," she said, "I assume the guy behind the wheel owns it."

She turned to the driver.

"When you get to own one," she said, "I'll be more polite to you."

Dave stepped out of the car. She slammed the door shut. The thrust of her arm made her left nipple bounce. It could have been a finger probing for a way out of the cloth of the T-shirt. Dave had a swift thought about the nipple on the right.

"I'm Dave Dehn," he said.

"Nice to meet you," she said. "Mr. Singer told me you'd be along. I'm Bella Biaggi."

She put out her hand. Dave took it.

"I'll take that back now," she said.

Dave dropped her hand.

"Would you like to come in for a minute?" she said. "Or do you want to walk around and have a look at what you're buying?"

"I'm buying the house as well as the land," Dave said. "I might as well see all of it."

What Dave saw, as he followed her up onto the sagging porch, was that there was more to Bella Biaggi than the stuffed T-shirt. Not much more. Just enough to fill a man's two cupped palms.

"Would you like some coffee?" she said when they came into a big room that was clearly, Dave saw, the center of the household. "It's all perked."

"That would be very nice, thanks," Dave said.

She walked to a gas range at one side of the room. She had to strike a match to get it going. From the blue-black splotches chipped out of the once-white enamel, Dave guessed it was possible pilot lights had not yet been invented when this number had joined the Biaggi household.

"The best chair is over there," she said. "By the radio."

The radio was on an upended wooden Schaefer's beer crate. The crate sat near the pillow of an unmade bed. The headboard was made of vertical strips of tarnished brass piping. It looked like the door of a prison cell. When Dave sat down, his foot hit something he had not noticed: a small hill of bedside reading matter. It broke and scattered across the splotched linoleum floor like pins going down at the end of a bowling alley.

"Sorry," Dave said.

He leaned over to pull the stuff together.

"Don't bother," Bella Biaggi said from the stove. "It's just junk."

Dave managed to shove back into place a Sears, Roebuck catalogue: "Winter 1940–Spring 1941." Under it was a copy of *Life*. The picture on the cover showed four Marines raising the Stars and Stripes over Mt. Suribachi on Iwo Jima.

"Were you in the Pacific?"

Dave looked up. She was coming across with two steaming cups.

"No," Dave said. "Europe."

He took one of the cups.

"Thanks," Dave said. "How did you know I'd been anywhere?"

She shrugged and sat down with her cup of coffee on the edge of the bed. Dave noticed there was only one hollow in the soiled pillowcase.

"At your age," she said, "you would have had to be somewhere. You look too healthy to get out of the draft."

Dave looked around the room. There were no curtains. Just green window shades. They were so old and worn the sun stabbed yellow pinpoints of light through the spider web of cracks in the exhausted oilcloth.

"You want the bathroom?" she said.

"No," Dave said. "I was wondering if you live here alone."

"Not yet," she said. "Grandpa is still dying upstairs."

"I'm sorry," Dave said.

"I'll bet you are," she said. "If he wasn't dying, I wouldn't be selling. Three nurses around the clock up there. You know what a private nurse gets these days? For an eight-hour shift? Plus two square meals? Not the kind of garbage I eat. To private nurses square meals means meat."

Miss Biaggi's laugh was a surprise. It sounded like the bark of a puppy on whose tail a thick boot had come down heavily. She kicked savagely at the copy of *Life*. The magazine went slithering across the linoleum floor. It sounded like a small animal running through tall dry grass.

"The businessmen in this town," she said. "The butcher told me he couldn't arrange his prices to accommodate three private nurses just because they were taking care of an old wop who is dying around the corner from the First Beechwood Bank and Trust."

"Did he actually use the word wop?" Dave said.

Bella Biaggi gave him a hard look across her coffee cup.

"Mr. Dehn," she said. "Do you have to hear someone use the word kike before you catch on that the son of a bitch is calling you one?"

The next time it happened, Dave Dehn would see to it that the son of a bitch paid for the privilege.

"How did you get to live in a place where your neighbors can call you a wop?" Dave said.

"I was born here," Bella Biaggi said. "At a time when all my neighbors were wops." She put down her cup. "Let's go look at the place where I was born."

It took longer to look at than Dave had thought. One reason was that all he knew was a number Sid Singer had given him. But Dave did not know what 180 acres meant. He soon learned it meant more walking than in his city shoes he was accustomed to. The hike did not seem to bother Bella Biaggi in her bare feet.

"What did your father do on this place?" Dave said.

"The same thing his father did," she said. "Grow onions."

"Onions?"

Dave was surprised by his own surprise. The whole world ate onions. Obviously, somebody had to grow them.

"When my great-grandfather came here from Eboli," Bella Biaggi said, "this whole area was full of onion farms. The soil was good for that particular crop, and a lot of Italian immigrants like my great-grandfather knew a lot about growing onions. There isn't much else you can grow around Eboli."

"A hundred and eighty acres," Dave said. "He must have come over from Italy with more money than my father brought over from Russia."

"He came with so little," Bella Biaggi said, "he had to borrow from the bank the two hundred bucks to buy his first four acres. In those days up around here the wops owned the banks."

"How did four acres become a hundred and eighty?" Dave said.

"My great-grandfather was a good onion farmer," she said. "He believed in land. Every nickel he made he put back into Turkey Hill Road. After a while he owned Turkey Hill Road. He was the biggest landowner in this area when he got his ass shot off following Teddy Roosevelt up San Juan Hill."

If he'd followed Teddy Roosevelt up San Juan Hill, and his son was now dying on the second floor with three meat-eating nurses in attendance, Dave figured there was a missing actor in the drama.

"Where's your father?" he said.

"He died at Bastogne," Bella Biaggi said. "My God-damn family is as full of patriotism as a rice pudding is full of raisins. Don't ask about my mother. She went during the flu epidemic in 1920. I was less than a month old. I don't remember anything about her. Not even a picture."

Dave did a bit of mental arithmetic. 1920 to 1946.

"That means you've been here on Turkey Hill Road for twenty-six years," he said.

"Does that make me too old to close this deal?"

"No," Dave said. "But it might make you too young."

"Don't worry about that," Bella Biaggi said. "I'm sure Mr. Singer told you I got myself some first-rate legal advice. These one hundred per cent Americans who have taken over this area, they'll sell you anything. Even pieces of their Harvard law degrees. All you have to do is fork over a high enough price. They'll take money from anybody. Even a wop."

"I guess that settles it, then," Dave said. "You've got a deal, Miss Biaggi."

"Before I sign," she said, "I want to know something."

"Tell me," Dave said.

"I can understand these greedy patriots taxing me out of here," she said. "Onions give you bad breath. Suburban housing developments give you a fat bank account. What I can't understand is why a Jew would want to buy a piece of property in the middle of these bastards who practically invented anti-Semitism."

How could she understand? She was not a Jew.

"I happened to be with the Third Army back on April thirteenth of last year," Dave said. "The day we liberated Buchenwald."

3

It was the word liberated that lingered, reminding Dave of
something he had been trying to forget since he was thirteen.
A memory that sometimes faded, leaving him momentarily
at peace. But never for long. And never at all since that April
day in Buchenwald. It was a memory that always came alive
in the same way, with the sound of his father's voice.

"David?"

His father never meddled with the Old Testament. Into
the tent of Saul had come a boy named David. He carried a
harp that promised the tormented king relief from despair.
Into the Albany tenement of the disappointed immigrant had
come a son. The child carried the last hope of fulfilling the
broken promise that had lured the father to America. The
father named the boy David. Not Dave. Men of God did not
tamper with the names of the anointed.

"David?"

The boy pulled his head out from under the tap in the
kitchen sink.

"You call me, Pa?"

"The neck," his father shouted from the bedroom. "Scrub
good the neck. It's a new *tallis*."

What else could it be? On the day of his bar mitzvah no boy was ever presented with an old *tallis*. But Dave kept the irritation out of his "Sure, Pa."

He sent the words toward the bedroom, and ducked his head back under the tap. It was the only source of water in the three-room tenement flat. The toilet was out in the hall. Dave was certain the back of his neck was clean. Clean enough not to soil the brand-new white satin prayer shawl that would be presented to him officially at the ceremony in the synagogue. Just the same, Dave gave his neck a few extra scrubs. The old man was okay. Dave liked his father.

He had to. Dave had no mother. But that was not the only reason. Dave liked his father because the old man left him alone. This too was not exactly a matter of choice. Six days a week the old man was downtown, standing on a ladder or swaying on a scaffold, spreading paint on the walls of some apartment house or office building. It was only on Saturdays that Dave saw his father. What he saw he liked. The old man was a calm type.

Except, of course, today. The old man's nervousness was understandable. Dave was a little nervous himself. It was easy enough to rehearse for three months with Rabbi Goldfarb. Just the two of you in a small room back of the *cheder*. But then came the big day. You had to get up there on your hind feet. Out in the open. In front of all those people in the synagogue. Dave shivered.

"A cold you caught already, God forbid!"

Dave turned off the tap and looked up through his dripping eyelashes. His father had come in from the bedroom.

"No," Dave said. "It's just the cold water."

He reached for the Hecker's flour sack on the wall over the sink.

"No, here," his father said. Mr. Dehn shoved Dave's hand away from the flour sack. "Use this."

He held out one of the two real towels the Dehn family owned. The Dehn family had two members. One towel for each.

"The sack is clean, Pa."

"Not clean enough," Mr. Dehn said. "Today you become a man. When for the first time the *tallis* touches the back of a brand-new man, his skin should be cleaner than it ever was when he was still a boy."

Dave took the towel. His father went back into the bedroom. Dave scrubbed his neck. When he came up out of the folds of the towel, his father had reappeared with the boy's clean white shirt.

Mr. Dehn held the shirt aloft with both hands, thumbs and forefingers pinched like tweezers at the seams where the sleeves were sewed to the shoulders. He could have been a salesman in an expensive haberdashery, exhibiting a rare item for a prospective buyer. The shirt had come from an inexpensive haberdashery. Stuermer's Men's Shop, around the corner on Ten Eyck Avenue. But the shirt was rare enough. Dave had never worn it, yet his father had washed and ironed it the night before.

"For a bar mitzvah," the old man said, "everything must be new, from the inside out. But it shouldn't *look* new."

He helped Dave into the shirt, then stepped back, out of the way, leaving the tie-knotting ceremony to Dave. Mr. Dehn knew the boy did not like to be fussed over. As Dave worked on the knot, he could see from the way his father's fingers worked along with his own that the old man's restraint was being achieved with an effort. Dave felt it only right to repay the effort.

"How's that?" he said, standing back.

Mr. Dehn's fingers did not stop twitching. But neither did he step forward. Better to reach man's estate with a not-quite-perfect knot in your tie than to fumble part of the ceremony because your father's excessive fussiness had made you nervous.

"Perfect," the old man said. "Now the suit."

The jacket was just a jacket, but the pants were long—Dave's first pair. Dave climbed unassisted into his new station in life.

"Okay, Pa," he said. "Now you get dressed. I'll go get the rolls."

Mr. Dehn released the first sign that he was not quite under control.

"No," he said, "I'll get the rolls."

Dave released the first sign that he accepted the responsibilities which would become permanently his in a couple of hours at the ceremony in the synagogue.

"I get the rolls for breakfast every day," he said. Not as calmly as he would have wanted to say it, but he said it. "I'll get them today."

Mr. Dehn hesitated, then scowled and nodded crisply.

"All right," he said.

He wheeled like a guardsman on parade and walked firmly back into the bedroom. Dave suspected his father had turned so abruptly because he did not want the boy to see his face. The boy did not, however, waste time on thinking about it. During the three months of rehearsal, Rabbi Goldfarb had come down hard on the responsibilities of maturity.

It was the theme of the "Today I Am a Man" speech the rabbi had written for David to deliver after the *tallis* was placed around his shoulders. Dave was not sure he understood everything in the speech he had memorized. He was, however, certain about one thing. Fetching the breakfast rolls had always been his job when he wore knickers. Nobody was going to do the job for him now that he wore longies.

Dave walked out of the kitchen and down the four flights of gray stone stairs. He stepped out into Westerlo Street.

It was a moment that always gave him pleasure. Not because Westerlo Street was a spectacular thoroughfare. Even to a boy who had thus far lived all thirteen years of his life in a corner of Albany no larger than several football fields laid end to end, Westerlo Street was not physically impressive.

Two long rows of tenements, all pretty much alike, stretching up from Ten Eyck Avenue toward South Broadway. Halfway up the block, a synagogue. Next to it, a vacant lot. Down near the Ten Eyck corner, a couple of beat-up old trees trying to remain alive. Almost no traffic. No people to speak of. Or rather, to. The few figures moving in the distance up near South Broadway seemed lifeless even though they were in motion. The truth was that Westerlo Street was not really a street. It was a setting. A place waiting for something to happen.

This was the source of Dave's pleasure. The empty landscape was his to fill.

He filled it every morning the way a painter fills a canvas. Beginning with a bold slash of color that jolted the blank rectangle into immediate life: "I'm here. It's me. Dave Dehn. I just came out into the street from 1075. What have you got to show me?"

The first thing Westerlo Street had to show Dave every morning was his buddy. Sid Singer was always waiting on the stoop of 1077 when Dave came out into the street from 1075. On this important morning in Dave's life, Sid's reputation for dependability took an unexpected blow. There was no sign of Sid.

Dave was confused. Several moments went by before he decided with reluctance that he'd better accept the incredible fact that his friend, who was always there, on this morning was not. On the heels of the decision, Sid appeared.

Not from the doorway of 1077. Sid appeared from the vacant lot beyond the synagogue, halfway up the block, and he appeared on the run.

"Dave!" he yelled, scooping both arms toward himself. "Dave, come on!"

Two jumps took Dave down the stoop and on the run up the block. He met Sid in front of the synagogue.

"What's the matter?"

"In the lot!" Sid said, panting. "Look!"

He dragged Dave up the block, past the synagogue, to the sidewalk in front of the vacant lot.

"The son of a bitch!" Sid said. "Look what he's doing!"

Dave looked. Not at the son of a bitch. Dave knew Dutch Stuermer, the kid whose father owned the men's-apparel shop on Ten Eyck Avenue, the way a puppy knows a toe that kicks. Dutch was two years older than Dave and Sid. Two years older and God knew how many years meaner.

Like most kids on Westerlo Street, Dave was scared of Dutch Stuermer. He hated to look at the big, lumpy kid with the sagging, always wet lower lip and the small, restless, hard-bright eyes that never stopped probing for a place to inflict pain. Dave looked instead at what Dutch Stuermer was doing, and Dave's heart turned over.

"Hey!" he yelled. "Cut that out!"

Dutch neither looked up nor cut it out. He went right on pouring liquid out of the big silver can onto the pile of wood. The pile had been assembled painstakingly by Dave and Sid and their friends on the block. For weeks every kid on Westerlo Street had been scouring the neighborhood, dragging back to the empty lot packing cases, broken wagon tongues, orange crates, egg boxes, empty grocery cartons—anything that would burn.

After Rosh Hashanah, the Election Night fire was the big event to which the kids of Westerlo Street looked forward. This year Election Day came three days after Dave's bar mitzvah. In his mind he had been seeing the fire as something personal, a celebration of his becoming a man. Dave had not told this to anybody, not even to Sid, but he had been living with the secret feeling for weeks.

Now, in front of his eyes, Dave could see the secret being destroyed. What that son of a bitch Dutch Stuermer was pouring on the pile of wood was not water. Dave could smell the kerosene all the way out on the sidewalk.

The smell grew stronger as he ran across the empty lot and grabbed Dutch's arm. The mean face came around in a slow arc.

"Look who's here," Dutch said. "The bar mitzvah mocky."

"Get away from that wood," Dave said.

"Who's gonna make me?"

Dave hesitated. Who indeed? The hesitation proved fatal. Dutch reached down with his free hand and grabbed the front of Dave's jacket.

"Where'd you get the suit?" Dutch said.

Dave squirmed to pull free. Sid stepped in. He shoved Dutch's arm.

"Mr. Dehn bought it downtown," Sid said. "Where my old man bought mine. We don't wear that kraut's crud your old man sells."

"You will, you little Jew bastard," Dutch said.

He shoved Sid aside. Sid stumbled. Dutch swung the silver can up and out. A rush of evil-smelling kerosene came down on Dave like water out of the shower head in the school locker room. He screamed. His hands shot up to shield his eyes. A moment later it was Sid who was screaming. Dave opened his eyes.

"Take it back downtown," Dutch Stuermer said. "For alterations."

He tossed the lighted match. Sid tried to knock it aside. He missed. The small flame hit Dave on the arm. There was a terrifying whoosh. Sid screamed again. The whoosh came roaring over Dave like a wave at the beach. Then the heat began to dig into him and he could not hear his own screams. He started to run, back to the sidewalk, trailing flame, and he thudded into the arms of Rabbi Goldfarb.

"Don't run!" the old man screamed in Yiddish. "Don't run!"

He whipped from under his arm the blue velvet pouch he always carried to the synagogue on Saturday mornings. With a savage tug Rabbi Goldfarb tore open the pouch and pulled out his *tallis*. He shook the folds free, wrapped them around Dave as though folding him in an embrace, and hurled the boy to the ground.

"Help me!" the rabbi panted in Yiddish to Sid. "Quick!"

Sid jumped in. Together he and Rabbi Goldfarb rolled

Dave like a salami across the sidewalk. Dave could feel the heat, but he could no longer see the flames. He saw Dutch Stuermer.

The mean little eyes gleamed. He raised the can. Dave screamed again. The kerosene poured down on the head and neck and shoulders of Rabbi Goldfarb, soaking big black wet stains into his coat.

Then Dave's eyes lost the picture. The rolling motion had carried his face around to the ground. His eyes came up to the sky again just in time to see Dutch drop the lighted match on Rabbi Goldfarb and jump clear.

The terrifying whoosh exploded again. Rabbi Goldfarb was hurled up and away, as though a giant foot had kicked him from Dave's body. When Dave sat up, still wrapped in what was left of Rabbi Goldfarb's *tallis,* the boy's ears had stopped recording.

He saw the old man running away from him, down the block, trailing flame like the torch carried by the runner who opened the Olympic Games in the newsreels. Dave became aware of another figure. Sid. Racing after the old man. Then Dave's ears seemed to come unplugged. The sounds came through.

Sid Singer yelling. Dutch Stuermer laughing. Rabbi Goldfarb screaming.

4

Almost nineteen years later, sitting beside Sid Singer on the rear seat of the Carey Cadillac that was carrying them up from New York to Westchester, Dave could still hear that screaming.

The Cadillac stopped. Dave came up out of the recurring horror. He looked out into the sunlit street. It was not the street on which Rabbi Goldfarb had burned to death. Dave's mind came back slowly to the moment in which he was now living. His eyes began to focus. He saw the building toward which for an hour he and Sid had been moving. The sight was pleasant. It eased the horror back into the secret drawer of Dave's mind where for so many years he had tried to keep it hidden.

He concentrated on the building in front of which the Carey Cadillac had stopped. White clapboard. Brightly painted green shutters with crescents cut into the corners. Under the fanlight over the door, a big bronze knocker cast to depict Paul Revere clattering through the Middlesex night. A flagstone walk leading up from the Main Street pavement. The whole thing set in a neatly barbered lawn protected by four gigantic elms. The trees had obviously been planted about the time William Bradford was getting himself elected Governor of the Plymouth Colony.

Dave gave the bronze knocker a couple of raps. A discreetly pitched buzzer clicked the lock free. They walked into the sort of anteroom in which the emissaries from the Continental Congress had waited for Betsy Ross to finish sewing.

"Good morning," a girl said cheerfully. "May I help you?"

"My name is Singer," Sid said. "This is Mr. Dehn."

"Oh, yes," she said. "You must be the two gentlemen from New York."

She went out and came back almost immediately.

"Mr. Babington will see you now," she said.

He saw them in a room that looked so much like the rest of the cottage that the shelves of bound law reports looked incongruous. Like a pile of catcher's mitts on the floor of the nave in St. Patrick's.

"Do sit down, gentlemen," Mr. Babington said.

While Sid and Dave got themselves settled around his desk, Mr. Babington tamped tobacco into a pipe from a round tin of Dunhill's "My Mixture" on his desk.

"Good of you to come all the way up from New York," he said.

Dave thought Mr. Babington made it sound as though he and Sid had crawled all the way up the Merritt Parkway on their hands and knees, bringing him his Congressional Medal of Honor.

"It's only a forty-minute drive," Dave said.

"You were obviously not troubled by the official speed limit," Mr. Babington said. "It usually takes me pretty nearly an hour, door to door."

"You lose time once you get into the city traffic," Dave said. "They put that Yale Club front door in a pretty inaccessible spot."

The wintry smile changed slightly. Mr. Babington chuckled.

"Actually, I'm Harvard," he said. "But the door of the Harvard Club is equally inaccessible. By the way, Mr. Dehn, are you Yale?"

"No," Dave said. "Ethan Allen High School."

Mr. Babington's wintry smile changed seasons. It sank into his leathery, golf-tanned face. He gave Dave a sharp look, as though until this moment he had not really seen his visitor. Dave was sure he hadn't. Goys never really saw Jews. What they saw was a picture inside their heads. A picture of a Jewish face they had painted for themselves years ago and had been carrying around ever since. Like an Army dog tag: instant identification. Once he owned the Biaggi property, Dave figured, he would fix that.

Mr. Babington stared at him across the match flame from which he was sucking a light into his pipe. The flame, pumping up and down, seemed to add a little more yellow to Mr. Babington's white hair. It looked like a tobacco-stained mustache, parted in the middle.

"I've heard of Ethan Allen," Mr. Babington said.

"He's not an obscure man," Dave said. "He captured Fort Ticonderoga from the British."

Sid Singer came in with his throat-clearing bit. He sounded like a railroad spike being pulled out of a waterlogged telegraph pole. "Perhaps we'd better get on with it," he said.

"I wish we could," Mr. Babington said.

Dave's gut jumped. The smile on Mr. Babington's face had gone back to wintry.

"What's to prevent us?" Sid said.

"An unforeseen circumstance," Mr. Babington said.

Dave recognized the goy euphemism for *Up Yours!*

"Miss Biaggi's grandfather has finally died?" Sid said.

Mr. Babington nodded. He did it with his whole body. The springs in the swivel chair under him squeaked. It was a small performance, but an impressive one. Dave had the feeling Mr. Babington had cultivated the movement to intimidate juries. It was like seeing Lincoln dip down from his marble seat on the Potomac to tie his shoelace.

"Late last night," Mr. Babington said.

"As circumstances go," Sid said, "I don't think that one

hangs up much of a record for being unforeseen. The old man was eighty-six. Sick as hell for almost a year. In a coma for a month. All during our negotiations for the property, Mr. Babington, it was clearly understood that the old man would be unable to attend this closing, or sign the transfer papers, because he was incompetent, and so his granddaughter would sign for him."

Mr. Babington nodded again. Teacher grudgingly giving minority-group pupil a good mark.

"True enough," he said. "You and I, Mr. Singer, were geared for a closing by proxy. Now, however, we must retool our thinking. As her grandfather's sole heir, my client, Miss Biaggi, is now the technical owner of the property."

"How come technical?" Sid said.

"She cannot dispose of it until her grandfather's will is probated," Mr. Babington said.

"Oh, Christ," Sid said.

It seemed to Dave that Sid was calling on the wrong boy.

"I'm sorry for the delay," Mr. Babington said. "I know how impatient Mr. Dehn is to take possession of the property."

"How long a delay?" Sid said.

Mr. Babington did something Dave had never seen before. He shrugged with his eyebrows.

"Who can say?" he said. "You're a lawyer, Mr. Singer. You know what executors and surrogates are like."

"I know what they're like down in New York," Sid said. "I've had no experience with them up here in Westchester."

"The breed is universal," Mr. Babington said. "Cautious, hesitant, nervous, ponderous, timid, and fearful. Terrified of making the slightest move that might commit them. Slow as molasses in the month of January."

"Could you make a guess about how long it will be before my client will be able to take title?" Sid said.

"Any guess I made would be silly," said Mr. Babington.

"Let's try to narrow it down," Sid said. "A week?"

The wintry smile came back.

"Mr. Singer, you know better than that."

"Ten years?" Sid said.

Mr. Babington chuckled.

"Mr. Singer, you're pulling my leg."

"So it won't take ten years?" Sid said.

"Of course not," Mr. Babington said.

"Then it must be somewhere in between those two figures," Sid said. "A week, and ten years. Is that correct, Mr. Babington?"

The sharp look came back into Mr. Babington's eyes. He clearly did not like being treated like a witness on the stand.

"Of course it's correct," he said. The edge in his voice could have been used to sharpen a pencil. "I don't know what you're driving at, Mr. Singer."

"A date," Sid said. "You have led me and my client to believe we had a deal. Everything was agreed on. We came up here from New York this morning expecting to sign the deal, and now you tell us you can't tell us when your client will be able to sign."

"I have explained why," Mr. Babington said.

"Then what we're dealing with is merely a legal delay?" Sid said. "That's the only reason?"

Mr. Babington's eyes spread out like a couple of poached eggs.

"What other reason could there be?" he said.

Suddenly, in that sunny room full of Early American furniture, Dave could smell something. Something he had smelled on that April day in Germany.

"Mr. Babington," Dave said. "When Mr. Singer entered into these negotiations with you, were you aware that his client was a Jew?"

The look of surprise was so smooth that Dave knew it was not real. Mr. Babington had brought it out of a secret pocket and hung it on his face like a beard.

"What difference does that make?" he said.

Dave decided to let Mr. Babington worry about that one himself.

Instead, Dave said, "You're not answering my question."

Mr. Babington shrugged.

"Frankly, no," he said. "I was not aware Mr. Singer's client was a Jew."

"When did you find out?" Dave said.

Mr. Babington hesitated. So Dave knew he was going to lie.

"Just now," Mr. Babington said. "When you told me."

"I didn't tell you," Dave said.

A faint tinge of purple came washing up slowly out of the Brooks Brothers button-down Oxford shirt and climbed slowly across Mr. Babington's leathery face.

"I mean, Mr. Dehn, that it seemed logical to draw the inference from the way you asked the question."

"Suppose I tell you that you have drawn the wrong inference?" Dave said. "Suppose I tell you I asked the question merely to test you?"

"About what?"

"Whether you're telling the truth," Dave said. "Whether you can't tell us how long the delay will be in signing this deal because executors and surrogates are unpredictably slow, or because the prospective purchaser is a Jew."

The purple eased slowly back down from the leathery face into the Brooks Brothers shirt collar. Mr. Babington was under control again. To prove it, he struck another match.

"Mr. Dehn," he said, "I am a lawyer. I am concerned, of course, for the best interests of my clients. But I am equally concerned for my fees. In this instance it is in the best interests of Miss Biaggi for this sale to go through. It is also in my best interests for the sale to go through. Both of us can use the money."

Dave stood up.

"Let's go, Sid," he said.

The match flame stopped on its way to Mr. Babington's pipe.

"Mr. Dehn," he said, "what are you going to do?"

What Dave Dehn had come to Beechwood to do.

"Protect your interests," he said. "You'll get your fee, Mr. Babington," Dave said. "I guarantee it."

5

It was a stupid boast. The boast of an angry, frustrated loud-mouth. Nobody knew this better than Dave Dehn, who did not enjoy thinking of himself as a loudmouth, or stupid. What he enjoyed was knowing he had what it took to beat the ass off Colin Babington. He intended to do precisely that.

Which was why he was starting to get sore about being held up. His anger was just beginning to work up a head of steam when he saw her come up out of the subway kiosk on the 79th Street corner. Anyway, he saw a girl. She was too far away for him to make out any details, but the outline was unmistakable. Especially to a man with twenty-twenty vision.

She came down Broadway in high heels the way she had gone across Turkey Hill Road in bare feet. Leaving no doubts in the mind of the observer about who owned the ground on which she was walking. Dave moved away from the front of the apartment building and walked up to meet her. The details came into focus.

"You're late," Dave said.

"I had to get something to wear," she said.

Dave examined the details. The top of the dress was red. The skirt was blue. They were held together by a wide white patent leather belt.

"Where do you think you're going?" Dave said. "A Fourth of July picnic?"

"Don't let's get started on this deal with you telling me what to wear," she said. "This is all they had for ten bucks in The Dress Box on Main Street, and ten bucks is all I had to spend on this clambake."

"Did they throw in the shoes for free?" Dave said.

She looked down at her feet. So did Dave. Without shoes they had looked like something a man wouldn't mind massaging for a while. In black patent leather, with double straps and copper buckles across the insteps, they left a man no alternative. He waited for the wearer to make the proposition.

"They're from my high school graduation," she said. "They're the only things I own that I could wear down into the city, and they hurt like hell. Why couldn't we have this thing done up in Beechwood?"

"Because Judge Martelli lives here in New York," Dave said. "He puts in a full day downtown in court. Since he's doing this for us as a favor, we couldn't exactly ask him to come up to Beechwood after work. He told Sid he'd be glad to help us out, but it would have to be done in his own home. Any other questions?"

"Yes," she said. "Why don't you stop wasting time with cracks about my clothes? Why don't we just get on with what you dragged me all the way down into New York for?"

Dave took her elbow and walked her back to the apartment house. It was one of those huge gray stone forts that had been started along upper Broadway soon after the First World War, and finished in time for stockbrokers to jump out of the upper floors during the 1929 Wall Street crash. The visitor came in off the street through a huge three-story arch. It was decorated with carved gargoyles and complicated signs of the zodiac. The structure would not have been inappropriate for shielding the eternal flame at the top of the Champs Elysées. What this arch shielded, however, was a courtyard in which the tenants parked their cars. Dave and Bella Biaggi circled the massed Cadillacs and came into a pink marble lobby.

"Yes, sir?" said an old man in a blue-and-gold uniform.

"Judge Martelli," Dave said.

"Are you expected, sir?"

"Yes," Dave said. "Mr. Dehn."

The old man went to a wall switchboard. He pressed a button, waited, and then said into a small brass grille, "Mr. Dehn in the lobby, and a lady."

"How did he know?" Bella said to Dave.

"Pipe down," Dave said.

"Yes, sir," the old man said into the grille. He punched another button and said to Dave, "The elevator on your right, sir."

"Thanks," Dave said.

The elevator on the right was in the hands of the old man's twin brother. He ran it up to the twelfth floor and slid back the bronze gate.

"Twelve A, sir," he said.

"Thanks," Dave said.

"You're pretty generous with those thanks," Bella said as they walked down the hall. "Up in Beechwood we don't thank anybody unless they do something for you that you don't have to pay them for."

"Maybe that's why those greedy one hundred per cent Americans taxed you out of existence," Dave said. "You're entering a new world. Learn to say thank you as often as you can. It may hurt a little, like learning to wear shoes, but it costs nothing, and now and then it may get you something for free."

"How did you collect this knapsackful of Dale Carnegie crap?" Bella said.

"By not spending my entire life on an onion farm," Dave said. "Now shape up. Here they come."

The door opened. A little white-haired old woman peered out at them through a pair of glasses that had been put together with strips of gold wire and the bottoms of two milk bottles. She was wearing a black silk dress embroidered with beaded white calla lilies. They grew up and out of her waist, then crawled haltingly across her tiny shoulders.

50

"Mr. Dehn?" she said.

"And lady," Dave said.

"Of course," the little old woman said. "Come in. Come in. I'm Mrs. Martelli. His Honor is expecting you."

He didn't look expectant. In fact, His Honor looked stoned. Sid Singer, however, looked like Man o' War waiting to break away from the barrier. He came up out of the chair facing Judge Martelli as though he'd been stabbed with a red-hot thorn in the world's most famous target.

"Hi, kids," he said. Sid turned to Judge Martelli. "Your Honor, this is my partner, Dave Dehn, and this is Miss Bella Biaggi."

His Honor moved, and Dave saw that the judge was not stoned at all. It was merely that he had the tight little face, thick blubber lips, and gaping pink nostrils of a rhesus monkey. The couch on which he sat was upholstered in the same pale brown furry material from which nature had cut the simian's suit. When His Honor came away from the camouflage, Dave could see his eyes. Shoe-button brown. Not bright, but glowing. Like a night light in the bathroom. Nothing to do the crossword puzzle by, but enough to keep you from breaking a toe on the way to the throne. No dope he, Dave decided.

"A pleasure," Judge Martelli said.

He stood up. He was not much taller than a rhesus monkey of, say, high school age, but he was dressed like the principal at the graduation ceremonies: striped trousers, a black cutaway, and gray spats. The last time Dave had seen clothes of this kind was when as a kid he used to follow "Bringing Up Father" in the *Albany Daily News*. Jiggs wore spats.

His Honor swung himself forward. He could have been moving through the branches of a banyan tree in Malaya. He took Bella's hand and looked up into her face. He did it as though he were reading the clock set on the black marble mantel near the window behind him. Through the window Dave could see all of Broadway stretching down to the Paramount Building.

"You're pretty," Judge Martelli said. "When I meet an Italian girl, if she's ugly my heart cries a little for my people. But if she's pretty my heart sings for all Italians."

"Thank you," Bella said.

"See?" Dave said.

"Shut up," she said.

The little monkey face wrinkled in puzzlement.

"You said something to me?" His Honor said.

"I said holy smoke, Your Honor, what a view!" Dave said. "I can see the Paramount Building."

Slowly, as though he were mounted on a swivel, His Honor turned around completely. Dave stole a quick look at the rear wings of the cutaway. Too bad. No tail.

"You should see it at night," Judge Martelli said. "When the clock is lighted. Before I go to sleep every night I check my watch with the Paramount clock. That's why I rented this apartment. When I was a boy down on Mulberry Street I used to walk all the way uptown with my shoeshine box. Nobody gets their shoes shined on Mulberry Street. You wanted to make a few nickels to bring home for Mama to set the table? You had to come uptown to Times Square. The first time I saw the Paramount clock I like you could say fell in love with it. Someday, I made up my mind, someday, I said to myself, someday I'm going to live where I can see that clock all the time. The day after the Governor appointed me to the State Supreme Court bench I rented this apartment. Didn't I, Angela?"

"Didn't you what, Your Honor?"

Dave turned. The little old lady came through the beaded portieres that hung down over an arched doorway at the far side of the room.

"The day after the Governor appointed me to the Supreme Court bench," Judge Martelli said. "I rented this apartment, didn't I?"

"The very next day, Your Honor," said the little old lady. Then, in a sudden squeal, "No! No! Stay away from me!"

She was carrying a small round cut-glass tray edged with

filigreed silver flowers. On it sat a bottle of rum and five small glasses with matching silver stems.

"But I want to help you, Angela," said Judge Martelli.

"Nobody can help me," said his wife. "When I'm carrying something I have to do it myself. If anybody tries to help me I drop it. There!"

She set the tray on a squat round mahogany table. Snarling lion's heads were carved at the points where the four feet touched the complicated Oriental rug.

"Congratulations, Angela," said Judge Martelli. "You did that beautifully. Didn't she?"

"Never saw a bottle of rum carried better," said Sid.

Dave gave him a sharp look. Sid did not, as a rule, make jokes in business meetings. Only when he and Dave were alone. Since this meeting was being held in Judge Martelli's home, Dave had assumed it was not going to be as strictly business as the meeting up in Mr. Babington's Beechwood office. Dave now felt a little confused. A condition of mind he disliked.

"Angela," said Judge Martelli. "Look at this girl. Did you ever see such a beautiful Italian girl?"

Mrs. Martelli had picked up the bottle of rum. She paused to peer at Bella.

"Never," she said.

"All right," Judge Martelli said. "Everybody please sit down."

He swung back through the branches of the imaginary banyan to his place on the couch. When he had wheeled himself into position he lowered himself slowly. Then he patted the place beside him.

"Here, you beautiful Italian girl," His Honor said. "You sit here."

Bella sat down beside him. Dave felt a poke on his biceps. He turned. It was Sid. With a sharp thrust of his forefinger Sid indicated the chair on the right of His Honor. Dave walked over, sat down, and found Mrs. Martelli standing over Bella with one of the small glasses.

"It's rum," Mrs. Martelli said. "I hope you like rum?"

"Thank you," Bella said, "I don't drink."

"But this you've got to drink," Mrs. Martelli said. "His Honor and I, we brought it back last month from our vacation in Haiti."

"They took us up into the hills to see the real voodoo," Judge Martelli said. "Not the junk they show tourists. They knew I'm a judge of the New York State Supreme Court, so they gave us a guide and he said we will show you and Mrs. Martelli the real voodoo, Your Honor."

"They did," Mrs. Martelli said. "And they gave us this bottle of rum as a souvenir. Take a sip."

Bella took the glass. Mrs. Martelli gave the second glass to Dave.

"Sidney here tells me you have a problem," Judge Martelli said. His wife went back to the mahogany table to fill more glasses. "If Sidney says you have a problem, you have a problem."

"Yes, sir," Dave said.

"I trust Sidney," Judge Martelli said. "He clerked for me for two years before he got drafted. Didn't you, Sidney?"

"Yes, sir," Sidney said.

"Did you enjoy it, Sidney?" Judge Martelli said.

"The happiest two years of my life," Sid said.

Judge Martelli nodded.

"Mine too," he said. He turned to Bella and patted the part of the American flag that covered her thigh. "I never had a clerk as good as Sidney before or since." He turned to Dave. "Sidney says you want to buy a piece of property up in Westchester but they won't sell because you're a Jew."

"They didn't exactly say it in so many words," Dave said.

"Did they say it to Jesus in so many words?" Judge Martelli said.

Dave hoped it was a rhetorical question. Fortunately, at this moment Mrs. Martelli appeared over Sid with one of the glasses.

"Drink it, Sidney," she said. "It's from the real voodoo."

Sid tossed off the drink in one swallow.

"Wow!" he said, and held out his glass. "Any chance for seconds?"

The crinkled smile on Mrs. Martelli's face moved the milk-bottle bottoms half an inch up her nose. The beaded calla lilies on her shoulders wiggled.

"For you?" she said. "Of course, Sidney."

She took his glass and moved back to the mahogany table.

"What was I saying?" said Judge Martelli.

Sid's forefinger exploded away from his body. It pointed at Dave. His confusion about Sid's role in this meeting went out the window that faced the Paramount clock. When that "Greeting" from the President of the United States had sent Dave off to war, the world's greatest stage director was widely believed to be Max Reinhardt. Now that he was home from the battlefields, Dave saw that the title could very well have passed to his old buddy Sid Singer. Dave took his cue.

"When Sid and I went to the closing in the office of Miss Biaggi's lawyer," he said smoothly, "he said he was sorry but the closing could not take place because Miss Biaggi's grandfather had died the night before."

Sid's hand went up. The forefinger of his other hand stabbed at his necktie. Dave shut up. Sid came in without causing a ripple.

"You see, Your Honor," Sid said, "title to the property was vested in Miss Biaggi's grandfather. However, because the old man had been rendered incompetent by physical and mental ailments, his granddaughter, Miss Biaggi, was going to sign for him."

The stiff forefinger darted at Dave. He came in like the ghost in *Hamlet*.

"Since the old man died the night before the signing," Dave said, "the lawyer told us Miss Biaggi, who was his sole legatee, is now the sole owner of the property, but she can't dispose of it until the estate is probated."

Judge Martelli nodded and inched himself forward on the couch. Dave had the feeling His Honor was zeroing in on a particularly luscious coconut.

"And there was no telling how long that would take," he said.

"You got it, Your Honor," Sid said.

"Why shouldn't I have it?" His Honor said. "In my years on the bench haven't I seen enough of these disgusting cases of veiled anti-Semitism to make a person sick?"

"Remember *Imbesi v. Imbesi?*" Sid said.

"Remember it?" Judge Martelli said. "I decided it."

The stiff finger stabbed toward Dave.

"What was *Imbesi v. Imbesi?*" Dave said.

Judge Martelli shook his head. Dave guessed that, on closer inspection, the coconut had looked not so luscious after all.

"A case involving a situation not dissimilar to yours," His Honor said.

"Historic," Sid said. "There were, of course, a few differences between that situation and the one in which my partner and Miss Biaggi are involved."

"Spell them out, Sidney," His Honor said.

"In *Imbesi v. Imbesi* it was not an onion farm but a big private estate," Sid said. "Mr. Imbesi's great-grandfather had been a sewer contractor in New York under Boss Tweed. Also, it was not in Beechwood but in that Westchester town that's nearer Long Island Sound."

"Sequesta," Judge Martelli said.

"My God, Your Honor," Sid said. "It's amazing how you remember things, sir."

"A boy from Mulberry Street who once shined shoes in Times Square," Judge Martelli said. "A boy who then grew up to be a Justice of the New York State Supreme Court. Such a boy does not forget things."

"Especially in historic cases," Sid said.

"You can say that again," Judge Martelli said. "The lower court threw the case out because it held the plaintiff and the defendant had made a mockery of the law."

Sid's finger stabbed in the direction of Dave's navel.

"In what way, sir?" Dave said.

"To beat the anti-Semites who would not allow Mr. Imbesi to sell to Miss Yetta Horowitz, the two people got married," Judge Martelli said. "Thus, Mr. Imbesi, who had always had title to the property, continued to hold the title, and the anti Semites around that town could do nothing about it, but they were furious, because now Mr. Imbesi had a Jewish wife and she was living right there in the middle of those anti-Semites."

Sid gave Dave the signal.

"What was the nature of the suit?" Dave said.

"Divorce," Judge Martelli said.

Again the signal.

Dave responded: "Divorce?"

Rising inflection.

"Divorce," Judge Martelli said. "Miss Horowitz and Mr. Imbesi were not in love. They just got married to beat the anti-Semites. A few weeks after the wedding she sued him for divorce, and he gave her the property as a settlement instead of alimony. So now they had a full-fledged fourteen-carat Jew owning a big piece of property in the heart of a community that had never allowed Jews to buy into the area. The First Selectman of Sequesta entered an *amicus curiae* brief, claiming fraud. The lower court said he was right, and it threw out the case. Mrs. Imbesi appealed, and the case came to me."

Judge Martelli's huge simian lips wrapped themselves around the mouth of the small glass and he threw back his head. The rum went down like a bowling ball dropping into a well. Dave heard the glug.

"They came to the wrong party," Sid said. "Didn't they, Your Honor?"

"Depends on whose side you're on," Judge Martelli said. "If you're a Sequesta anti-Semite, I was the wrong judge. If you're a Jewish girl named Horowitz who wants to live in Westchester, I was the right judge."

"His Honor has a long record as a champion of civil rights," Sid said.

"No," Judge Martelli said. "I have a long memory. Any boy born on Mulberry Street knows about discrimination. He doesn't have to study. There's a first-class teacher on every uptown street corner. Teaching poison. I didn't know much about Jews when I was a boy. But I knew about wops. Every place I went uptown, beginning with my shoeshine box, I got it rubbed into me. Then I learned I wasn't the only one. I learned about kikes. And I made up my mind. Just like I made up my mind someday I was going to live where I could see the Paramount clock from my window, I made up my mind I was going to do as much as I could to clean out this poison. So I reversed the lower court in *Imbesi v. Imbesi*."

Sid's forefinger gave Dave the stab signal.

"So what Miss Biaggi and I have planned?" Dave said. "You are in sympathy, Your Honor?"

The little monkey face seemed to fall apart. Dave had a moment of terror. Then he saw that Judge Martelli was smiling.

"A beautiful Italian girl like this?" he said. He patted Bella's thigh. "I'm not only in sympathy," His Honor said. "I'm jealous."

Sid leaned forward.

"Here are the medical certificates, sir," he said.

"And the license?" Judge Martelli said.

"Here, sir," Dave said.

"Angela," His Honor called across the room. "Please stop fussing and come over here. For this we need two witnesses."

6

While Dave Dehn was trying to figure out what to do about a wife he did not want, a brand-new neighbor of his was struggling with another problem. A problem Dave in his nearly thirty-two years had not yet encountered.

Mike Palgrave was troubled by his family's weight.

When the Palgraves, soon after they were married, had come to live in Beechwood, Mike had weighed 175. Not bad for a six-footer. And Sally had fluctuated between 120 and 123. Which was even better. After all, Sally was a tall girl, who had played center on the Brearley basketball team before she went to Bennington.

"How'd you make out?" Sally called from the kitchen.

"Lousy," Mike called back. "Up a pound and a half."

For another few moments he watched hopefully, allowing the balance bar to shiver gently. But it did not move out of its tiny orbit. Mike knew it wouldn't. It never did. The scale had come from a doctors'-equipment supply house. It was probably the most expensive piece of machinery in the Palgrave home. It was loathsomely accurate.

Mike stepped off the scale with a feeling that shocked him. Months ago he had begun to step off the scale every morning with a feeling of discomfort. Then it had become a feeling of uneasiness. Now, this morning, Mike had stepped off the scale with a feeling of terror. What the hell was happening to him?

"I don't understand it," Sally said from the kitchen. "All day yesterday we ate exactly the same things, and this morning I was up only three-quarters of a pound. Unless you cheated at lunch?"

"I didn't have any lunch yesterday," Mike said. "I turned down an invitation from Colin Babington for the City Club because it was Thursday, and on Thursdays the specialty is eggs Benedict. I forced myself to stay in the office, working on the plans for the Blaisdell garage. Miss Royko brought me two cups of black coffee. That's all I had. Honest."

"Well," Sally said, "it's damned peculiar."

It had been for some time. But now, to his astonishment, Mike saw that it had become something worse. Mike Palgrave did not like that. He hated terror. Years ago he had worked out a small trick for jolting himself out of unpleasant moments. He set it in motion now. With great deliberation, as though he were setting the lens speed and aperture reading on his Leica, he looked at his wrist watch.

"For the record," Mike called to Sally, trying for a light tone, "as of 7:28 A.M., October 21, 1946, your fat husband weighs two hundred and forty-two pounds."

He stepped across to the ledger on the Formica counter beside the basin. He and Sally kept the ledger open at all times, pencil at the ready. Mike made his regular morning entry. In the column next to the one in which he wrote his 242 he saw Sally's just-entered 219. Mike's mind was trained to handle the world in mathematical terms. It automatically added together the two figures. As of this moment the Palgrave family weighed 461 pounds. Deep in his belly Mike felt a small shiver.

"Breakfast in a minute," Sally called.

"Right," Mike called back.

Putting on his shirt, he noticed that the seventeen neck was beginning to feel tight. When he and Sally had come to live in Beechwood, Mike Palgrave had worn a size fifteen collar.

He walked to the window to knot his tie. The view always soothed him. The view was the reason he and Sally had come to live in Beechwood.

The house was an ingeniously designed sprawling one-story structure. Its principal material was weather-beaten California redwood slabs, in which at irregular intervals were embedded rough gray flagstones. The house had porthole windows framed in white and, on the long flat roof, a widow's walk fenced by a delicate wrought-iron cage painted black. It was one of the earliest appearances of modern construction in that area of Westchester, and the first in Beechwood. Any one interested in architecture would probably have suspected on first sight that the house had been built by an architect for his own use. In spite of its eye-catching oddity, it looked like a home.

The house sat at the crest of Cavalry Road, facing, far below, Sequesta Pond. It was not really a pond. It was actually an impressive body of water into which the Sequesta River, after its long, unhurried trip down from the Berkshires, paused to sun itself, so to speak, before moving on to Long Island Sound. The Sound gleamed and danced magnificently in the near distance, catching the sun like a million shattered mirrors. Mike Palgrave yielded to no man in his admiration for the Sound. But it was not in the same league with Sequesta Pond.

The Sound was all sailboats and Chris-Crafts and sunlit waves or, in the winter, rough white-capped sea. But the Pond was always the same. A placid sheet of dark glass with a jagged shoreline full of secret little coves. Over them hung maple and weeping willow and pin oak and trembling aspen. Through the leaves in the summer, and through the branches in the winter, Mike could see the old Colonials and the boathouses and the swimming docks that wealthy New Yorkers had started building at the turn of the century. They had built them as summer places from which they could commute to their Wall Street offices. Most of these were now year-round residences from which the sons of those early builders commuted to the same offices.

Pep DeJong, with whom Mike Palgrave had roomed at M.I.T., had been born in one of those houses. When Pep got married, the wedding present from his father had been five acres on the crest of Cavalry Road. Pep got started at once.

By the time his dream house was half finished, Pep was no longer married. He was bitter about the divorce. He stopped work on the dream house and moved into an apartment on Sutton Place.

When Mike and Sally got married, Pep offered them the dream house for their honeymoon. Their first morning on Cavalry Road, as they looked down on the misted surface of Sequesta Pond, they knew this was where they wanted to live.

Before they could broach the subject to Pep DeJong, Pearl Harbor shifted his interests from Sutton Place to the Navy, and Pep offered to sell the place to the Palgraves for whatever they considered a reasonable price. The figure was set at a meeting between Sally's father, Mike's father, and Pep's father. Pep went off to get himself killed at Peleliu. Mike and Sally settled into the unfinished dream house. It was still unfinished.

Not because during the almost five years they had lived in it Mike and Sally had done no work on the place. On the contrary. They had done a lot. What they had done had been fun. Pep and Mike had shared the same architectural ideas. Nothing Pep had done, therefore, had to be torn down. It was simply a matter of addition, but it was a bad time for dream houses: the war had brought a severe shortage of building materials. Also, there was the matter of time. Soon after they arrived in Beechwood, Mike had opened an office on Main Street.

To his and Sally's pleased surprise, commissions had been plentiful almost at once. Plentiful and exciting. Every assignment was what Sally called a challenge. She had majored at Bennington in applied psychology. The word was not inaccurate. If to design and build a house for a client without the availability of bricks and lumber was not a challenge, what was?

"Breakfast!" Sally called.

Mike came into the kitchen. It had a deep, high fireplace surrounded by blue-and-white Dutch tiles, and was equipped with a functional roasting spit that could accommodate a small pig. The cooking section of the kitchen was on the left, under a picture window that seemed to bring Sequesta Pond right up the hill into the room. The dining area was at the far end, under another picture window. This one looked out on the west side of Cavalry Road. It ran downhill for almost two miles, all the way into Main Street. The view was no match for Sequesta Pond, but it had charms of its own.

From this window Mike could see the big clock on the square tower of Town Hall; the green-and-white cottage that was Colin Babington's office; and the piece of Main Street on which Sally's "Sally Palgrave Interior Designs" shop sat between Bohack's and the First Beechwood Trust. Mike could not see his own office. It was up Main Street, going toward Larchmont, just beyond the sight lines from the dining alcove on Cavalry Road. But Mike found it pleasant to know it was there. Anyway, he had always found it pleasant. Until this morning.

"Your lunch with Bella Biaggi's new husband," Sally said. "This man named Dehn, is it?"

"David Dehn, yes," Mike said. "What about him?"

"I don't know anything about him," Sally said. "Except that he's as rich as God, or so Avis Babington told me yesterday when she came into the shop to pick up the brass shelf strip for her étagère."

"How does Avis Babington know how rich Mr. Dehn is?" Mike said.

"Her husband is Bella Biaggi's lawyer," Sally said. "You know that. What's the matter with you?"

Mike wished he knew.

"Nothing," he said. "I was just trying to remember if my date with Mr. Dehn is for lunch or if it's just a regular business appointment."

"Avis Babington says this Mr. Dehn is killingly handsome," Sally said.

"Has she met him?" Mike said.

"No, but Colin told her," Sally said. "He had a meeting with Mr. Dehn in his office last week, and Colin says he looks a little like a Jewish Gary Cooper."

"Oh, come on," Mike said. "Nobody in the world ever looked less Jewish than Gary Cooper."

"I'm just quoting what Avis says Colin told her," Sally said.

"A man who resembles Gary Cooper," Mike said. "And who is as rich as God, Avis says. Why should a man like that come poking around a decaying old onion farm in Westchester to find and marry a barefoot girl without breeding or education or a dress to her back or a dime to her name?"

"When we were kids," Sally said, "why did Daddy Browning, that old man with all those real estate millions, why did he marry that sixteen-year-old illiterate blob of vulgarity out of Hell's Kitchen named Peaches Heenan?"

"My classmates at Ethical Culture knew the answer to that one," Mike said. "They maintained Peaches was the possessor of a fur-lined twat."

"Maybe Bella Biaggi is similarly equipped," Sally said.

"I wouldn't know," Mike said.

"I should hope not," Sally said. "But I'll tell you who could supply the information."

"Who?" Mike said.

"Tony D'Alessandro," Sally said.

"Isn't he the kid who knocked up the Rinaldi girl and had to marry her?" Mike said.

"He had to marry her," Sally said, "but he didn't have to live with her. He swore he'd never been in the sack with the Rinaldi girl, but nobody believed him, so after the wedding he just went his merry way as before, and his merry way was

Bella Biaggi. Everybody in town knows Bella and Tony have had a thing going since they were in high school."

Mike could suddenly see the slender figure in the man's T-shirt. As slender as Sally had been when they first met. Tony D'Alessandro was one lucky son of a bitch.

"I guess this is so-long-Tony time," Mike said. "Rich men from New York have a tendency to frown on their brides' continuing to put out for wop building contractors who take their girls to the movies on Saturday night in pickup trucks."

"I hope Mr. Dehn does not frown on commissioning you to build a lovely mansion in which to house his brand-new bride," Sally said. "At this moment in its financial life the Palgrave family could use a nice big fat commission."

7

Peering through the windshield as the jeep bumped along the cracks and potholes of the worn black-top, Mike Palgrave saw up ahead a man standing on the sagging porch of the Biaggi house. He was watching Mike's approach. The sun was directly overhead, so it was impossible to make out details. But Mike could see from the sunlit silhouette what Colin Babington had meant.

The outline was tall and slender. Broad shoulders. A slight stoop, which was a surprise: Mike Palgrave had always associated a stoop with the unconscious attempt of a tall, shy man to minimize his height in a world of shorter people. Mike's only contact with Mr. Dehn had been the telephone call inviting him to this meeting. Mr. Dehn on the phone had not sounded shy.

He certainly did not look shy. He was standing with his hands resting easily on his narrow hips. Mike grinned. It was as though Mr. Dehn had overheard Colin Babington's description of him and he was doing a burlesqued imitation of it. He was standing the way almost every movie actor in Westerns, including Gary Cooper, stands while awaiting the arrival of a horseman cantering toward him through the chaparral, resting his hands easily on the holsters of his gun belt. Then Mike pulled the jeep up to the porch. The sun was cut abruptly by the canvas top. Mike saw Mr. Dehn's face, and he saw also that Colin Babington was not so far wrong in his description.

Like Mr. Dehn's body, his face was long and lean. A square chin jutted just enough to give the impression of a not unpleasant toughness. Pale blue eyes—so very pale that, like the eyes of Orphan Annie in the comic strip, they did not seem to have pupils. A widow's peak of sandy hair. A strong, slightly hooked nose. And the one feature that had obviously moved Colin Babington to his description: two long, deep creases that might have been a surgeon's incisions. They ran down Mr. Dehn's cheeks like a pair of parentheses from the backs of his nostrils to the corners of his mouth.

"Mr. Palgrave?"

"Yes," Mike said.

He climbed out of the jeep.

"Mr. Dehn?"

"Yes," Mr. Dehn said. "Good of you to come."

He came down the two sagging porch steps. They shook hands. Mr. Dehn did it as though Mike's hand were a lobster claw out of which he was determined to crack the last scrap of meat. Mike winced and examined the envelope, so to speak, in which the tall young man was encased. He saw at once that it had cost money.

Mike Palgrave was aware of clothes. Until he was ten he had worn, like all the other kids at Ethical Culture, chinos and pull-overs and sneakers. At ten his mother enrolled him in Miss De Santo's dancing school. Mike's father took him to Brooks Brothers for his first formal suit. Mike had been going there ever since. He could see that Mr. Dehn had been going there too.

The blue blazer, the button-down white Oxford shirt, the three-stripe tie, the Peale shoes could have come from no other store. As a Brooks Brothers man, Mike Palgrave felt he had to approve of another man who got his clothes in the same place. Why, then, did Mike feel there was something wrong about the way the very correct Mr. Dehn was dressed?

"I'm not going to invite you in," he said. "The place is a dump. I'm going to tear it down and start all over again. I wouldn't want to insult an architect by showing him the inside of this pile of garbage."

Mike's first thought was for his rumbling stomach. If Mr. Dehn was not going to invite him in, it looked as though Mr. Dehn was not going to give him lunch. Mr. Dehn did not seem to be dressed for supervising a cook-out. Mike's already roiling insides growled a sharp warning. How long could he last before he was able to make it back to the Burger 'N' Shake Shop on Main Street?

"It's pretty hard to insult an architect," Mike said. "By showing him bad or old construction, I mean. In fact, sometimes it helps. If you see what your clients lived with before you were called in, quite frequently it gives you some inkling of what they might want to replace it."

"Seeing the inside of this junk heap won't help you," Mr. Dehn said. "Not in the direction I want to go. What I have in mind is totally different from anything you've ever done, Mr. Palgrave."

"From that, Mr. Dehn, I would have to assume you know everything I have ever done."

"The assumption is correct," Mr. Dehn said.

Mike waited for more. But there wasn't any more. Mr. Dehn's interest in the point seemed to have been exhausted.

"There aren't even any chairs inside on which we can sit and talk," he said. "You mind if we walk down the road a bit? There's a place we can sit in reasonable comfort. It's certainly more comfortable than the chairs inside, and it gives you a view of the house and the area around it on which I want to build after the house is cleared away. It'll make it easier for you to grasp what I have in mind."

He started up the road. Mike fell in beside him.

With his first step, Mr. Dehn tapped the knot in his tie and fooled delicately with its location in the inverted V of his collar. A few yards farther along the black-top, he checked his cuff links. A couple of moments later, Mr. Dehn looked down at his shoes. They gleamed so brightly in the sunlight that Mike knew this was Mr. Dehn's first venture outdoors that day. Turkey Hill Road was a dusty thoroughfare. Then Mr. Dehn shook his shoulders more comfortably into the fit of his navy blue blazer, and he touched the gold button that held the coat closed around his lean, muscular frame.

When Mike caught the glance Mr. Dehn sent him out of the corner of his eye, Mike knew at once why he had felt there was something wrong about the way the very correctly dressed Mr. Dehn was dressed.

Mr. Dehn obviously knew the right shop to which a man of parts should go for his clothes. But it was knowledge recently acquired. Mr. Dehn was still checking what he wore against what other men of parts were wearing. Mike was willing to bet that Mr. Dehn, who was clearly rich, had not been rich very long.

"How about this?" he said.

Mr. Dehn was pointing to a ten-or-twelve-foot length of partly decayed elm trunk. It lay at the edge of the road, backed by a tangled growth of sumac.

"Fine," Mike said.

"It's clean," Mr. Dehn said. "I've been sitting on it quite a lot these last few days."

It might have been clean, but Mr. Dehn was obviously a careful man. He pulled a handkerchief from his pocket, shook out the folds, and slapped from the top of the log nothing Mike could see. He wondered if the small performance was a calculated bit of elegance intended by Mr. Dehn to impress his visitor. Mr. Dehn gestured for Mike to sit, then sat down beside him. Mr. Dehn pulled his gray flannels up a couple of inches on his knees so that the crease would not be damaged. He gestured toward the house they had just left behind them.

"Quite a sight," he said, "isn't it?"

"Well, it's pretty old," Mike said. "And nothing much has been done to it in the way of paint for many years."

"I don't mean the house," Mr. Dehn said. "That's junk. I mean the view."

Mike looked beyond the house. It wasn't nearly the view he and Sally had from their kitchen window. Turkey Hill sat lower than the crest of Cavalry Road. There was no sign of Sequesta Pond. Only the Sound. Perhaps the word only was not fair. From the log on which Mike and Mr. Dehn were sitting, Long Island Sound in the October sunlight was a breathtaking sight. It did not, like Sequesta Pond, exude peace. It trumpeted magnificence. Mike guessed that that was what Mr. Dehn had meant.

"Yes," Mike said. "My wife and I have been living here in Beechwood for almost five years. We never get tired of it."

"People looking out at a thing like that," Mr. Dehn said. "I don't mean tourists stopping to snap a picture of the view. I mean people living here. Seeing a sight like that all the time. Even when they're not looking at it. Just being aware of it. While they're cooking or working or praying or whatever they're doing. It would give them a feeling of confidence. They'd have the guts not to be scared."

Mr. Dehn paused. Mike wondered if he was expected to comment. Mr. Dehn had not put his words in the form of a question. His last sentence had not ended on a rising inflection. But Mike felt there was something odd in Mr. Dehn's statement.

The people for whom Mike designed houses always talked about the view. Mike had learned how to reply. It was part of the architect's bedside manner. But Mike had never heard a potential client, in discussing the view he wanted from the windows of his house, speak about enjoying the view while praying, or because of the view finding in himself the guts not to be scared.

Again, since he didn't know what to say Mike followed his rule: he said nothing. Mr. Dehn did not seem to be aware of Mike's silence. Mr. Dehn had retreated from the lump of decayed elm on which they were sitting. Mr. Dehn had gone off into a private place inside his head. Watching him out of the corner of his eye, Mike was sure Mr. Dehn was not even seeing the Sound. The Dehn eyelid nearest Mike did not blink.

Astonished, Mike saw that Mr. Dehn seemed to be in the grip of something not unlike a trance.

Mr. Dehn's body was shaking. Beads of sweat had come up on his forehead. His hands, resting on the knees covered with impeccably tailored gray flannel, were clenched into fists. The knuckles had gone white. The unblinking eyes stared out and out and out, beyond Long Island Sound. Mike Palgrave suddenly felt the way he had felt that morning when he had stepped off the scale. Scared. Then Mr. Dehn seemed to come back from wherever he had been.

"Do you know the Statue of Liberty?" he said.

The voice was casual. Mr. Dehn's hand came up and, even more casually, brushed away the beads of sweat.

"You mean the Statue of Liberty?" Mike said. "Down there in New York Bay? The lady with the torch?"

"Yes, on Bedloe's Island," Mr. Dehn said. "Do you know it?"

"If you mean have I ever visited it, no," Mike said. "But of course I know it. I mean, in the sense that I know what it is, and what it means, and how it was a gift from France. All that, yes, I certainly do know it. I must say I didn't know the island it's on is called Bedloe's."

"You ought to go down someday and go over on the ferry and have a look," Mr. Dehn said. "Close up. The way you're now looking at that pile of junk down the road. I don't mean you should go for patriotic reasons. I mean you should go as an architect. It would interest you professionally."

"In what way?" Mike said.

"For the house I want to build here," Mr. Dehn said.

"You want to build a house here on Turkey Hill Road that will look like the Statue of Liberty?" Mike said.

"Not the entire statue," Mr. Dehn said. "Just the pedestal."

"I see," Mike said.

"No, you don't," Mr. Dehn said. "You can't, since you've never been on Bedloe's Island."

"I was just using a figure of speech," Mike said. "To indicate that I understand you want me to build a house for you that will look not like the entire Statue of Liberty but only the pedestal."

Mr. Dehn turned and smiled at him. The smile caused the vertical creases to cut more deeply into Mr. Dehn's cheeks. My God, Mike thought, the son of a bitch does look like Gary Cooper.

"I know you think I sound like a nut," Mr. Dehn said. "I've talked to quite a few architects these past few months, and I got the impression the good ones know how to take nuts in their stride. Now, I'm not a nut, Mr. Palgrave, but I'm aware that what I want you to do for me may sound nutty. So I urge you to stop hunching over the handle bars. Just relax and listen. I think you'll like what I have in mind. I think you'll enjoy building it. Okay?"

There was always a moment in a first encounter with a new client when Mike Palgrave's caution, his uneasiness and indecision, his concealed but very real fear of all strangers turned a corner about the particular stranger with whom he was dealing. This was such a moment. Abruptly, Mike knew that he liked Mr. Dehn.

"Okay," Mike said.

"When you visit Bedloe's Island," Mr. Dehn said, "you'll notice something that is not very noticeable when you see the statue from the distance. Say from the deck of a ship coming up New York Harbor. Or standing by the rail in Battery Park. From the distance what you see is this gigantic woman, in flowing robes, holding up a torch, because that's what you're supposed to see. You may be aware that the statue is standing on a low flat platform, but who cares about platforms? It's the statue that counts. Well, for me, Mr. Palgrave, it's not the statue that counts. It's the platform."

"In what way?" Mike said.

"Up close," Mr. Dehn said. "When you're actually standing there on Bedloe's Island, you find that that platform is an impressive piece of architecture. Anyway, I did."

"The design?" Mike said. "The construction?"

"Both," Mr. Dehn said. "It looks like a fort. From the way

it's positioned there in the bay, I wouldn't be at all surprised to learn that the architect who built it as a resting place for this statue that was a present from France—I have a sneaking suspicion he had that in mind. A fort. A stone structure commanding New York Harbor. Something from which with enough guns you could hold off an invader. It impressed me. Sitting here on this log and looking out at that view, I've given it a lot of thought since I came up here from New York. I've come to the conclusion that what I saw on Bedloe's Island is closer to what I have in mind than anything I've seen these last few months. Anyway, I'm tired of hunting. I want to get started."

"Let's see if I've got this straight," Mike said. "Up here on Turkey Hill Road, on that site in front of us where the old Biaggi house now stands, you want to build a reproduction of the base of the Statue of Liberty?"

Mr. Dehn smiled again.

"Scared?" he said.

Mike Palgrave could feel his face grow hot.

"No, of course not," he said.

"Then what?" Mr. Dehn said.

"What do you mean, what?" Mike said.

"I'm waiting for positive waves," Mr. Dehn said. "I don't feel any of them coming out of you."

"They're not negative either," Mike said. "What you're sensing is a little confusion."

"Okay," Mr. Dehn said. "Ask clarifying questions. I'll answer."

"While you were on Bedloe's Island," Mike said, "did you happen to note how big the statue is? And how much it weighs?"

"I bought one of those souvenir booklets," Mr. Dehn said. "As I recall, it says the statue measures 156 feet from her sandals to the top of her torch, and the lady weighs 450,000 pounds."

"Do you remember the dimensions of the pedestal?" Mike said.

"No, I don't," Mr. Dehn said.

"I don't know what they are either," Mike said. "But it's my business to know a good deal about the stresses and strains of building materials. We have an object 156 feet high that weighs about half a million pounds, or approximately 250 tons. To support such an object would require a platform roughly two hundred feet square. You know where Brooks Brothers is located? The store?"

Mr. Dehn's hand darted involuntarily to the knot in his three-stripe tie. He shot a sharp, slanting glance at Mike.

"Sure," he said. "Why?"

"Forty-fourth and Madison," Mike said. "Walk north to Forty-fifth. Turn left into Forty-fifth. Walk west two hundred feet to the first lamppost. They're set by city ordinance two hundred feet apart. Left again, and imagine yourself walking south, through the bricks and mortar of all those office buildings. You come out on Forty-fourth. Left once more, and down to Brooks Brothers on the Madison Avenue corner. You know what you've just done, Mr. Dehn?"

"What?" Mr. Dehn said.

"You have just walked around the perimeter of the platform on which the Statue of Liberty stands," Mike said.

"I see your point," Mr. Dehn said. "If I'd made myself clearer, Mr. Palgrave, you wouldn't have had to make the point. I've got a pretty big place here. One hundred and eighty acres. I've never measured, but when I walk from that crummy house up this way, toward the end of my property, I have a feeling I'm walking several city blocks. It doesn't matter, because I don't want a building here as big as the pedestal of the Statue of Liberty. What I want is a building that looks like the pedestal of the Statue of Liberty. The size is something that I'll leave to my architect. Within limits, anyway. I'll give you the guidelines. You tell me how big it will have to be."

"To fit that cleared space up there?" Mike said. "Where the Biaggi house now stands?"

"Yes and no," Mr. Dehn said. "I want it on that spot because I want the building to command the entrance to Turkey Hill Road, but I also want it to have room for a meeting hall on the ground floor."

"A meeting hall?" Mike said.

"A place where a group of people can get together and hold meetings," Mr. Dehn said. "A meeting hall. An auditorium. A council chamber. I don't care what you call it. I just want that kind of ground floor."

"That means what you have in mind," Mike said, "I *think* what you have in mind—Mr. Dehn, you're not thinking of a family dwelling?"

"Upstairs, maybe," Mr. Dehn said. "I'm not sure yet how many floors I'll want above the meeting hall. We can come to that later. Right now I'd like you to fix the meeting-hall ground floor in your mind. So you can work out the dimensions."

"That will depend on how many people you plan to bring together in this meeting hall," Mike said.

Mr. Dehn squinted out at Long Island Sound. Once again Mike had the feeling Mr. Dehn had gone away from Turkey Hill Road. To a secret place somewhere inside his head. It might have been the place to which he had gone earlier, but Mike didn't think so. Mr. Dehn's hands on his knees were not clenched into fists. His forehead was dry. He was not shaking. Mr. Dehn obviously had more than one secret place inside his head. The one into which he had now retreated was apparently the one in which he did his arithmetic.

"Let's say a couple of hundred people," he said finally.

"Doing what?" Mike said.

"I don't understand," Mr. Dehn said.

"A couple of hundred people playing basketball calls for a room of a certain size," Mike said. "A couple of hundred people sitting on benches listening to a lecture, that's a room of a different size."

"Of course," Mr. Dehn said. "Let's say a room that could accommodate a couple of hundred people listening to a lecture."

75

"Then I think we won't need a building as big as a city block," Mike said. "We'll want something bigger than that Biaggi house up there right now, but I think we can utilize quite a lot of space around the plot on which that house now stands without creating something disproportionate to the setting."

"Good," Mr. Dehn said. "Before you go off to tackle sketches, then, I think I'd better summarize. I don't want you wasting your time because I haven't made myself clear. So, then, first, a building that will accommodate on the ground floor an auditorium large enough to seat at least two hundred people. Right?"

"Right," Mike said.

"With, of course, adequate space up front for a stage or its equivalent," Mr. Dehn said.

"Of course," Mike said.

"The structure to be as close as possible to the shape of the Statue of Liberty pedestal," Mr. Dehn said. "Made of stone, naturally."

"Have you seen the bank on Main Street?" Mike said.

"Yes," Mr. Dehn said. "Why?"

"It's made of gray fieldstone," Mike said. "Fieldstone is indigenous to this area. A great many houses not only here in Beechwood but also in Rye and Larchmont and Mamaroneck, most of Westchester, they're built with gray fieldstone. Part of my own house on Cavalry Road is made of fieldstone. If we use that, you have my assurance your structure will blend with the landscape beautifully."

"Okay," Mr. Dehn said. "You've sold me. Now, there's one more thing."

"Yes?" Mike said.

"The man who does the outside of my building," Mr. Dehn said: "I'd like the same man to design and build the inside."

"That's customary with all architects who build homes," Mike said.

"I'm not building a home," Mr. Dehn said.

"What are you building?" Mike said.

"A synagogue," Mr. Dehn said.

Mike Palgrave did not know if at this point there was a pause in the conversation. He did know that he made it a point to come in with a prompt reply. Mike always did, when in a face-to-face meeting he was jolted by something the other man said.

"Well," he said, feeling not only the pause, but also Mr. Dehn's pale blue eyes turned full on him, "you said earlier that you'd done a little investigating about me, and you knew pretty much everything I had done professionally, so I assume you know I've never before built a synagogue."

The tops and bottoms of Mr. Dehn's pale blue eyes disappeared as his eyelids came together to form a couple of slits.

"It's time you did, Mr. Cohen," he said.

Mike Palgrave's first reaction came from his stomach. It growled a protest so angry and loud that he was certain Mr. Dehn could hear it. Mike was glad he was sitting down. His stomach had been hollow when he turned the jeep into Turkey Hill Road. Now the emptiness made him feel faint. But he carried on. He knew how to do that. He and Sally had been carrying on for almost five years. Ever since they had come to Beechwood.

"Your investigation has obviously been thorough," Mike said.

"Do you mind my knowing your real name is Meyer Cohen?" Mr. Dehn said.

Curiously enough, Mike was not sure. This astonished him. Brutally, speaking for himself, the answer was yes. Of course he minded. You didn't hide something from your neighbors for almost five years without minding when somebody comes along and, without warning, rips your beard off. But there was that thing about Mr. Dehn. The thing that had made Mike decide he liked him.

"I do and I don't," Mike said. At once he felt better. "I know I'm not the first Jew who changed his name, but that doesn't cover it all the way. When you do something like that, you're always aware not of the other guys who've done it.

You're always aware of yourself. You're the first *you* who has done it. If you know what I mean."

"I do," Mr. Dehn said. "And I want you to know what *I* mean. I'm not criticizing you. I don't have the right to. If you're born with a name like mine the issue doesn't have to be faced. I'm not a MacIntosh or a Saltonstall or a Babington. But I am a D, e, h, n. Dane. Hell, I could be anything from a Dutch Catholic to a Blackfoot Indian. I mean, for business reasons. Not socially. Just as a name to front for you in business, Dehn is no handicap. It's the Garfinkels and the Finkelsteins who have it tough."

"Not to mention the Cohens," Mike said.

"Forget it," Mr. Dehn said. "To me you're what you are to everybody else in this town. An architect named Palgrave."

Somehow, Mike felt, that was not enough. What he had said to Mr. Dehn had made him feel good. So he wanted to say more.

"Would you mind telling me how you happened to choose me for this job?" he said.

"On one condition," Mr. Dehn said.

"What's that?"

"From here on in, what I tell you," Mr. Dehn said, "and what you tell me, it goes no further than the two of us."

"The condition is met," Mike said.

"Okay, then," Mr. Dehn said. "Just as I checked you out, before I even thought of an architect I checked out Beechwood. Not a synagogue in town. That told me all I had to know. So I hunted around New York for an architect, and I came across some pretty good ones, but something about all of them bothered me. I didn't know what it was until my partner pointed it out to me. They were all goyim, and for what I had in mind that was no good. To build a synagogue I wanted a Jewish architect. I checked out all the architects in Beechwood. No luck. All goyim. Then a funny thing happened. Your name reminded my partner of something."

"Which one of my names?" Mike said.

"The only one we knew at the time," Mr. Dehn said. "Your

goy name. Palgrave. My partner is a guy named Sid Singer. Wall-to-wall brains. You'll meet him. Anyway, Sid said he'd heard the name Palgrave only once before in his life. When we were in Ethan Allen High school together. In English class we used a poetry anthology called *Palgrave's Golden Treasury.* And Sid remembered the introduction to the book. It was written by a man named Louis Untermeyer. He said Palgrave's real name had been Meyer Cohen. Purely on a hunch, Sid said I'll bet this Michael Palgrave, this architect up in Beechwood, I'll bet he's a Meyer Cohen. So we checked you out and like they say, the rest is history."

Mike laughed. Not a business-meeting laugh. Good point, ha, ha. None of that. Mike really laughed. With pleasure.

"There's just a slight error in your partner's analysis," he said. "Meyer Cohen is my father's name. Me, I'm Morris Cohen."

Mr. Dehn grinned and put out his hand.

"Shalom," he said.

Mike grinned.

"Next year in Jerusalem," he said.

They shook hands.

"Okay," Mr. Dehn said. "I'll have Sid get in touch with you to fix the terms and arrange for a retainer. In the meantime, keep all this under your hat. Until the ground floor is built, nobody in Beechwood has to know what the inside is going to be."

"May I tell my wife?" Mike said.

"Is she Jewish?" Mr. Dehn said.

"Sylvia Mersky that was," Mike said.

Mr. Dehn laughed again.

"I insist that you tell her," he said.

They walked back to Mike's jeep.

"I'll go down to New York tomorrow and have a look at Bedloe's Island," he said. "I might have a preliminary sketch for you next week."

"Great," Mr. Dehn said. "I don't want to sound as though I'm rushing you, but I don't want you to pay any attention to the way I don't want to sound. That's just insincere politeness. The truth is I'm in one hell of a hurry."

Mike turned the ignition key.

"So am I, Mr. Dehn," he said.

It wasn't until he turned the jeep out of Turkey Hill Road that Mike realized his empty stomach was no longer growling. He wouldn't have to sneak into the Burger 'N' Shake for the bootlegged lunch about which he had been lying to Sally for over a year. For the first time since his weight had begun to scare him, Mike knew his 140-calorie breakfast would without strain carry him through to dinner.

8

What he did not know was that Mr. Dehn was grinning happily as he stood at the Biaggi end of Turkey Hill Road, watching Mike Palgrave's jeep bump its way up to the low rise. From this high point the smooth part of the road fell away down to Main Street.

Dave watched with a sense of exhilaration. He had found the right man. It was luck, of course. If this fat boy had proved to be the wrong man, Dave was sure before long he would have found someone who would have been the right man. He had the money. It not only, as advertised, talked. It also attracted. Money made its own luck. The way rich people made their own weather. So if it was luck, of course it was also the right kind of luck. Luck that triggered a domino reaction. Other luck was on the way.

The jeep topped the low rise, dipped down, and disappeared. Dave looked at his watch. Ten minutes after one. A year and a half ago, when he was still in Germany and the plan had begun to take shape in his mind, Dave had assumed getting the right architect would hold him up for weeks, maybe months. It had taken one hour and ten minutes.

If all the other parts of the plan clicked along at this pace, he would be in operation by Yom Kippur of next year.

The feeling of exhilaration was followed by what was always for Dave the inevitable sequel: hunger. The familiar knotting in his stomach brought with it a thought that made Dave grin as he turned into the house and climbed to the second floor.

His marriage was different from that of other men. It provided him with something other men might not have prized: the solid rock he could trust to support what he had learned in Germany he wanted to do with the rest of his life.

The bedroom in which Bella's grandfather had died had not changed much since she had become Mrs. Dehn. What little change there was had been caused by Dave. It was the sort of change that took place in a hotel room when a man checked in for the night. The changes did not affect the decoration. They were merely signs of a human presence. Razor and toothbrush in the bathroom. Pajamas and robe in the closet. A change of shirts in the open bureau drawer. Dave had to sleep in the room a couple of nights a week.

Now that he'd set Mike Palgrave in motion, other aspects of the project would begin to move out of the planning phase. Dave would have to spend more time in Beechwood. He'd probably have to bring up a couple of extra suits and a few more shirts. Bella would notice. But she would not comment.

She did not get in his way. He tried not to get in hers. He might have been a boarder to whom she had rented the upstairs room on condition that they did not interfere with each other's comings and goings. Dave could not help noticing, however, that she was a slob at heart. The day after they were married, Dave had put a substantial deposit into Bella's checking account in the Beechwood Bank & Trust.

"If that's not enough," he had said, "let me know."

"It's enough," she had said.

"When you need more," Dave said, "speak up."

"Why would I need more?" Bella said.

"Women always need more," Dave said. "Clothes. Jewelry. The beauty parlor. You know what women spend money on."

"I never had any to spend."

"You have it now," Dave said. "You're no longer Bella Biaggi. You're Mrs. David Dehn. Get yourself organized to look the part."

"Why?" Bella said.

"I'm about to start rebuilding this place," Dave said. "I'm going to make this run down dump into something that will turn those Wasp anti-Semites down on Main Street the color of a great big fat ripe cucumber. Something your great-grandfather and your grandfather and your father would have been proud of. I want you to be proud of it too."

"You mean you want me to get to look like the rest of those titless bitches down the hill," Bella had said. "So you won't be ashamed of me."

"You've grasped the point," Dave said. "Now act on it. I'm a rich man. You're now a rich man's wife. Start wearing shoes."

"When I get ready," Bella had said.

Dave wondered what she meant by that, but he did not wonder about it very often. He had too many other things chasing around in his head. As he picked up his topcoat and his hat, those other things in Dave's mind stopped chasing one another just long enough for a simple fact to surface. As of today, almost a full month after Judge Martelli had married her to Dave, Bella was not yet ready to wear shoes. Dave went downstairs to the waiting car.

"How's Mrs. Dehn?" the driver asked as Dave climbed in.

"Fine," he said casually.

Dave did not want people speculating about his relationship with his wife. Certainly not the drivers of Carey Cadillacs.

"The usual, Mr. Dehn?"

Dave made a mental note. Next time he asked Sid to lay on a car for him he would ask Sid to make sure it was not driven by Cliff.

"No," Dave said. "Two changes today. First, don't turn around and go back down Turkey Hill Road into Main Street. Keep going the way you're headed. Up that way. This property ends at the Post Road. When we reach it, turn left. A couple of hundred yards down, on the right, there's a lunch wagon."

"I know," Cliff said. "Patsy's Place."

"We'll stop there for a few minutes," Dave said. "I haven't had any lunch."

"I recommend the chili," Cliff said. "Patsy makes the best bowl of chili between Mt. Vernon and Westport."

Dave wondered about the chili west of Mt. Vernon and east of Westport.

"Chili gives me heartburn," he said. "Then, when we get to where you usually make your turn for the East Side, don't make it. I want you to go down the West Side Highway."

"How far?" Cliff said.

"Pier 91," Dave said. "Fiftieth Street."

"Where the *Queen Elizabeth* docks?" Cliff said.

Inside Dave's head the alert signal flashed red.

"Among other ships," he said. "I don't know how many the Cunard owns."

"I see some others once in a while when I drive by," Cliff said. "But it's the *Elizabeth* everybody notices. Like this morning. I had a call for the Federal Court House in Foley Square. Judge Martelli. I drive him a lot. Passing Pier 91, there she was. The *Elizabeth*. Beautiful."

If she was in, then Dave did not have to drive down to check on her arrival. But he did not want to change his instructions to Cliff. He was a nosy bastard.

"That's where I want to go before you take me up to my apartment," Dave said.

"Check," Cliff said. "Wow. This is a rough piece of road."

"It wasn't made for Cadillacs," Dave said. "It's a cut-through across the farm. They shoveled it out for the wagons. They used to pick up the onions stacked by the pickers at the edges of the fields, then take them to the root cellars. After horses went out of style, pickup trucks came in. The tires cut the road a little wider. After onions went, this road went. Now it's just a short cut up to the Post Road. Nobody uses it except me and Mrs. Dehn. It's posted."

"Looks like you got yourself a trespasser, Mr. Dehn."

Cliff nodded toward the windshield. Dave slid over on the back seat so that he could see past Cliff's head. A pickup truck was parked on the grass outside the big squat root cellar.

"Stop the car," Dave said.

Cliff hit the brake. Dave climbed out.

"Want me to come with you, Mr. Dehn?"

"Why?" Dave said.

"If it's a trespasser," Cliff said, "I don't know, there might be a fuss."

"Not on my property," Dave said. "Wait in the car."

He was aware, as he moved down the dirt road, that if it had been paved he would be moving on his toes. This root cellar was one of fourteen that had been built by Bella's grandfather at strategic points on the 180-acre tract when onions had been a paying crop. The cellars were all alike. One-story affairs, half sunk in the ground. To enter you had to crouch very low. When Bella had been showing Dave the various buildings on the property, she had entered this one on her hands and knees. There were no windows. Only narrow ventilation slits under the overhang of the stone roof. The onions that used to be stored in these cellars, waiting to be trucked down to the produce markets in New York, had to be kept cool to prevent rotting.

The pickup truck had not had the attention the Biaggi onions used to get. It was a battered Ford with fenders rusted away to almost feathery brick red screens of rotted tin. As a vehicle it had probably seen its best days long before Pearl Harbor. Now, in late 1946, it was not so much a vehicle as a miracle of survival.

Dave walked around to the side. The identification on the cab door had been hand-painted by someone to whom fashioning the letters of the English alphabet did not come easily.

ANTHONY X. D'ALESSANDRO
GENERAL CONTRACTOR
BEECHWOOD, N.Y.
BEECHWOOD 7384

Dave stood there for a few moments. He didn't really want to do what he knew he was going to do. He knew also that he wanted to do it more than he did not want to do it. So he did it.

He moved quietly around to the back of the root cellar, dipped down, and peered through one of the ventilation slits. At first it was like peering into the inside of a cow's belly. Then his eyes grew accustomed to the faint light that seeped in through the slits cut into the other three walls.

First Dave became aware of the sheets of rotted chicken wire nailed across the front of the storage bins. Once they had kept rats and other field animals away from the stored onions. Now they just rotted. Then Dave saw the mattress on the earth floor. It was gray with darker gray stripes. Or that was what the colors had probably been when the mattress was new. Now it was as old and exhausted as the pickup truck outside. Tufts of dirty gray wadding poked out of holes in the corners where the once tough fabric had worn away.

What had worn it away could very well have been the activity for which it was at the moment providing a platform. The people involved were as naked as a couple of peeled bananas.

They must have been involved for some time, because, moments after Dave began to see them clearly, the figure on top shuddered like a train braking too late in a desperate effort to avoid overshooting a station platform.

After a pause, she pushed herself up from the mattress with one hand, shoved hard, and flopped over on her back. Like a pancake done on one side plopping into position on the griddle for browning on the other side. Long before he saw her face Dave knew the identity of this actor in the performance.

Even when it was encased in pedal pushers, Bella's ass was a unique signature.

Dave narrowed his eyes to sharpen the view. He had seen Tony D'Alessandro several times behind the wheel of his pickup truck as it passed on Main Street. But Dave had never seen him in repose or this close up. The close-up view was not revealing. Anyway, it didn't last long. Mr. D'Alessandro, from the state of his erection, had clearly not yet come to climax.

He rolled over on top of Bella. She used both hands to help him get into firing position, then swung her arms and legs up and around him, like a couple of pairs of huge pincers, and Mr. D'Alessandro got on with the job.

Dave carried his own erection away from the root cellar, around the pickup truck, and back to the Cadillac.

"Something funny?" Cliff said.

"Funny?" Dave said.

Then, as he dropped back into the rear seat and pulled the door shut, he realized he must have been grinning.

"No," he said. "Just a local contractor doing his regular service job."

The Cadillac started. Dave could feel the grin start coming up again on his face. He enjoyed discovering the answers to questions that had been running unanswered through his mind. Until they were nailed down they were a distraction. Like loose gear that had not yet been lashed tight rolling about on the deck of a ship in a storm.

Ever since their wedding night, when Bella had made it clear that she had accepted him as a husband but not as a lover, Dave had wondered where she was getting it, and from whom.

Now he knew.

9

What Dave did not know was something he believed was more important than his wife's sex life. What Dave did not know was how Marian Singer felt about the Beechwood project.

Marian's feelings were the only area in Dave's relationship with his partner that worried him. The worry was a new experience. New and troubling. He had never worried about Sid. Not when they were kids on Westerlo Street, or soldiers in Europe, or starting out on Madison Avenue.

In all those years Dave had dealt with only one person. A man he trusted so completely that it never crossed Dave's mind to identify his feeling about Sid with the word trust. Then Sid got married, and he ceased to be one person.

Before Dave's eyes, it seemed, Sid Singer split down the middle. One half of Sid remained the man Dave had known all his life and saw every day in their office. The other half became somebody else: a man who every day at noon walked five blocks to have lunch with his wife.

What did they talk about, Dave wondered.

"How about another cup of coffee?" Marian said.

"You kidding?" Sid said. "I've already had the two you never allow me to have more than, or is it more of, for lunch."

"Just this once you can have a third," Marian said. "You're entitled because I just heard you tell Dave on the phone you're going out to Jersey City to straighten out the Noonan boys, whatever that means."

"It means Dave and I have invested some money in their business on certain conditions, as we invest in a lot of businesses, but the Noonan boys are not meeting their conditions. People who don't meet their conditions have to be straight ened out. Thanks." Sid took the cup of coffee and said, "Okay, now you can make your speech."

"What speech?" Marian said.

"We haven't been married for very long," Sid said. "Due to a slight interruption in our plans caused by our little yellow brothers' dropping the old Sixth Avenue El back on us at Schofield Barracks. But we've known each other practically all our lives. I can tell when you've got something on your mind and you are working your way up to getting it off."

"How?" Marian said.

She said it with genuine interest. All her life she had been trying to understand herself. The trouble was that she never knew if in the endless quest she was ahead or behind. No sooner did she get something straightened out than something else came and hit her. Something so upsettingly incomprehensible that it washed back over and swept away the thing she had been so certain she had finally got straightened out. Marian thought of the inside of her tortured brain as not unlike Penelope's Web. Everything she wove during the day came unraveled at night. She was fascinated by anybody who indicated even a fragment of absolute certainty about anything. Fascinated and envious. How could Sid tell when she had something on her mind that she wanted to get off?

"You abandon a principle," Sid said. "To get off your mind whatever it is you have on it you always abandon a principle."

"I wish you'd explain that," Marian said.

"Easy," Sid said. "What were we talking about during lunch?"

"Dave and his plans for Beechwood and how they were coming along," Marian said.

"Okay," Sid said. "So we're talking about Dave and Beechwood, and the next thing I know you're offering me a third cup of coffee."

"What's the connection?" Marian said.

"It's a matter of principle with you that I must never have more than two cups of coffee at one time," Sid said.

"It's not a matter of principle with me," Marian said. "It's a matter of strict orders from Artie Steinberg."

"Artie's orders are your principles," Sid said. "And since my health is involved, I admire you for sticking to this principle. But all of a sudden, for what seems like no reason at all, you offer me a third cup of coffee. You want me to sit still, sipping coffee, while you're unloading your mind. Okay, honey, unload."

Sid took a sip from his cup.

"I don't think—" Marian began.

"Yes, you do," Sid said. "You think more than anybody I've ever met. Now that you've set me up for it, let's have it. I really must get with those Noonan people out in Jersey City this afternoon."

Marian drew a deep breath.

"I don't think we should move up to Beechwood after the baby is born," she said.

"You don't like Dave," Sid said. "You never did."

"Oh, Jesus," Marian said. "Now you're mad at me."

"Not mad," Sid said. "Sad."

"I'm sorry, darling."

"So am I," Sid said. "You love someone, you want them to love all the other people you love. I don't love Dave the way I love you. I couldn't love anybody the way I love you. But I do love Dave. Not because he saved my life near Remagen. I didn't think there was anything unusual about that. A guy's been a part of your life all of your life, when the necessity arises you take it for granted he'll save your life. If the opportunity ever came up I'd do the same for Dave without even thinking about it. You've turned on the water works. Why?"

"Because I feel so inadequate," Marian sobbed.

"You're not inadequate," Sid said. He pulled a handkerchief from his pocket and tossed it into her lap. "You're a great girl. I've never known a greater one. You're just not tuned in to the same wave length about Dave that I am. It's a matter for regret. Not tears. So blow hard, and dry your eyes, and cut this out."

Marian blew hard and dried her eyes.

"If I cut this out," she said, "I abandoned my principle about you and three cups of coffee for nothing."

Sid laughed.

"Okay, baby," he said. "Talk."

"I don't think we should move up to Beechwood after the baby is born because it's an unknown quantity," Marian said. "I don't know anything about the place."

"How much did you know about Tudor City before we moved in here?" Sid said.

"It's not the same thing," Marian said. "This is New York. Since we got married and I came down here from Albany, I've got to know this place. It's become my turf. I breathe good here. I don't keep looking back nervously over my shoulder here. It's become part of me."

"Do you want these three postage-stamp-size rooms on Forty-second Street to become a part of our kid?" Sid said. "This setup is okay for a couple of newlyweds just starting out. But in six months we're not going to be newlyweds. We're going to be a family. I hope we'll have more kids after this one. Where are we going to raise them? Here?"

"Why not in some other part of the city?" Marian said. "You and I were raised on Westerlo Street."

"Do you want our kids to be raised in a place like Westerlo Street?" Sid said.

Marian hesitated.

"No, of course not," she said.

"Park Avenue?" Sid said.

"You're not being fair," Marian said. "There are lots of places between Westerlo Street and Park Avenue."

"But they're all part of New York," Sid said. "And New York is becoming every day and every hour a more terrible place to raise kids. Damn near every couple we know, all of them our age, they've all moved or are moving to the suburbs to raise their families. Why not us?"

"Because we're not moving to the suburbs," Marian said. "We're moving to some sort of crazy idea Dave Dehn has in his head."

Bull's-eye. Sid looked down into his coffee cup. She had zeroed in on the one point about Beechwood where, in spite of his closeness to Dave Dehn and the project, Sid Singer was flying blind.

"We're not going to live in Dave's head," Sid said. "We're going to live on a beautiful tract of land overlooking Long Island Sound. And it's but beautiful, baby, believe me. Everywhere you look you're up to your navel in trees. Wait till you see it. It's absolutely and positively the most gorgeous place you've ever seen."

"It's also Gentile," Marian said.

It was not what she meant to say. What she'd wanted to say was something else. Something she didn't have the courage to say. Something that had been driving her crazy for more than a year. Ever since Sid had come home from Germany. To say it would have been an act of which she was incapable. It would have torn her apart. Because it might have torn both of them apart. It would have been the first time she had questioned the solid rock on which she and Sid stood as a team. She couldn't do that. Marian knew it in her guts. And the knowledge had been hounding her into desperation.

She couldn't let Sid into the den of her doubts. Because the doubts were about him. That was the twist that was killing her. Always it had been her guilt. Now, since the end of the war, it was Sid's guilt. The possibility of Sid's guilt, anyway.

Both she and Sid had been brought up as nickel pinchers. They had to be. There were so few nickels to go around. Then Sid had come home from the war and they had got married and the nickel had vanished from their thinking. There was enough money for everything. Even buying huge tracts of land up in Westchester that were up to her navel in trees.

Where had the money come from? Why hadn't Sid told her? Why didn't she have the guts to ask? Why did she have to hide behind the Gentiles?

"What difference does that Gentile crap make?" Sid said.

He said it sharply and firmly. Because Sid felt neither sharp nor firm. He knew what difference it made. Sid Singer had been a Jew all his life.

"This is 1946," Marian said. "And the people up in Beechwood have kept Jews out of the place since about the time the Pilgrims hit Plymouth Rock. Roughly three hundred years. That statistic alone would seem to indicate they're pretty good at keeping Jews out. I don't want to come up there with my husband and my baby and watch those fucking Wasps demonstrate on me and my baby and my husband just how good they still are at it. I'm not sure that New York is such a terrible place to raise kids. You and I were raised in Albany, which is worse. I'm willing to concede times have changed. I'm willing to agree to move to a suburb. But why can't we choose a suburb where Jews are already part of the landscape? Why do we have to break new ground?"

Sid hesitated again. She was not a very calm girl. She had her demons. But she was an honest girl. She had her principles. He could not live up to them. But neither could he damage what they had between them. He could not lie to her.

"Because Dave wants to break new ground," Sid said. "And I'm his partner."

"I'm not," Marian said.

"No," Sid said. "You're *my* partner."

"If I said no?" Marian said.

"You know the answer to that," Sid said. "I couldn't go alone."

"You're the nicest man I've ever known," Marian said. "And you can be the biggest son of a bitch. Don't finish that coffee. Three cups are bad for you. Of course I'll go."

10

Whenever Hella Drachenfels set foot on the gangplank of the *Queen Elizabeth,* and with her overnight case started down the incline to the dock of Pier 91, she became Helen Drake. Not actually. Not on her passport. Hella was too smart to tamper with that. For a German girl to have obtained a British passport at that time was almost a miracle.

Hella had achieved the miracle the way many miracles were then achieved in Germany. She had peddled what the British occupation forces seemed to treasure more than their desire to avenge the bombing of the Wren churches in London: her ass.

It was one of the prettiest asses in Hamburg. For almost a year it had been one of the most sought-after in London. Now, twice a month, whenever the *Queen Elizabeth* docked at Pier 91, that ass did very well for Hella Drachenfels in New York. She was careful, therefore, about seeing to it that when she became Helen Drake the change should take place only in her own mind.

"Taxi, ma'am?"

"You will take me, please, to an apartment house called The Dakota," Hella said to the driver. "It is located at the corner of Seventy-second Street and Central Park West. Understood?"

"Gotcha," the driver said. "Heil Hitler."

Hella examined him in the mirror over the windshield. He was looking up into the mirror, examining her as closely as she was examining him. Hella dropped her glance to the license card next to the meter. Irving Mendelowitz. Hella was not surprised. The Buchenwald ovens had not been allowed to complete the final solution. The lice were everywhere.

"Heil Hitler," she said coolly.

When the driver stopped the cab, Hella gave him a one-dollar bill.

"Keep the change," she said.

Irving Mendelowitz crumpled the dollar bill into a ball and threw it in her face.

"Stick it up your ass," he said. "You Nazi cunt."

Calmly Hella picked up the crumpled dollar bill. She got out of the taxi.

"Your time will come," she said quietly to the driver. "When it does, I will find you. It is your ass up which this dollar bill will be stuck. I will remember to drive it home with the end of a red-hot poker."

The driver gunned his motor, so she did not hear the pig's parting obscenity. Hella carried her overnight case into The Dakota. The concierge announced her on the switchboard in the gatehouse. She went across the courtyard and up the stairs and stopped in front of a rectangular brass plate set over a massive knocker shaped like the head of a snarling tiger. On the brass plate was engraved one word: DEHN.

Hella lifted the tiger's head and gave the signal. Four fast taps. Pause. Three fast taps. Pause. Two fast taps. Pause. One final tap. Pause. Mr. Dehn opened the door.

"You're prompt," he said.

"It is the ship that is prompt," Hella said.

"Come in."

Mr. Dehn held the door wide for her. The way he did it always made her heart tumble into a tiny shivering flutter. Many men had been polite to Hella Drachenfels, but none had ever treated her the way David Niven treated women in the movies. This funny little feeling in her heart was another reason why she was determined that when the day of retaliation arrived, Mr. Dehn would be among the first to be taken care of. No Jew had the right to do this to the pure heart of an Aryan girl.

"May I have your coat?"

She slipped out of it and Mr. Dehn carried it to the closet.

"You have a new picture," Hella said.

She was standing in front of a large glossy enlargement of a snapshot. It showed a shabby old frame house that had once been white. Behind it was a large body of water that stretched away to the horizon. If the house had been made of stone instead of wood, and the body of water had been the North Sea, Hella would have guessed it was a farmer's house somewhere in the fertile basin between Hamburg and the Kiel Canal. Near Elmshorn, perhaps. Or Bad Oldesloe. The sort of farmhouse in which she had been born.

The picture confirmed her belief that Jews were more than dangerous. They were also peculiar. Why would Mr. Dehn spend what must have been a large sum of money on the elaborate frame that held the snapshot of such a house to his living-room wall? Even more peculiar was the fact that the snapshot filled only the left half of the frame. The half on the right contained the same sort of expensive matting that surrounded the snapshot on the left, but the space on the right was empty. Mr. Dehn came up beside her.

"You like it?" he said.

The question was even more peculiar than the picture or its setting.

"I don't know what it is," Hella said.

"Is that what they taught you when you were a kid?" Mr. Dehn said. "To make sure you know what something is before you allow yourself to feel you like it?"

"Nobody had to teach me that," Hella said.

She spoke casually. A friendly tone. She had to be careful how she spoke to a profitable customer. On American soil Mr. Dehn was her most profitable. Almost as important, he paid her in crisp, new American bank notes. Buried in a box of

Kleenex, they went through customs at Southampton without a hitch. Mr. Dehn was responsible for a respectable part of the hoard she had accumulated in her safe-deposit box at Barclays Bank on Portman Square. When *Der Tag* arrived, Hella Drachenfels would be ready to do her part for the Fatherland. Now, however, she spoke softly to the pigs. In a servile voice. Later they would pay extra for her personal humiliation. All of them would pay. But Mr. Dehn would pay the most.

"Nobody had to teach me that," Hella said. "I worked it out for myself. I don't like being gypped. Dead beats make bad lays. A good fee makes a good screw. I like it that way."

"Let's go settle the fee for today," Mr. Dehn said.

Hella gave him the smile that had got her the job as second hairdresser in the beauty salon on the *Queen Elizabeth*.

"Please tell me what it is," she said. "You must like it or you would not hang it in such a place of prominence in your living room. I want to like it too."

Mr. Dehn smiled back at her. She wished he had not. Even though he was a Jew he was a very handsome man. His smile worried her. She did not want the relationship to go beyond money.

"It's a piece of property I just bought," Mr. Dehn said. "North of the city." He nodded toward the snapshot. "That's what it looks like now. I'm about to tear the place down and build something new. When it's finished I'll put a picture of the new house here, on this blank space."

Mr. Dehn touched the snapshot. "Before," he said.

He moved his hand to touch the blank square in the frame. "After."

He picked up Hella's overnight case.

"Let's see what goodies you've brought me this trip."

She followed him into the bedroom. Mr. Dehn placed Hella's overnight case on a table at the foot of the bed.

"Let's go," he said.

Hella went to the case and opened it.

"How many did you bring this time?" Mr. Dehn said.

"Wait and see," Hella said.

She pawed about in the case and came up with a doorknob. It was made of badly tarnished gun metal. The screw holes in the short square rod on which the knob was mounted were crusted with red rust. Hella held it out. Mr. Dehn took it by the rod and held the knob upright. It looked like a medium-sized metal mushroom.

"Is this what I think it is?" Mr. Dehn said.

"It is," Hella said.

Mr. Dehn went to his closet. He dragged out into the bedroom a beautiful pigskin suitcase fitted with a silver combination lock. Fifty quid at Austin Reed, Hella figured. Maybe even a hundred. Mr. Dehn worked the numbers on the lock and pulled the suitcase open. He spread both halves on the carpet and dropped to his knees. The suitcase was full of Manila clasp envelopes. Each envelope had a sentence or two written on the outside.

Mr. Dehn moved the envelopes about carefully. He could have been candling eggs, hunting for a particular one. When he found it, Mr. Dehn got to his feet. He undid the clasp and pulled from the envelope a tarnished gun-metal doorknob. It looked like the one Hella had just pulled from under her tumbled nightgown and robe. She had a feeling Mr. Dehn was holding his breath as he fitted the knob from the envelope onto the end of the short square metal rod attached to the knob Hella had given him.

"It fits," Mr. Dehn said.

No excitement in his voice. Mr. Dehn was that rare customer: a cool Jew.

"Last month I told you it would," Hella said.

"Now tell me what it is," Mr. Dehn said.

"You remember the north entrance?" Hella said.

"The one that faced the railroad spur?" Mr. Dehn said. "Where they unloaded the boxcars?"

"No," Hella said. "That was the east entrance. The north entrance had double steel gates. It was the only entrance that had a Buchenwald sign."

"Yes, now I remember it," Mr. Dehn said. "The first time my jeep went through I remember seeing the sign and wondering why they'd put it up."

"They had to," Hella said. "It was the side of the camp where they unloaded the vans. By that time in the war even the S.S. was suffering from manpower problems. They were sending out the vans with inexperienced drivers. Men who had never driven anything but cows to pasture until they got into the army. A lot of them had never lived anywhere outside Berlin and some of the other big cities. Most of those knew how to drive, but they didn't know their way around the country. But all of them, they had all heard of Weimar, and they could manage to find that. It was the next five miles that caused the trouble. They were always getting lost. For those of us on the staff of the camp it was a terrible nuisance. We would get our orders to receive a certain number of bodies on such and such a date at such and such an hour, and we would gear up for the arrival, but they would not appear. We had to send men out on motorcycles to roam the roads and find them and guide them in. The north entrance was nearest the road down which the guides sent them, so the Commandant decided to hang a sign on the gate. When the guides found those stupid drivers and set them right for Buchenwald, the guides told them to watch for the sign."

"What does that have to do with this doorknob?" Mr. Dehn said.

"You say you remember the north entrance?" Hella said.

"Clearly," Mr. Dehn said.

"Then you may remember there was a stone gatekeeper's hut just inside the first set of steel gates," Hella said. "On the left."

"Yes," Mr. Dehn said. "I remember."

"You're holding in your hand the doorknob from the toilet in the gatekeeper's hut," Hella said.

"What else did you bring this trip?" Mr. Dehn said.

Again she pawed about in the overnight case.

"The Commandant, in his office, he had a private bathroom," Hella said. "Whenever he came back from a tour of the camp grounds he always washed his hands with soap and hot water." She came up with a tarnished oval silver box. "This is his soap dish," Hella said. "You will note his initials on top."

"What else?" Mr. Dehn said.

During the next quarter hour, following the ritual they had established seven months ago, Hella brought out from the overnight case four more of the souvenirs she had gathered hastily on the day the wireless had reported advance units of the U.S. Third Army eighteen kilometers from Weimar and orders had come from Himmler personally to abandon the camp in the morning. Hella had not known on that hysterical day that a year and a half later she would be selling some of those souvenirs to a wealthy Jew in New York.

Hella did remember clearly, however, why she had gathered them. In the First War, when she was a child, her father had been wounded at Verdun. When he was patched up and invalided home, he had brought with him the four brass balls he had stolen from the tops of his hospital bed posts. A few years later, during the bad times that followed the war, Hella's father had sold those brass balls to a British tourist for a sum that fed the Drachenfels family for almost all of the bad winter of 1921. The lesson had made a deep impression on Hella. While the rest of the staff had spent the last day at Buchenwald moaning about their fate at the hands of the approaching Allied armies, she had prowled the camp with a small canvas sack.

"What's this thing?" Mr. Dehn said.

"A belt buckle," Hella said.

"From a prisoner?" Mr. Dehn said.

"Yes," Hella said. "All that was left of him."

"Anything else?" Mr. Dehn said.

"That's all this trip," Hella said.

"When will you be back?" Mr. Dehn said.

"In two weeks," Hella said.

"What will you bring me?" Mr. Dehn said.

"Wait and see," Hella said.

"You've chosen the things already?" Mr. Dehn said.

She smiled at the Jew pig's stupid eagerness.

"I've chosen one of the things already," Hella said.

"Something good?" Mr. Dehn said.

"The best yet," Hella said.

"What?" Mr. Dehn said.

"I said wait and see," Hella said.

"Tell me now," Mr. Dehn said.

"No," Hella said.

"I'll give you a dividend," Mr. Dehn said.

"No," Hella said. "That would spoil things. I like the way it's been happening now for seven months."

"How much do I owe you for what you brought today?" Mr. Dehn said.

"As always," Hella said, "I will tell you later."

"All right," Mr. Dehn said. "Take off your clothes."

11

Mr. Dehn's sex life was more complicated than Mike Palgrave's, but Mike was aware of certain compensations.

He stepped off the scale with a feeling of confidence that had become familiar and expected. It had been with him for almost three months. Since that day in October on Turkey Hill Road when he had first met Mr. Dehn.

Mike moved jauntily across the bathroom to the ledger on the Formica counter. He made his regular morning entry. In the column next to the one in which he wrote his 219 Mike saw Sally's just-entered 196.

"Hey!" he called toward the kitchen.

"What?" Sally called back.

"As of this morning the Palgrave family weighs four hundred and fifteen pounds," Mike said.

"That means you're down from our all-time high exactly as much as I'm down," Sally said. "Twenty-three pounds each."

Swiftly, studying the ledger, softly whistling "Zip-a-Dee-Doo-Dah," Mike did the computation.

"That's right," he called. "Our all-time high was last October twenty-first, when I was two forty-two and you were two nineteen, for a total of four sixty-one. This morning you're one nine six, and I'm two one nine, for a total of four fifteen."

"Come on in and have your breakfast, skinny," Sally called.

"I'm on my way," Mike called back.

Sally was seated at the kitchen table, measuring out his breakfast. Mike stopped and waited. Sally looked up.

"Anything wrong?" she said.

"Not yet," Mike said. "But in four seconds flat there will be if you don't notice."

"Notice what?" Sally said.

Mike spread his arms wide. He arched his back, like a swan diver at the apex of his trajectory. And he pirouetted in a complete circle.

"My blue blazer," he said. "I haven't been able to get into it for over a year."

Sally laughed.

"Darling, it looks great," she said. "I'm proud of us. So will Mr. Dehn be, when he sees you in it at your meeting today. If we keep going at this rate I figure I'll break a hundred and eighty by Lincoln's birthday, and you should make two hundred by St. Patrick's Day."

"I've set Purim as my goal," Mike said.

The statement took him by surprise. It came out of a memory that had once been vivid but, since he had begun living in Beechwood, had vanished from his consciousness.

It belonged to the winter of his first year at Ethical Culture. His father had almost died from a severe bout with pneumonia. The doctors ordered him to Florida for a month of convalescence. Mrs. Cohen would not allow her husband to go alone, even though her notion of alone meant two private nurses in constant attendance. Nor would she allow young Morris to accompany his parents.

He had just entered Ethical Culture. Dumbbells did not get into Ethical Culture. Just keeping up with his classmates was difficult enough, and Mrs. Cohen did not expect her son to settle for just keeping up. Morris was expected to surpass his classmates. A month in Florida, away from his school work, could put him so far behind that he might even flunk out, God forbid. So Morris could not go with his parents to Florida. Nor could his mother leave him in the apartment at The Carlyle with only a handful of servants to take care of him. The solution, which Morris' father suggested, did not please his mother.

It was not that she disliked her husband's parents. It was merely that the way old Mr. Cohen and Mrs. Cohen lived had nothing in common with the way their son and their son's family now lived. Mr. and Mrs. Cohen's son Meyer was no longer a poor boy living in a tenement on South Broadway in Albany. Meyer Cohen was now one of the wealthiest and most successful dress manufacturers on Seventh Avenue. *House Beautiful* did a color spread on the Cohen duplex in The Carlyle every time Morris' mother redecorated it. A boy who had been brought up in The Carlyle, a boy who went to Ethical Culture, to send such a boy to live for a month in Albany, God in heaven, it could ruin him.

It did not ruin Morris. It did not even make an impression on him. As soon as his parents came back from Florida and he returned to his life in The Carlyle, Morris forgot all about his month in Albany with his grandparents. At any rate, the experience had never in later years crossed his mind. Not until now. Now, on this January day in 1947, sitting at the breakfast table with Sally in their dream house on the crest of Cavalry Road, it crossed Michael Palgrave's mind. No, it didn't cross. It entered his mind like floodwaters coming in over a window sill. Giving him a chance to examine it. Not the whole month. Just that one moment.

It had been a Saturday morning. His first Saturday morning on South Broadway. Morris' grandfather, who went to synagogue every Saturday morning, on this morning took his grandson along. Morris went the way he went everywhere when he was asked to accompany an adult. Without objection or enthusiasm. It had never yet occurred to him to say no to an adult. Sometimes, he had learned, the places to which adults led you were dull. Sometimes surprisingly pleasant. The visit to his grandfather's synagogue proved to be one of those surprises.

Morris had never been inside a synagogue. He was not even aware that such places existed. So everything he saw was new to him. He did not understand what he saw, but he watched with interest. Then, unexpectedly, what was merely interesting became electrifying.

A velvet-draped closet up front was opened. Out of it a man lifted a long, thick, heavy object covered with a blue velvet sheath embroidered with metallic threads of gold and silver. The man carried the heavy object to a table, set it down, and walked to the sort of lectern from which the principal of Ethical Culture every day spoke to the student body gathered for morning Assembly. Except that the man in the synagogue, when he took his place at the lectern, spoke to someone Morris could not see. The man kept his back turned to the people on the benches. It was the ceiling in which he was interested.

Then, without warning, addressing the ceiling, the man's voice rose in a long, wailing chant. The people on the benches, including Morris' grandfather, sent their voices to the ceiling in what Morris perceived as a long, wailing reply. The man at the lectern took the reply and wove it into a series of musical phrases that made Morris gasp. Again the people behind him replied, their voices soaring, as though to reach something Morris could not see, but he could feel.

An invisible, shining place, where nothing bad happened, where he did not have to worry about beating his classmates, or be ashamed of his thoughts about Miss Tulchin's ass or his mother's swaying blouse. A place the boy suddenly wanted, with all his heart, to be in. There was something in the singing voices around him that made the small hairs on the side of Morris' jaw tingle. A feeling of peaceful warmth swept through him. He stole a glance at his grandfather. The old man's eyes were closed. He rocked gently back and forth as he chanted. Soon the whole room was a single mass of beautiful sound. Morris' throat grew tight.

The tightness eased away during the walk home. But the sense of well-being remained. He remembered thinking he never wanted to lose it. But he had.

And now, years later, he had found it again.

12

Mr. Dehn's New York apartment was in a building well known to Mike Palgrave.

The man at the window of the stone gatehouse put a phone to his ear and pressed a small lever on the desk switchboard.

"Mr. Dehn?" he said. "A Mr. Palgrave to see you?" Pause. "Very good, sir." The concierge put down the phone. "Do you know the way, sir?"

"First landing on the left?" Mike said. "Then up one flight?"

"That's right, sir," the concierge said. "Mind the step at the end of the courtyard. It's being mended."

"Thanks," Mike said.

"Excuse me, sir," the concierge said. "I haven't seen your father for some time. I hope he's well?"

Astonished, Mike nevertheless managed to say smoothly, "He's fine, thanks."

"I don't see him very often any more," the concierge said. "I was afraid perhaps he might be ill."

"Just age, that's all," Mike said. "He's slowing down a bit."

"Pity," the concierge said. "Do give him my best."

"I will indeed," Mike said.

He said it like Mike Palgrave. But he walked into the courtyard the way he used to: as Morris Cohen. In the days when many of his Ethical Culture classmates lived in The

Dakota. The big apartment house was known to them as Kike's Peak.

Morris had never told this to his father. When Morris was a boy Mr. Cohen used to come across town from The Carlyle three or four times a week to play chess in The Dakota with his garment-center cronies or listen to amateur string quartets play Brahms.

Mike could not understand the concierge's remembering him. How had he connected Meyer Cohen, an old man he no longer saw very often, with Mr. Palgrave, a young man he had not seen for at least five years?

Mike did not, of course, know the answer. Asking the question, however, brought with it a feeling of surprise. How many Jews were walking around, as he was, carrying in front of them the shield of a Gentile name? Thinking they were safe? Only to discover that they were not fooling even an apartment-house doorkeeper who had not clapped eyes on them for half a decade.

On Mr. Dehn's mahogany door Mike rapped a brass knocker shaped like the head of a growling tiger. A few moments later the door opened.

"Come in," Mr. Dehn said. "Sorry to drag you into town in this weather. Let me take those."

"No trouble," Mike said. He flipped open the buckles of his galoshes. "Living in the country you get used to snow in January."

Mike slipped out of his parka. Mr. Dehn put it with the overshoes in the closet.

"Let's go to my study," he said. "I've got some things there I want to show you."

On their way through the living room, Mike stopped in front of a framed picture hanging over a large blue couch. The left side of the frame contained a blown-up snapshot of the Biaggi house on Turkey Hill Road as it had looked until two weeks ago, when the bulldozers had wiped it out of existence. The right side of the frame contained a photostat of Mike's drawing for the large stone structure Mr. Dehn planned to build on the site. Mike had given the drawing to Mr. Dehn a week ago in Beechwood.

At the far end of the room Mr. Dehn seemed to become aware that Mike was not following him. He turned back.

"How does it look?" he said.

"I wish you'd told me you planned to frame it," Mike said. "I would have made you a more attractive copy."

"I like it as is," Mr. Dehn said. "It's exactly what I had in mind that day last October when I told you about the Statue of Liberty. You've given me what I want. I'm pleased with you, Mr. Palgrave."

Mike felt a small hot sensation in his stomach. Like heartburn.

"Speaking for Morris Cohen," he said, "Mr. Palgrave says thank you."

"Okay, Morris," Mr. Dehn said. "Now that you've got the shell looking the way it looks in my head, let's see what we can do about the inside of the shell."

Mike followed Mr. Dehn down a carpeted hall into the room in which he obviously worked.

"Take that chair," he said. "It's comfortable."

It was also, Mike noted when he was in it, set so that it faced directly toward the chair behind the desk into which Mr. Dehn had dropped.

"While you were working on the shell," he said, "I didn't want to bother you with my ideas for the inside."

"I went around to look at some synagogues," Mike said. "The first one I looked at was Temple Emanu-El, because that's the famous one. I mean, everybody knows it's on Fifth Avenue."

"My father didn't know it," Mr. Dehn said.

Mike could feel the surprise invading his face.

"My father didn't know very much about anything except three things," Mr. Dehn said. "The corner of Russia from which as a young man he escaped to America. The corner of Albany where he stopped being a young man. And his relationship with God. Russia was a bad memory. My father spent very little time on it. Albany was where my father spent most of his time. He had to. I'm talking in terms of clock time. If you're poor, making a living takes quite a lump out of the twenty-four hours. On that third thing, his relationship with God, my father spent all the hours he had left. He had no time to visit the places where other men worked out their relationships with God. I don't think my father ever heard of Temple Emanu-El. I doubt that he knew there was such a place as Fifth Avenue. Am I confusing you?"

"Not if you're making the point that I went to the wrong synagogues," Mike said. He tapped the batch of papers that contained his notes and sketches. "None of these is what you have in mind because your father didn't know any of them. What you have in mind for Beechwood is the kind of synagogue your father did know."

"Exactly," Mr. Dehn said. "The kind of synagogue my father started taking me to when I was a kid."

Mr. Dehn pulled open the bottom drawer of his desk. He brought from it a small package of folded white satin. He shook out the folds and placed the satin around his shoulders with a proud arching movement of his neck, like a bullfighter going in close with the cape.

"My *tallis*," Mr. Dehn said.

He dipped down into the drawer again and brought up a blue velvet pouch. It was about ten inches square. The velvet was decorated with gold-braided Hebrew lettering set off by red, yellow, and green embroidery.

"My *tfillim*," Mr. Dehn said.

A third dip into the desk drawer produced a small book. It was bound in ivory-colored Celluloid. The spine was embossed with a golden star of David. The covers were held together by a golden clasp.

"My *siddur*," Mr. Dehn said.

Mike had never used any of these objects, but he had seen them. Ethical Culture did not view with favor the sort of Judaism practiced by Mr. Dehn's father. In its enlightenment of its students about all religions, however, the school Did Not Compromise. Mike's enlightenment had been so thorough that he felt he probably could have told Mr. Dehn a few facts he had never suspected about the history and meaning of his prayer shawl and phylacteries and prayer book. It was clear, however, that nobody could add to Mr. Dehn's knowledge of what his possessions meant to him.

"I don't know what they give a kid when he gets bar mitzvah in Temple Emanu-El," he said. "In my father's synagogue this is what they gave me. The place is gone now, of course."

"There must be other synagogues like it all over the city," Mike said.

"Not in my city," Mr. Dehn said. "But Albany is not the only city in the country with synagogues like the one I knew as a boy. There are lots of them here in New York. Up in the Bronx, down on the East Side, over in Brooklyn. I've gone to look at some of them. They're pretty much like my father's used to be. Pretty much, but not quite."

"And you don't want pretty much," Mike said. "Or not quite."

"I want exactly," Mr. Dehn said.

"Exactly is a tough assignment," Mike said. "You're asking me to reproduce something that no longer exists."

"It exists up here," Mr. Dehn said. He touched his temple with a corner of the *siddur* bound in Celluloid and gold. "If I give you a description of what I still see clearly in my own mind, I think you can do it."

"I'd like to try," Mike said.

Mr. Dehn turned with the *siddur* and stared out the window.

"You have to picture a kid," Mr. Dehn said to Central Park. "Seven or eight. Maybe nine. A kid whose mother died in childbirth. So he's never known anybody but his father. The kid goes to school. The father goes to work. He's a house painter. So the kid and his father don't see very much of each other. The father comes home from work around seven o'clock. Sometimes later. He's pretty bushed, but he cooks the evening meal, and then the kid helps with the dishes.

"By the time the dishes are finished the old man has to go to bed. He gets up at four-thirty every morning. So the kid doesn't see very much of his father during the week. That's what makes Saturday so special. Saturday is built solidly around the synagogue. Morning prayers. Home for the big meal. A couple of hours to sleep it off on the leather couch in the front room. Then back to the synagogue. And in the evening, after the dishes, plenty of time for *meises* because the next day is Sunday and they can both sleep late.

"The word *meises* means stories, but for this kid it means religious stories. Pinocchio and Br'er Rabbit and Little Red Riding Hood you don't take in with mother's milk in Minsk. Religious stories were the only kind this kid's father knew, and he knew how to tell them. The stories were a part of Saturday the way the synagogue was a part of Saturday. It was not separate things. It was all one piece. I mean the day and the things that took place on that day. All of those things were as much a part of the synagogue as the bricks and mortar and lumber with which the building had been put together."

Mr. Dehn swung his glance away from the window, back to his visitor.

"You see what I mean?" he said. "Why these other synagogues I went to look at, even though they looked pretty much like my father's used to look, they were all no more than that? Pretty much, but not quite?"

"Yes," Mike said.

His feeling of excitement had taken a new turn. Mr. Dehn was telling him something Mike felt he knew.

"I understand what you mean," Mike said.

Mr. Dehn nodded and smiled. They were almost the same age. Sally had done one of her research jobs. Mr. Dehn had turned thirty-two in November. Mike would be thirty-two in April. Yet there was in Mr. Dehn's nod and smile what Mike remembered in the smiles he used to get from his own father.

"I thought you would," Mr. Dehn said. "That's why I decided to call you Morris."

"Morris is listening," Mike said.

"Here's what I want you to capture," Mr. Dehn said. "What that eight-year-old kid saw when he came into that synagogue in Albany. A long, high tunnel. Not very clearly defined. Fuzzy at the edges, but nice. Nice like a school assembly hall. Where somebody is in control. Teachers, the school principal, people who could get rough if you didn't behave, but when you obeyed the rules they were friendly. They liked you. They were people you were glad to be with. You felt safe with them.

"There were no doors to this tunnel. I mean, once you came through the street doors it was there, up front, waiting for you behind a wooden arch. I don't know what it is that makes an arch give you the feeling it's making you welcome, but this arch in my father's synagogue gave me that feeling. This synagogue you're going to build up there in Beechwood, that's the feeling I want."

"You'll get it," Mike said.

Mr. Dehn's glance had not been fixed on anything in particular. Certainly not on Mike. Now it seemed to catch up with Mike's words. The crinkles smoothed away from the corners of his eyes. Mr. Dehn smiled.

"Yes, I think I will," he said. "I wouldn't waste time telling this to somebody who couldn't deliver."

Mike's heart walloped up against the wall of his chest.

"After you went through the arch," he said. "There were benches on the left and right. Dark brown. Then about halfway down the tunnel, a square platform. Four steps leading up to it."

"No," Mr. Dehn said. "Three."

Mike closed his eyes and counted.

"One, two, three," he said. Mike opened his eyes. "That's right," he said. "Three steps. With a railing all around the platform. Then, in the middle of the platform, a slanted table. So that when they brought the Torah out of the ark and they unrolled it, the men on the platform could read the words without bending over."

"What were the men wearing?" Mr. Dehn said.

"Prayer cloths," Mike said. "They were heavier and not exactly white like yours. They may have started out white, but after years of use they were now a little faded. That kind of color."

"What sort of hats?" Mr. Dehn said.

"Black Homburgs," Mike said. "Yes, and wait," he added quickly. "When they read aloud from the Torah, these men in the black Homburgs, they used a large silver pointer. It was big and long, like the rung of a heavy kitchen chair, and it was cut square. It was made of filigreed silver, and it narrowed down at the tip to a small silver human hand, with an outstretched finger. The men at the table held the pointer like a fountain pen, moving the silver finger along the parchment; stopped at every word, and they—"

"Morris."

Mike's mind came back into the room.

"Sorry," he said. "I was remembering the only synagogue I'd ever been in. One winter when I was a kid my father had pneumonia, and my mother took him to Florida for a month. I was sent up to Albany to stay with my grandparents. Every Saturday morning my grandfather went to the synagogue, and while I was staying up there in Albany with them he took me along."

"Where in Albany?" Mr. Dehn said.

"They lived on South Broadway," Mike said.

"No, I don't mean where they lived," Mr. Dehn said. "I mean where was the synagogue?"

"On the next street over," Mike said. "My grandfather and I used to walk from his house down South Broadway to a big wide street, a sort of avenue. It ran at right angles to South Broadway and it had trolley cars."

"Ten Eyck Avenue," Mr. Dehn said.

"That's it," Mike said. "That was the name. My grandfather and I, we'd walk one block alongside the trolley tracks and then turn left into this street that had the synagogue on it."

"Was there an empty lot next to the synagogue?" Mr. Dehn said.

"Yes," Mike said. "Full of all sorts of junk, I think. Yes, old cartons and broken wagons. Things like that."

"Westerlo Street," Mr. Dehn said.

"I don't know," Mike said. "I don't remember the name."

"I do," Mr. Dehn said. "I was born on Westerlo Street."

The two things came together inside Mike's head with an almost audible slap.

"Then that synagogue," he said slowly, "the synagogue my grandfather took me to, it must have been—?"

"It was," Mr. Dehn said. He smiled. "I told you I knew I'd picked the right man for this job. You've obviously got inside your head exactly what I have inside mine. Your next job is to get it out of your head and onto paper."

"This synagogue we both seem to remember," Mike said. "How big was it?"

"I never thought about the size," Mr. Dehn said. "Is size important?"

"It could be," Mike said. "I have a feeling it was a small place. I remember I wasn't overwhelmed. The way you are when you go into St. Patrick's or Emanu-El. Those places, they make you feel like a tourist. You want to shoot a Kodachrome slide to take home as proof to your friends you were there. Just the sheer size overwhelms you. But this synagogue on Westerlo Street, what I remember is it was cozy. What I liked was the feeling that it was a part of my home. I don't know if I'm making myself clear."

"You're doing fine," Mr. Dehn said.

"Well, then, you can see the problem," Mike said. "When we first talked about your plan in October, you said what you had in mind was a room in which a couple of hundred people could sit around in comfort and listen to a lecture."

"What makes that a problem?" Mr. Dehn said.

"A room in which a couple of hundred people are sitting

around in comfort does not exactly give you a feeling that the place in which they're sitting is a part of anybody's home."

"It will," Mr. Dehn said. "When the other things I have in mind for the building are added."

"Such as?" Mike said.

"A cornerstone," Mr. Dehn said.

Mike looked down at the cuticle on his left thumb. It did not seem the right moment to come up with the words "You must be kidding." Did Mr. Dehn expect Mike to take seriously the suggestion that a room capable of accommodating two hundred people could be made to feel like part of anybody's home by the addition of a cornerstone?

"Isn't that a little unusual?" Mike said.

"This whole thing I'm doing up in Beechwood is unusual," Mr. Dehn said. "You know about cornerstones?"

"The kind that get into the papers, yes," Mike said. "People are building something, a bank or a city hall or an office building, and they get a lot of things together to seal in a block of cement so that a couple of hundred years later or whenever, if people open the block they'll get some idea of what life was like when the building was put up."

"My cornerstone is not too different from your description," Mr. Dehn said. "Except for the things I'm going to put into it."

"Like what?" Mike said.

"First," Mr. Dehn said, "these things."

His hand moved across the desk in three separate movements, as though he were bestowing a benediction. He touched his prayer book shawl, then his phylacteries, and finally his prayer book.

"The next things that are going in," Mr. Dehn said, "are the same things that belonged to my father. His *tallis,* his *tfillim,* and his *siddur.* Then the third group of things." Mr. Dehn pressed a button on his desk call box and said into it, "Fanny, would you come in a minute, please." He released the button and said, "Fanny Mintz is my secretary. She's coming up to live in Beechwood as soon as her house is ready."

The door opened. Through it came a small, skinny hump-backed woman. Hunting for a phrase that would make her come alive for Sally when he described this meeting to his wife at dinner tonight, Mike decided to postpone the hunt until he was on his way home. For the moment he settled for recording that Miss Mintz was without doubt the ugliest human being he had ever seen.

"Fanny," Mr. Dehn said, "would you bring in the suitcase from my closet?"

"Of course," Miss Mintz said.

After the door closed behind her Mr. Dehn said, "Most efficient woman I've ever known. Better than that, she's the first person I've come across who is in complete sympathy with my motives."

Mike knew he would never get a better opening.

"You could come across a second person," he said. "If he knew what your motives are."

Mr. Dehn's eyes did that funny thing that apparently always accompanied an attempt to pull together his complete attention. His eyes irised down. Mike held his breath. From the look on Mr. Dehn's face it seemed obvious that his only preoccupation at the moment was trying to decide in which direction to pitch Mike out of the apartment. The decision was postponed by Miss Mintz. She came back into the room carrying a large pigskin suitcase fitted with a silver combination lock.

"Just set it down, Fanny," he said. "Thanks."

Miss Mintz set down the suitcase in front of the desk and left the room.

"Did you ever hear of Masada?" Mr. Dehn said.

"Sure," Mike said. "A.D. 73."

He didn't know what Mr. Dehn was driving at, so he rattled off the remembered facts as though he were back in history class at Ethical Culture.

"Three years after the sack of Jerusalem and the destruction of the Second Temple," Mike said glibly. "Masada was the last pocket of Jewish resistance to Rome. Just as the defenses were about to be breached by the Romans the Jewish commander, a man named, if memory serves, Eleazar Ben Yair, he worked out what he called a death of glory. He had his men draw lots. The ten men who won, what they won was the duty to kill every man, woman, and child in Masada. Then these last ten men drew lots, and the winner this time, his job was to kill his nine buddies, and then finish the job by falling on his own sword. He did the job."

Thank God for Ethical Culture, Mike thought. When they taught you history they made it stick to your ribs.

"Where did you learn all that?" Mr. Dehn said.

"School," Mike said.

"I learned it two years ago," Mr. Dehn said. "Not out of a book. I was there."

The suspicion that Mr. Dehn might be a bit off his rocker invaded Mike's mind like an unexpected rain cloud coming in over Sequesta Pond on a sunny summer morning.

"At Masada?" he said in what he hoped was a normal tone of polite inquiry.

"No, in Germany," Mr. Dehn said. "When I saw the place, the Germans were calling it Buchenwald."

Mike's reluctant suspicion about Mr. Dehn's sanity moved a notch or two toward confirmation.

"I don't see the connection," he said. "Masada is generally considered to be one of the most heroic acts of mass martyrdom in all history. Buchenwald is generally considered to be the worst case of mass murder in all history. They are two different things."

"Not to the victims," Mr. Dehn said. "They both acted the same way. If those men at Masada had fought they would have ended up just as dead as they did by not fighting, but at least they would have taken a few Romans with them. They would have left a few less of the enemy for the rest of us to fight later. Those people at Buchenwald and the other camps, there were six million of them. They could have squashed those Nazi bastards like a bunch of cockroaches. Just by walking into their machine guns. A lot of them would have been killed before the sheer weight of their numbers choked off those machine guns. But so what? If you get killed walking bare-handed into a gun you get yourself no more dead than you get by crawling on your knees into a gas chamber. Both of them, at Masada and at Buchenwald, instead of standing and fighting, they let themselves get slaughtered like a bunch of sheep. What was the name of this commander?"

"Eleazar Ben Yair," Mike said.

"Yes," Mr. Dehn said. "Him and his death of glory. One of the most heroic acts of mass martyrdom in all history? I read it another way. One of the most shameful acts of mass cowardice in all history. What that son of a bitch did, he laid down a pattern that's been misleading us for two thousand years. When those Romans were coming over the walls, why didn't this Eleazar Ben Yair scream at his men *Come on, let's go, nobody lives forever!* If he'd done that, for two thousand years we would have had a different tradition to follow. Instead of bowing our heads and crawling into those God-damn gas chambers, one of us to whom Masada was the right kind of tradition would have waved his fist at the six million of us behind him and he would have screamed what this Eleazar Ben Yair didn't have the guts to scream. *Come on, boys, let's get these Nazi bastards!* Some would have been mowed down, sure. But when you've got an army of six million what do a few thousand matter? If we'd fought at Masada we would have fought at Buchenwald. You don't throw your life away. You fight to keep it. It's an instinct. Animals have it. Why not Jews? If not for Masada we would have had that instinct going for us at Buchenwald. There would have been blood, but a lot of it would have been Nazi blood, and there would have been no gas chambers."

Mr. Dehn paused. To catch his breath, Mike thought. Then he saw that what Mr. Dehn was catching was not his breath. He was fighting for something else—something inside, something Mike figured Mr. Dehn had taught himself how to handle. Something that, in spite of what he had learned, had just got away from him. The struggle ended with a deep, hard, open-mouthed intake of breath. Mr. Dehn held it for a long moment. Then he pursed his lips, as though he intended to whistle, and his chest deflated slowly.

"Sorry," Mr. Dehn said. "I didn't mean to say it that way."

"If you had said it any other way," Mike said, "I don't think I would have understood."

Mr. Dehn's eyes did that thing again. When he had Mike fully back in his sights Mr. Dehn seemed a little surprised by what he was looking at.

"You got it?" he said.

"How could anybody not get it?" Mike said.

"It's a goy world," Mr. Dehn said. "Jews are scared to live in it."

"You don't sound scared to me," Mike said.

"I didn't know I was, until the day I walked into Buchenwald," Mr. Dehn said. "I was young. I was full of piss and vinegar. I was just beginning to make it. In a small way, of course. But when you're a kid you don't measure. You just feel. You feel yourself coming up out of the sewer. Nothing ever again smells as fresh as those first whiffs of the goy world when you're twenty.

"I'd known goyim in school, of course. I'd seen and talked with them in stores. The women who ran the public library. The guys you met in the park when we chose up a baseball game. After school, when I got my first job, I started to know some *shiksehs*. I even banged a few, when I could. But I'm talking business. The business world. When I came down to New York, I mean. There was a depression on, but only for the average guy. For the guy with brains, if he knew where to look, the dough was lying around to be picked up. There are plenty of Jews picking it up, of course, but those money streets—Madison, lower Park, Wall Street—they have a Gentile smell. To a kid of twenty from Albany, anyway. Those streets, to me they smelled of goyim. Goyim in Brooks Brothers suits. A whole new breed of cat to Dave Dehn from Westerlo Street. And a whole new feeling that I was moving into it, learning to handle it, getting on top of it. There's nothing like it when you're twenty.

"It's like booze. Afraid? I never even heard of the word. Then the war came, and at first I was sore. It stopped me from going up. But the Army opened my eyes. I found the Army was just an extension of the goy world. If you can lick something in a sack suit you can lick it in khaki pants. It didn't take me long to get on top of it. I stayed there, on top of it, enjoying every God-damn minute. Even the eight pieces of shrapnel I caught in my thigh at Aachen. I loved that shrapnel. When they shipped me back to my outfit I carried those pieces of shrapnel wrapped in toilet paper, hidden in my helmet liner. Then came that day at Buchenwald, and I knew what every Jew learns long before I did. How to be really afraid."

Mr. Dehn stood up and came out from behind the desk. He dropped to his knees beside the pigskin suitcase.

"I didn't like that," Mr. Dehn said, working the numbers of the silver combination lock on the suitcase. "Being afraid was a new experience for me. I hated it. I worried about it for a while, and then one day it came to me. I knew what to do."

Mr. Dehn paused to pull apart and spread open on the floor the two halves of the suitcase.

"Do what?" Mike said.

"Reverse a two-thousand-year trend," Mr. Dehn said. "Wipe out the damage that was done to us at Masada. Fix it so there can be no more Buchenwalds. No more deaths of glory. No more crawling into death chambers. Never again."

"How?" Mike said.

"I decided to start a whole new breed of cat," Mr. Dehn said. "Like doctors in a laboratory. Create a new kind of animal. A Jew who doesn't know what it means to be afraid."

From the suitcase Mr. Dehn lifted a half dozen Manila clasp envelopes. He spread them on the carpet. Each envelope, Mike noticed, had a couple of lines inked on the outside.

"I started collecting these things," he said.

"What are they?" Mike said.

Mr. Dehn handed him one of the envelopes. It was marked, "Doorknob from toilet in gatekeeper's cottage, north entrance, Buchenwald."

"Look at this," Mr. Dehn said.

He handed over another envelope. Mike read the words lettered neatly on the outside: "Oval silver soap box. From private bathroom attached to office of Commandant, Buchenwald."

Mr. Dehn saw the puzzled frown on Mike's face. Mr. Dehn released a short, harsh laugh.

"The son of a bitch was sensitive," he said. "Whenever he came back from a tour of the camp grounds he washed his hands with hot water and soap. Take a sniff."

Mike sniffed the envelope. It smelled like one of those bottles Sally had on her perfume tray.

"Chanel?" Mike said in surprise.

"Number Five," Mr. Dehn said. "He had the stuff shipped by the carton from Paris. Here."

Mike took the next envelope. The neatly lettered marking read: "Belt buckle cut from body of a Jew a few minutes after he was shoveled out of the gas chamber and placed on a butcher's block in the dismembering room, where the corpses were cut into pieces of the correct size to allow the ovens to achieve maximum efficiency, Buchenwald."

"Here's one to haunt your choicest nightmare," Mr. Dehn said.

"Never mind," Mike said. "I get the point. How did you get these things?"

Mr. Dehn squatted back on his heels, like a Boy Scout getting into position to toast a marshmallow on a stick at a campfire.

"I laid down my lines of communication year before last," he said. "Before I left Germany. People bring things to me. There's no problem about customs. Except to the courier the things look like perfectly harmless junk."

"What are you going to do with them?" Mike said.

"They're going into my cornerstone," Mr. Dehn said. "Along with my father's *tallis* and *tfillim* and *siddur*."

"Is it a secret?" Mike said.

"Almost," Mr. Dehn said. "Aside from me, three people know about it."

"I guess I shouldn't ask," Mike said.

"Wrong guess," Mr. Dehn said.

Puzzled, Mike said, "You mean I should?"

"You don't think I've told you all this about my project because all of a sudden I fell into an attack of stupidity?" Mr. Dehn said.

"Who are the three people?" Mike said.

"Sid Singer, of course," Mr. Dehn said. "Number two, Fanny Mintz."

Mr. Dehn's voice stopped. He seemed to feel there was more to be said but he would not say it unless he was asked.

"Who's the third person?" Mike said.

"You," Mr. Dehn said.

Mike realized how odd it was that he did not feel astonished. He felt like that kid with the tuft of chest hair sticking up out of his work shirt, sitting on the kibbutz tractor and grinning cockily at the *Life* photographer.

"Why me?" Mike said.

"If something happens to me," Mr. Dehn said, "Sid may not be able to handle it because his wife might get in the way. He loves us both, but I also love Sid, so I don't want to put him in the position of choosing up sides between me and Marian. With Fanny Mintz there will be no problem of choosing up sides. Physically, however, anything requiring muscle would be beyond her. Which leads me to you. Underneath what looks to me like forty pounds of flab you can do without, I'd say there's the makings of a pretty good defensive tackle."

"Right guard, actually," Mike said. "When I was in prep school. Football was out at M.I.T. because they don't field a team, but I was not exactly the worst man on the Charles

River at single sculls. What sort of physical things could happen to you?"

"Until it did happen to Lincoln did he know what sort of physical things could happen to him?" Mr. Dehn said. "That sort of thing, whenever it happens—we learn again and again that the best-protected people in the world can't be protected against the unexpected nut from left field who wants to get him."

"Somebody wants to get you?" Mike said.

"Now, no," Mr. Dehn said. "It's too early. I haven't really surfaced yet. But when I do, the synagogue is only the beginning. When this cornerstone goes in, and the synagogue becomes a place people start coming to, and the other things I've planned move out of the planning stage, there will be people who won't like David Dehn. When people don't like someone and they find they can't stop him by legal means, they hunt up some other means. You can take my word for that. It's a subject I know quite a lot about."

Mike didn't doubt it. All at once what in an abstract way he had suspected about Mr. Dehn from the beginning seemed to become hard reality. He had accepted the fact that Mr. Dehn was a rich man. But Mike had not been able to learn what Mr. Dehn was rich at. The Fords made automobiles. Heinz made pickles. Mike's father manufactured dresses. What did Mr. Dehn make? Where did his money come from? All at once it occurred to Mike that Mr. Dehn was one of those people about whom you did not ask that kind of question. Mr. Dehn, Mike grasped, knew a lot about a lot of things that came to Mike's attention only when they became lurid headlines.

Mr. Dehn seemed to sense—not for the first time, Mike noticed—what was going through Mike's mind.

"You don't have to put in with me," Mr. Dehn said. "It's not going to be easy. It might be dangerous. If you say no, okay. You don't lose the assignment to build Beechwood for me. That involves your talent as an architect and your recollections about that synagogue on Westerlo Street. I'm sold on both. But I think it's only fair to say that if you don't put in with me I'll be very disappointed."

"Why?" Mike said.

"Because I'm sold on you," Mr. Dehn said.

"All of a sudden?" Mike said.

"In a way, yes," Mr. Dehn said. "The things that were going for it started earlier. But the actual sale, yes, it happened this morning, here, in this room."

"Why?" Mike said again.

"You're a boy who has been there," Mr. Dehn said. "Five years behind the beard as Michael Palgrave. I figure you're ripe to come out of your corner as Morris Cohen and start swinging."

"Can you take one more question?" Mike said.

"Shoot," Mr. Dehn said.

"Why did you pick Beechwood?" Mike said.

Mr. Dehn came to his feet slowly, as though the marshmallow he had been toasting were ready.

"If you're going into the business of breeding a race of people who won't know what it is to be scared of wild animals," he said, "the best place to set up your training school is in the heart of the Matto Grosso."

13

"Who?" Dave said into the phone.

"It's me. Bella."

Dave had not seen or heard from her for months. It took a couple of moments to adjust to the fact that the voice at the other end of the wire belonged to his wife.

"It's nice to hear your voice," Dave said. "How are you, Bella?"

"You really want to know?"

He considered the question. Dave was not surprised by how quickly his mind came up with the truthful answer.

"I do," he said. "After all, you are Mrs. David Dehn."

She laughed.

"I forget it for a long time," Bella said. "Weeks, sometimes. Then I remember it and, well, like now. It's funny."

"It's not funny for me to want to know how you are," Dave said.

He had not even thought about her during the months of her absence. Now that he couldn't help thinking about her, Dave couldn't help the direction his thoughts were taking.

"I'm fine," Bella said. "Really I am. Florida was a good idea."

Now he remembered. The bills from Saks in Miami, and Neiman-Marcus in Bal Harbour. Fanny Mintz had wanted to know if it was okay to pay them.

"That's what everybody seems to say about Florida," Dave said. "I've never been."

"You ought to go sometime," Bella said. "The sun and the ocean and the, I don't know, all that God-damn grapefruit. It's different. It makes you feel good, and it gives you time to think. I mean really think."

"When I was a kid," Dave said, "at this point the smart-ass in the crowd used to say a penny for your thoughts."

Bella laughed again. It occurred to Dave that her laugh had changed. He remembered the short, sharp bark that had had no mirth in it. The laugh that had reminded him of a puppy's yelp when its tail is stepped on. Bella's laugh now sounded as though she had seen or heard or remembered something that gave her pleasure.

"For my thoughts," she said, "I'd get arrested if I charged you even a penny. I'm your wife. Remember?"

He wondered how he could have forgotten. Dave could suddenly see her as he had seen her on that first day. Barefoot. Her tail stuffed into those cheap robin's-egg blue pedal push-ers. Her nipples pawing maddeningly for a way through the cloth of that sleazy T-shirt.

"I sure do," Dave said. "Am I going to see you?"

"Do you want to?"

"What do you think?" he said.

He was surprised by the ease with which he fell back into the mindless old teen-age boy-girl banter. Mindless and curiously erotic. The innocence had in it a tantalizing excitement. Things were waiting for you. All you had to do was probe. It turned him on more effectively than the around-Broadway, no-nonsense, t.o.t. call-girl talk to which he had grown accustomed.

"Don't get a swelled head," Bella said. "But yes, I do want to see you."

"Are you tanned?" he said.

"Anybody who's been in Florida as long as I was and is not tanned gets arrested," Bella said. "What kind of question is that?"

"The kind of question anybody with brains would ask if he heard the way you sound," Dave said.

"How do I sound?" she said.

"Like Lena Horne," Dave said.

"I'm not that tanned," Bella said.

"Where are you now?" Dave said.

"The Israel Putnam Motor Inn," Bella said.

"Oh, up there," Dave said. "On the Post Road."

"There wasn't any other place to go," Bella said. "The old house is gone."

"I told you I was going to tear it down," Dave said.

"You didn't tell me you were going to replace it with a stone fort," Bella said.

"You didn't stick around to listen," Dave said.

"Would you have told me?" she said.

"Would I have kept a thing like that from my wife?" Dave said.

"I don't know," Bella said. "I didn't stick around long enough to find that out either."

"Do you mind my tearing down the old house?" Dave said.

"Does anybody mind seeing the garbage get carried out?" Bella said.

"I meant because of your family," Dave said. "Your parents, your grandfather. Being born there. Your memories is what I mean. Old associations, people call it. All that."

"Listen," Bella said. "My memories and my old associations about that place you can roll them up and stick them. I got in late last night, so I didn't get a chance to see much of what you're doing over there on Turkey Hill Road, but whatever it is, believe me, it's an improvement."

"I'd like to show you around," Dave said.

"I'd like that," Bella said.

The pleasure in her voice added a notch to the pleasure he already felt.

"How did you get my number here in New York?" Dave said.

"I called Mr. Singer," Bella said.

He and Sid now had another thing in common. Bella had not stuck around long enough to call either of them by his first name.

"Well, now, look," Dave said. "I usually drive up to Beechwood about eight o'clock. Gets me there a little before nine for our morning staff conference. It's now, let's see . . ." He glanced at his wrist watch. "Quarter after seven," he said. "How about this? After the staff conference I'll come over and pick you up at the Israel Putnam, and we'll take it from there. That okay?"

"I'm looking forward to it, Dave."

Well, that put him one up on Sid Singer. She had finally called him by his first name. It was not a name that rolled trippingly from the tongue. It seemed odd, therefore, that the sound she had made of the single syllable should hang around inside his head all the way up to Beechwood and all through the staff conference. The sound was still there when he pulled his Cadillac into the parking area in front of the Israel Putnam Motor Inn.

Dave parked the car, started across the asphalt apron to the front door, and stopped. A girl had come out the front door and was walking toward him.

It was like that moment in front of Judge Martelli's apartment house on upper Broadway, when she emerged from the subway kiosk on the 79th Street corner. She had come toward him down Broadway in high heels the way she had gone across Turkey Hill Road with him in bare feet. Leaving no doubts in the mind of the observer about who owned the ground on which she was walking.

Now it was the same observer, and the same girl. Except that now the high heels seemed to be a part of the absolutely smashing legs. And the skirt of the Royal Pastel mink swung with casual elegance to each movement of the slender body. And the shoulder-length hair, curled upward at the edges by about forty dollars' worth of a good hairdresser's attention, swayed to the rhythm that kept her coming toward him.

"My God," Dave said. "Did I pay for all that?"

"This too," she said.

She put her hand on the front door of a fire-engine red Cadillac convertible. It made his own car look like a stunted jeep.

"My feelings are hurt," Dave said. "You told me when you got ready to wear shoes you'd let me know."

"You told me I was no longer Bella Biaggi from a beat-up old onion farm in Westchester," she said. "You told me now that I was Mrs. David Dehn you wanted me to dress like Mrs. David Dehn."

Bella smiled. He had never before noticed she had dimples. Probably because she had never before smiled at him. She swirled the skirt of the mink.

"Is this what you had in mind?" she said.

"Among other things," Dave said.

She laughed. He laughed with her, falling into the same easy rhythm of pleasure. He took her arm. It fitted his hand.

"My," she said, looking up at him. "I never realized what a big, tall, handsome son of a bitch I married."

She pulled his elbow close.

"I guess you're not the only one in this family who never realized certain things," Dave said.

Then they both laughed again. In the same way. For no particular reason.

"Now that we've both caught up," Bella said, "what do you want to do first?"

"You know what I want to do first," he said.

"So do I," Bella said.

She turned, moving him with her. They walked into the inn side by side. They went down a long corridor, turned right, and stopped in front of a door marked "114." Bella opened it with a key, locked it behind her, and pulled up her skirt to get at her girdle.

Later, when they were both lying back in the bed, Dave said, "Now what do you want to do second?"

"Get you to promise me something," Bella said.

"Anything you want," he said.

"After I hung up on you this morning," she said, "I drove over to Turkey Hill Road and took a look at the old homestead. That's an awful lot of work you're doing there."

"We've just scratched the surface," Dave said.

"Who's your contractor?" Bella said.

"Kerner-Hirsh," Dave said. "A New York outfit."

"You'd better fire them," she said.

"Why?" Dave said.

"From now on," Bella said, "I want all the work on our place done by Anthony X. D'Alessandro, General Contractor, Beechwood 7384."

It took a couple of moments for the words he heard to make contact with the things he remembered. When they came together, Dave did not wait to move his body into position. Swinging as he lay, almost totally supine, with a single, hard, slashing chop of his open palm Dave Dehn broke his wife's nose.

14

"What are her grounds?" Dave said.

Colin Babington took the pipe from his mouth. He examined the ash.

"In this state there is only one ground for divorce," he said. "Adultery."

"She'll have to prove it," Dave said.

"She has no intention of doing that," Babington said.

"Then she won't get a divorce from me," Dave said.

"Not in New York State," Babington said.

"She can try the other forty-seven," Dave said. "If Hawaii and Alaska make it into the Union, she can take a shot at all fifty. This girl could use a project that will keep her off the streets."

"Bella plans to go to Mexico," Babington said.

"Getting your client out of the country is the best idea you've come up with so far," Dave said. "If I ever run into her again I'll break a few of her more important bones."

"I don't see what purpose that would serve," Colin Babington said.

"You might," Dave said, "if you were married to a bimbo."

A faint purple tinge came washing up out of the Brooks Brothers button-down Oxford blue shirt. The color climbed slowly across Colin Babington's leathery face.

"I cannot, of course, expect you not to be rude," he said. "I can, however, expect you to stick to the matter in hand."

"You happen to be talking to a man who can do both," Dave said. "Your client can go to Mexico or to Madagascar. She can file on grounds of physical cruelty or virulent halitosis. I'm staying in Beechwood, and I'm sticking to adultery."

The purple eased slowly back down from the leathery face into the Brooks Brothers shirt collar. Mr. Babington was under control again. To prove it, he struck a match.

"You don't seem to grasp the point," he said. "In your wife's suit for divorce, she is the one who selects the grounds on which she chooses to file."

"In her suit she can do any God-damn thing she pleases," Dave said. "Not in mine."

Colin Babington stared at him across the match flame from which the lawyer was sucking a light into his pipe. The flame, pumping up and down, seemed to add a little more yellow to the hair parted in the middle. It looked more and more like a tobacco-stained mustache that had been pressed into service as a wig.

"I don't understand," he said.

"If she files in Mexico," Dave said, "I will file a countersuit here in New York."

"On what grounds?"

Dave pulled an envelope from his pocket.

"These," he said.

He tossed the envelope across the desk. It hit the green blotter and slid bumpily toward Babington. The envelope came to rest against the leather middle button of his tweed jacket. Babington put down the pipe and picked up the envelope. He pulled out the pictures and started through them, one by one. After the first run-through, Babington put the pipe back into his mouth and examined the prints more slowly. Finally, he looked up at Dave.

"How did you get these?" Babington said.

"The way most people get things like that," Dave said.

"By hiring a firm of ex-goons who now call themselves private investigators. They specialize in infrared photography. Some of those shots were taken in the root cellar that used to be on Turkey Hill Road. Some were taken last December in the gazebo of the Embrie house down on the shore of Sequesta Pond when the house was shut up for the winter. The six underexposed ones were shot in the cab of his pickup truck while it was parked in the Mamaroneck Drive-In Movie Theatre. The picture they paid to watch but didn't was *Stairway to Heaven* with David Niven. I don't blame them for turning to other forms of entertainment. I saw that movie. The best shots, of course, are on the bed. They were taken in the Israel Putnam Motor Inn on the Post Road. If you want more prints, just call Mr. Lou Lasquadro at the Twenty-Four Hour Surveillance Service, Inc. They're in the Knickerbocker Building, 250 West Forty-second Street. You'll find them listed in the yellow pages as well as in the regular phone book. The negatives are in their Chase Manhattan safe-deposit box down in the lobby. Any questions?"

"Yes," Colin Babington said. "What are they doing?"

Dave leaned across the desk and spread out the prints on the green blotter.

"In this one she's giving him a head treatment," Dave said. "Sometimes known as a blow job. At Harvard you probably called it fellatio. At Ethan Allen High we called it cocksucking. Here, in this one, he's eating her. At Harvard it's probably not done, but if it is the participants identify it as cunnilingus. At Ethan Allen it was very popular but never discussed. Cunt lapping was considered unmanly. These others are variations of those two basic positions. The variations are included because photographers always get carried away on a job like this and they shoot more film than is necessary. Also because it's important for the purpose of evidence in a divorce court to get in very clear focus not only the sexual organs of the players but their faces as well. This one of my wife is, I think, very flattering. This one flatters not only Mr. D'Alessandro's cock but his profile as well."

Dave stood up.

"Just so you won't feel disappointed," he said, "I'm now going to be rude, as you expect all Jews to be. I'm cutting out of here. I've got a lot of work waiting on Turkey Hill Road. We're pouring concrete this morning for the swimming pool and the tennis courts back of the Center. I hope your client has a nice trip to Mexico. You can tell her that I don't give a damn who she screws so long as she doesn't try to fool around with the title to the Turkey Hill property. It's in her name, and as long as it is she's going to remain my wife. The minute she takes another crack at fucking me up I'll take the property away from her and throw her out on her ass. While you're carrying messages, which it seems to me is just about all you're good for, Mr. Babington, you might add a footnote for the little lady. As long as she remains my wife her monthly allowance will continue going into her account here in the First Beechwood Bank and Trust. That ties it, I think."

15

Colin Babington's thinking was somewhat different. Studying the prints Mr. Dehn had left with him, Colin Babington found his mind wandering.

He glanced at his watch. Ten minutes to noon. Colin Babington pressed the key on his interoffice call box.

"Audrey, bring me the Truscott file."

"Mr. Babington, today is only Tuesday."

"I know," he said. "But something has come up."

He flipped the key back into place. On his direct wire Babington dialed the number he usually dialed at this hour on Wednesdays.

"Hello?"

"Lola, it's me."

"Oh," she said. "Is anything wrong?"

"On the contrary," Babington said. "Something very interesting has happened. Instead of waiting until tomorrow, I thought I'd come up now. Is that all right?"

"Of course," Lola said. "What is it?"

"Not on the phone," Babington said. "I'll tell you when I get there."

"I've got a pumpkin bread in the oven," she said. "I'll need five minutes."

"Lola, after all these years surely you must be aware that it takes me at least a quarter of an hour to drive from my office to Magruder Crescent."

"Come along, then, darling, and stop sounding like Hector."

Hector Truscott and Colin Babington had been Leverett House roommates at Harvard. Soon after graduation they had borrowed money from Hector's father and bought the old Paternoster wheelwright shop on Main Street. In it, after a considerable amount of restoration, they had set up their law practice. Five and a half years ago, after a long and prosperous relationship, a freak accident on the Hutchinson River Parkway had broken up the partnership.

Hector and Lola had been on their way home from a dinner party in Rye when a trailer truck, coming toward them on the eastbound side of the road, lost one of its front retreads. The truck jackknifed, leaped the divider, and came down on the Truscott Pontiac. Both the driver of the trailer and Hector were dead on arrival at the hospital. Lola lost her right foot at the ankle.

Colin Babington did not have to think twice about his course of action. He kept Hector's name on the letterhead, and from the list of clients on the firm's books at Hector's death he allocated fifty per cent of the firm's profits to Hector's wife.

The accident did more to Lola than make her a widow and a cripple. It turned her into a recluse. She resigned from her chairmanship of the local chapter of the Girl Scouts. She was never seen again at the monthly meetings of the Beechwood Historical Society. The paper on Women in Westchester Local Government that Lola Truscott had been preparing for more than a year was never read before her fellow members of the Beechwood chapter of the League of Women Voters. All her once considerable executive ability seemed to abandon her.

There was some comment. A few people made inquiries. Some heads were shaken. Soon, however, she was pretty much forgotten by the fellow citizens among whom she had once been so active. Lola Truscott clearly did not mind that. Or seem even to be aware of it. She seemed to have forgotten her fellow citizens. She was perfectly happy with her new life, which centered around a totally new interest: cooking.

Lola spent most of her day in the kitchen. She rarely ate what she cooked. At best she could have consumed only part of what she produced. Most of it went into the garbage pail soon after it emerged from the oven. Lola went out into the garden occasionally to pick a few tomatoes or green beans, but most of her life was now lived almost entirely within the walls of the house on Magruder Crescent. This new life was made possible by the devotion of Colin Babington.

Lola would not face a bill. She refused to keep a checkbook. And she either had forgotten or could no longer be bothered with simple household chores such as calling Keefe Schlossberger to come put up the storm windows for the winter and replace them with screens for the summer. Colin Babington took care of everything.

Every Wednesday he drove up for lunch. He brought Lola enough petty cash to see her through the week. Tips for the Bohack's driver who delivered the enormous quantities of food she ordered by phone and consumed in her culinary experiments. Pennies for the postman to pay for the postage-due stamps on an occasional letter. Colin called Keefe Schlossberger when necessary, and took care of other chores that had accumulated during the week. Neither the money nor the chores added up to much, but they kept Lola from entanglement with the outside world. It seemed to Colin Babington it was the least he could do for her.

Avis Babington thought her husband was a fool to carry his loyalty to Hector to such lengths, but Colin was aware that Avis had never liked Lola. Besides, the weekly visits had compensations for Colin that Avis would not have understood. He did not enlighten her.

As always when he drove up to Magruder Crescent, Colin left his office and headed east, as though he were going to Rye.

Safely out of Beechwood, he cut across to the Hutchinson River Parkway and doubled back, coming at the Truscott house from the north. Very little of Beechwood's local traffic came from that direction. Most houses on Magruder Crescent were set so deeply in their own not inconsiderable acreage that they could not be seen from the road. This was one of the charms of the neighborhood, and the source of much of Colin Babington's ease of mind about these weekly visits. He had never encountered a pedestrian or a car on his way to or from the Truscott house.

Colin saw nobody today as he turned into the driveway. He drove down to the garage and parked the car inside. On his way out he pulled down the overhead door. Colin walked across the back yard to the kitchen and let himself in with his key. He saw the pumpkin bread cooling on the counter beside the oven and, next to it, the can of Campbell's Pepper Pot out of which would come his lunch. Lola's passion for cooking never fed Colin Babington. What she served him every Wednesday always came out of a can.

"Colin, is that you?"

"Yes, Lola," he called up the back stairs as he walked out into the living room.

"Make the drinks, darling," she called. "I won't be a moment."

In the living room Colin went to the bar. There was ice in the bucket, and slivers of lemon peel lay on the tiny Spode plate. Colin made two martinis. He set one on the black marble top of the Empire table next to the chintz-covered tub chair in which Lola liked to sit. He carried his own drink across to the secretary. Sipping slowly, Colin went through the papers Lola had weighted down neatly with the bronze reproduction of Notre Dame she and Hector had brought back from their honeymoon in Paris.

The long brown envelope containing Lola's bank statement. She had urged Colin long ago to have it sent to his office, since he made the deposits and wrote the checks, but Colin had thought it more seemly to have Lola's account listed under the Magruder Crescent address. Keefe Schloss-berger's bill for removing the storm windows, putting up the screens, and two months of lawn trimming. The telephone bill. The Westchester Light & Power bill. Hagedorn's Fine Meats & Poultry. Le Gourmet Food Shoppe. Finizetti's Fish Market. The usual bag.

Colin finished the papers neatly and put them in his pocket. He took some money from his wallet, put it on the secretary, and anchored it with the bronze reproduction of Notre Dame.

"You've finished your drink."

Colin turned. Lola had come in. She was wearing the long red velvet hostess gown he had given her for their first Christmas. Colin had never told her why. When he saw it in the window of The Dress Box on Main Street, it had reminded him of the gown Emma Bovary had worn to her first assignation with Léon Dupuis in Rouen. Colin had never told her, but Lola obviously knew the gown had a special significance for him. She never wore anything else for their Wednesday meetings.

"Not quite," Colin said. He lifted his glass to the light from the window. Not much martini was left. "Anyway, I always have two. So I'll slow down while you catch up."

Lola sat down in the tub chair. He pushed the matching chintz footstool into position. He waited until she had her right foot on the stool before he sat down facing her. A stranger, seeing Lola Truscott for the first time, would not have known the red velvet outstretched on the stool con-cealed an artificial limb.

Lola picked up her martini, took a sip, and smiled at him across the rim of the glass. It was just a woman's smile. The smile of a woman who had never been beautiful and was now no longer young. A smile to which Colin suspected Lola gave no more thought than she gave to the tip she handed the delivery boy from Bohack's. Both were polite acknowledg-ments for a service rendered. And Lola's smile had never meant anything to him. In fact, for years he had never really been aware of Lola. Until the accident in which she lost her foot. From then on, Lola's smile always did something to his heart. He carried around the small, delicious pain from Wednesday to Wednesday, like a bright but carefully hooded secret.

"Now tell me what's this unexpected thing that's come up," Lola said.

"I've run into a feeling that a long-held belief has been held too long," Colin said. "It's been taking up room in my mind for years. Maybe all my life. This morning I was jolted into an awareness that maybe it should be tossed out onto the ash heap to make room for something new."

"Start from the beginning," Lola said.

They had been through this before. Many times. Colin knew his role. Lola knew hers. The moves were as stylized as a minuet. First came his call for her to dip into her research files, so to speak. She knew at least something about everything, and a great deal about many things.

"It's about Jews," Colin said. "Tell me what the word means to you."

Last Wednesday he had wanted to know what the word artichoke meant to her. A client with a successful business that packaged luncheon meats had decided for no very good reason to invest a substantial sum in a vegetable-trucking firm. He then discovered that the firm was going broke because its customers had unexpectedly developed a puzzling indifference to artichokes. The client had come to Colin for help. Colin had come to Lola.

"Jews," Lola said, and she paused.

Not to think. The thinking had been done long ago, when she was unaware she had been doing it. In the years before her accident. When she had been living life. Not remembering it. Lola paused to let the coded knowledge break through to her. She had nothing to do with the act of bringing it to the surface. The knowledge was buried deep in her mind.

Like last Wednesday's knowledge of artichokes. All she had to do was trip the trigger. Out of the accumulation of years the knowledge would explode.

All she had to do was say the word. "Jews."

It exploded.

"Real estate values," she said.

Colin nodded.

"That's what I used to think," he said. "Until this morning."

"What changed your mind?" Lola said.

"I had a visit from Mr. David Dehn," Colin said.

"The man Bella Biaggi married?"

"She wanted to divorce him," Colin said.

"Why?"

"He's broken her nose."

"That's odd," Lola said. "There's nothing in my mind that identifies Jews with violence."

"Nor in mine," Colin said. "I've had this thought about them for years. The same thought I've had all my life about Negroes. People who should not be allowed to move into your neighborhood because they send real estate prices down."

"They always do," Lola said.

"Not always," Colin said. "I think Beechwood is going to be an exception."

"I don't see why," Lola said.

"You would if you saw Mr. Dehn," Colin said. "He doesn't fit that thing I've had in my head for years about Jews. So I've decided the time has come to get rid of that thing in my head and put in something else."

"Tell me," Lola said.

"You get the right Jew in the right neighborhood and the wrong thing will happen," Colin said.

"Like what?" Lola said.

"Real estate prices won't go down," Colin Babington said. "They'll go up."

142

"Mr. Dehn must have done something to you this morning besides sit in that chair by your desk," Lola said.

"He did," Colin said. "He beat me at my own game. Anybody who can do that stops being a Jew. He becomes somebody from whom I can learn."

"Learn what?" Lola said.

"The only thing worth learning from a Jew," Colin said. "How to make money."

"What game were you playing?" Lola said.

"I thought I had Bella Biaggi's divorce wrapped up," Colin said. "Mr. Dehn unwrapped it for me."

"How?" Lola said.

Colin Babington took the envelope from his pocket, stood up, and dropped it in the lap of Lola's red velvet hostess gown. He crossed to the bar and made his second martini while she went through the pictures.

"These aren't particularly extraordinary," she said finally. "Actually, it's all rather common, everyday, garden-variety fellatio and not very adroitly executed cunnilingus. Without much style, either. I would have thought a couple as young and well endowed as Miss Biaggi and this D'Alessandro boy seem to be would show more verve and daring."

Colin came back with the drink and set it on the table. He took the batch of pictures from Lola and shuffled them until he found the one that puzzled him.

"Here, look at this," he said. "Can you tell me what in God's name they're doing?"

"Of course," Lola said, "but I won't."

She slid down the zipper of her hostess gown and she unhooked the fastening of her artificial foot.

"I'll do better than that," Lola said with the smile that always gave him that funny little feeling in his heart. "I'll show you."

16

Ten months after work had begun, a visitor from the Matto Grosso would not have recognized what had happened to Turkey Hill Road.

The main building had been topped off. Mike Palgrave was supervising the wood carvers who were putting the paneling into the sanctuary on the ground floor. The two houses on Saul Street had not yet been completely finished, but they had been in good enough shape for Sid and Marian Singer and their baby to move into their new home in Beechwood. The following day, Fanny Mintz had moved herself and her parents up from New York into the second Saul Street house. Best of all, the subdivision plan was working.

On the day Fanny Mintz caught him on the field phone near the Post Road, one hundred and eight lots had already been spoken for. And at their staff conference Sid had reported he expected to close seven more before the end of the week.

"Who?" Dave said into the phone.

The instrument sat on an empty wooden crate that only the day before had been full of dynamite caps. The crate sat at the bottom of a trench that was ready to receive a twenty-four-by-six septic tank. It would service, Mike said, the eight lots that faced the Post Road.

"*Time* magazine," Fanny said.

"Tell them my subscription is paid up," Dave said.

"D.D., they're serious," Fanny said.

"Fanny, for God's sake, tell them anything. I'm up to my ears. Sid is waiting for me at the bank on Main Street."

"Sid won't run away," Fanny said. "*Time* might."

"What do they want?" Dave said.

"They want to send a reporter out to interview you," Fanny said.

"About what?" Dave said.

He knew about what. The question was a stall for time. Dave had not expected the reporters so soon.

"D.D., you know about what," Fanny said. "I think you ought to see them. *Time* Magazine is big stuff."

Too big, Dave was suddenly thinking. He did not want that kind of publicity. He had not given much thought to the p.r. end. There had been too many other things to think about. Dave saw now that he had to think about it. And he had to think fast. *Time* not only marched on. Like opportunity, it knocked only once. Those Yale boys in Radio City would not call twice.

"Give them the brush," Dave said.

"D.D.," Fanny said. "Please concentrate. This is *Time* mag—uh—zeen. They can do us a lot of good."

Not the right kind of good. Dave's mind was beginning to turn over. It told him he could do better than *Time* magazine.

"Give them the brush," Dave said again.

"You sure?" Fanny said.

"Positive," Dave said, although he wasn't. He was still riding a hunch.

Later in the day, at the afternoon staff conference, Dave knew he was riding in the right direction.

"*Newsweek* called," Fanny said.

"Same answer," Dave said.

"If you say so," Fanny said.

"What's this all about?" Sid said.

"Publicity," Dave said. "Fanny thinks I'm making a mistake."

She shrugged and said, "What about *The New York Times?*"

"When did they call?" Dave said.

"They haven't," Fanny said. "But with *Time* and *Newsweek* sniffing around, the *Times* is next. They print all the news that fits."

"When they call," Dave said, "same answer."

Looking troubled, Sid said, "Dave, we could use a little publicity."

"Not a little," Dave said.

The next morning, from his apartment in The Dakota, Dave called *The Jewish Daily Forward.* Getting the city editor on the phone was not difficult. Getting him to understand what Dave wanted took a little longer. When he did, the city editor was interested. When Dave said he would pay all expenses, the city editor was enthusiastic.

"There's an eleven-twelve from Grand Central in the morning," Dave said. "It gets to Beechwood at twelve-five. Tell your man I'll meet him."

When he did, Dave was pleasantly surprised. He had no idea what a reporter for *The Jewish Daily Forward* should look like. It had not occurred to Dave that the man would look like Hildy Johnson in *The Front Page.*

"I'm Dave Dehn."

"Krauss with a double s," the reporter said, putting out his hand. "Ted Krauss."

They shook hands. As he led the reporter to the brand-new powder blue convertible, Dave examined his visitor. He looked clean, alert, and aggressively baggy. Dave had a feeling that when Mr. Krauss sent out his ancient tweed sports coat, his instructions to the tailor were Dry-clean and rumple.

"Any special place you'd like to eat?" Dave said when they were in the car and heading down toward Main Street.

"These Westchester towns always have some kind of businessmen's club," Mr. Krauss said. "But you have to be a member to get in, and I don't suppose you are."

"Why not?" Dave said.

"You're a Jew, aren't you?" Ted Krauss said.

"If I were not," Dave said, "would I call *The Jewish Daily Forward* for this interview?"

"You'd be surprised by the people who call *The Jewish Daily Forward*," Ted Krauss said. "Just before the war, when he was shoveling out his garbage from a radio station in Washington we had a call from Fulton Sheen. The prick wanted to know why we weren't giving him any coverage."

Mr. Krauss's pleasant voice had clearly come to maturity somewhere in the Bensonhurst section of Brooklyn.

"What did you tell him?" Dave said.

"Not me," Ted Krauss said. "That kind of call Abe Cahan handles himself."

"What did Mr. Cahan say to Fulton Sheen?"

"Nobody on the staff really knows," Ted Krauss said. "Old Abe took the call in his private office. But there are plenty of Yiddish euphemisms for go fuck yourself."

Dave laughed and said, "Then there's Floyd Klenczewski's Steak Pit on Main Street."

"I know," Ted Krauss said. "Steaks Chops Sea Food Sixty-five cents a Shot of Bourbon Businessmen's Blue Plate Luncheons."

"The food's not bad, and the bourbon is bourbon," Dave said. "But Floyd is only six months up from his former greasy-spoon dog wagon on the Post Road, with mortgages up to here, and he's desperate to hold onto his monthly Catholic War Veterans lunches and the rest of the Rotary Club crap."

"So he examines the noses of his customers to make sure he screens out the more obvious heebs," Ted Krauss said.

"Something like that," Dave said.

Ted Krauss turned to examine him.

"I think he probably lets you in," the reporter said finally.

"Actually, we've become pretty good friends, Floyd Klenczewski and I," Dave said.

"Would he let your friend in?" Ted Krauss said.

"Let's have a look at the profile," Dave said.

Ted Krauss turned on the front seat and stared straight ahead through the windshield. Dave studied the reporter's nose.

"Well," Dave said finally. "You don't look like Ben-Gurion, but you're not a dead ringer for Ray Milland either."

"You game?" Ted Krauss said.

"For what?" Dave said.

"A little research," Ted Krauss said.

"On what?" Dave said.

"What you asked me to come up and interview you about," Ted Krauss said.

"I haven't told you about that yet," Dave said.

"You've told me plenty without knowing it," Ted Krauss said. "Now let's see if my mere presence can tell both of us a little more."

"Like what?" Dave said.

"The intensity of this town's screw-the-Jews movement," Ted Krauss said. "Some of these Wasp assholes would keep Jesus out of their dog wagons because he doesn't wear pants with a zipper. So keeping out Ben-Gurion is easy stuff. So is welcoming Ray Milland. It's the guys in between that tell the story. Guys like me."

"You want to eat at Floyd Klenczewski's Steak Pit?" Dave said.

"I'd like to try," Ted Krauss said.

"Let's go," Dave said.

"Introduce me any way you want," Ted Krauss said. "Just in case you have to, I mean. And invent some reason for why I don't talk. Only don't make me a deaf mute. I might believe it and not hear anything."

Dave guided the Cadillac down Main Street and parked in front of the Steak Pit. When they walked into the restaurant, Floyd came across to meet them at the door. He was carrying an armful of menus and wearing his toothy headwaiter's smile.

"Hello, Mr. Dehn," he said.

Then Floyd Klenczewski saw Ted Krauss. Floyd's eyes narrowed. He turned to Dave, then quickly turned back for another look at Ted Krauss. The reporter obliged by moving his head so that Klenczewski could get a better view of his profile.

"Hello, Floyd," Dave said. "Two, please."

The restaurateur ran his catcher's-mitt-size hand across his naked skull. His Adam's apple bobbed like a sinker when a trout takes the bait.

"You mean, to eat?" he said.

"No, to play a game of two-handed pinochle," Dave said. "What else do people come to your place for? How about that booth over in the corner? We want to talk."

Floyd's Adam's apple plummeted. It churned around somewhere in the vicinity of his epiglottis, then came hurtling back into place.

"Mr. Dehn," he said.

His voice stopped.

"Mr. Dehn," Floyd said again.

He shot into the rear of the restaurant two desperate backward glances, one across each shoulder, as though he suspected armed marauders were closing in on him.

"Mr. Dehn," he said a third time.

The third attempt seemed to get Floyd off dead center. He grabbed Dave's arm and said, "Come over here a minute."

Dave resisted Floyd's tug.

"It's all right," he said. "You can speak in front of my guest. He doesn't understand English."

"He doesn't?" Floyd said.

"Did your father understand English the day he got off the ship from Poland?" Dave said.

Floyd looked hurt.

"It's not the same thing," he said. "My old man wasn't Jewish."

"That means probably you're not Jewish either," Dave said.

Floyd shook his head, as though to clear it of the confusing thought Dave had dropped into it.

"What else could I be?" he said.

"Half Jewish," Dave said. "If your father married a Jewish girl."

"No, no," Floyd said. "My mother was Catholic. She still is. I could introduce you to her."

"Some other time," Dave said. "We're hungry."

"Listen," Floyd said. "Mr. Dehn, do me a favor. For lunch, just this once, just today, please go some other place."

"Something wrong with your kitchen?" Dave said.

"Mr. Dehn, please," Floyd said. "It's not I'm against Jews. Some of my best friends are Jews."

"Don't I know that?" Dave said. "I'm one of your best friends."

"Ain't that a fact?" Floyd said. "Absolutely, Mr. Dehn. This town, the few months you've been here, you're one of my best friends."

"One of your best friends is hungry," Dave said. "Put a steak on, Floyd. For my guest, a kosher apple and a glass of Manischewitz Royal Mountain Claret."

"Mr. Dehn," Floyd said, "I can't."

"Why not?" Dave said.

"If your guest looked, you know, if he looked like—like—"

"Like the son of a Polish immigrant with a Catholic mother who owns a steak joint on Main Street?"

"Now, that ain't fair, Mr. Dehn. Especially to a friend. You know what I mean, Mr. Dehn."

"On an empty stomach I'm never sure," Dave said. "Tell me."

"Okay," Floyd said firmly. "To you it's a joke, Mr. Dehn. To me it's my bread and butter. I let you in, okay. But you start bringing other guys. My regular lunch crowd comes in. They take one look, Mr. Dehn, and I'm dead. It's curtains for Floyd Klenczewski. I might as well hang a lock on my door. I'm out of business. Finished in this town for good. Please be reasonable, Mr. Dehn."

Dave looked at Ted Krauss.

"What do you say, rabbi?"

"Let's blow," the reporter said. "Anything I ate in this joint, it wouldn't stay down."

"Hey!" Floyd said. "I thought you said he doesn't understand English!"

"He doesn't," Dave said. "He just reacts to bad smells."

Out in the car, the reporter said, "You know what I want now?"

"What?" Dave said.

"A nonsectarian double Scotch," Ted Krauss said.

"We're five minutes from your first sip," Dave said.

He sent the car east on Main Street, past the turnoff into Turkey Hill Road. He drove down to the Hutchinson marker; turned right, away from the Parkway, toward the Sound; and came out on the Post Road. Then he headed south and pulled into the parking space next to Patsy's Place.

They went around to the back of the dog wagon. Dave led the way in through the kitchen. Patsy was opening the cupboard over the refrigerator.

"I saw you coming," she said.

She brought down Dave's bottle of Scotch. She set it beside the two tumblers on the drainboard. She poured them both full.

"Hey, wait," Dave said. "This is lunch. I can't take that much this time of day."

"You don't have to," Patsy said. "I can tell from your buddy's sports coat he can finish what you leave over."

"I'd better buy myself another bottle," Dave said. "I'll bring it over tomorrow."

"I already did," Patsy said. "I'll put it on the check. I saved the corner booth for you."

"Thanks, Patsy." Dave picked up the two glasses. "Come on, Mr. Krauss."

Dave shouldered his way through the swinging door. He held it with his hip for Ted Krauss to precede him. Except for a truck driver soaking his pancakes in maple syrup at the counter, the place was empty. Dave led the way to the corner booth. He set down the two tumblers.

"If anybody asks what you're drinking," Dave said, "it's Dr. Brown's Celery Tonic. Patsy doesn't have a liquor license."

Dave sat down. The reporter moved toward the chair against the screen. Dave pulled him back.

"No, take this one," he said. "I brought you here for a reason."

Ted Krauss sat down in the chair that faced the Post Road. Dave took the chair on his right. Patsy appeared with two glasses of ice water and a couple of menus.

"You want to order?" she said.

"You kosher?" Dave said to the reporter.

"Not when I'm out on assignment," Ted Krauss said. "But don't go squealing to Abe Cahan."

"My God," Dave said. "Don't tell me Abe Cahan is still running the place?"

"Okay, I won't tell you," the reporter said. "But that won't make Abe Cahan go away."

"If your buddy's not kosher," Patsy said, "why don't you order? When I'm on my feet I like to spend the time working. There's a lot to do out in the kitchen. Listening time comes after the day's work is finished."

"Patsy makes a great T-bone," Dave said. "I recommend it."

"In that case," the reporter said, "I'll take two."

"Chili and a glass of milk," Dave said.

Patsy made a note on her pad. She picked up the menus and waddled off to the kitchen.

"Probably going right to the phone," the reporter said. "To call Abe Cahan."

"Not a chance," Dave said. "Patsy hasn't been able to wedge her way into a phone booth since Dempsey married Estelle Taylor." He picked up his glass. "Here's to Abe Cahan. That column he used to write? 'A Bintel Brief'? When

I was a kid up in Albany, my father used to read aloud from it every night after we finished the supper dishes."

"My father used to read from an endless comic saga on the facing page about a character named Yenta Telibenda," Ted Krauss said.

"Written by B. Kovner," Dave said.

"Let's drink to all those heart-warming old farts of yesteryear, God bless them," the reporter said.

They did. Dave chased his belt with a swallow of ice water. He could tell Ted Krauss was a seasoned reporter. He chased his belt with another belt.

"Before we start swapping the names of our public school arithmetic teachers," he said, "I might as well tell you, what I've seen and heard so far up here in Beechwood I could have seen and heard where I've seen and heard it dozens of times before. In any reasonably affluent suburban town in any part of these here United States. If I'm going to get an interview up here that's going to justify your underwriting those T-bones and this Scotch, Mr. Dehn, you'd better start by telling me what's so special about Beechwood."

"The fact that I've chosen it for my experiment," Dave said.

"A reporter for the *Times* would now show he was one of Carl Ackerman's prize pupils up at the Columbia School of Journalism by asking you to tell about your experiment. But I haven't made it to the *Times* yet. I'm a leg man for *The Jewish Daily Forward*. And *The Jewish Daily Forward* is called the *Forward* because it's read backwards. So I'm going to ask the last thing first. What's so special about the town of Beechwood?"

"What you just said about it," Dave said. "It could be any reasonably affluent suburban town in any part of these United States."

"Like the Lynds you're doing?" Ted Krauss said. "A *Middletown*?"

"No," Dave said. "What they were after, they were doing a

sociological study of a small American city. Muncie, Indiana, the way I remember it from Eco Two in Ethan Allen High School. We had the book as a supplementary text. Employment figures, crime statistics, educational facilities, how the different social classes live and think and eat and fuck. Lower lower. Middle lower. And upper lower. Lower middle. Middle middle. And upper middle. Lower upper. Middle upper. And upper upper. I'm not interested in that crap. Up here in Beechwood, I mean. I'm interested in only one level of Beechwood society."

"Which one is that?"

"The Jews," Dave said.

"Before I went to Grand Central to catch the train," Ted Krauss said, "I did a little research. There are hardly any Jews in Beechwood."

"There are going to be a lot more," Dave said.

"When?" the reporter said.

"As soon as I can arrange to bring them in," Dave said.

"A lot of Jews?" Ted Krauss said.

"It's got to be a lot," Dave said. "Jews are my business."

"What's a lot?" the reporter said.

"A thousand, for starters," Dave said.

"A thousand like in ten times a hundred?" Ted Krauss said.

"Or twenty times fifty," Dave said.

"A thousand Jews?" Ted Krauss said. "Here in Beechwood?"

"To get the ball rolling, yes," Dave said.

"According to my research," the reporter said, "the population of Beechwood at the last census was a little short of thirteen thousand."

"Twelve thousand eight hundred and seventy-two," Dave said.

"Into the middle of twelve thousand eight hundred and seventy-two goyim," Ted Krauss said, "you plan to inject a thousand of our people?"

"As I said," Dave said, "for starters."

"Boy," the reporter said, "when it comes to looking for trouble you go out with searchlights."

"I'll find it," Dave said. "Don't worry."

Ted Krauss took a pull at his glass and chased it with another pull.

"Don't worry, he tells me," the reporter said to his ice cubes. "What else do I know how to do?" he said to Dave. "I'm a Jew."

"If you were the right age," Dave said, "I'd include you in my first thousand. You could learn what I'm going to teach the other nine hundred and ninety-nine."

"What's that?" Ted Krauss said.

"How to be a human being as well as a Jew," Dave said.

The reporter gave him a sharp look.

"That means taking the worry out of being a Jew," he said.

"Correct," Dave said.

"That's like taking the bubble out of champagne," Ted Krauss said. "What's left?"

"A human being," Dave said.

Ted Krauss shook his head.

"It won't work," he said.

"Why not?" Dave said.

"If you take the worry out of a Jew," the reporter said, "you also take out the fear."

"What's wrong with that?" Dave said.

"A Jew without fear is not a Jew," the reporter said. "There's no such animal."

"I'm going to breed one," Dave said.

The reporter's glass stopped on its way to his mouth.

"Here in Beechwood?" he said.

"Here in Beechwood," Dave said.

"How?" Ted Krauss said.

Dave hiked his elbows forward over the table. He nodded toward the wide window that ran along the front of Patsy's Place.

"Look directly out across the Post Road," he said. "To the land on the other side."

"Okay," the reporter said.

"What do you see?" Dave said.

"An excavation," Ted Krauss said. "That big gray thing, that's a septic tank. I've seen them on construction sites. Is that what you mean?"

"Yes," Dave said. "You can't see much beyond it, so you'll have to take my word. That septic tank is sitting on the northwestern end of a piece of land that bellies out from Long Island Sound just south of Main Street for one hundred and eighty acres."

"How do you know?" Ted Krauss said.

"I own it," Dave said.

"One hundred and eighty acres," the reporter said slowly. He gave Dave another sharp look. "The number means something?"

"Yes," Dave said.

"What?" Ted Krauss said.

"Buchenwald was just one point eight acres smaller," Dave said.

For the first time since he had met Ted Krauss at the train Dave could see he had captured the reporter's complete attention.

"What are you doing with that land?" Ted Krauss said.

"Subdividing it," Dave said. "Into quarter-acre building lots."

"For one thousand Jews?" the reporter said.

"For starters, as I told you," Dave said.

"From what you've told me so far," Ted Krauss said, "I'm going to make an educated guess."

"I'm listening," Dave said.

"These one thousand Jews are going to have to meet certain requirements to put their hands on one of those quarter-acre lots," the reporter said. "Requirements laid down by you."

"If I run into Abe Cahan," Dave said, "I'm going to tell him he's got at least one smart reporter on his staff."

"Tell him some other time," Ted Krauss said. "Right now tell me what those requirements are. Aside from the fact that every purchaser has to be a Jew."

"He has to be an ex-G.I.," Dave said. "He has to be married. And he has to be at least first-generation American."

The reporter looked down into his glass. He seemed to be doing an arithmetic problem in his head. Finally, he looked up at Dave.

"The way I work that out," Ted Krauss said, "I figure it means you don't want anybody like my old man."

"Or mine," Dave said.

"No immigrants," the reporter said.

"No immigrants," Dave said.

"All native-born," Ted Krauss said.

"Every one of them eligible to run for President of these United States," Dave said.

"And all fairly young," the reporter said.

"I was in the war," Dave said. "And I'm thirty-four. Fairly young, yes."

"Young enough to start raising families on these quarter-acre lots," Ted Krauss said.

"If they've already got a family under way, that won't keep them out," Dave said. "So long as the kids they come here with are young enough to start growing up here."

"Their first memories, then," the reporter said. "These kids. You want all of them to know nothing earlier than Beechwood."

"I want Beechwood to be the starting place," Dave said. "For all of them."

Ted Krauss nodded and took another sip from his glass.

"I think I've got it worked out," he said.

"Tell me," Dave said.

"No," the reporter said. "You tell me."

"I want a community of kids who won't know what you and I knew," Dave said. "Immigrant parents. Memories of pogroms. Sweatshops. Stinking tenements on the lower East

157

Side in New York and on Westerlo Street up in places like Albany. Being called kikes in school. None of that. I want them to start off like other middle-class American kids."

"You want your Jewish kids to grow up like Wasps," Ted Krauss said. "In the suburbs. Playing Little League baseball. Later, tennis. Wearing blue jeans and penny loafers and T-shirts. Going to camp in the summer and dancing school in the winter. Studying arithmetic in buildings that look like ranch houses. With those kitchens where Betty Crocker without a hair misplaced in her hair-do and an apron she could wear to the Coronation Ball is testing a seven-layer fudge cake made of her new nonsifting buttermilk mix. Earning pocket money not by selling newspapers on Delancey Street but by working in the supermarket after school. Am I close?"

"Close enough," Dave said.

"What have I left out?" the reporter said.

"Every Saturday morning every one of those kids has to attend services in the synagogue that will be the center of the community," Dave said. "Every Sunday morning every one of those kids has to come to Sunday school at the Center. At the end of thirteen years, every one of the boys must be bar mitzvah."

"Suppose a boy doesn't want to be bar mitzvah?" Ted Krauss said.

"His father will change his mind," Dave said. "Those conditions are part of the contract of sale my lawyer has worked out. When a man signs on for one of those quarter-acre lots, he signs on for the religious education of his children."

"Your idea of their religious education," Ted Krauss said.

"Why not?" Dave said. "I'm paying for it."

The reporter again devoted a few moments to a scowling study of the contents of his glass. Again he seemed to be working out a problem in mathematics. And again he apparently came up with a solution.

"Quarter-acre lots in a community like Beechwood are not cheap," Ted Krauss said. "Building appropriate housing on them will cost money. More money than most ex-G.I.'s can afford. Even with veterans' financing from the Government, for most of them Westchester is going to be more than they can swing. You've covered that?"

"Of course," Dave said.

"How?" the reporter said.

"I'm banking the whole deal," Dave said. "Any man who meets the specifications can have the services of my architect free of charge, plus all the mortgage money he wants, even up to one hundred per cent of purchase price, at a rate of interest set at one-half of whatever is the going rate at local banks."

"Where did you get that kind of money?" Ted Krauss said.

"My grandfather invented the wheel," Dave said. "I've kept the basic patents rolling."

"If you don't want to tell me how you got to be Al Capone's bagman, that's fair enough," Ted Krauss said. "Every guy has a right to be curious about how the next guy got rich. It's the American way. Every man also has the right to tell the curious to mind their own God-damn business. So forget my question. I'll shift to uttering a simple declarative sentence. Mr. Dehn, you must be but loaded."

"I manage to put chicken on my table on Sundays," Dave said.

"And you want this thing pretty badly," the reporter said.

"Badly enough to back it with every dime I've got," Dave said.

"Is that the story you want me to print?" Ted Krauss said.

"I could have had it printed in *Time*," Dave said. "Or in *Newsweek*."

"But you preferred *The Jewish Daily Forward*," Ted Krauss said.

"I'm paying for your T-bone," Dave said.

"Very few ex-G.I.'s read *The Jewish Daily Forward*," Ted Krauss said.

"No, but their fathers do," Dave said. "Their fathers will tell them. The way my father would have told me, and your father would have told you. I want that special clout."

"You've covered everything," the reporter said.

"I think so," Dave said.

"There's one thing you've left out," Ted Krauss said.

"What's that?" Dave said.

"Your twelve thousand eight hundred and seventy-two neighbors," the reporter said.

17

Several months later, one of those twelve thousand eight hundred and seventy-two neighbors chose not to be forgotten.

"Go see the guy," Sid Singer had urged. "What can you lose?"

"Time," Dave said.

"We're ahead of schedule," Sid said. "We can afford to waste a little, and there's always the chance it won't be wasted. You might learn something."

The first thing Dave learned, as he guided his car into the tunnel of carefully pruned poplars, was that Mr. Don Fortgang was a man who clearly wanted his visitors to know at a glance they were not coming to see a citizen who carried his lunch to work every day in a paper bag.

What Mr. Fortgang had invested in the compound that exploded into view at the top of the avenue of poplars was anybody's guess. For the most informed guess Dave thought it would have been wise to choose somebody on the staff of the architect who had laid out Boston Common. Mr. Fortgang's home on the River Lane hill overlooking the western shore of Sequesta Pond looked like a scale-model reconstruction of the Massachusetts Bay Colony.

"Come up this afternoon and have a drink," Mr. Fortgang had said to Dave on the phone. "I'd like you to see my home."

What Dave saw first was what his host was wearing: a bright

red kimono and green wooden-soled sandals. Don Fortgang looked like an actor having a few last puffs on his straight-grain briar before going out on stage as Nanki-Poo in *The Mikado.*

"Nice place you've got here," Dave said.

Mr. Fortgang waved the stem of his pipe at the house facing them.

"Maybe so," he said. "But before you call a place like this nice you have to work your way around the word sensational. Come take a look."

He led the way into a large, high, airy hallway. Perhaps it was more than a hallway. Dave could not be sure. The area reminded him of a ground-floor wing at the Met. Doorways stood open at regular intervals on both sides. Dave could almost see the red velvet ropes that were strung from jamb to jamb on visitors' days.

"This room here," Mr. Fortgang said, pointing with the stem of his pipe. "See that thing? That's a silversmith's table. You know Paul Revere?"

"Not personally," Dave said.

"I mean in the poem," Mr. Fortgang said.

"One if by land and two if by sea?"

"Him, yeah," Mr. Fortgang said. "He was a hot-shot silversmith. Made most of the stuff standing on that table. Look at this."

Dave looked at cobbler's benches, clocks, lamps, and dozens of other artifacts—all Early American, all displayed with expensively chilling care, and all contributing to a general feeling that he was slowly losing his mind.

Finally Dave said, "Where do you and Mrs. Fortgang do your actual living?"

"Follow me," Mr. Fortgang said.

Dave followed him across the parking court to a tall hedge. They entered a concealed arch and emerged in front of a structure that looked like a bright red Japanese pagoda.

"Y'ever seen a thing like this?" Mr. Fortgang said.

"What is it?" Dave said.

"A bathhouse," Mr. Fortgang said. "We have two. This one is for the pool. People they want to swim in Sequesta, we have one the other side of the house. Come have a look."

Mr. Fortgang opened the pagoda door and led the way into a locker room. A bronze incense burner was going full blast on a bamboo towel rack. Dave coughed.

"You'll get used to it," Mr. Fortgang said. "How about a sauna?"

"I was invited for a drink," Dave said.

"All my guests, I insist they have cocktails in the sauna," Mr. Fortgang said. "That's how they learn what good is. Here, try one of these."

From a row of hooks shaped like a series of Japanese ideographs Mr. Fortgang took down a red kimono.

"You don't know what comfort is until you get into one of these," Mr. Fortgang said. "Back in 1945? Right after MacArthur got the Japs to put their John Hancock on those surrender papers on the deck of the *Missouri*, Charlene and me, our oldest boy Marvin, he's on MacArthur's staff. We hadn't seen him almost two years, right after he was wounded at Tarawa and they flew him to the hospital in Bethesda. You don't know my Marvin. That boy is but on his toes. He pulled a few strings and Charlene and me, we got the air lift, and we flew over to Tokyo for a visit. You never saw anything like those Japs. You learn when you hear the word relaxation what it means it means a Japanese kimono. Then a couple of drinks in the sauna and believe me you feel ten years younger. Go ahead, try it. You'll find out if I'm not right. Use the locker at the end. It's got a side door leads right into the lounge."

The lounge, Dave saw when he came into it wearing the kimono, had been designed for lolling.

"See?" Mr. Fortgang said. "You look more relaxed already." He sprawled into a more relaxed position on a cherry red chaise longue. "Why'n't you put it there?"

The pipe stem tapped the plump cushion of an avocado green chaise longue set at right angles to the cherry red number.

"Put your feet up," Mr. Fortgang said.

Dave put his feet up. This brought his bare toes within touching distance of Mr. Fortgang's bare toes.

"Don't worry," he said. "I won't tickle. This is the way the Japs do it. You'd be surprised how it makes the talk come easier."

"When does it start?" Dave said.

"What interests me," Mr. Fortgang said, "from what I hear about you I know you have brains. Then I meet you and I right away know you have something else. Personality. But you put on a Japanese kimono and like it does to everybody it does something to you. Hello, sweetheart."

He tossed the words across his shoulder, toward the swinging door with the bamboo *mezuzah* on the jamb.

"Hello," said a woman in a yellow wig. "I see your guest arrived."

What Dave saw was that identifying this woman would have taxed the ingenuity of the more sophisticated electronic devices employed by the F.B.I. Mrs. Fortgang was dressed to blend with the tiles on the pagoda wall. Her red caftan was decorated with endlessly repeated silhouettes of Fujiyama embroidered in gold.

"Don't he look good in that kimono?" Mr. Fortgang said. "Mr. Dehn, I want you to meet my wife, Charlene."

Dave slid off the chaise longue.

"How do you do?" he said.

He could have said it to the huge green-and-gold paper dragon lantern that swung from the ceiling. Relentlessly Mrs. Fortgang addressed her husband.

"It's time like maybe for a drink, no?"

"Name your poison," Mr. Fortgang said to Dave.

"Scotch if it's going," Dave said.

"Why shouldn't it be going?" Mrs. Fortgang said to her husband. "Your guest thinks maybe we live like pigs?"

Mr. Fortgang's guest thought his hosts lived like a couple of characters Walt Disney was working on, but had not yet sharpened enough to allow them off the drawing board.

"On the rocks, then, please," Dave said to the only thing in the room that seemed to be willing to face him: a silver-foil mobile of Hirohito over the sauna door.

"And you know mine," Mr. Fortgang said to his wife.

"A question," she said. "Tell your guest to sit down."

Dave dropped back into Japanese talking position. Mrs. Fortgang went to the bar. It was almost as wide as the room, not quite as wide as the painting over it. The painting depicted a young man in U.S. naval uniform. Marvin, no doubt, Dave guessed. The boy's shoulder was circled by the braided loafer's loop of a C.O. staff aide.

"Your son?" Dave said to Mr. Fortgang.

"You wouldn't know it from the way up there the stupid artist made the boy look," Mr. Fortgang said.

Mrs. Fortgang came across from the bar. She carried a small red-and-black lacquered tray. Like her caftan, it could have been a tile torn from the walls of the room.

"Tell your guest if he wants another drink he should not be bashful but go up to the bar and make it himself," Mrs. Fortgang said. "I have other things to do. Now I'll leave you and your guest to your talking."

The caftan glided back across the room. Mrs. Fortgang vanished.

"I guess if I was running for mayor," Dave said, "Mrs. Fortgang wouldn't vote for me."

"Don't be too sure," Mr. Fortgang said. "She could end up making speeches to Hadassah and addressing envelopes for you. The fact she didn't talk to you just now, that's only a sign what a fair-minded person Charlene is. With my wife, impartiality it's like a religion with her. When somebody comes here to talk a deal with me she's so impartial you wouldn't even know she's in the room. She'll give him a drink or to eat, but to speak to him? Not so much as a syllable. Not till she gets from me the signal the deal is set."

"Why don't you fill in for her?" Dave said. "I'll finish my drink and then I've got to get back to my staff. I'll sip slowly. You can talk until my glass is empty."

"It won't take that long," Mr. Fortgang said. "I called your office and asked to set up a meeting because I want to make you an offer."

"I'm listening," Dave said.

"The Biaggi property," Mr. Fortgang said. "The whole hundred and eighty acres. I want to buy it. Name your price."

"I can't," Dave said.

"Why not?" Mr. Fortgang said.

"I don't own it," Dave said.

"Your wife is the owner of record," Mr. Fortgang said.

"A lot of wives own title to property their husbands can't sell," Dave said.

"You're not one of those husbands," Mr. Fortgang said.

"How do you figure that?" Dave said.

"Colin Babington told me who rules your roost," Mr. Fortgang said.

"Colin Babington is a friend of yours?" Dave said.

Mr. Fortgang raised two fingers, held close together.

"Me and Colin," Mr. Fortgang said. "We're like that."

"As a result of what?" Dave said.

"Life," Mr. Fortgang said.

"Life is like ketchup," Dave said. "It covers too much for my taste. You better be more specific."

"Okay, for starters, then," Mr. Fortgang said. "Colin Babington and me we grew up together. He made Eagle and I made Life Scout the same year in Beechwood Troop Number One. I caught for him when he pitched for the Ravens in Little League. We went to Miss Flyte's Dancing Academy together. I coached him through fractions in seventh grade. Christmas we did like all the other kids in town. We went to parties, and we swapped presents, and we delivered baskets to poor families that were made up in the church, and we skated on Sequesta Pond, and when the old folks weren't around we played doctor with the same girls."

"How many of them were Jewish?" Dave said.

"None," Mr. Fortgang said. "The Fortgangs were the only Jewish family in town, and I'm an only child. Does that answer your question about me and Colin Babington?"

"For what you call starters," Dave said. "There's at least half a century between playing doctor with *shiksehs* when you're a Boy Scout and getting information about my private life out of Colin Babington. You could hold my interest in your autobiography a lot more firmly if you filled in the time gap."

"Easy," Mr. Fortgang said. "Colin filled his half century with St. Paul's and Harvard Law and the daughter of the president of the First Beechwood Bank and Trust, a girl named Avis Falconer. Me, I filled in my half century with Mamaroneck High and Penn State and the daughter of the president of the Norwalk Real Estate and Insurance Corporation, a girl named Charlene Holzapfel whom you just met. Every second Tuesday Colin and I meet in the upstairs council room at Town Hall, where we have the regular meetings of the Board of Selectmen."

"They let you attend those meetings?" Dave said.

"How can they stop me?" Mr. Fortgang said. "All members of the Board of Selectmen must attend those meetings."

"Oh," Dave said.

It was not a comment he was proud of.

"Fooled you, huh?" Mr. Fortgang said with a grin.

"It won't happen again," Dave said. "Before I got involved with the Biaggi property I did some research on Beechwood. Population a little short of thirteen thousand. Not a synagogue in town. In the phone book not a single Garfinkel, Rosen, Levy, Ginsberg or Hershkowitz. It didn't occur to me to look up Fortgang, but I now learn if I had I'd have found only one. Say there are some *landsleit* in Beechwood who don't own phones, I'd say without making an actual head count before I arrived here there were probably less than fifty Jews in this town. There couldn't be more. Am I close?"

"Close enough," Mr. Fortgang said. "There are a few businessmen on Main Street. Ray Schnur, who owns The Dress Box. Harry Honig, who manages the Daitch Shopwell. Mort Blumenfeld, he's got the Beechwood Art Movie Theatre. Leo Narvik, he's Beechwood Carpets and Rugs. Ludwig Bloch, that big camera place across from the Episcopal church on Main Street. All those boys, people like me, they're in business here in Beechwood, but most of them they live down in Mt. Vernon or up around Norwalk. They find it more comfortable. In terms of people who actually live in Beechwood, until you showed up I'd say twenty Jews is a fair count. That includes wives and kids too, of course."

"Twenty into almost thirteen thousand population," Dave said. "That comes out about roughly one Jew in every six or seven hundred citizens. The Board of Selectmen consists of seven members. One of them is a Jew. You must admit that puts a strain on the word disproportionate. How come in a town like this, with only seven spots available on the Board of Selectmen, one of them goes to a *landsman?*"

"Remember Mecca Temple?" Mr. Fortgang said.

"Remember what?" Dave said.

"You're probably too young to remember the place," Mr. Fortgang said. "It's where they held all those meetings for the causes. The Scottsboro boys. Sacco and Vanzetti. The Gastonia strikers. Henry Ford with his Protocols of Zion. Free Tom Mooney. Those things. And at those meetings they always had that prop nigger."

"That what?" Dave said.

Mr. Fortgang unplugged his pipe to make room for a chuckle.

"In Mecca Temple," he said, "whoever was running the meeting, what they wanted was everybody should understand right away it was a liberal meeting. The way they did that, they always had this black boy. I don't know where he came from or who he was, but every meeting you went to, there he was, down in front, so everybody the minute they came in they could see him and they knew right away they were at a liberal meeting. A sort of prop, like, and that's why I got to

think this black boy, for the liberals he was their prop nigger."

"What's he got to do with your being one of the seven
members of the Board of Selectmen here in Beechwood?"
Dave said.

"These goyim up here like Colin Babington, the Wasps
who run this town," Mr. Fortgang said, "I'm their prop Jew."

Dave was not sure about the expression on his face. It must
have shown more, however, than he wanted to reveal. Mr.
Fortgang did not bother to remove the pipe from his mouth.
This time, with reckless abandon, he chuckled around the
stem.

"Beechwood is no different from most places in this country," he said. "The guys who own the place they don't want
Jews around, but they're ashamed of feeling that way. It's
sort of against all those Norman Rockwell posters about
America the melting pot, give us your tired, your poor, the
land of opportunity, that crap. I mean, they hate Jews but
they have this uncomfortable feeling hating Jews is un-Amer-
ican. It's like knocking General Motors. They don't want
outsiders pointing the finger at Beechwood, or wherever it is
they happen to live, and saying, That town? Christ almighty,
they're nothing but a bunch of lousy Jew-haters. It doesn't
sound nice. So they pick themselves a prop Jew, and they let
the guy live right there along with them, doing all or nearly
all the things they do, so outsiders they won't be able to accuse the town of anti-Semitism."

"Do you have to put on much of a campaign to get yourself
elected prop Jew?" Dave said.

"From the tone of your voice," Mr. Fortgang said, "I can
tell already you don't understand. Nobody gets elected prop
Jew. To be a prop Jew you have to get yourself born to the
job. In this town I happen to have been born to it because
my father got to Beechwood when there weren't enough people in the town to think about things like Jews. As the town
grew and they started thinking, the smart cookies understood
the problems involved in choosing a prop Jew. Well, at that

point there was Don Fortgang, ready-made for the job. I wasn't a pushy wise guy trying to bull my way into an exclusive club. I was a guy the club members had grown used to from the time they were this high. Like the shoeshine kid in the locker room. They didn't have to go out and bring me in. All they had to do was let me stay. But they'd never feel that way about a newcomer. That's why no matter how much dough you sink into the Biaggi property you haven't got a chance. To Beechwood you're superfluous. They don't need you. They've got me. You made a mistake coming here. It's a mistake you had no way of knowing you were making, but the result will be the same."

"What result?" Dave said.

"They will run you out on your ass," Mr. Fortgang said. "You haven't got a prayer."

"I'm not counting on prayer," Dave said.

"Once these boys up here in the tweed sports coats get started on you," Mr. Fortgang said, "that's all you'll have to count on, and it'll do you about as much good as a box of Band-Aids in a leper colony. Take my advice. Name your price."

"You couldn't pay my price," Dave said.

"I can pay any price," Mr. Fortgang said.

"You look like a pretty smart apple," Dave said. "How can a guy with brains and business sense say he can pay a price he hasn't even heard yet?"

"If the price is too big for me to swing alone," Mr. Fortgang said, "I got friends ready to chip in and help."

"Why would Colin Babington and his friends chip in what could be a king-size bundle of cash to help you buy me out of the Biaggi property?" Dave said.

"Because Colin and his friends they're comfortable with the prop Jew they've got. So far as they're concerned Beechwood doesn't need another one."

"What does Don Fortgang get out of living in a town where he serves as prop Jew to his thirteen thousand anti-Semitic neighbors?" Dave said.

"He gets peace," Mr. Fortgang said. "He gets a chance to live in the place where he's respected. A place where Don Fortgang's neighbors invited him to join them in running the community. He wants to keep it that way. He doesn't want to have his boat rocked by pushy smart-aleck heeb wise guys coming in with new money that nobody knows how they got hold of it, and getting his neighbors sore so that all of a sudden they're remembering what they were taught to believe as kids, namely, that all Jews are vulgar pushy loudmouth kikes. Don Fortgang wants to live his life the way he always lived it before you came along."

"Knowing his place," Dave said.

"Knowing his place," Don Fortgang said.

"Which has been assigned to him by his Wasp caretakers," Dave said.

"What they assigned him is not exactly a dump," Mr. Fortgang said. "What they assigned him is a pretty desirable chunk of real estate. I'm the only one who knows how desirable. I don't want my neighbors beginning to take closer looks at me and getting jealous at what I've got. I don't want to attract attention."

The sunlight came slicing in across the two chaise longues. Dave turned. Mrs. Fortgang was pushing her way into the room. Then Dave saw what she was pushing. A little old man. He might have been an obstruction that had rolled into Mrs. Fortgang's path as she was clearing a driveway with a snow shovel. The swinging door eased noiselessly shut.

"I'm too early?"

Mrs. Fortgang hurled the statement at her husband like Zola sounding the opening notes of "J'Accuse."

"No, no, sweetheart," Mr. Fortgang said. "You're on the button." To Dave: "I want you to meet my father."

Dave was unaware that he had already come to his feet. The little old man wore a brown leather windbreaker zipped up to his scrawny throat. It was a copy of the garment Dave's father used to wear on cold mornings in Albany when he went off to work.

"Hello, Pa," Dave said.

The greeting brought joy to Don Fortgang's face.

"See?" he said to the little old man. "I told you."

"Hold the tongue," Mr. Fortgang's father said. "What you tell me it turns out always I knew it before you were born."

Without taking his sharp glance from Dave's face, the old man made in the direction of Mrs. Fortgang an impatient backward sweeping motion.

"Stop slapping with the hands," he snapped across his shoulder. "You're not making a matzoh ball."

The well-stuffed red caftan behind the old man reminded Dave of a helicopter probing for the proper settling position a few feet over a landing pad.

"You look like in my head I made up my mind you would look," the little old man said. "Disappointed I'm not."

"Tell your guest Papa is eighty-seven years old," Mrs. Fortgang said to her husband.

"Tell your wife to hold the tongue," the old man said to Mr. Fortgang. "What does she think Mr. Dehn he thinks I am? A bar mitzvah boy?"

"How did you think I would look?" Dave said.

"Like the man he gave that interview to the reporter for *The Jewish Daily Forward*," the little old man said.

Borrowing his tone from Secretary of War Stanton advising the world over the body of Lincoln that "Now he belongs to the ages," Mr. Fortgang said, "My father reads *The Jewish Daily Forward* every day."

"What else should I read?" the little old man said. "*Mein Kampf?*"

"Tell your guest Papa is a big admirer of Abe Cahan," Mrs. Fortgang instructed her husband.

"Who else is there to admire?" the little old man said. "It was because of Abe Cahan sixty-three years ago when I first came to this country that I came to Beechwood. On Ellis Island they said to wait. I sat down to wait and on the bench I found the first *Jewish Daily Forward* I ever read. In those days on Ellis Island when they said to wait you learned what waiting means. But who cared? I was in America and I had *The Jewish Daily Forward*. I read every word, from back to front. On a page in the middle there was 'A Bintel Brief,' by Abe Cahan."

"Tell your guest how Papa read Abe Cahan's advice," Mrs. Fortgang ordered her husband.

"Instead of talking all the time you should listen a little," the old man said in the direction of his hovering daughter-in-law. "In this way you would learn how little room there is when people talk for most of the things you have to say."

The words changed direction. Again they came tapping up out of the small walnut face directly into Dave's eyes.

"That day on Ellis Island," the little old man said, "I read in 'A Bintel Brief' a letter from a man like me, a young man, just new in America. He said to Abe Cahan in this letter, he said, this is America? Bending twelve hours a day over a sewing machine in a pants shop on Allen Street? What Abe Cahan said in his answer it changed my whole life. Abe Cahan said no, twelve hours a day over a sewing machine in a pants shop on Allen Street, no, that is not America. In this country America, Abe Cahan said, in America there's more than Allen Street. Don't go to the East Side, he said to this young immigrant. Go somewhere out of New York, he said. So from Ellis Island I took my few pennies and I went out of New York. I went as far as my few pennies would take me. They took me to Beechwood. Here I stopped, and now, today—"

The voice of the little old man died away. The small walnut face moved left and right. The sharp, bright eyes raked the red tile walls, the red tile bar, the red-and-green Japanese lantern, the bronze incense burner, the avocado green and the cherry red chaise longues set at right angles, the mobile of Hirohito over the sauna door, the bamboo *mezuzah*. The eyes came to rest finally on Mr. Fortgang's red kimono.

"Tell your guest to sit down," Mrs. Fortgang barked at her husband. "Papa doesn't sit unless the guest sits."

"I should sit in this room?" the little old man said. "What am I? A Dzep?"

"My father has his little jokes," Mr. Fortgang said to Dave.

"My whole life it's a joke," the little old man said. "From Abe Cahan and 'A Bintel Brief' sixty-three years ago to now here in this *mishugahs*."

The little old man leaned forward. The long bony forefinger tapped at the front of Dave's red kimono.

"That's why I liked what you told that reporter in *The Jewish Daily Forward*," Mr. Fortgang's father said. "Here is a young man, I said to myself, a young man he's not afraid to be a Jew. A young man he doesn't go sit and hide in a corner from the goyim, a corner the goyim gave him to sit in, like they give a dog a bone, a corner they'll let him sit in so long as he's a good boy. And by the goyim you know what that means. To them a good boy is a Jew who doesn't open his mouth. A Jew who he stays in the corner. So he has to make his corner look like this—"

Again the little old man's voice stopped. Again the small, tight walnut face swiveled left and right. Again the bright little eyes raked the preposterous room.

"From *The Jewish Daily Forward*," the little old man said, "I went to my son. Did he listen? Not for three months. Three months it took till he read what you told Abe Cahan's reporter."

"In Yiddish?" Dave said.

"In my house nobody talks Arabic," the little old man said. "I told my son I wanted to see the young man that Abe Cahan's reporter wrote about in *The Jewish Daily Forward*."

"Why?" Dave said.

"I'm too old in the feet to go to the store every day," the little old man said. "But in the head I'm not too old to understand what's important. Sixty-three years I live here in Beechwood, but when it comes Yom Kippur and I must go to *shul* I have to pay a shabbas goy to drive me to Mt. Vernon. This for sixty-three years it hurts me. But to my neighbors here in Beechwood I'm a good Jew, so I never say to anybody how it hurts. Then I read in *The Jewish Daily Forward* a new young man he's here in Beechwood and he's building a *shul*.

This takes away the hurt. Now I know what I want to do. I want to help that young man."

Dave gave himself time for a separate glance at each of the three faces in the room. It didn't take long, but it was long enough for him to pull it all together. Dave brought his glance back to the only face that mattered.

"You want to help me build a *shul*," he said to the little old man. "Your son wants to buy me out of town. Tell me which."

"My son and I don't see everything the same way," the little old man said. "That's because I have Jewish eyes and he, his, they're not the eyes I gave him when he was born. In that special corner that the goyim give to the good Jew, my son he hasn't lived there as long as I have. So he still has hope that someday the hurt will go away by itself. Me, though, me I've lived in that corner so long I know the hurt it will never go away by itself. How long I have left I don't know. But how long it is, that time I want to give to you if you'll take it."

"I accept," Dave said.

"From what you told Abe Cahan's reporter in *The Jewish Daily Forward* I understand money you don't need," the little old man said.

"Not yet," Dave said.

"If you ever do," the little old man said, "you'll know where to come. But to help now we have to do things that don't need money. First, all these young Jews that it said in *The Jewish Daily Forward* you're selling to them the land very cheap, they need furniture, no?"

"I've been advancing the money for whatever they need as their houses go up," Dave said.

"To go buy any place they like?" the little old man said.

"What's wrong with that?" Dave said.

"What's wrong is they're paying big fat prices to goyim," the little old man said. "They're throwing away your money. From now on you tell them they must buy only from Fortgang's Furniture Mart here it's on Main Street. We guarantee they'll get first-class quality, and from Fortgang's the discount they get it's money you'll save in your own pocket. You can take it out of your pocket and put it in the *shul*." The little old man turned to his son. "Now you," he said.

"Mr. Dehn," Don Fortgang said. "At last week's meeting of the Board of Selectmen your name came up for discussion."

"Did I pass?" Dave said.

"You got put on probation," Don Fortgang said. "Colin Babington suggested your name should go on the permanent agenda."

"Meaning what?" Dave said.

"It's like if you were, say, a book, and the Pope puts you on that list: All Faithful Harps Forbidden to Read."

"You make it sound like the F.B.I.," Dave said. "Their Most Wanted List."

"The farm where they grow the boys who run the F.B.I.," Mr. Fortgang said, "it's the same place they get the boys who run the Beechwood Board of Selectmen."

"Except you," Dave said.

"From now on I'm your F.B.I.," Don Fortgang said. "The Board makes a move? I tip you off where and when."

"What else do you recommend?" Dave said.

"Sign up at once for an immediate crash course in a *boy-chik* named Rocky Riordan."

18

For about a month the press of work kept Dave from enrolling in this course.

Then, one morning when he turned the Cadillac off Turkey Hill Road into the compound, something caught his eye on the west wall of the unfinished main building. This was not unusual.

Every morning, when he arrived from New York for his day in Beechwood, many things caught Dave's eye. They were always things that had been added the day before. When he and the staff had been so preoccupied with planning for what was going to be done tomorrow that there was no time to pause for the pleasure of examining what had been done yesterday. It was a pause Dave missed.

That was why, even though staff meetings were set for nine sharp, Dave always reached the compound at eight-thirty. The next half hour was a form of self-indulgence to which he did not feel he was entitled but which he could not resist.

Dave would run the Cadillac into the still unpaved parking area, get out, and walk around. Slowly. Circling the main building. Then he would move through the ground floor. Looking. Touching. Tapping. Pushing. Occasionally, as on the morning after the first panel of stained glass had been set in the west wall of the sanctuary, stroking. Dave did it with a sense of wonder. It was like watching himself grow up.

On this morning, the sense of wonder did not have a chance to get off the ground. What had caught Dave's eye on the west wall of the main building did not belong there. He was too far away to make out precisely what it was. Even from twice that distance, however, he would have known it was something that had not come from Mike Palgrave's drawing board.

Dave eased his toe from the brake, pushed down on the gas, raced the car up into the parking space, and jumped out. Running around to the west wall, he could feel his heart start to go. He suddenly knew what he was going to find. He was not wrong.

Staring at his discovery, Dave knew something else. It was not the only thing he would find. He was not wrong about that, either.

Swiftly Dave circled the building twice, making mental notes as he moved. Then, on the run, he carried the horrifying inventory up the steps of the still unfinished front entrance. He moved more slowly through the ground floor. It was more vulnerable than the outside of the building. There would be more to note.

Dave noted it all, with the sick feeling expanding slowly in his gut. Then, more quickly, the feeling seemed to turn a corner and take a new direction, into familiar ground. By the time Dave had crisscrossed the ground floor twice, and opened the door for a hurried look into the gym, the nausea had disappeared. It had been replaced by something Dave Dehn knew how to handle: cold fury.

He marched into the meeting room at nine sharp knowing exactly what to do. So, apparently, did the staff.

"Jesus!" Sid was saying.

Mike was pulling open the curtains on the windows in the east wall. They were the only windows in the room on which curtains had already been hung. Until noon the sun off the Sound came in so powerfully on this side of the building that unless the glare was cut it was impossible to work in the conference room. Mike's hand dropped from the plastic knob at the end of the draw rope. The sun shot into the room.

"Jesus!" Sid said again.

"This is just the tip of the iceberg," Dave said. "They've worked us over inside and out. I've just gone through the place pretty thoroughly."

"We saw a lot of it on the way in, but we haven't had a chance to examine it all. Mike saw all the broken glass first, and—"

"My God," Mike said.

He was staring at the upper frame.

What emerged from Fanny's throat defied phonetics. A low, moaning gasp of anguish and disbelief.

Dave stepped delicately through the mounds of shattered glass under the window sill. The lower frame had been wrenched halfway out of the casement. The glass in the upper frame, however, although badly cracked, was still holding together. On it, in large crude red letters, was painted:

!TUO TƎ⅁ ꙅⰄᴙATꙅAꓭ WƎႱ

"For anybody who has trouble reading backwards," Dave said, "I will—"

"I can read that no matter what direction it goes," Sid said grimly. "It says Jew Bastards Get Out!"

"There are similar messages on other windows on the ground floor," Dave said. "All have been smashed at the bottoms and torn from the casements. Just in case we don't get the point, the message is repeated, in bigger letters, on the outside wall.

"Inside the building, on the ground floor, the message is painted on the walls and floors of the reception room, Fanny's office, my office, the foyer, and the kitchen area. The big electric ranges in the kitchen and all the sinks have been torn out of the walls and smashed with what looks like sledge hammers. The Formica counters have been sliced to ribbons with

what I guess are those curved knives they use for cutting linoleum. The porcelain fixtures in the washrooms have been
given the sledge-hammer treatment, including the tile floors.
The first two panels of the stained-glass windows in the sanctuary are a pile of practically powdered glass scraps on the
floor.

"I haven't had time to check out anything upstairs because
I got here at eight-thirty and I wanted to be on time for this
meeting. I did get a quick look into the gym. I had time to
notice only that the flooring of the overhead track has been
ripped up like the Formica counters in the kitchen area. The
heating machinery for the steam room has been smashed, and
the south end of the pool has a hole in the tiling you can drive
my Cadillac through.

"They must have had a busy night. Not too busy, however,
to remember to leave their signature. On the west wall of the
building—it was the first thing that hit my eye when I drove
into the compound—on the west wall our visitors have burned
into the fieldstone a great big swastika with what I would
guess is an acetylene torch, and they filled in the ruts with the
same red paint."

Dave turned back to his desk.

"Jesus," Sid said again.

He came out of his chair with a jump.

"No, wait," Dave said.

Sid stopped moving.

"For what?" Mike said sharply.

With the words, he too came up out of his chair.

"Until we think this through," Dave said.

"Let the cops think this one through," Mike said.

He was wearing his heavy black-and-red flannel lumberjack
shirt. It made him look more aggressive than he did in his
blue blazer.

"What cops?" Dave said.

"The Beechwood cops," Mike said. "We're taxpayers. We
pay them to protect us."

"You know any of the Beechwood cops?" Dave said.

"Not intimately," Mike said. "Just to say hello. What difference does that make? All we have to do is what any taxpayer in this town would do. Put in a call."

"To whom?" Dave said.

"I don't know," Mike said. "I've never had to call the cops before. But this isn't just minor vandalism. This is major stuff. Why not go direct to the top? Why not call the Chief of Police?"

"Because when I was up at Fortgang's last month," Dave said, "I learned about our Chief of Police."

"Rocky Riordan?" Mike said.

"That's the boy," Dave said.

"What did you learn?" Mike said.

"Mr. Riordan's feelings about Jews," Dave said.

"I've lived in Beechwood for more than six years," Mike said. "Riordan's been our police chief for four of those six. In all that time I've never heard a word about him and Jews and how he feels about them."

"In all that time there haven't been enough Jews in this town to pay attention to," Dave said. "We've just arrived."

"Dave," Sid said.

His only concession, sartorially speaking, to the shift from the planning stage to actual construction was a shift from his neat three-button Broadstreet's charcoal gray to a poplin zipper golf jacket. It made him look like a caddy.

"Yes?" Dave said.

"I don't know what Fortgang told you," Sid said, "but it seems to me—"

"He told me we could expect a message from Mr. Riordan," Dave said. "We've had to wait a few weeks for it, but it's up there on the window. If you can still read backwards."

"Are you saying Riordan is responsible for this?" Sid said.

"I'm sure he had help," Dave said. "So will you when you take a look around."

"Now, listen," Sid said. "I'm talking as a lawyer. You can't go accusing the Chief of Police of staging this thing unless you have hard facts. Have you?"

"How much harder do you want them to be?" Dave said.

"Harder than inference," Sid said. "Drawers of inferences end up with damage-suit judgments for false accusation. When you're dealing with cops only hard facts count. If we don't have them we have to go through channels to get them. We've got to report this to Riordan the way anybody else in this town would report a crime. It's his job to find out who did it."

"He won't," Dave said.

He was holding on to his voice as he said it. He had not counted on what he was suddenly getting: resistance.

"How do you know?" Mike said.

"Because Mr. Fortgang's father told me," Dave said. "And he's lived in Beechwood a little longer than you have. Sixty-three years to be precise."

Mike's face flushed. Seniority was the one thing he had over all the rest of them. He was jealous of the advantage this gave him.

"Then what the hell are we going to do?" Sid said.

"Nothing," Dave said.

"Oh, for Christ's sake," Sid said.

Inside Dave's head the alert signal went off. Sid's resistance was turning to anger. Dave had come into the room expecting what it had never occurred to him he did not have the right to expect: cooperation. He saw now that he would have to do this himself.

"Nothing Rocky Riordan expects," Dave said. "First we'll clean up the mess. The crews are working up at the Post Road end of the compound. Bring them all down here right away. Get that thing off the west wall. I don't want to see that fucking swastika ever again. Then scrub away those God-damn painted signs around the building. Sweep up the glass and the smashed porcelain. Everything. Get rid of all the crap those bastards left behind. Tonight, when our men come home from work, I want you to arrange a meeting. Get them all up here. We'll organize our own police force. We'll set up night watches. Every man takes his turn. This thing won't happen again. We'll see to that. One last thing. What happened last night, don't let it throw you. Everything the bastards destroyed can be replaced and will be."

"You can't replace the way I feel about it."

Mike. Sullen.

"Me too."

Sid. Tart.

"Don't be so sensitive," Dave said.

He considered the four words a triumph of self-control. He fought the impulse to tell them he didn't give a fuck what they felt about it. They clearly did not grasp the point: the only thing that mattered was how Dave Dehn felt about it. And Dave Dehn knew what to do about his feelings.

"I'll replace your feelings too," he said. "With something better. Something to put in the place of your sense of outrage."

"What's that, if I may ask?" Mike said.

Dave wondered if along with the closet Jew what was emerging in his architect was also the closet prick.

"A sense of pride," Dave said. "We'll keep this in the family. In my neighborhood up in Albany, when there was trouble you didn't go running to the police station. You handled it yourself. We'll handle this ourselves."

Fanny's head dipped in a short, crisp nod of approval. Dave's heart moved. There was always one person he could count on. There was always Fanny.

"For Christ's sake, how?" Mike said.

"Not like Eleazar Ben Yair," Dave said. "I'm not putting together this thing up here on Turkey Hill Road to turn it into another Masada."

19

"Okay, men," Dave said that night from the front of the jam-packed room. "I'm glad you all share my feelings about this. Now I'll turn the meeting over to Sid Singer and Mike Palgrave. They will work out with you the schedule of watches, the number of men on each watch, the problem of who carries weapons and who doesn't, and all other details of our night patrols. Fanny and I have to get going. We're half an hour late for another meeting."

There was a round of applause as Fanny followed him out of the room. In the hall, on the way to Dave's office, she pulled his sleeve.

"Something just occurred to me."

"What?" Dave said.

"I think you know who did it," Fanny said.

Dave grinned and with his forefinger gently pressed the tip of her nose.

"You keep your thoughts to yourself," he said.

"Anything more I can do right now?" Fanny said.

"One thing, yes," Dave said. "Go home and tuck your parents into bed. Daisy Sternshus promised to get over to your house at two-thirty, and I'm sure she will. She's an efficient girl. She says she knows about old people; she took care of her grandparents for years."

"What about you?" Fanny said.

"Pick me up as arranged," Dave said. "I've got some things to do."

By the time he finished doing them it was ten minutes to three. Dave snapped off the storm lantern by the light of which he had been working. He crawled out of the root cellar, dragging the attaché case behind him. He stood up and stretched and thanked God there was no moon.

There was enough light for him to see the old Chevrolet crawling toward him down Turkey Hill Road even though it showed no lights. Dave stepped back into the shadow of the root cellar. The Chevy eased off the road and bumped across the grass toward him. When the car came to a stop, Dave emerged from the shadows. He opened the door, shoved the attaché case onto the floor of the car, and slid in beside the driver. He pulled the door toward him, but caught it with his other hand. He worked the door gently into the latch without a bang.

"Okay?" Fanny whispered.

"Okay," Dave whispered back. "Anybody see you?"

"Not unless they were watching from behind curtains," Fanny said. "Not a light showing anywhere."

She eased the motor back to life.

"Now what?" she said.

"Head for the Post Road," Dave said. "Sid and Mike have probably got their first patrols working. This is the wrong night for our boys to demonstrate how efficient they are. We don't want to be caught by anybody—friend or foe, pro or con, Jew or goy. What we're doing is something private. Just you and me. Nobody else."

"You and me and Daisy Sternshus," Fanny said.

"All she knows is you asked her to come over for a while to keep an eye on your parents because you had to go out on a business matter."

"In the middle of the night?" Fanny said.

"Why not?" Dave said. "Something you forgot to do at the office. Everybody knows you're a bloodhound for work. Let's go."

Fanny eased the car back out onto Turkey Hill Road. She drove with her nose a few inches from the steering wheel. Seeing her every day on sunny construction sites and in lighted offices, Dave had forgotten her deformity. He had no longer seen her as a humpbacked woman. She had faded into being just Fanny. Now, in the semidarkness, she was something else. A silhouette hunched over the wheel, her nose almost touching the horn button. It was as though the Chevy were being driven by an educated turtle.

"Daisy ask any questions?" Dave said.

"No," Fanny said. "She got to the house at two-thirty and started making coffee."

"Your parents?" Dave said.

"Corking off," Fanny said.

"You will be too," Dave said. "In less than an hour."

"Then we can't be going very far," Fanny said.

"We could walk it in twenty minutes," Dave said.

"Why don't we?" Fanny said.

"I don't want us to take twenty minutes getting you back home," Dave said.

"Don't worry about me," Fanny said.

It occurred to Dave that he never did. He suddenly wondered guiltily if he should.

"Scared?" he said.

"Cut it out," Fanny said. "But I'd feel better if I knew what I was doing."

"What you're doing—or should be doing, if you stopped asking questions and paid attention to your work—is making a right turn into the Post Road," Dave said.

Fanny eased the car from Turkey Hill Road into the Post Road. It was like coming out into one of those scenes in a bad dream when the whole world seems suddenly to have run away, leaving you alone in a vast, brightly lighted stretch of nowhere. The Post Road was deserted as far as Dave could see in both directions.

"Go up to the Israel Putnam," he said. "Then turn right into Main Street."

Main Street looked as abandoned as the Post Road. Except for the light from the street lamps, it could have been a fragment of an evacuated city.

"Now what?" Fanny said.

"Go up to just past The Dress Box," Dave said. "Then left into the alley next to the courthouse."

The alley separated the courthouse from Eckerd's Drug Store. Both structures were tall enough to form a narrow canyon into which the light from the stars and the street lamps did not penetrate.

"Stop here," Dave said.

"Here" was one of Eckerd's side doors. Through it during the day the drugstore received in bulk the goods that eventually wound up on its shelves. Attached to the base of the door was a low ramp. It provided two triangular corners, about three feet high. In them a man could squat and be totally concealed from Main Street or, at the other side of the ramp, from Hermit Crab Square, which opened up back of Main Street. Dave slid the attaché case up into his lap.

"As soon as I get out," he said, "I want you to start circling the block. Move slowly and try not to bump anything. In this part of town at this time of night the chances of anybody running into you are pretty remote. Just the same, the less noise the better. Keep your lights off and keep going. Don't stop. On one of your circles I'll be back here, ducked down behind this ramp, waiting. If you move at ten miles an hour it will take you almost exactly three minutes to complete each trip around the block. I checked it out this afternoon. That means when I get back here I shouldn't have to wait for you longer than three minutes. Less, if you've already started on one of your circles. The important thing is that under no circumstances should I have to wait more than three minutes. That's the nitty gritty. I must not be kept waiting more than three minutes. That clear?"

"Perfectly," Fanny said.

"Any questions?" Dave said.

"One," Fanny said.

"Shoot," Dave said.

"Where are you going?" Fanny said.

"I'll tell you after I've been there," Dave said.

He opened the door and slipped out of the car. He reached in for the attaché case and patted Fanny's shoulder. Then he closed the door the way he had closed it twenty minutes before outside the root cellar. No slam. Just a click.

"Ready?" he said into the car.

"Ready," Fanny said.

"Go!" Dave said.

For a few moments he watched the Chevy creep up the alley into Hermit Crab Square. Then Dave turned and moved swiftly down the alley toward Main Street. At the eastern edge of Eckerd's big front windows he paused to look left and right. Nothing.

Dave stepped briskly across the sidewalk into the gutter. He trotted across to the two-story frame structure that faced Eckerd's at the north side of Main Street. On the street floor the entire front of the structure was taken up by a store front. Two large plate-glass windows separated by a door. On both windows, in gold-leaf lettering, appeared the same legend:

CATHOLIC WAR VETERANS ASSOC.

391

BEECHWOOD, N.Y.

At the left of the structure was an alley. It looked not unlike the alley across the street except that this one separated the home of Beechwood's Catholic War Veterans from the In At 10 Out At 4 Dry Cleaners.

Bending low, Dave slipped quickly into the alley. The buildings it separated were not as tall as the courthouse and Eckerd's across the street. The light from the stars and the street lamps, therefore, penetrated more deeply into the alley. To avoid it Dave had to move in a crouch that was almost a crawl.

At the back of the building there was a service door. It was flanked by four galvanized-iron garbage cans, two on each side. Dave ducked down into the shelter the cans provided and went to work on the lock.

He did it with a chisel he had borrowed from the toolbox of Mr. Zwilling, the custodian engineer Sid had hired last week to handle minor repairs on the compound.

It was the sort of lock Dave's father had hung on their coal-bin down in the cellar of the tenement on Westerlo Street. Getting the chisel into position was easy. Getting the proper leverage was a little tougher. It took three shoves. The hasp made a thin, screeching noise when it broke from the door.

After he closed it behind him, Dave got out his flashlight. The back room was a kitchen. The front room was obviously a meeting hall. There were shadowy pictures and posters on the wall, but Dave didn't want to risk lifting the flashlight beam to identify them. Besides, he knew what Pope Pius looked like. He kept the small circle of light close to the floor as he moved around both rooms.

It took him four minutes by the radium dial of his wrist watch to find the six crucial areas. He opened the attaché case and pulled out the first of the six devices he had spent the three hours in the root cellar putting together.

Dave staked it down on the floor with thumbtacks in the first position. He cocked the pin, then led the thin strand of wire along the floor to the second position. He checked his watch. A few seconds more than two minutes.

Dave figured he could finish all six in fifteen minutes. He beat his calculation by a full minute and ten seconds.

By the time he was back across the street, crouched with the empty attaché case in the corner behind the Eckerd's ramp, he and Fanny had been separated for exactly nineteen minutes. That meant she had completed six three-minute circuits of the block and was well into her seventh. According to Dave's wrist watch, the Chevy should be pulling up beside him in about ninety seconds.

"D.D.?"

He came up from his knees in the ramp corner.

"You're early," he whispered.

He slipped into the front seat beside her.

"You all right?" Fanny said.

"No problem," Dave said. "Get going."

"Where?" Fanny said.

"Home," Dave said. "By way of the Minuteman and Beach Road. Not too fast down Main Street, but once you make the turn at the Hutchinson marker you can let her rip."

The Chevy was just coming into the south end of Turkey Hill Road when Dave heard it. A low, roaring boom like summer thunder rolling toward them from somewhere down below the forest of maple and oak and trembling aspen that shielded the compound from Main Street at the bottom of the hill.

"What's that?" Fanny said.

"Shhh," Dave said.

He had taped the wires three and three. The clock on the detonator had only two outlets. Listening hard, Dave counted carefully: *"One chim-pan-zee, two chim-pan-zee, three chim-pan-zee."*

Boom!

The second explosion of roaring thunder came in across the maple and oak on time. Dave blew out his breath and leaned back. He reached up and slowly massaged the lump of muscle at the base of his neck.

"Sorry," he said. "I didn't hear you."

"I asked, what have you done?" Fanny said.

"Left an invitation for Mr. Rocky Riordan to come visit," Dave said.

20

What Rocky Riordan liked about Beechwood was the way the people dressed.

It wasn't like Los Angeles, where all the time everybody looked like it was payday and on the way home from work they just couldn't resist stopping in at Bullock's to buy that jazzy new sports shirt they'd been drooling over in the window all week.

That was the thing about Beechwood. Nobody drooled. Certainly not over clothes. The things the people wore here in Beechwood, they looked like they'd been wearing them a long time, and they weren't about to send them back to the stables and start all over again with new stuff just because of the snappy ads in the current issue of *Esquire*. Rocky Riordan wondered how Mr. Dehn dressed.

Since the bulldozers had started tearing up the Biaggi farm Rocky had driven through Turkey Hill Road a number of times, but he had never run into Mr. Dehn. On this morning it struck Rocky as not inappropriate that he was coming to Turkey Hill Road not to run into Mr. Dehn but to run him over. It was the only way to deal with Jews. Hit them before they could reach their shyster lawyers and take the Fifth.

"I called Mr. Dehn this morning," Rocky said to the weird-looking secretary in the office on the ground floor. "He asked me to come over at eleven."

"Of course, Mr. Riordan," the ugly broad said. "Mr. Dehn was called upstairs for a couple of minutes. He asked me to apologize for the delay. He won't be long."

"No sweat," Rocky said. "I'll just have me a look around."

There was a lot to see, but none of it was in a finished state. The office of Mr. Dehn's secretary was equipped with bookshelves and filing cabinets, but the door to the hall had not yet been hung, and the lower half of the window was missing. Half the hall floor was paved with sheets of tan marble, but the other half was still a brownish mess in which busy workmen knelt among buckets and trowels and stacks of marble tiles. Across the hall from the secretary's office, four men were easing a plate-glass window into place in front of what was probably going to be an information booth. The window had a beveled square hole at mouth-high distance from the floor.

"Mr. Riordan?"

Rocky turned. He felt a twinge of irritation. The Jew boy coming toward him was wearing a blue blazer.

"Mr. Dehn."

They shook hands. Rocky's irritation eased. The blazer was not a Beechwood blazer. There was no sign of imminent fraying at the cuffs. Mr. Dehn's blazer was brand new.

"Sorry to be late," he said.

"No problem," Rocky said.

"It's a mess, as you can see," Mr. Dehn said. "But we're moving along. The trouble is, the moment you stop to catch your breath somebody grabs you and hangs a new one on you that has to be solved or moved or admired but this very minute. Would you like to see what made me late just now?"

Knowing what he knew, Rocky now knew something else. This Mr. Dehn was a smart-ass. The bombing of the Catholic War Veterans' headquarters would not be allowed to enter the conversation until Mr. Dehn was ready to give it a visa. Or so he thought. Rocky would give this ass-hole enough rope so there would be no slippage when he decided to pull the knot tight.

"I'll look at whatever you show me," Rocky said.

"This way," Mr. Dehn said.

He led Rocky back up the hall to the round foyer through which Rocky had come into the building from the still unpaved parking area. He noticed something he had not seen on his way in: a jagged hole in the middle of the white marble floor.

"What's that?" Rocky said.

"Oh, just a prank somebody played on us a couple of nights ago," Mr. Dehn said.

"Looks like that prank was played with a sledge hammer," Rocky Riordan said.

"That's what it looked like to me too," Mr. Dehn said. "I'm glad to have my opinion confirmed by an expert. Let's see if the elevator is working. It took me up and brought me down, but the Otis man said it was only a test run. Something about cable adjustments in the basement."

He punched a button on the half-finished marble wall. A pair of bronze doors slid open.

"We're in luck," Mr. Dehn said.

He waited for Rocky to precede him. The panel on the elevator wall was a bristling tangle of wires. They did not seem to intimidate Mr. Dehn. He touched the end of a red wire to the end of a black. The elevator came to life.

"You're pretty handy around electrical gadgets," Rocky Riordan said.

"When I was in the Army I did a hitch with the Signal Corps," Mr. Dehn said.

"Any bomb-disposal work?" Rocky said.

"Enough to know my way around h.e.," Mr. Dehn said. "I was downstairs in my office waiting for you when our architect came along. I think you know him. Mike Palgrave?"

"I sure do," Rocky said. "Up on Cavalry Road."

"Among the million things he's doing on the place," Mr. Dehn said, "he's building an apartment for me on the third floor."

"Then it's true you haven't moved in yet?" Rocky said.

"How do you know that?" Mr. Dehn said.

Rocky shrugged.

"Being top cop in a place like Beechwood you get to know a lot of things," he said.

"Must make for quite a load on your mind," Mr. Dehn said.

"That kind of weight never bothered me," Rocky said.

"Anyway," Mr. Dehn said, "a few minutes ago Mike came running into my office and said they'd just put something into my apartment and I had to come up and see it."

The elevator stopped. Mr. Dehn guided Riordan out into a hall with a complicated pale blue lattice ceiling. Three of the center panels had been torn away into hanging shreds.

"More pranksters?" Riordan said.

"The same, I would imagine," Mr. Dehn said. "They seem to have grown more efficient as they made their way through the building. Watch your step. Plasterers leave things in funny places. Just over here."

He opened a door into a small foyer. He led Riordan across the foyer to an unpainted room with a wide picture window that looked out on the Sound. Most of the glass had been smashed out of the frame.

"Industrious bastards, whoever they were," Mr. Dehn said. "Over there, if you will."

He nodded toward the unpainted wall to the left of the smashed window. Over a square hole that would someday be a fireplace hung a large oil painting in a gold frame.

"This is what Mike wanted me to see," Mr. Dehn said. "It just came up on the truck from New York."

For a few moments Rocky Riordan studied the painting.

"Who's the boy?" he said.

"My father," Dave Dehn said.

"Good-looking son of a gun," Riordan said.

Dave wondered about Don Fortgang's assessment of Mr. Riordan's character.

"A Nazi, American style," Don had said. "But subtle. The rule, *boychik,* is eyes open wide at all times with this *utzpay.*"

"It started as a snapshot," Mr. Dehn said. "He was nineteen when it was taken. A conscript in the Russian army. He died while I was in Germany. When I came home I went through his things and I found the snapshot. It was the only picture I had of him, so I took it to this friend of mine, he's a painter, and I asked him to copy it. He'd known my father, and he knew how my father hated war and everything connected with it, including uniforms, so he had this idea. The painter. In the snapshot my father was wearing one of those sloppy khaki army blouses, and one of those little stiff hats without a brim, sort of like a fez. In those days army privates all over Europe wore them. What my friend did, he painted out the fez and put in the skullcap. Then he covered up the khaki blouse with my father's prayer shawl and he put the phylacteries on his arm."

"You mean what's up there in the painting," Riordan said, "that's your old man's own *yarmulke* and *tallis* and *tfillim?*"

Inside Dave's head the warning bell went off.

"He used them every day of his adult life," Dave said. "Sort of surprising that you should know about things like that, isn't it?"

"Like I said," Riordan said. "Cops know everything. This painter, you happen to know if he put in that *tallis* as is, or did he touch it up?"

"As is," Dave said. "I wouldn't let him fool with it. Why do you ask?"

"If he didn't touch it up," Riordan said, "it means your father brought that *tallis* with him from Europe."

"How can you tell?" Dave said.

"By the color," Riordan said. "The color shows it's old. I can also tell by the knots in the tassels. An American-made *tallis,* over here they can't afford to put in the time any more making knots like that. Labor. It would price the *tallis* way out of range of the average man's pocketbook."

"I never knew that," Dave said.

He made no move to keep the irritation out of his voice. It was too early in the morning to be taught things about Jews by a Nazi in full uniform.

"Neither did I," Riordan said. "I learned it from a rabbi out in L.A. There was a fire in this synagogue, see, and we got most of the stuff out, when he said he had to go in for his *tallis*. I said ixnay. By now the place was a furnace. We were lucky nobody was killed. I didn't want to lose any people on my beat. You can always buy another one of those things, I said. I didn't know the word yet. But the old man shook me off, and he ran into the synagogue, so I had to go in after him. We got out just in time, him and me and his *tallis,* and I was pretty sore about it. I mean, we both could have been fried like a couple of potato chips. So he explained to me why he had to go in after it. The knots, I mean."

Dave thought for a few moments about this bull of a man in the Americanized uniform of an S.S. officer. Dave knew why the police chief had called and asked for an appointment. What did the bombing of the Catholic War Veterans' headquarters have to do with the *tallis* of a rabbi in Los Angeles?

"He had to go in after his *tallis,*" Dave said. "You didn't have to go in after him."

Under the skin-tight olive tunic the huge shoulders moved in a shrug.

"You're a cop, you got a job," Riordan said. "You got a job, you do it. What else you got to show me?"

Dave showed him the sanctuary on the ground floor. The wood carvers were working on the ceiling.

"That's good stuff," Riordan said. "Out in L.A. there's a synagogue on La Brea. Sephardic Jews. You know, from Spain. They had the only hand-carved ceiling I ever saw."

"This is the only hand-carved synagogue I ever saw," Dave said. "Stained-glass windows telling the story of the Old Testament will be going up over there. Until yesterday morning we had the first three panels in place."

He could feel rather than see the sharp turn of the policeman's head.

"What happened to them?" Riordan said.

"Your friends the pranksters," Dave said.

"My friends?" Riordan said. "What does that remark mean?"

"If they're not your friends, you wouldn't be wasting the taxpayers' time paying me visits," Dave said. "You'd be out there trying to round up and arrest the bastards for vandalism. Let's take a look at the gym."

He moved toward it without waiting for Riordan's reaction to the remark. There was time enough for that.

The gym flooring was down. Two men were guiding big circular waxers toward each other across what was obviously going to be marked out as a basketball court.

"That's something," Riordan said, pointing up at the banked track. "How big?"

Apparently he was not yet ready to indicate a reaction to Dave's remark.

"An eighth of a mile," Dave said. "Mike Palgrave is trying something new. He read a piece by a French architect who says it's much healthier to run barefoot instead of in sneakers, and he worked out this cork flooring for indoor tracks. Mike had it imported. The other night the pranksters exported it, you might say. But we've reordered. I hope the kids like it. The stuff isn't cheap. How about the basement pool? It's Olympic length."

"I've never seen one," Riordan said. "Let's take a gander."

They took a gander at the basement pool, the main feature of which was, of course, the huge hole the sledge hammers had beaten out of the south wall.

"Jesus," Rocky Riordan said.

"No," Dave said dryly. "Pranksters. I could show you more. The steam rooms, the various arts and crafts rooms in the basement and on the ground floor, but I'd rather show them to you in a few weeks, after we've repaired the signature the pranksters left behind."

"Yeah," Riordan said.

It seemed a not inappropriate comment for a man who was obviously marking time. Dave wondered for what.

"Out back, facing the Sound," Dave said, "we've got twelve

tennis courts staked out, and another Olympic-length pool which will be heated. It's still intact. The pranksters apparently ran out of time. You want to see?"

"Not really," Riordan said. "One thing that's no novelty to a guy from L.A. who now works in Westchester, and that's heated swimming pools. Let's take a look at what's happening where the onions used to grow."

"My car or yours?" Dave said.

"The people you're selling quarter acres to," Riordan said. "They scared of cops?"

"If they were," Dave said, "I wouldn't want them on the place."

"Then let's go in my car," Riordan said. "It's a brand-new Buick. The Board of Selectmen just shelled out four grand for it. Let your tenants see they've got a police department with equipment that inspires confidence."

"They're not my tenants," Dave said as he climbed in beside Riordan on the front seat. "Every family on the compound owns its own land and its own house."

"Except for the big fat mortgages you own on every one," Riordan said.

"They own more of their homes than they would if the mortgages were held by the First Beechwood Bank and Trust," Dave said.

"You ought to hear Sykes Falconer, the president of the First Beechwood Bank and Trust," Riordan said. "You ought to hear what he has to say about the interest rates you're handing out."

"Since the pranksters smashed all the glass out of our windows," Dave said, "I can now hear Mr. Falconer morning, noon, and night."

"He wants to know how come you can afford to lend these people the money for their homes at half the interest he has to charge to keep his bank going," Riordan said.

"Did Falconer send you over to ask me?" Dave said.

It was a pleasantly warm day for March, but Riordan was

wearing black leather gauntlets. Dave could see the gloved fingers tighten on the steering wheel.

"What does that remark mean?" Riordan said.

"For a literate man you seem to need an awful lot of translations of Basic English," Dave said. "What that remark means is I expect the police department in the place where I pay my taxes to maintain law and order. I don't expect it to carry messages from disgruntled bankers."

"I'm not carrying messages for anybody," Riordan said. "I just can't help wondering the same thing Falconer and the other citizens of this town are wondering."

"What's that?" Dave said.

"Where do you get your money from?" Riordan said.

"The same place Falconer and his fellow citizens get theirs," Dave said. "Any time they want to sit down at a table with me I'll be glad to match my method for getting mine with their methods for getting theirs. Think you can carry that message back accurately to Sykes Falconer?"

"I won't omit a syllable," Riordan said.

"Good," Dave said. "Now would you mind pulling the car up around to the north side of the building?"

"Anything you say," Riordan said.

He pulled the Buick around to the north side of the building.

"Here?" Riordan said.

"This is fine," Dave said.

Riordan stopped the car.

"Up there," Dave said. He pointed to the scars in the fieldstone. "We got the red paint out with benzine, but the torch marks won't come out. The fieldstone will have to be replaced. We've ordered seven new slabs from the quarry."

Riordan extended the shade from the sun his hat provided by putting his hand up to the rim of the visor.

"What the hell is it?" he said.

"The signature the pranksters left behind the other night," Dave said. "Recognize the handwriting?"

"How's that?" Riordan said sharply.

"The handwriting," Dave said.

"What about it?" Riordan said.

"They borrowed it from the son of a bitch whose brains we finished beating out three years ago in Germany. Does that refresh your memory?"

"Oh," Riordan said. "It's a swastika."

"I see you weren't kidding when you said a cop gets to know everything," Dave said.

"What's it doing up there?" Riordan said.

"I thought maybe that's what you came over here this morning to tell me," Dave said.

Riordan gave him a long, hard look.

"Let's get going with the guided tour," he said finally.

"If that's what you came for," Dave said.

"That's what I came for," Riordan said.

"In that case," Dave said, "turn left and head up toward the Post Road."

They moved up Turkey Hill Road slowly. Riordan drove in silence. Dave waited. The ball was in the cop's court.

"Hi, Mrs. Weisberg!" Dave called out the car window. "Your nursery furniture come yet?"

Riordan slowed the car. The pretty girl in the bulging blue house dress moved away from the dish towels and pillowcases on her clothesline and came around the raw lawn toward the police car.

"Look!"

She pointed up Turkey Hill Road, behind Dave and Riordan. They turned. A big brown van was easing toward them. The lettering on the sign over the windshield read "Fortgang's Furniture Mart."

"Just in time," Dave called.

The pretty girl laughed and tapped her swollen belly.

"I told my husband I refuse to pop until the Fortgang's truck shows with the bassinet."

"If the pains are starting," Riordan said, "the Beechwood

Police Department would consider it an honor to drive you to the hospital."

The pretty girl laughed.

"Mrs. Weisberg," Dave said. "This is our Chief of Police, Mr. Riordan."

"Gee, this is a thrill," she said. "Wait till Steve comes home from work and I tell him. Thanks, Mr. Riordan. I'm not cutting it that fine, but the Weisberg family appreciates your offer."

"Any time," Riordan said. "I hope it's a boy."

"I won't tell that to my husband," Mrs. Weisberg giggled. "He wants a girl."

"We better make way for Fortgang's," Dave said. "Good luck, Mrs. Weisberg."

"Thanks, Mr. Dehn," the pretty girl said. She blushed. "I mean," she said, "you know, for everything."

"Forget it," Dave said. "My best to Steve."

"Take care," Riordan called, moving the police car up Turkey Hill Road, clearing the way for the Fortgang van. "She's cute."

"They're all cute," Dave said. "Because they're all young."

"I've known some young ones," Riordan said, "they had faces you could rent them out to haunt houses."

"Not when they're pregnant," Dave said.

"All the chicks up here pregnant?" Riordan said.

"Pretty damn near," Dave said.

"Must keep you busy," Riordan said.

"I'm not a cop," Dave said. "I never dump on my own doorstep."

Again the gloved fingers tightened on the steering wheel.

"You're a touchy son of a bitch," Riordan said.

"About some things," Dave said.

"All I was doing," Riordan said, "I was trying to make a joke."

"Keep trying," Dave said. "When you hit a funny one I'll laugh."

Riordan eased the car to a stop in front of a black-top driveway that wound up in an arc to a gray clapboard ranch house with fire-engine red shutters. A skinny kid in blue jeans and a floppy white T-shirt was pushing a lawn seeder across the freshly dug earth.

"Anybody you know?" Dave said.

Before Riordan could reply, a pretty girl in a red-checked apron appeared in the doorway. Daisy Sternshus was carrying an aluminum percolator.

"Hey, Mr. Dehn!" she called. "You get arrested or something?"

Dave wished she hadn't said that. Not on this morning. He hoped Mrs. Sternshus had enough brains to remember that Fanny had pledged her to keep her mouth shut about last night.

"Not yet," Dave called back as casually as he could. "Come meet our Chief of Police."

Aside from the fact that she was wearing red checks instead of blue, Daisy Sternshus was a dead ringer for Mrs. Weisberg. In silhouette, anyway. She was just about as far along in her pregnancy.

"Mr. Riordan, our Chief of Police," Dave said when she reached the car. "Mr. Riordan, Mrs. Sternshus."

"My pleasure, ma'am," Riordan said.

"I see you all the time on Main Street when I go over to Daitch's," Mrs. Sternshus said. "I mean, driving by, but you look even more handsome close up."

"Why, thank you, ma'am," Riordan said.

"I like a place that appreciates its handsome Chief of Police enough to get him a car that matches his looks. That's a honey of a gas buggy, Mr. Riordan."

"Thanks to you," Riordan said. "And all the other taxpayers of this town."

Mrs. Sternshus lifted the percolator to the height of her swollen belly.

"I just perked this fresh," she said. "Could I interest you gentlemen in a cup?"

"Not for me, thanks," Dave said. "Chief?"

"Just had one, thanks," Riordan said. "Satisfied with your gardener?"

Mrs. Sternshus turned to look at the skinny kid pushing the lawn seeder.

"Boy, am I," she said. "The nurseries up here in Westchester, what they charge to put in a lawn I could write a letter to Truman."

Riordan nodded toward the boy in blue jeans and the floppy T-shirt.

"How'd you get him?" the police chief said.

"He came to the door and asked if we could use any help," Mrs. Sternshus said. "Luckily, it was Sunday and Ernie was home, so they had a talk and it turns out Roger knows a lot about gardening. Ernie got the stuff for him at The Green Thumb up on Main Street, and he's done it all himself, the whole thing. Bushes out back, something I can't pronounce over here for the borders, and he raked the ground himself for the lawn and now he's seeding it. Ernie and I are crazy about him. Hey, Roger!"

The boy stopped pushing the seeder and looked up.

"Yes, ma'am?"

"Come meet the Chief of Police!"

The boy dropped the handle of the seeder and wiped his hands on his jeans as he came across slowly.

"We have two celebrities to offer you this morning," Mrs. Sternshus said. "This is Mr. Riordan, our Chief of Police, and this is Mr. Dehn, our Jewish Santa Claus."

The boy smiled shyly and murmured greetings as he shook hands with both men. The way he did it made Dave's heart move. He was suddenly reminded of himself, the day before his bar mitzvah, thanking Rabbi Goldfarb after the last rehearsal for the time and trouble the rabbi had taken with Dave's training for the big event. The words had been prepared for Dave the night before by his father, but he remembered now that as he spoke them the feeling had been his own. It was a funny feeling to be remembering unexpectedly twenty years later. On the morning after he had bombed the headquarters of the bastards who had vandalized the sanctuary he was building to the memory of his father and Rabbi Goldfarb.

"I better go," the boy said. "The weather forecast said rain, and I have to get the seed in before it starts coming down." He bobbed his head, smiled shyly again, and said as he backed away from the car, "It was nice meeting you gentlemen."

Mrs. Sternshus kept her eyes on the boy until he dipped down to retrieve the handle of the seeder.

"Funny kid," she said.

"In what way?" Riordan said.

"He's like, I don't know, sort of like Bambi, if you remember the movie," Mrs. Sternshus said. "Like a fawn, I mean. Scared to death of people. Very sweet boy, though. Ernie and I are crazy about him. Sure you won't have some coffee?"

"Thanks, no," Riordan said.

"Give Ernie my best," Dave said.

Mrs. Sternshus waved as the car pulled away.

"You know the Metuchen place?" Riordan said.

"Down there on Beach Road?" Dave said. "Just south of us?"

"Yes," Riordan said.

"What about it?" Dave said.

"Mrs. Metuchen comes out from New York only on week ends. The rest of the week the place is locked up. It's on our surveillance list. We check it out regularly, the way we do for anybody in town who is going away and wants us to keep an eye on their house. You ever meet Mrs. Metuchen?"

"No," Dave said.

"Rich as hell," Riordan said. "A widow. Runs a big public relations outfit in New York. I've never had much to do with her. Just seen her around on Main Street week ends. That's her son."

Startled, Dave said, "Who?"

"That boy Roger we just talked to back there," Riordan

said. "The one putting in the lawn for your Mrs. Sternshus."

"If his mother is rich as hell," Dave said, "what's he doing knocking on doors asking for gardening jobs?"

"I don't know," Riordan said. "Since he's working here on your compound, though, I feel you ought to know the background. Just in case."

"Just in case what?" Dave said.

"These situations," Riordan said. "I've seen a lot of them out in L.A. They go off in screwy directions sometimes."

"What cases?" Dave said.

"This Metuchen kid was badly shot up on Guadalcanal," Riordan said. "A lot of pain for a long time. The medics put him through one of those complicated series of operations that are supposed to patch you up. Judging by the look of the kid, they seem to have succeeded. I mean, he looks like they got all the pieces back in place. By the time they finished, though, the kid was hooked."

"On what?" Dave said.

"Morphine," Riordan said. "They put him on the stuff to kill the pain, the way they do with a lot of these cases. When he was discharged a few months ago, the Navy doctors said the kid was clean. But judging by my experience in L.A. with a lot of these kids just out of V.A. hospitals, there's always the chance that the doctors are full of tutti-frutti. Not that I blame them. They put the kids on the stuff for a perfectly valid reason, to keep them from going nuts with pain, and when the pain is gone they're sort of embarrassed, the medics, by what they've done to the kids, so they say they're cured and discharge them to get them out of the way."

"It can't be they're all not cured," Dave said.

"Lots of them come through fine, but lots of them don't," Riordan said. "This Metuchen kid may be one of the lucky ones and he's okay, but there's one thing bugs me."

"What's that?" Dave said.

"His mother, like I said, she's in New York all week," Riordan said. "Comes out only week ends. The house is supposed to be locked up. She asks us to put it on the surveillance list and check it out regularly. We do that, and so far as we can tell the place is locked up like a bank vault. No sign of life. Nothing."

"Then what's your problem?" Dave said.

"If the house is locked up five days a week," Riordan said, "where's the kid sleeping those five nights?"

"I thought a cop knows everything," Dave said.

"Sooner or later," Riordan said. "Because what he doesn't know he makes it a point to find out. That's why I'm telling you this. The kid's working for one of your pregnant ladies here. You could do a little detective work without the kid or anybody else catching on. Whatever you learn you could pass on to your Chief of Police if you were so inclined."

"Why should I be?" Dave said.

"Good-neighbor policy," Riordan said. "It keeps away pranksters."

"Is that a guarantee?" Dave said.

"It could turn into one," Riordan said.

"I'll think it over," Dave said.

"Good," Riordan said. "And that crack I made about all the pregnant ladies you're surrounded by?"

"What about it?" Dave said.

"That's all it was," Riordan said. "A crack. A guy can't help thinking. Sometimes he says what he's thinking when he shouldn't. You're a bright boy. You ought to recognize an apology when it's laid in your lap."

It was not what Dave's lap had been prepared to receive from this visit.

"You can take it out of my lap," he said. "I just had the pants dry-cleaned."

"Good," Riordan said. "Because there's something real nice up ahead."

He stopped the car at the top of Saul Street. He nodded down beyond Sid Singer's house and Fanny Mintz's house. Through the gap in the oaks at the bottom of the street the sun came bouncing in like quicksilver off the waters of Long Island Sound.

"The view up here is great from any angle," Dave said.

"You could do me a favor," Riordan said.

"If I can," Dave said.

"My kid brother," Riordan said. "Out in L.A. He just got married and he's got a good job offer here in New York. The only trouble is his wife doesn't want to live in the city. When they were out here last week they looked us over and they fell for Beechwood. They'd like to come live here if I can find a nice place in their price range. The mortgage interest you charge, it's in anybody's price range. If that lot out there is available how about selling it to my kid brother?"

Like all sons of bitches, Riordan had finally made it: he had got to the point.

"I could say it's not available," Dave said.

Riordan gave him that quick, sidelong glance. The seasoned player giving the carefully studied green a final wrap-up look before he swung to sink his putt.

"Don't bother with alternatives," he said. "Just give me the real reason."

Dave wondered if at this stage the bastard had expected to get a fake one.

"I can't sell it to him," he said.

"Why not? The kid's a G.I. like all the other guys you've been selling to."

"His name is Riordan," Dave said. "The other guys are named Weisberg and Sternshus."

"Then it's true what I've been told," the police chief said.

"I don't know what you've been told," Dave said.

"You're running a restricted operation," Riordan said.

"Aren't you?" Dave said.

"There's no sign outside police headquarters that says no Jews need apply," Riordan said.

"There's no sign at the foot of Turkey Hill Road that says all goyim stay out," Dave said.

"But that's what it means," Riordan said. "Visible or invisible."

"Except for one word," Dave said.

"What word is that?" Riordan said.

"All," Dave said.

"Who are the exceptions?" Riordan said.

"Brothers of police chiefs are a possibility," Dave said.

"What would the brother of a police chief have to do to get a crack at buying that lot?" Riordan said.

"He'd have to get his brother the police chief to tell the owner of the lot why he called me this morning and asked for this appointment," Dave said.

Riordan squinted against the sun hurling itself in from the Sound across the lot at the foot of Saul Street.

"The Catholic War Veterans," the police chief said finally. "Somebody blew the ass out of their headquarters last night."

"Pranksters?" Dave said.

"No," Riordan said. "This was a professional job."

"How do you know?" Dave said.

"A cop knows everything," Riordan said. "Including how to spot the work of a man who knows his way around h.e."

"Then why don't you nail the pranksters who night before last gave us a going over with sledge hammers and acetylene torches?" Dave said.

"I thought you knew who they are," Riordan said.

"Check me out," Dave said.

"The Catholic War Veterans," Riordan said.

"When did they tell you?" Dave said. "Before or after?"

"They're not dumb enough to tell that to anybody," Riordan said. "Any more than you're going to be dumb enough to tell me who blew them up last night."

"Which leaves us where?" Dave said.

"Me, in the position to carry a message," Riordan said. "You, in the position to dictate it."

"Okay," Dave said. "Here's a message for those creeps."

"Shoot," Riordan said.

"They've had their fun," Dave said.

"Anything else?" Riordan said.

"Yes," Dave said.

"What?" Riordan said.

"If they try again," Dave said, "any rebuilding they do on their headquarters at 391 Main Street will be a waste of time."

"You could be wasting your time too," Riordan said.

"How?" Dave said.

"Ordering new slabs of fieldstone from the quarry," Riordan said.

"I'm rich," Dave said. "I'll take my chance on that."

"You don't have to take a chance," Riordan said. "What you can do is take out an insurance policy."

"How?" Dave said.

"By selling that lot to the brother of your Chief of Police," Rocky Riordan said.

21

Two things Dave was going to miss. The early-morning drives up from New York. And those first glimpses of the compound when he turned the Cadillac into Turkey Hill Road in time for the nine-o'clock staff meeting. For a year both had been pure pleasure.

The drives were what Dave had in secret named his "How Much Yesterday?" chart. Running through in his mind what had been accomplished the day before.

And those first glimpses of the compound were what Dave would have been embarrassed to tell Sid and Fanny and Mike he called his "Up to Now" scoreboard. How far they had come since that January day in 1947 when the first Kerner-Hirsh bulldozer had taken its first bite out of the old Biaggi house.

They had come so far that Dave could no longer absorb all of it from behind the steering wheel of the Cadillac. Living in the apartment on the third floor made up for this. From the bathroom window Dave had a view of the compound that could have been improved only from a plane.

Mike Palgrave, who was not yet Morris Cohen, had built the apartment where Dave had wanted it. Directly over the sanctuary, in the southwest corner of the building. So that while he shaved Dave could see it all.

The Sound on the left. The tennis courts and swimming

pool at his feet. The neat little streets filling up steadily with ranch houses that stretched up and out, all the way to the Post Road. And best of all, the wooded area on the right. The massed trees that shielded the compound from Main Street and the rest of Beechwood. The small forest of maple and oak and elm through which, when they were ready, the bastards would have to come.

Dave didn't doubt that they would. Rocky Riordan had made that clear. When they came they would not necessarily be wearing green uniforms with two small strokes of jagged lightning embroidered in silver on the collars. But when they came it wouldn't matter what they wore. The effect would be the same. And they would come. The sledge hammers of the Catholic War Veterans had been the first probing skirmish. They were not going to sit by indefinitely and watch a bunch of Jew boys take over their ball park. Not sons of bitches like Colin Babington and his selectmen and their buddies in the City Club and their gauleiter Rocky Riordan.

Dave was not fooled by the fact that there had been no further trouble since his meeting with Riordan. Babington and his gang, they were all still in a state of shock. Dave had sensed that as he sat beside Rocky Riordan in the brand-new Buick. They were just about due to come out of it. When they did, Dave Dehn would be ready for them.

The phone rang. He went to the small table near the shower and picked it up.

"Yes, Fanny?"

"How did you like your first night in your new home?"

"I slept like a baby," Dave said.

"Is there anything you need?" Fanny said.

"I'll want the cash figures on rebuilding the gym," Dave said. "Call Sid and ask him to bring them to the meeting."

"I already did," Fanny said. "I didn't mean that. I meant is there anything you need upstairs? I've been housekeeping for two old people for so long I have no idea what a young bachelor needs. I got as far as soap and towels and sheets and tooth paste, and then I ran out of steam."

"You did fine," Dave said. "I came up with a suitcase from The Dakota last night, so I'm okay for the time being. After the meeting we can make a list. And, Fanny."

"Yes, D.D.?"

"That was pretty sneaky," Dave said.

"What was pretty sneaky?"

Dave grinned at her inept attempt to reproduce the innocence of a wide-eyed little girl.

"That *Britannica*," Dave said. "It was the first thing I noticed when I came in last night and turned on the lights. You shouldn't have done it."

"If you go around doing only the things you should have done," Fanny rapped out, "that's all you will ever do. You'll go around. In circles."

Jimmy Cagney, scoutmaster, gruffly fending off the thank-yous of the troop for a Good Deed.

"A person moves into a new place," Fanny said, "he's entitled to a housewarming present. By me a house is not a house without an encyclopedia. Ma and Pa said to tell you to use it in good health."

"Tell them I promise not to look up anything when I have a cold or a toothache," Dave said. "Anything else?"

"Staff meeting in twenty minutes," Fanny said. "That okay?"

"Perfect," Dave said.

It was better than that. He could tell as soon as he walked into the office downstairs. For months after the ground floor was usable, and while Mike had the contractors working on the apartment upstairs, Dave had come into these staff meetings at nine in the morning directly from the Cadillac he had just parked outside. This was the first time he had come into a staff meeting from the apartment upstairs.

He walked to the electric coffee urn on the table behind his desk and picked up a cup. "Fanny?"

"Thanks, no," she said. "I've had my two cups."

"Anybody else?"

"And get Marian reporting me to Artie Steinberg?" Sid said.

"Sally won't let me, either," Mike said. "She says, you slip sugar into it while I'm not looking. That's sixteen calories per teaspoon."

"You get any skinnier," Dave said, "I'll have Artie put you on an all-starch diet."

He drew a cup for himself.

"Let's get the cost figures on the gym out of the way first," he said. "It's been on my mind. I may have been a little ambitious about replacing that French corking on the indoor track."

Mike read off the figures while Dave brought the cup of coffee to his desk and sat down. Mike finished the figures. He thought repairing the indoor track would work out, dollars-and-cents-wise, as estimated. Sid wondered if it wouldn't be a good idea to check with the Beechwood Fire Department. Occupancy ordinances could be tricky.

"I got all that squared away last year," Mike said. "When I designed the new gym for St. John's Episcopal."

Sid read out the figure on mortgage applications for the week. Mike whistled.

"Boy," he said, "you'd think we're giving away those quarter acres for free."

"For all practical purposes we are," Dave said. "Even so, that's one great big Yankee Stadium–size figure for a single week. Your legal mind see any special reason?"

"Of course," Sid said. "The follow-up story on your interview in *The Jewish Daily Forward*. Half our applicants report they heard about us from their immigrant fathers who read nothing but Yiddish and only the kind written by Abe Cahan and his staff."

Quickly and smoothly they worked their way through the agenda. There were no disagreements. Everybody knew what everybody else wanted. There were only additions and subtractions. Fanny set them all down in her notebook. Once she made a note she did not go back. She kept things moving forward.

"That's it," she said. "Except for extras."

"Okay," Dave said. "Speak up with the extras."

"Me first," Mike said.

"Shoot," Dave said.

"When can I start calling myself Morris Cohen?"

"When I give the word," Dave said. "I'm keeping you illegitimate for a very good reason. When your turn comes to emerge as a heeb you will cover yourself with glory. That's a promise. Meantime, if you don't stop bringing it up every morning I will put the double whammy on Sally's diet recipe book and start you back on the road to looking like William Howard Taft. If you want to continue looking like Charles Atlas, shut up about being Michael Palgrave. Remember Milton."

"Milton who?" Mike said.

"*They also serve who only stand and wait,*" Dave said. "While you're waiting, stop being so completely irrational, meaning so God-damned typically Jewish. Half the Morris Cohens between here and the Hillcrest Country Club in Los Angeles would give their right arms to be called Palgrave. Isn't that right, Sid?"

"I wouldn't know," Sid said. "I'm an authority only on Jews named Singer, and if we can stop the clowning for a minute I'd like to bring up something serious."

"If Mr. Palgrave will button his lip," Dave said, "the floor is yours."

"It's the Metuchen place," Sid said.

"Our neighbor?" Dave said. "Down on Beach Road?"

"The same," Sid said.

"What about her?" Dave said.

"About her, nothing," Sid said. "She's in New York, as she always is, except on week ends. It's her son. He's just out of the Army and he's hiding out in Mama's house all by himself. I say hiding out because even the cops didn't know he was there, and they have the house on their surveillance list.

They've been checking it out regularly. I don't know what made them suspicious, but five nights ago Rocky Riordan and three of his cops came calling. They had a search warrant and they searched, and they found enough morphine stashed in the kid's bureau drawer to carry a full-blown addict through a week of fixes."

"Oh, Jesus," Mike said.

"Five nights ago?" Dave said.

"Five nights ago," Sid said.

"I haven't seen it in the papers or heard anything," Fanny said. "I always pick up stuff from the delivery boys, but not a word about this. Where did you get it, Sid?"

"From our gauleiter himself," Sid said. "I was in the Records Room over at Town Hall yesterday, checking out the zoning maps on the Furthgast property, when I ran into our affable hard-nosed Chief of Police."

"Riordan told you?" Fanny said.

"He brought it up," Sid said. "Without prompting."

"That's funny," Fanny said.

"Not so funny as the fact that it hasn't been in the papers in five days," Dave said. "Drug busts are big stuff even in big towns. How can a thing like that be kept under wraps for five days in a place like Beechwood?"

"Mama is loaded," Sid said. "And she's got friends in high places. Oliver Stehli owns the Beechwood *Bugle* and he's a member of the Board of Selectmen. Riordan told me he heard Mrs. Metuchen promised the Board if they kept it quiet she'll sell the house and get the kid out of town."

Dave tracked back over his talk with Riordan when they were touring the compound. It was like working your way across a field with a bloodhound, losing the spoor at a certain point, then picking it up later some distance away. The gap was a puzzle. Dave could understand Riordan's telling him about the Metuchen boy. That was an obvious setup. Dave could understand Riordan's making the drug search that same night. That was to nail down in Dave's mind, when the information became important later, that the setup had been made. At this point Dave lost the spoor. Because at this point Sid entered the picture. Why would Riordan confide voluntarily to Sid news that he'd suppressed from the rest of Beechwood for five days? The confidence had not been accidental. It had been deliberate. Why? Dave's tracking mind refused to come up with an answer. He wondered if he should call Don Fortgang.

"I'm all for her selling it," Dave said. "The house sits in five point seven acres, almost five point eight. The way we're getting cramped for space up here, this could be a real break. Hold off on the Furthgast property for a few days, Sid, and find out what Mrs. Metuchen will take for hers."

"Too late," Sid said. "Colin Babington closed the deal yesterday for a client named Mrs. Truscott. Riordan told me she's the widow of Babington's former law partner."

"Now, there's something that can really be called funny," Dave said.

"Make us laugh, leader," Sid said.

"The Metuchen property abuts on ours," Dave said. "According to the thinking of these Wasp thinkers, owning property cheek by jowl with heebs is a losing proposition."

"I have suspected for some time that maybe we don't know as much about Mr. Colin Babington's thinking as we should," Sid said. "If you spend your time creeping around the Records Room in Town Hall, you learn very soon that this boy has a real zip on his fast one. Babington's name is peppered all over the deeds of this town like a case of chicken pox."

"May I?" Fanny said.

"Speak up," Dave said.

"You say it happened five nights ago?" Fanny said.

"According to Rocky Riordan," Sid said.

"If Babington bought the property yesterday," Fanny said, "I'd say he was in an awful hurry. Anybody moving that fast, he probably didn't want any competition. It could be Babington had something to do with keeping the story about the kid out of the papers."

"I wouldn't be surprised," Sid said.

"Too bad," Dave said. "We could have used those six acres. Oh, well, as we used to say at Ethan Allen High, if you'll pardon a bit of Latin, Fanny, *nil desperandum,* or screw it. There are other acres."

"We may not be around to buy them," Sid said.

It was as though the fire bell out in the hall had exploded. Dave was looking at Sid, but he could see what was happening to Fanny's face and to Mike's face.

"You better explain that," Dave said.

"According to our Chief of Police," Sid said, "the Metuchen kid's contact is one of our owners."

"Here?" Fanny said. "The boy is buying his morphine from one of our people?"

"So Mr. Riordan informs me," Sid said.

"Which one?" Mike said. "Who's selling it to the Metuchen kid?"

"Riordan said they don't know yet," Sid said. "But they're damn well going to find out."

Dave had a moment of uneasiness. Maybe he should have taken out the insurance policy Rocky Riordan had offered. But it was only a moment. You didn't buy protection by allowing the enemy to plant a Catholic War Veteran in the middle of your compound at the foot of Saul Street. What you bought that way was an infection. Then the moment of uneasiness vanished. His mind had leaped the gap. It had picked up the spoor.

"Okay," Dave said. "I'll handle this."

He knew quite a bit about how to prevent the spread of this kind of infection. On his mental agenda Dave scratched out the note to call Don Fortgang. Now that he knew the connection between what the police chief had told him in the red Buick and why Riordan had volunteered the information to Sid Singer yesterday in the Hall of Records, Dave also knew what to do about it. His mind came back into the meeting.

"My God," Mike Palgrave was saying. "If they can pin dope addicts on us—"

217

Dave did not hear the rest of Mike's remark. The alert signal was clanging away inside his head. He had been expecting them. But it had never crossed his mind that the bastards would come from this direction. Dave could feel the panic start to invade the room. The waves began to reach him. He stepped right into it. Fast.

"Cut it out," Dave said. "All of you. I'll take care of this."

"How?" Sid said.

"I've been holding off my meeting with Dr. Bieberman," Dave said. "I wanted more bricks and mortar in place. I see now we'll have to work with what's already on its feet. Fanny, set up a date for me with Bieberman in New York."

Fanny flipped to tomorrow's page in her agenda notebook. At the top she wrote two words:

Rabbi, expedite.

22

Silas Bieberman liked to quote Churchill.

Not that Dr. Bieberman admired the British statesman.
How could any Jew admire a man who had dragged his feet
about honoring the Balfour Declaration?

No. Silas Bieberman did not quote Churchill out of admiration. He quoted the wartime Prime Minister the way a
chemist used litmus paper. A person's reaction to a Churchill quotation was as revealing to Dr. Bieberman as it was
revealing to a chemist to observe the color to which a piece
of litmus paper changed when it was dipped into a liquid.

To Silas Bieberman, people who drooled over Churchill
sallies were frauds, scalawags, nitwits, dastards, Litvaks, pol-
troons, phonies, wretches, smart alecks, adventurers, *shmucks,*
mountebanks, crooks, or just plain God-damn fools.

People who reacted to a Churchill quote with skepticism,
or merely refrained from falling down on the floor in a fit of
quivering ecstasy, such people were not necessarily admirable
or even honest. But for such people there was hope.

"Churchill once remarked that one Jew is a Prime Minister," Silas Bieberman said. "Two Jews are a Prime Minister
and a Leader of the Loyal Opposition."

Dr. Bieberman's guest scowled slightly. He crossed his
long legs in the chair beside Dr. Bieberman's desk. He was
obviously thinking about Churchill's words.

"What does the statement mean?" Mr. Dehn said.

Dr. Bieberman decided this husky young man had something more than matzoh balls between his ears. Perhaps doing business with him was not an impossibility.

"I'm damned if I know," Dr. Bieberman said. "I have a feeling when he made the statement Churchill didn't know either."

"Nothing wrong with that," Mr. Dehn said. "Lots of people say things they don't understand. When I was in the Army I used to issue orders most firmly and convincingly when I didn't know what the hell I was talking about. What I meant was, why did you quote him? What does Churchill's remark have to do with what we've been discussing?"

"It shows that even a brilliant man can sometimes say something that's far from brilliant," Dr. Bieberman said. "Have I got you good and confused?"

"You've certainly taken a big step in that direction," Mr. Dehn said.

"Good," Dr. Bieberman said. "Then we've both made a start." He opened the bottom drawer of his desk and pulled out a box of cigars. "Have one?"

"Thanks, no," Mr. Dehn said. "I don't smoke."

"One of these could change your mind," Dr. Bieberman said. "They're Upmanns. A present from the wife of a young man I placed with a congregation in Newark two weeks ago. She wanted a sophisticated metropolitan city. She was afraid they would end up in some godforsaken little prairie town in North Dakota. The wives of rabbis are a peculiar breed. These days most of them are college graduates, yet on the one hand they think a little prairie town in North Dakota has enough Jews to form a congregation that can afford an eight-thousand-a-year-or-more rabbi, plus medical benefits and pension plan, and on the other hand they think Newark is a sophisticated metropolitan city. Anyway, she's happy, and it's my job as chairman of the Placement Committee of the Central Rabbinical Assembly to keep the wives of rabbis happy. Besides, I got a box of Upmanns out of it, which is not bad for a White Owl smoker, so who's complaining? Sure you won't have one?"

"Positive," Mr. Dehn said.

Dr. Bieberman liked the way the young man said positive. Not as if what he really meant was *efsher*—maybe. Dr. Bieberman chose an Upmann for himself, then replaced the box in the bottom drawer of his desk. Out of his next two small acts he made a ceremony as calculated as his quotations from Churchill. A performance as graceful and adroit as any by Fred Astaire guiding Ginger Rogers across a ballroom floor.

First, from the pocket of his vest, which was trimmed with black silk piping, Dr. Bieberman pulled a small gold instrument. It was fastened to the end of his watch chain. With this instrument he devoted to cutting off the tip of his Upmann the sort of care and precision that had brought Harvey Cushing to world eminence in the field of brain surgery. After replacing the cutter in his vest pocket Dr. Bieberman took a wooden kitchen match from a white leather box on the desk. He struck the match alight on a sandpaper square set in the box lid. Holding the cigar in his left hand and the match in his right, Dr. Bieberman swung his swivel chair toward the window. Always, at this stage, he was careful to keep his head in profile to his visitor. Dr. Bieberman inserted the end of the Upmann between his Mark Twain mustache and his Joseph Conrad goatee as though he were a doctor slipping a thermometer into the appropriate orifice of a feverish member of the House of Windsor.

For the final phase of the performance, Dr. Bieberman stared out into Fifth Avenue toward the public library across the street. He liked to make his visitors feel that as he sucked what was intended to be a perfect light from the match flame into the cigar, he drew inspiration from the stone lions crouched on the library steps.

When the cigar was going well Dr. Bieberman tossed the match into his wastebasket. He touched the *yarmulke* on his bald head to make sure it had not been dislodged during his performance. And he swung back to his visitor.

Dr. Bieberman was pleased to note that his visitor's good-looking, somewhat goyish face reflected no hint of annoyance or impatience. Dr. Bieberman's opinion of Mr. Dehn went up another notch.

A man who did not hesitate to question the validity of a Churchill quotation, a man who had the *sitzfleish* to wait calmly through an old man's foolish ritual with a cigar, such a man was no ordinary Jew. Ordinary Jews were a dime a dozen, and not infrequently, Dr. Bieberman had noted, great big roaring pains in the *zudik*. He had learned to keep his eyes open for the exception.

"Now let us see if we understand each other," he said. "You have just established a new congregation up in Westchester, and you have come to me to help you find a rabbi. Is that correct?"

"That is correct," Mr. Dehn said.

"Do you know what a rabbi is?" Dr. Bieberman said.

"I think so," Mr. Dehn said. "We had a rabbi attached to the synagogue on my block when I was a kid in Albany. After school every day I went to his *cheder*, and when I started creeping up on thirteen he coached me for my bar mitzvah."

"May I ask how many summers you count to your credit, Mr. Dehn?"

"Thirty-three," Mr. Dehn said.

"So you were bar mitzvah," Dr. Bieberman said, "some twenty years ago."

"November 1927," Mr. Dehn said.

"What part of Albany, may I ask?" Dr. Bieberman said.

"A place called Westerlo Street," Mr. Dehn said.

"I know the area," Dr. Bieberman said. "And I know the kind of rabbis who flourished on Westerlo Street in 1927. It's all changed, Mr. Dehn. Completely."

"In what way?" Mr. Dehn said.

"In every way," Dr. Bieberman said. "Your rabbi was probably a man born in Russia or Poland or some other part of Central Europe."

"Russia," Mr. Dehn said. "Like my father."

"He had a full long beard and long curly *payess*?"

"Yes," Mr. Dehn said. "And on Saturdays and holy days he wore to *shul* a long black caftan. It was made of alpaca, I think. He also wore a fur-trimmed *shtreimel*."

"So did my father," Dr. Bieberman said. "And if your rabbi spoke English it was with an accent?"

"Very thick," Mr. Dehn said. "But we had no trouble understanding him, and I don't remember that he had any trouble understanding us."

"The rabbi you get today will be cut from an entirely different bolt of cloth," Dr. Bieberman said. "He will be native born. He will be a college graduate—usually at least *cum laude,* frequently more impressive than that. And on top of the college degree he will have had five years of hard study in the seminary. He will be a young man. Perhaps younger than you, Mr. Dehn. Your congregation is new and, from what you've told me, quite small. In rabbinical-placement circles anything less than a thousand members is considered a small congregation. An older man would not accept a job with your congregation, Mr. Dehn. This would be no reflection on you or the members of your congregation. It's just that being a rabbi in this country today is a career like any other American career. Like being a doctor or a lawyer. For a successful career a rabbi must peak in his middle years. If he does not succeed in landing a congregation of a thousand or more in a big city by the time he is, say, forty-five, he will never get one. So he must push up from the sort of small congregation like yours, where he probably got his start."

"I would have no objection to a young man," Mr. Dehn said. "The members of my congregation are all about my age. Many are younger. I think they'd like their rabbi to be a young man."

From Mr. Dehn's tone of voice Dr. Bieberman picked up something Mr. Dehn might not have been aware he was conveying. If it turned out that the members of his congregation did not like a young rabbi, Dr. Bieberman was certain Mr. Dehn would straighten them out on the point. Authority

could not be faked. Not for long, anyway. A man had it or
he did not have it. Dr. Bieberman could see that Mr. Dehn
had it. Dr. Bieberman heaved an inward sigh of relief. He
could take the rest of the day off. He had finally found a congregation for Peretz Vogel.

"In that case I have just the man for you," he said.

"That's great," Mr. Dehn said.

"There is, however, a problem," Dr. Bieberman said.

"What's that?" Mr. Dehn said.

"The man I have in mind is married to a Gentile girl,"
Dr. Bieberman said.

Mr. Dehn's goyish face became, in an instant, radiantly
Jewish. He smiled.

"That's no problem," Mr. Dehn said. "So am I."

23

Amanda Cahill Vogel was a Sarah Lawrence girl. She had never been asked to address the graduating class at one of her alma mater's commencement exercises. Not yet. She was, after all, only twenty-six years old. The opportunity, however, might still come her way.

If it did, Amanda anticipated no difficulty with the subject matter of her speech. Already she had very clearly worked out in her mind the three sentences with which she would begin the traditional address to her fellow alumnae:

"Kids, if you've got to marry a Jew, make sure you're not a Gentile. Your husband will always be ahead of you. Especially if the little wonder is a rabbi."

Amanda had not yet worked out the rest of her speech because she had not yet worked out the rest of her life. This small drawback had not deterred her husband.

Perry Vogel was only six months older than his wife, but he had all of his life mapped out in advance. Even including the number of years he would be granted in which to complete the grand design he had set for himself.

The only parents Perry had known were his maternal grandparents. Perry's grandfather had made it to ninety-one. His grandmother, left with nobody to punch around, had hung up her gloves a year later, on her eighty-ninth birthday. Perry Vogel's grasp of the laws of heredity might have made

Gregor J. Mendel do a bit of spinning in his grave, but that would not bother Perry. He invented his own laws. Even about heredity. The ones Perry invented for this situation were based on simple arithmetic.

His grandfather's ninety-one and his grandmother's eighty-nine added up to one hundred and eighty. Since he was the only surviving product of their union it seemed to Perry obvious that the way to determine his own life span was to divide one hundred and eighty in half.

"That gives me ninety years in which to get all my work done," he had told Amanda on their wedding night. "Bernard Shaw just passed the ninety-one mark, and I see talk in the papers he's supposed to be working on a new play for next summer's Stratford Festival. So I don't think ninety is an unreasonable figure to set for a Jewish boy from Bushwick Avenue who has a first-rate digestion, open bowels, and a limitless supply of lead in his pencil. Roll over, honey. Time to play another chukker. This is very good for the Jews."

Amanda had to admit it was not bad for Gentiles either. Perry's complete confidence in himself could be irritating, but not in the sack. Amanda sometimes wondered where he had learned it all.

"Learned it?" Perry said when she made a joke about his sexual prowess. "What you're getting, honey, is brand-new stuff. Nobody taught me anything. I started from scratch and made it all up. Watch this."

He adjusted the triple mirror on the bureau near the bed, and he moved her left leg into what seemed an awkward position. It wasn't. Not even remotely.

"Okay, tell me," Perry said later. "You ever read anything like that in *A Marriage Manual*?"

"No," Amanda said, "I must admit I didn't."

"Don't admit it, honey," Perry said. "Be grateful for it. You're plowing new ground. Or maybe I've got the verbs hooked to the wrong pronouns. I'm the one doing the plowing. You're the one reaping the harvest. All the girls you went to Sarah Lawrence with, none of those chicks is ever going to get anything in the same league with what you're having served up every hour on the hour."

"Not unless you start conducting seminars," Amanda said.

"That's unfair," Perry said. "You know me well enough by now to realize that I believe in the vigorous pursuit of nookie, but not in promiscuity. I'm a one-woman man, and Bess you is my woman now. Remember that."

"Porgy," Amanda said, "I'll remember if you will."

"How can I forget?" Perry said. "I am a man of God. I live by the Torah, and I check out every inch of the way I'm doing it in the Talmud. They tell me that skirt chasers get nothing but a lot of telephone numbers in their little black books, plus an occasional dose of clap in their shooting irons. A man who works on one number, honing it regularly like a good razor, such a man is sure of getting a good ride every time he goes to the corral, and the good gets better and better."

It had, for almost two years. Until his last year in the seminary, when Perry was seized by a crisis of faith.

The desire to be a rabbi had been the inner motor of his life ever since childhood. Suddenly, when the goal was within his grasp, the desire fell away. It vanished as it had come, without so much as a warning tremor. One day Peretz Vogel had believed as he had always believed: in God and the truths of Judaism. The next day his beliefs were gone.

For a man of his almost abnormal self-confidence the experience was shattering. He had no way of knowing what his professors at the seminary knew: that the experience was quite common. If he had sought help, Peretz Vogel might have learned that what had happened to him was not unique, and that with time belief would return. He was, however, a man who had never sought help for anything. Help was something needed by weaklings. Strong men did not seek it. Indeed, it never occurred to a strong man that help was available.

It certainly never occurred to Peretz Vogel. He carried the horror like a dirty secret, concealing it from his classmates and his professors as though it were an obscene disease.

He could not, of course, conceal it from Amanda. She knew something was wrong the day it happened. Probably within hours after disaster struck. Perry came into their tiny apartment two blocks from Hebrew Union College in Cincinnati and he did not make his usual dive for the hook fasteners of her brassiere.

"Perry," she said. "You sick?"

"I seem to have caught something," he said in a voice Amanda had never heard before. "I'll be okay in a little while."

He wasn't. Not in a little while, and not for the balance of Perry's last year at Hebrew Union. After graduation, when they came back east to the home of Amanda's parents in Scarsdale, she and Perry had not slept together for eight months. Nor had they discussed the problem.

This was simple enough. Perry pretended there was no problem. It was driving Amanda crazy, and she could only guess what it was doing to Perry, but it had one unexpected compensation.

Mr. and Mrs. Cahill had been shocked when Amanda had told them she was going to marry a Jew. The shock deepened when they learned the Jew Amanda planned to marry had plans of his own: to become a rabbi. It was a peculiar form of shock. It survived Mr. and Mrs. Cahill's confusion, protests, shouts, pleas, screams, tears, threats, and ultimate bow to the inevitable.

The Cahills bowed, but they did not bend. It would have been difficult for them to conceal their hatred of Perry. Perhaps that was why they did not try. They were obviously pleased when, immediately following the wedding, Amanda and her husband returned to his studies in Cincinnati.

During their remaining time at the seminary Amanda had not thought much about her parents. As graduation closed in, she was forced to think about them. The life-insurance money Perry had collected on the death of his parents had almost run out. They could not afford a hotel or a sublet in New York while Perry went job-hunting. Amanda and Perry were not happy about accepting the Cahills' offer to put them up, but there was no alternative. To her surprise and relief, Amanda's fears proved unfounded. She could not believe the attitude of her parents had changed toward her marriage, but it certainly seemed to have changed toward Perry. The Cahills were actually polite to him.

It did not take Amanda long to figure out the reason. The Perry her parents had first met was a self-confident smart aleck who knew all the answers and insisted on telling them to all within earshot in the boisterous, vulgar, offensive way Mr. and Mrs. Cahill believed was typical of all Jews. The Perry who came back from Cincinnati was quiet, soft-spoken, shy, considerate, and self-effacing. In other words, scared shitless. The Cahills were astonished, then reluctantly friendly. Amanda was pleased but not fooled.

Another person who was not fooled was Dr. Bieberman, the chairman of the Central Rabbinical Assembly's Placement Committee. After Perry's second interview, Dr. Bieberman asked to have a talk with Mrs. Vogel.

"In placing a rabbi with a congregation," he told Perry, "the prospective rabbi's wife is just as important to the congregation's pulpit committee as the rabbi himself. I'm free tomorrow at ten-thirty. I would like to have a talk with Mrs. Vogel."

"Okay," Perry said. "I'll bring her in."

"Don't bring her in," Dr. Bieberman said. "Send her. I want to see Mrs. Vogel alone."

The next day Dr. Bieberman came crisply to the point.

"Your husband's record at the seminary is brilliant," he said. "Placing him with a good congregation should be a fairly simple matter. It should be, but it's not. There is a grave problem."

"What's that?" Amanda said.

"He has come out of the seminary with something he should have left behind him," Dr. Bieberman said. "A crisis of faith."

"I didn't think it showed," Amanda said.

Dr. Bieberman removed the Upmann from his mouth.

"You mean your husband has discussed it with you?" he said in surprise.

"No," Amanda said. "But I can tell."

"Wives should, but they usually don't," Dr. Bieberman said. "It's the sort of thing that works a change in a man. Even obtuse wives have reasons to notice the change. The members of a pulpit committee have no reason to notice. When they interview a prospective rabbi for their congregation they are almost always seeing a man they have never seen before. They have no yardsticks by which to measure changes in him. When they discover later that there is something wrong with the man they hired, who catches it in the neck?"

"You, I imagine," Amanda said.

"Technically, who catches it is the Placement Committee of the Central Rabbinical Assembly," Dr. Bieberman said. "Actually, in the practical sense, the blame is dumped on yours truly and nobody else. I don't like blame any more than other people, so I try not to recommend a rabbi who I know in my bones is going to be a disappointment to the congregation that hires him."

"If you're not going to recommend my husband," Amanda said, "I don't see why you asked me to come and see you."

"Did anybody in this room hear anybody say I'm not going to recommend your husband?" Dr. Bieberman said.

"I'm sorry," Amanda said. "I assumed that was what you meant. I hope my assumption is wrong."

"It could be," Dr. Bieberman said. "I hope it is. I was impressed with your husband, Mrs. Vogel. I have seen enough of this problem to feel pretty confident he will recover from his crisis of faith. It is an entirely different problem that worries me."

"What's that?" Amanda said.

"What to do about your husband while he's weathering the hollow of the spiritual wave," Dr. Bieberman said. "And I'm not talking in financial terms. Even if your husband were

rich, which he tells me he is not, or if you were rich, which
you may be someday when your parents die but at present
you are not, if you both had all the money in the world is
what I'm saying, it would make no difference. It is a spiritual
problem. A man must work it out for himself. Until he does
he is not a whole man. When a congregation hires a rabbi
they have a right to believe they are hiring a whole man. Only
a whole man can truly supervise the spiritual needs of others.
That's what makes a rabbi. And that's what the congregation
is paying for. A man who is concerned with working out his
own spiritual needs rather than theirs, such a man is not earning the money they are paying him."

"I can see that," Amanda said.

"What, then, in the case of your husband, Mrs. Vogel—what
is the solution?" Dr. Bieberman said.

"I don't suppose there is one," Amanda said.

"Because you are inexperienced," Dr. Bieberman said.
"What you learn in a job like mine is that there is always
a solution. What you have to do is find it. Consider for a moment what the average pulpit committee is like. A dozen or
more members of the congregation. All of them very serious
people. All of them a trifle self-important. All of them adding
up to a very difficult hurdle for a prospective rabbi to get
over. They usually ask to see him two or three times. Sometimes more. They ask him all sorts of personal questions. A
lot of them quite embarrassing. Then they make a report
to the congregation. The congregation votes. Some vote yes.
Some vote no. Many of the votes have nothing to do with the
prospective rabbi. They reflect the way the voters feel about
different members of the pulpit committee. If the prospective rabbi gets a majority of the votes, he gets the job. At this
point his troubles are only beginning. From now on, the
people who voted no will be watching him. All the poor rabbi
has to do is stumble a little, make one mistake, and bingo,
they're on top of him. The rabbi lives in an atmosphere of
constant tension. In such an atmosphere, a man living
through a crisis could fall apart."

"Then I was right," Amanda said. "A man going through what my husband is going through would not have a chance with any normal congregation."

"But with an abnormal one?" Dr. Bieberman said.

"An abnormal congregation?" Amanda said.

"Why not?" Dr. Bieberman said.

"I never heard of such a thing," Amanda said.

"Neither did I," Dr. Bieberman said. "Until two days ago. A man came to see me. Not a pulpit committee. Not the chairman of a pulpit committee. A single man. Acting on his own. He is just starting a small congregation up in Westchester, and it is something unique in my experience. This congregation in the town of Beechwood is a one-man show."

"Is there such a thing?" Amanda said.

"There is if you've got the money to pay for it," Dr. Bieberman said. "This man not only has the money to choose his own rabbi without the help of a pulpit committee or putting the choice to a vote of his congregation. This man has one other thing that it seems to me would make your husband the ideal rabbi for his congregation."

"What's that?" Amanda said.

"I have a feeling this man is not particularly interested in spiritual problems," Dr. Bieberman said. "I would not be surprised to discover that this man never heard of a spiritual problem. If he has, he left me with the impression that he can take care of his own without the help of a rabbi, and I suspect he wouldn't give a damn about any spiritual problems his rabbi might be struggling with."

"Then why does he want to hire a rabbi?" Amanda said.

"Why does a sharecropper who strikes oil want right away to hire an English governess for his children?" Dr. Bieberman said.

PART III

24

Dave had the car window rolled down. He was watching for the Cross County marker. The phone box beeped his signal. He reached over for the instrument and put it to his ear.

"Yes, Fanny?"

"Bad news, I'm afraid, D.D.," Fanny said.

"Tell me."

"Riordan's men just picked up the Metuchen boy's contact."

"Who?" Dave said.

"You'll never guess."

"I think I can," Dave said.

"D.D., are you kidding?"

"I'm afraid not," Dave said.

"Who's your guess?"

"Ernie Sternshus?"

"My God," Fanny said. "How did you know?"

"I didn't, but I see now I should have," Dave said. "Remember a couple of weeks ago? When Riordan came around to look us over and he and I went for a tour in his brand-new red Buick police car?"

"What about it?" Fanny said.

"At one point Riordan stopped the car in front of the Sternshus house," Dave said. "I didn't think about reasons because we were just on a random tour, stopping at other houses along the way, but I see now that Riordan stopped the car because he saw the Metuchen boy seeding the lawn. Nothing happened. Just hello and goodbye with Daisy Sternshus and the boy. But at the staff meeting five days later, when Sid told us what Riordan had told him in the Hall of Records about the Metuchen boy's arrest, that visit came back to me. I couldn't put the two things together. It just came back to me, and it stayed with me, hanging around in my mind, waiting for an explanation. The minute you just said bad news, it clicked."

"What clicked?" Fanny said.

"Riordan was setting me up," Dave said. "If I didn't snap at what he called his insurance policy, if I didn't sell that Saul Street lot to his brother, Riordan was going to show me his muscle by nailing the kid and then going after Sternshus. I didn't snap at the bastard's insurance policy, so first he nailed the kid and now he's nailed Sternshus. When he goes into court Riordan can now tell the judge he warned me there was drug traffic on the compound but I did nothing about it. So now I've got to do something about it. Before I get started you better tell me exactly what happened."

"Just about what you would expect," Fanny said. "If you're expecting that kind of thing to happen is what I mean. As soon as the Metuchen boy was arrested his mother came out from New York. She went bail, of course, pending trial, and Judge Elphinstone released the kid in her custody. The kid asked if he could finish his gardening job at the Sternshus place while he was waiting for the trial, and the judge said sure if his mother kept an eye on him. Mrs. Metuchen said she would. What else could she say? So the next morning the kid went back to work at the Sternshus place, and he's been going back every day, and all the time Riordan and his boys were doing what you would think the kid and Ernie Sternshus would have had enough brains to realize the cops would be doing."

"What's the exact evidence?" Dave said.

"Pretty bad, according to Sid," Fanny said. "It happened about five o'clock. Sternshus came home early from his job in New York. His wife picked him up at the train, which she does every day. When they turned into their driveway the Metuchen kid was working on some bushes he'd been putting in. Sternshus got out of the car to talk to him and his wife ran the car into the garage. While Sternshus and the kid were talking, Riordan's boys arrived and jumped them. Sternshus had a canvas package in his pocket. It was full of small white envelopes. A few of those envelopes were still in the boy's hand. The silly little dope hadn't even had time to slip them into his pocket."

"Where are they now?" Dave said.

"In the clink," Fanny said. "Waiting for Judge Elphinstone. He's playing golf down in Scarsdale, but they reached him on the fourteenth hole. He said he'd come right up as soon as he finished his round. Sid figures he ought to be here in Beechwood by six-thirty. Where did I catch you?"

Dave looked out the car window.

"I'm coming off Bruckner Boulevard into Cross County," Dave said. He glanced at the dashboard clock. "It's ten to six," he said. "With luck I could be at the office by six-thirty. Say six-forty the latest."

"I think you should be at that arraignment," Fanny said.

"I've got to be," Dave said.

"Then you better not waste time coming here," Fanny said. "You better go direct to the courthouse. Elphinstone probably won't be right on the button, but if he has some luck with his last four holes he might be. I'll tell Sid to stall as long as he can."

"Tell him not to make it obvious," Dave said. "I don't want the judge to feel I'm anything more than a spectator."

"D.D., I don't think you'll get away with that," Fanny said. "The judge is doing this after hours because Riordan asked for it. He didn't want to wait until tomorrow morning. Only interested parties know the arraignment is taking place.

There won't be any off-the-street spectators, D.D. While this thing is happening in the courthouse Beechwood will be home eating its dinner."

"Let me handle that on the spot," Dave said. "You got the rabbi's number?"

"Of course," Fanny said. "I put it in my book the day their phone was installed. Hold it."

A few moments later she was back on the phone with the number.

"Thanks," Dave said.

"D.D., you want me to meet you there?"

Dave thought fast.

"No," he said finally. "I think you better stay by the phone, Fanny."

"Will do," she said.

Dave clicked her off. He gave his full attention to the task of guiding four thousand dollars' worth of brand-new Cadillac through the piled lumps of torn concrete that were still technically Bruckner Boulevard. When he was safely out on Cross County Highway and he had the car heading for Beechwood at sixty, Dave beeped his signal into the call box and gave the operator the Vogel number.

"Rabbi Vogel's residence."

Dave had a moment of shock. Since Mrs. Vogel and her husband had moved onto the compound, Dave had stopped by several times on Isaac Street to ask if there was anything he could do to help them get settled. Mrs. Vogel had been pleasant. Dave now realized he had never heard her voice on the phone.

"This is Dave Dehn," he said.

"Oh, hello, Mr. Dehn," she said. "Amanda Vogel here."

"Yes, I know," Dave said, and then wished he hadn't. He tried for a more businesslike approach. "Is the rabbi there?"

"Sorry," she said. "I didn't hear that."

"It's the traffic," Dave said. "I'm calling you from my car on the way up to Beechwood. It's noisy as hell."

"I hear you now," she said.

"Is the rabbi there?" Dave said.

"Of course," she said. "One moment."

Dave wondered what it was in her voice on the telephone that didn't show up when he talked to her face to face.

"Dave?"

He didn't have to wonder about her husband's voice. Peretz Vogel came on the blower like Graham MacNamee announcing Ed Wynn on the *Texaco Comedy Hour*.

"Yes, hello, Perry."

"I suppose you're calling about the Sternshus thing?"

"I just got the news on my car phone," Dave said. "Fanny Mintz reached me here on the Cross County."

"Now, Dave, I don't want you to worry."

Dave couldn't understand why he should find it annoying that Rabbi Vogel addressed him by his first name. They had known each other for about a week. As a rule, if a newcomer on the compound was not addressed by his first name three hours after he moved in, he went to the office and ordered Fanny to tell Mr. Dehn he felt his new neighbors were anti-Semites.

"I never worry," Dave said tartly. "I always check out my orders. I'm calling to find out if you're clear on yours."

"Everything tickety-boo, Dave."

"Everything what?" Dave said.

"Cockney slang for everything under control," Peretz Vogel said.

Christ, Dave thought, this is a rabbi?

He said, "Here it is in Beechwood slang, so listen, please. I may be late getting there. Sid will try to stall if he can, but it's not important. One way or another, on time or late, I'll show up. You go ahead without me. If I'm late pay no attention when I walk in. I'm just a face in the gallery. That clear?"

"Crystal clear," the rabbi said.

When his next free moments surfaced, Dave thought irritably, he would have to introduce this rabbinical wise guy to the words yes and no.

"Okay," Dave said. "Carry on as planned. I'll see you in about an hour."

He was off by four minutes. The clock on Town Hall showed six minutes to seven when Dave parked his car in Hermit Crab Square and walked around to the courthouse entrance on Main Street. There were a few cars up the street in the City Club parking lot, and the usual bar noises were coming from Floyd Klenczewski's Steak Pit down the street, but nobody was walking the sidewalks. Dave climbed the courthouse steps.

The prosecuting attorney, who was on his feet when Dave came tiptoeing into the courtroom through a rear door, was wearing a jazzy four-in-hand.

"That concludes the prosecution's case, Your Honor," Wes Dicey was saying as Dave sat down in the back of the room.

"Mr. Singer?" Judge Elphinstone said from the bench.

At the defense table Sid came to his feet with the slight halting jerks of a stoic who lives with the nagging, constant twinges of pain from an old battlefield injury about which he wants no comment from sympathetic observers. Sid helped himself erect by pushing down on the table with both palms. It was his courtroom manner. In real life, as Dave knew, Sid was as spry as Charley Paddock responding to the crack of the starter's pistol.

"The defense interposes no objection to the evidence as stated by the prosecuting attorney," Sid said.

"The court will proceed with the arraignment," Judge Elphinstone said.

"If Your Honor please."

The judge had been lifting a glass of water to his lips. The gesture caused the folds of his black robe to fall away from his right forearm. His Honor had obviously come directly from the golf course. The forearm was encased in a tweed sleeve of boldly patterned black-and-white hound's-tooth.

"Yes, Mr. Singer?"

"If Your Honor please," Sid said. "Before the court pro-

240

ceeds to arraignment I would like to make a statement, if I
may."

"No objection, Your Honor," said Wes Dicey.

He had not been asked if he had any. Dicey's knowledge
of the law had come out of Yale, but his awareness of how
it should be practiced had obviously been picked up in
places not unlike Dave's Odeon Theatre on Ten Eyck
Avenue.

"Proceed, Mr. Singer," said Judge Elphinstone.

"If it please the court," Sid said.

His voice was low and halting, but not quite as halting as
the movements that had brought him jerkily to his feet. The
voice, however, was not resonantly forthright, either. It was
the voice of an honorable man, a man who understood the in-
iquity of criminal acts, deplored them, and stood foursquare
behind the principle that if a free society is to survive, wrong-
doing must be punished. A man who was nonetheless troubled by the occasional consequences of such punishment. On
the hard bench at the back of the room Dave relaxed. Sid was
safely into his humble bit.

"On the surface," Sid said, "this would seem to be a simple
case, Your Honor. One of the defendants has been apprehended in his own home while under the influence of a drug
the use of which is in this state forbidden by statute. At the
same time the apprehending officers found in the young
man's possession a not inconsiderable supply of this same
drug which, again according to the statutes of this state, it is
illegal to obtain except on a doctor's prescription. The second young man was apprehended this evening, on the driveway in front of his own home, in the act of passing on to the
first young man a further supply of this illegal drug. The
defense, representing both young men, did not produce a
doctor's prescription to cover either of these two supplies of
drugs. On the face of it, therefore, the laws of this state have
been violated, and it is incumbent on the court to proceed
with arraignment."

Judge Elphinstone exposed at least a foot of hound's-tooth tweed as he glanced at his wrist watch.

"Which you, Mr. Singer, feel in this case the court should refrain from doing," he said, not without irony.

Sid gave a remarkably accurate impersonation of a man who, on his sedate way down a church aisle to his pew, is without warning stabbed from behind in a sensitive area with a red-hot poker.

"I beg your pardon, Your Honor?" he said.

"You don't have to beg the court's pardon," Judge Elphinstone said. "All you have to do is get on with your statement. The prosecution asked that this hearing be held now, in the evening, instead of waiting until the normal hour tomorrow morning, and the court is willing to co-operate. But surely it is not necessary to make the court miss its dinner."

"Your Honor is quite right," Sid said. "The defense will be brief."

"It is the most effective way to earn the mercy of a hungry court," Judge Elphinstone said.

"These two young men," Sid continued, "are not ordinary criminals, Your Honor. They are veterans who have recently been discharged from the U.S. Marine Corps. In the war just ended, these two young men served our republic bravely. Both were badly wounded on Guadalcanal. Their drug addiction was imposed on them by our U.S. Navy doctors in an effort to relieve them of terrible pain while their wounds were being mended by long and difficult surgery. In the process, their bodies were saved, but their nervous systems were enslaved by the drug that helped alleviate their pain. When they were discharged into civilian life they carried this enslavement with them. They also carried something else. A sense of responsibility for each other. Ernest Sternshus was the platoon sergeant who sent Roger Metuchen into the action that almost killed them both. They did not know each other before they met in the Marine Corps. They went their separate ways after they left the Marines. It is sheer coincidence that three months ago Ernest Sternshus came to live in this community where Roger Metuchen's mother has maintained a home since her son was a child. When Ernest Sternshus learned that the boy he had sent into battle had emerged from the war with the same terrible addiction from which Sternshus himself suffered, he felt he could do no less than help the boy. The defense does not approve of the nature of that help, nor does the defense ask the court to condone it."

"Please tell us what you want the court to do," Judge Elphinstone said.

"The defense asks the court in its mercy not to sentence these young men to prison, where they will be forced to break the law daily and dangerously in order to obtain the drug that is the only way for them to preserve their sanity."

Sid paused. He leaned forward over the defense table. His voice grew a bit stronger.

"There is another way out," he said. "It exists right here in our community. If Your Honor please, I would like the indulgence of the court for a brief statement by Rabbi Peretz Vogel."

Wes Dicey came to his feet.

"The prosecution objects," he said.

"Why?" Judge Elphinstone said.

"We have here an open-and-shut case," Dicey said. "A statute has been violated. The violators must be arraigned. What's all this irrelevant talk about other ways out?"

"Mr. Dicey," the judge said, "how much do you know about drug addiction?"

"I read the papers," Wes Dicey said.

He made it sound like an achievement to be ranked with the invention of the internal-combustion engine.

"So do I," Judge Elphinstone said. "Since the end of the war the newspapers have been telling me an increasingly appalling story about what is happening in this country. Drug addiction is rampant. It is accelerating at a terrifying pace, especially among the young. All efforts at eradication or even containment of this national disease have failed. Anybody who has even a suggestion of something helpful in dealing with this national epidemic will be heard, even if the court's dinner has to wait until it will take the place of tomorrow's breakfast. Mr. Singer, please ask Rabbi Vogel to come forward."

Sid turned and gestured. Perry Vogel stood up.

"Your Honor," Sid said, "Rabbi Peretz Vogel."

"Permit me to introduce myself," Perry said. "I am the rabbi for a congregation of one hundred and seventy-two families living in a new and expanding housing development on Turkey Hill Road. When I was a student at Hebrew Union College in Cincinnati, Your Honor, I was active for two years in a field-work program devoted to the rehabilitation of drug addicts, particularly young people. The one lesson with which I came away from this shattering experience, Your Honor, has already been stated by the defense attorney. Prison is no cure. On the contrary. Prison spreads the infection. What little success we had in Cincinnati was achieved not on an institutional basis but on a personal basis. Wherever we were able to place an addict with a family that was interested in him as a person who was sick and needed care, we were always at least partially successful and in a gratifying number of cases totally successful.

"As a rabbi I feel my duties to my parishioners extend beyond the merely spiritual. Because of my experience in drug-rehabilitation work, and because I am convinced this work will become increasingly important as the epidemic of drug addiction takes a greater and deeper hold on this country, I have worked out a rehabilitation program for our community on Turkey Hill Road. Mr. David Dehn, the developer of our housing project, has advanced the funds for the installation at once of a reputable doctor and nursing staff in residence.

"My wife and I want to start the program by taking one of the defendants, young Roger Metuchen, into our home. The other defendant, Ernest Sternshus, lives just around the corner from us. He is a married man, but on this level my wife and I would like to assume responsibility for him as well.

Mrs. Metuchen and Mrs. Sternshus, who are both here in court tonight, have granted their permission. With the medical assistance Mr. Dehn is in the process of laying on for us, plus my field experience in Cincinnati, I am certain as their spiritual adviser that we can bring these two young men out of the shadows of criminality into the fresh air of useful citizenship. I ask Your Honor to refrain from arraigning Roger Metuchen and Ernest Sternshus. I implore Your Honor to turn them over to the custody of my wife and myself. Thank you, Your Honor."

Judge Elphinstone went to work on his glass of water.

"Mr. Dicey," he said, "have you any comment?"

It was clear from Mr. Dicey's face that he had several, but none was fit for public expression.

"It's all pretty unusual," he said. "That's all I can say."

"So is the problem," Judge Elphinstone said. "You'll have to say more."

Wes Dicey didn't seem to know how to go about finding the words with which to say more, so Sid stepped in.

"If Your Honor please," he said, "I wonder if you would be good enough to indulge the defense to the extent of adding one more comment?"

"If it's helpful," Judge Elphinstone said.

Sid turned.

"Is Mr. David Dehn in the courtroom?" he said.

Dave stood up.

"Yes," he said.

"Would you be good enough, Mr. Dehn, to come to the defense table?" Sid said.

"Certainly," Dave said.

When he got there he saw Ernie Sternshus sitting beside his wife. Beyond them, Roger Metuchen was sitting next to an erect, handsome woman with gray-streaked blonde hair. She was wearing the sort of tweed suit Irene Dunne always wore in the scenes with Cary Grant where she played the successful business rival he had not realized, when he summoned her for the big stock-transfer showdown, was a woman. Mrs. Metuchen, no doubt. The sort of woman, Dave had learned long ago, there was only one way to handle: assassination.

"Your Honor," Sid Singer said, "this is Mr. David Dehn, our developer. If the court please, he has a few words to say."

"Proceed, Mr. Dehn," Judge Elphinstone said.

"Your Honor," Dave said, "I went through the war with the Third Army in Germany. After we liberated Buchenwald I was assigned for several months to work with the medics on a problem that was just beginning to surface in the E.T.O. Drugs. My experience was probably not so extensive as Rabbi Vogel's, but when you're dealing with drug abuse a little experience goes a long way. While still in Germany I made up my mind that if I ever could do anything about the problem here in my own country, I would.

"I did not realize when I came to Beechwood a year and a half ago for purely business reasons that I was walking into an opportunity to be helpful. I came to develop some real estate. I found I wanted to do something for the community in which my real estate is located. The program Rabbi Vogel has outlined is just getting under way. It will grow because the drug problem in this country is growing. The two young men in question happen to have been apprehended on my real estate. I therefore want to take care of them. But I would also like to help anybody in this community, regardless of creed, color, or national origin, who now needs or in the future will need drug-rehabilitation assistance. Your Honor is aware, I am sure, that the need for such assistance already exists and will grow stronger. Give us these two young people as a start, and we will take all the young people the town of Beechwood chooses to send us. All the financial responsibility involved will be assumed by me. Thank you, Your Honor."

Dave was aware, as his voice stopped, that Mrs. Metuchen had turned and was very coolly examining him. Not, Dave noted, with visible admiration. Hers was a look of assessment. Rocky Riordan had said Mrs. Metuchen ran a big public relations outfit in New York. Her assessment of the statement

Dave had just made would be subjected to more severe examination than Judge Elphinstone would bring to bear on it. Dave wished all at once that he believed every word he had just uttered.

"I am inclined to grant your request," the judge said.

"Thank you, Your Honor," Dave said.

"One thing, however, troubles me," His Honor said. "You are a comparative newcomer in Beechwood, Mr. Dehn. I would feel easier about doing what you ask if there were somebody in the community who is a friend of yours. To put it bluntly, Mr. Dehn, is there anybody in Beechwood who can vouch for your *bona fides?*"

"There is," Dave said.

"Who, please?" Judge Elphinstone said.

"A member of your Board of Selectmen," Dave said. "Mr. Donald Fortgang."

25

Don Fortgang felt a small shiver of excitement. This was the first time in his life he had ever set foot on the wooden steps that led up to the front door of the City Club.

It didn't seem possible. Don had been born in this town. He had lived here every day of his sixty-one years. In that time he had come to know almost every square foot of Beechwood. In fact, he had come to own more of those square feet than most of his fellow citizens realized. Yet Don Fortgang had never set foot on these steps. Never once. The small shiver of excitement stabbed through him again.

"Mr. Babington is waiting for you, sir," the headwaiter said when Don came through the front door.

The greeting brought with it a moment of shock. Don had known Paul Zwingli ever since the members of the City Club had imported the dapper little Swiss hotel manager before the war. Paul and his wife had purchased the furniture for their home in Fortgang's Furniture Mart. He and Don greeted each other whenever they met in the bank or the post office or on the street. Paul was a familiar figure to Don Fortgang. Yet he did not look familiar now.

It occurred to Don that Paul Zwingli was not unlike a bird that came every morning to the feeder outside Don's bedroom window. He had grown so accustomed to seeing the bird that

248

he no longer paid any attention to its presence. Until one day, on a visit to the zoo, he saw the bird inside the screening of a cage. Don Fortgang had never seen Paul Zwingli indoors at his post in the City Club.

"This way, Mr. Fortgang," the headwaiter said. He led Don into the dining room.

Colin Babington rose from his chair. "Hello, Don," said Beechwood's First Selectman. He took Don's hand.

"Hello, Colin," Don said. "Sorry to be late."

"Nonsense," Colin Babington said. He nodded toward the big mahogany grandfather's clock near the door that led to the bar. "You're a couple of minutes early."

"May I take your hat, sir?" Paul said.

Don could feel his face grow hot. He had forgotten he was carrying his hat.

"Thanks, Paul," he said.

Handing over the hat, Don realized he should not have worn it. None of the members of the City Club wore a hat on an ordinary business day. What the hell was the matter with him? What was he doing with a hat? He had been invited to lunch, not a Seder.

Since he was more flustered than he wanted Colin Babington to notice, Don could not help noticing something else. Colin Babington was wearing his beautifully aged heather-colored Harris tweed jacket with the worn leather buttons. Don Fortgang, the *shmuck,* was wearing his Dunhill's double-breasted blue pin-stripe. Christ, he thought, you sure are acting like a nervous bride calling for the first time on the groom's hostile parents.

"Let's get you a drink," Colin Babington said. "This thing I'm toying with is a martini. What will you have?"

"The same, please," Don said.

"Two more of these, Paul," Colin Babington said. "And then we'll order."

"Very good, sir," Paul said.

He walked away.

Don's eyes roved the room.

"See somebody you know?" Colin Babington said.

"No, no," he said. What the hell did he mean, no, no? He knew every son of a bitch in the God-damn room.

"Just admiring the place," Don said.

"Haven't you ever been here before?" Babington said.

"No," Don said.

"A pity," Colin Babington said. "You'd enjoy this place, Don. Thanks, Paul."

"Right, sir," the headwaiter said. He set down the two martinis and picked up Colin Babington's empty glass. "It's Thursday, sir."

"That means the special is eggs Benedict," Colin Babington said to Don Fortgang. "I recommend it."

"Eggs Benedict it is," Don Fortgang said.

In the stronghold of the goyim, what could be more appropriate for a Jewish boy's lunch than a dish made of both dairy and meat, plus the meat should be ham, yet?

"Two, Paul, please," Colin Babington said.

"Very good, sir," the headwaiter said.

He went away. Colin Babington raised his glass.

"Here's to the new Board of Selectmen," he said.

Don Fortgang's glass, on its way to his lips, jerked to a halt. For a moment he looked as though he were waving a flower toward someone at the other side of the room.

"What happened to the old one?" Don said.

"Nothing yet," Colin Babington said. "But we've got elections coming up in June."

"I thought it was agreed weeks ago the present slate was running for re-election," Fortgang said. "Like last year."

"They are," Colin Babington said. "All except one."

"Which one?" Don Fortgang said.

"You," Colin Babington said.

He took a sip. Don Fortgang remembered where his glass was. He set it back in motion, got it to his lips, and took a sip. He had trouble swallowing. When he managed to get the stuff down, it seared his throat. He coughed.

"I didn't realize I wasn't running for re-election," he managed to say.

"That's why I asked you to lunch," Colin Babington said. "The other members of the board didn't want you to find out on your own. They felt it would be less painful if I explained to you in person why you're not going to run."

For a moment it was as though Don Fortgang were lounging on his cherry red chaise longue in his bright red kimono in the pagoda Charlene had built for him on their private hill. The sense of relaxation allowed the resentment to dart past the carefully posted guards of caution.

"Nobody tells me when to run and when not to run for membership on the Board of Selectmen of this town," Don Fortgang said. "I make that decision myself."

Colin Babington released a chuckle. "Try not to be silly," he said quietly.

"Gee whiz," Don Fortgang said. "What's this all about?"

"It's about what happened two nights ago in Claude Elphinstone's courtroom," Colin Babington said. "I had calls yesterday from several members of the board. They don't like what you did, Don. They don't like it one little bit."

"For Christ's sake," Don Fortgang said. "I didn't do a Goddamn thing, Colin. I wasn't even there. That son of a bitch Dehn he never asked my permission. How could he? I don't know him. Would I vouch in court, in a court of law, for God's sakes, would I vouch for a perfect stranger? I never even met the bastard."

"Odd," Colin Babington said. "If you never met him, how does it happen that all those Jews up there on Turkey Hill are buying their furniture in Fortgang's Furniture Mart at a thirty-three and one-third per cent markdown across the board on every piece of your merchandise they want? Whereas the rest of us common folk in this town, when we go into Fortgang's for a chair or a bed we pay what it says on the price tag?"

"I didn't do that," Don Fortgang said. "It's not me, Colin."

"It's your store," Colin Babington said.

"Colin, believe me," Don Fortgang said. "It's not me, Colin. You know I wouldn't lie to you, Colin."

"There was a time when I thought I knew," Colin Babington said.

"You still know," Don Fortgang said. "When I say it's not me, Colin, I'm telling you the God's honest truth. Honest, Colin."

"In that case tell me something else," Colin Babington said. "If it's not you, who is it?"

Don Fortgang felt his mouth open. He felt the words start to come. But they didn't come very far. He could do a lot of things. To a lot of people. He had the bad memories to prove it. If he hadn't done those things he would not now be what he had been all his life. Beechwood's prop Jew. But there were limits. There was one thing he could not do. He could not shit on his own father.

"Okay," Don Fortgang said in a tired voice. "What do you want me to do, Colin?"

"Have a talk with Claude Elphinstone," Colin Babington said. "Not on the phone. You go see him in person. You tell him you don't know Dehn. You never intended to vouch for him. You resent Dehn's using your name the way he did. You make it clean and hard and tough. No room for doubt. As a citizen of this town, as a member of the Board of Selectmen, you are furious because an outsider tampered with your integrity. You do that, Don."

Colin Babington's voice stopped. He took a sip from his glass. Don Fortgang stared at his own glass. It reminded him how much he hated gin. His gut started to contract.

"After I do that," he said, "what about the rest?"

"The rest is none of your business," Colin Babington said. "You do your part. I'll see we do ours."

"What's your part?" Don Fortgang said.

"I said that's none of your business," Colin Babington said.

"You better tell me, Colin," Don Fortgang said.

Colin Babington gave him a sharp glance. As though it

had occurred to him he would be wise to check the identity of the person he had up to now assumed was the man he had invited to share his table.

"It's not important," Colin Babington said.

"It's important to me," Don Fortgang said.

Colin Babington hesitated, then shrugged.

"Dehn's wife still has title to the Turkey Hill property," he said. "Bella Biaggi has agreed to allow me to start eviction proceedings. It's going to be messy, because of some evidence Dehn has about her relations with Tony D'Alessandro, but that evidence would be operative only in a divorce court. It has nothing to do with this kind of civil suit. Bella hates the bounder. She's willing to face the scandal to get her hands back on her own property. I'll see to it she does. For your help in running Mr. David Dehn out of this town the Board of Selectmen has authorized me to tell you they will allow you to stand for re-election."

The waiter arrived.

"Very hot, please," he said as he set down the plates of eggs Benedict. "Very hot indeed, gentlemen."

The smell of hot hollandaise finished the job on Don Fortgang's contracting gut. He shoved himself away from the table and moved swiftly toward where he hoped the men's room was located. He made it without being aware that Paul's imperturbable guidance and sustaining grip had got him through the right door. Then Don Fortgang's stomach gave up its contents.

Knowing the provenance of his humiliation seemed to help. Don Fortgang did not understand why. He did not want to understand. He wanted only to remove all signs of his shame.

When he did, when the mirror over the basin indicated that the Dunhill's pin-stripe had not been soiled, Don Fortgang knew he was going to be all right. He had been handling this crap all his life. Today was no time to stop. Not when at long last he knew he had come out on top of it. Don Fortgang was smiling when he got back to the table.

"Sorry," he said. "The last of that damn twenty-four-hour flu that hit me day before yesterday."

"A lot of it's going around," Colin Babington said. He lifted a forkful of eggs Benedict. "Don't let your food get cold."

"I hate hot ham," Don Fortgang said.

The forkful on its way to Colin Babington's mouth did not get there. He gave Don Fortgang a sharp glance, then set the fork back on his plate.

"All right," Colin Babington said. "Let's have it."

"I'll do what you and the board want me to do," Don Fortgang said. "On condition that you do something I want you to do."

"What's that?" Colin Babington said.

"Put me up for membership in the City Club," Don Fortgang said.

26

The bathroom phone rang. Dave picked it up.

"Yes, Fanny?"

"Somebody finally answered at the Fortgang house."

"Who?"

"I don't think you've met this one," Fanny said.

"I met Don and Charlene and Don's father," Dave said. "Who did I miss?"

"There seems to be a son," Fanny said.

"That's right," Dave said. He could suddenly see the oil painting above the bar in the red-tiled sauna pagoda. "It must be Marvin. He's on MacArthur's staff in Tokyo. What's he doing here in Beechwood tonight?"

"Answering his parents' phone," Fanny said.

"Why aren't they answering it themselves?"

"Because according to the son his parents have gone to spend a long week end on some grouse shooter's estate in Aiken, South Carolina," Fanny said.

"I should have figured that," Dave said.

"Figured what?" Fanny said.

"Prop Jews do not come to meet new rabbis at parties given in Jewish Centers of the goy towns they service as prop Jews," Dave said. "Mr. and Mrs. Fortgang are in South Carolina like I am in the chair at the Congress of Vienna with Prince Metternich. They chickened out."

"You knew when you invited them, D.D., that the Fort-gangs do not want to be seen in public with a lot of Jews."

"What I didn't know is that leopard who can't change his spots," Dave said. "He's a world's-champion chameleon by comparison with the prop Jew who can't straighten up out of his cringe even for a celebration. To hell with the Fort-gangs."

"D.D., please calm down," Fanny said. "We've got to have a Fortgang at the party. Judge Elphinstone is coming. You know as well as I do His Honor is not showing up because he's dying to meet Rabbi Vogel. He met Vogel in court last month. Elphinstone is coming to see with his own eyes the man you said was vouching for you in this town. His Honor wants to see the act of vouching. So stop being angry and start thinking. There's not much time. The guests are beginning to arrive."

"Okay," Dave said. "I've got a nonangry idea."

"What?" Fanny said.

"Call Marvin Fortgang back," Dave said. "Ask him what he's doing tonight."

He put down the phone and went to the closet to choose a necktie. Dave was pulling the knot tight when the phone rang again.

"Guess what Marvin Fortgang is doing tonight," Fanny said.

"He's coming to our party," Dave said.

"He sounded pleased to be invited," Fanny said. "He asked if he could bring someone."

"He'd better," Dave said. "All the other chicks at this party are pregnant."

"Please hurry," Fanny said. "That Blumenfeld man? The one who owns the Beechwood Art Movie Theatre? Through the glass door I can see him pacing around outside, waiting. I'm not coming out until you come down, D.D., and stage a diversionary tactic."

Coming down in the elevator Dave tried to remember what he knew about Mort Blumenfeld. Then the elevator door opened, and Mort Blumenfeld vanished from Dave's mind. He had a moment of shock.

Dave had expected the noise. A couple of hundred people gathered in celebration, and doing it to the accompaniment of their own alcohol-brightened voices plus the rattle of ice cubes against glass, could not be expected to go unnoticed. What Dave had not expected was his reaction to the place where the celebration was being held.

Dave knew every inch of the arena in which the celebrants were making merry. He had planned it. He had supervised every piece as it went into place. He could have closed his eyes and walked without stumbling to any designated corner of the structure. He could have answered without thought any question about the multiplicity of functions for which he had planned and provided. Yet now that it was finished what he saw seemed as strange as a foreign city into which without briefing he had been forced to parachute.

A year of his life had burned away. For a dozen or more months he had been totally absorbed in fragments. Architects' drawings. Bulldozers digging. Cement pouring. Walls rising. Windows going into walls. Electricians laying wire. Decorators hanging draperies. Carpenters hammering down floors. Nurserymen putting in shrubs. Wood carvers cutting a ceiling. Plumbers installing fixtures.

He had bought every scrap of it. He had paid all of them. He had driven the materials and hounded the workmen in the direction of his fierce vision. He had seen it in his head in Germany. He had built it on the ground here in Beechwood. He was standing in the middle of his own creation. And yet inside his head, like an irritated metronome, the bewildered question beat back and forth: *Is this what I wanted?*

It was like that moment in a clothing store when the customer steps up to the triple mirrors and realizes for the first time in his life what he really looks like. Dave couldn't believe it.

For several long, long moments he remained motionless,

wondering what was wrong. The pieces he had so furiously assembled had come together into something he could absorb with his eyes. It did not seem enough. Something was missing. Something that was a part of what he had felt three years ago in Germany, when the vision had invaded his head and his heart. In the vision he had not been able to touch the as yet unbuilt temple, but he had been able to feel it. Now that he was able to touch it, Dave suddenly knew what was wrong. He could not feel it.

He felt instead the hands of Mort Blumenfeld dragging him out of the elevator.

"Listen, Mr. Dehn," Blumenfeld said. "I've just been talking to Rabbi Vogel."

"I hoped you two would meet," Dave said.

Across Mr. Blumenfeld's shoulder Dave sent a distress signal with his free hand toward the glass door through which he could see Fanny at her desk. She had the phone to her ear. As she talked into the instrument she signaled back to Dave: *In a minute!*

"Sure I met him," Mr. Blumenfeld said to Dave. "He's back there, in that big room, and a real sweetheart of a guy he is, too, I'm sure. He's got brains and a beautiful wife, which is a combo you can't beat, and I believe he's going to be a big addition to this community, but there's a problem."

"What's that?" Dave said.

Another signal to Fanny. Another frantically waved wordless reply: *One more sec!*

"When it comes to the silver screen as a medium for visual education," Mort Blumenfeld said, "your rabbi doesn't know from *bupkes.*"

"*My* rabbi?" Dave said. "I brought Peretz Vogel to Beechwood to be *our* rabbi."

"I'm ready to let him be," Mort Blumenfeld said. "But first the guy will have to wake up. He thinks like everybody. Movies to him they're Gable's Back and Garson's Got Him or Garbo Loves Taylor, that stuff. Sure it is. That's what keeps my theater full seven nights a week. But what about the days? I mean aside from the kids' matinees on Saturday afternoons? All the rest of the time, every day, my theater is closed. I pay the same taxes, the same janitor's wages, the same heating bills whether my theater is open or closed, so why shouldn't it be open?"

"You want me to help you open it," Dave said.

"Would I try to sell you a bill of goods to help me close it?" Mort Blumenfeld said. "This town, what's been wrong with it for years, where other people have brains the members of our Board of Selectmen have the stuff that's left over when out there in Chicago they finish packing a Swift's Premium Ham. The trouble with this town, I've said it for years, Beechwood will never get up off its ass and come into the twentieth century until we import a stiff dose of some good Jewish blood. So you come along and I say to my wife now we'll start going places. At last we got a Jewish head up there on Turkey Hill Road instead of all those onions. So I come to this party and I go to your rabbi a little while ago, over there in that other room, and I outline my plan for using the Government. Educational films you can get for free from every department in Washington, something most people don't know. I figure we lay out a program, let the rabbi do it. He picks the films, I provide the theater, and we charge the kids a minimum, just enough to cover my overhead, and what have you got?"

"What?" Dave said.

"The greatest step forward in education since the public schools gave up one teacher for all subjects and they started using departmental," Mort Blumenfeld said. "So I explain all this to your rabbi, just a few minutes ago over there in that big room with the pictures, and I'm I don't know how to say it, I'm flabbergasted, that's what. I'm talking to a Jew, a rabbi, someone with brains, and what do I get? The same fish eye I get from Father Boyle, and from that hammerhead Episcopalian we got in this one-horse town, the Very Reverend Hamish Flyte, to who, between you and me, Mr. Dehn, from brains he'll never die. What this plan of mine could do for the Jewish community, Mr. Dehn, I don't know how to tell you."

"I'm going to insist that you do," Dave said. "Fanny," he called as she came slinking out of her office. "Fanny, could I see you a minute?"

"Sure," she said, and came over.

"Will you set up a date for me to have a long talk with Mr. Blumenfeld? He's got some interesting ideas about education that I want to explore."

"Certainly, D.D.," Fanny said. "Right now, though, I think you'd better go in and say hello to Rabbi Vogel. He's talking to Judge Elphinstone. They've been asking for you."

"You mind running interference for me?" Dave said. He clapped the movie-theater proprietor on the back. "Nice talking to you, Mr. Blumenfeld. The bar is over that way, near the library."

"Please," Mr. Blumenfeld said. "To you it's Mort."

"We've got a date, Mort," Dave said. "There's another bar over this way, in the Small Crafts Room. Come on, Fanny."

"I can't," Fanny said. "I've got to stay here in the lobby and keep the traffic moving in the right direction. People keep wanting to go into the sanctuary. They think drinking martinis in front of the Torah is a fun thing. But wait. Marian!"

Dave turned to follow the thrust of Fanny's voice. Marian Singer had just come out of the kitchen area. She was carrying a large glass platter. She looked the way she always looked. As though she wished desperately she were somewhere else.

"You want me?" she called.

Fanny beckoned her with a crisp scooping wave of her hand and said, "Just for a second, Marian. Please."

Marian came toward them, her body bent forward, as though she were afraid if the edge of the platter touched her bright green dirndl she would explode.

"Honest, Fanny," she said.

For those who knew Sid's wife the petulance was scarcely noticeable. It was Marian Singer's normal speaking voice.

"Look how they've gone and sliced this sturgeon," she said.

An arm encased in crisp black decorated with two gold stripes came across Dave's shoulder and lifted a piece of sturgeon from the platter. Dave turned. The boy in naval uniform popped the sturgeon into his mouth and chewed vigorously.

"Mmm-mmm," he murmured. "Nothing wrong with this sturgeon, ma'am."

Marian Singer looked at the handsome young lieutenant as though he had said something in a foreign language. Was it a compliment? Could it be an insult? Had he made mock of her? How should she react? Dave saw the thin mustache of sweat beads appear on her upper lip.

"Marian," he said. "This is Lieutenant Marvin Fortgang. Am I right, Lieutenant?"

"Absolutely," the lieutenant said. "You must be Mr. Dehn."

"I am," Dave said. "And this is Mrs. Singer, my partner's wife."

"How do you do?" Marian said.

She took a nervous hop backward as Marvin Fortgang reached out for another slice of sturgeon.

"Pleased to meet you, ma'am," he said. "If I knew you were serving Barney Greengrass sturgeon I wouldn't have waited for an invitation. I'd have crashed."

Sharply, as though she were defending herself against an accusation, Marian said to Fanny, "Is it Barney Greengrass sturgeon?"

"Would we serve an officer of the U.S. Navy anything but the best?" Fanny said. The edge in her voice carried a footnote for Marian: *Stop acting silly and pull yourself together!* Fanny continued smoothly, "I'm Mr. Dehn's secretary, Fanny Mintz."

"Pleased to meet you, ma'am," the young man said.

"How did you know the sturgeon came from Barney Greengrass?" Dave said.

"My mother never serves anything else at her Sunday

brunches," Lieutenant Fortgang said. "She has it sent up from New York by pack mule. When she's not supplying her guests my mother has Barney Greengrass fly boxes of the stuff to me out in Tokyo. I never see much of it, though. Thanks to my mother Barney Greengrass sturgeon has replaced bourbon as the black-market favorite with General MacArthur's staff. I wangled a two-week pass home on condition that I bring a barracks bag full of it back to Tokyo. Another piece, ma'am?"

"What?" Marian Singer said.

"Just one more," Lieutenant Fortgang said. He took it from the platter and popped it into his mouth. "Thank you, Mrs. Singer."

"Marian," Fanny said, "could you take D.D. to Rabbi Vogel and Judge Elphinstone?"

"May I come along?" Lieutenant Fortgang said. "I understand His Honor wants to see a real live Fortgang rubbing elbows with the members of this *minyan*."

Dave gave the young man a quick glance. How did the kid know that?

"Marian!" Fanny said sharply.

Marian jerked up out of the dark place in her mind where her shapeless fears crawled about endlessly.

"Of course," she said, clearly relieved to escape from another of the totally meaningless dead ends of desperation in which she managed to trap herself regularly. "The rabbi and the judge are down at the end of the reception room, by the fireplace."

She wheeled sharply, like a cavalryman bringing his mount up on its hind legs for an abrupt change of course, and she hurried across the lobby.

"Better step on it," Fanny muttered to Dave. "She's wearing her running pants today."

Dave touched Fanny's shoulder, gave her a half wink, and took young Fortgang's arm.

"This way, Lieutenant."

The way was unexpectedly barred by a barrel of a man smoking a dollar cigar.

"Mr. Dehn," the man said, "I'm Ray Schnur, The Dress Box."

Business at The Dress Box was clearly booming. Men who smoked cigars that cost less than a dollar always tore off the paper band before they fired up.

"Glad to meet you," Dave said. They shook hands. "My people up here tell me you're treating them well."

"I'm treating them well?" Mr. Schnur said. "Look how they're treating me, the living dolls they should live to be a hundred and twenty, each and every one of them, God bless them."

The proprietor of The Dress Box patted the place on his belly where a bunghole would not have looked out of place.

"Since you came to Beechwood, Mr. Dehn, I've tripled the size of my maternity department. Keep them coming." Mr. Schnur's face contracted in a wicked wink. "The husbands, anyway."

"Dave!"

Marian Singer's desperate cry came soaring over the crowded entrance hall like an outflung handful of pebbles. She was standing in the reception-room doorway, dragged over in a crouch by the weight of the platter as though the slices of sturgeon had unexpectedly turned into ore samples.

"We better step on it," Lieutenant Fortgang said. "The lady looks desperate."

Dave took a firmer grip on the young man's arm. The end of the loafer's loop dangling from the shoulder of his tunic brushed Dave's knuckles.

"Here we go," he said, burrowing himself and Lieutenant Fortgang into the densely packed drinkers. "Where's your date?"

"In the can," the Lieutenant said.

"This way!" Marian shrieked.

By the time Dave and the lieutenant reached the entrance

to the reception room Marian was halfway into it, plowing her way toward the long oval table near the grand piano. On it sat two tall electric coffee urns, each one as big as the old milk cans that used to stand in front of Deutsch's grocery store on Westerlo Street. The urns stood guard over platters of corned beef and pastrami; towers of sliced rye bread; mounds of schnecken; bowls of green pickled tomatoes; jars of pickles, sweet and sour; pots of mustard; stacks of paper plates; clusters of forks; and piles of small white paper napkins imprinted in blue with the Star of David over the words "Beechwood Jewish Center."

"Now, that's what I call *eppes* but a layout."

Dave's body was tugged around toward the grating voice.

"Hello, Mr. Honig," Dave said. "Having a good time, I hope?"

"On my food who ever had any other kind of time?" said Harry Honig, the manager of Daitch Shopwell. "If you knew what that table does for me, just to look at it, Mr. Dehn, every penny you've spent up here on Turkey Hill Road you would consider it a *mitzvah*. For years I've been trying to get the people of this town to enjoy, to eat what's good, but with them it's boiled ham, it looks like wet Kleenex, and sliced white bread, it's like chewing gum without the spearmint flavor. Then you come along, and look."

Mr. Honig gestured toward the mounds of incipient gall bladder malfunction.

"I've got them eating civilized at last," he said. "We've just put in a deli department it's twice as long as our dry-cereals aisle already, and the new expanded bagels section alone is beginning to curl into our canned-soups area."

"Dave!"

Marian's voice was dangerously out of control.

"Let's go, Mr. Dehn," Lieutenant Fortgang said. "The sandbags on the levee are about to give way."

"She's all right," Dave said. "Crowds make her tense, that's all."

"Oh, Mr. Dehn!"

He turned. Amanda Vogel was signaling him toward the couple with whom she was standing under the large framed pictures of Chaim Weizmann and Harry Truman.

"You mind going it alone?" Dave said to Lieutenant Fortgang. "I'll catch up with you in a minute. I'd better say hello to our rabbi's wife."

"I wouldn't mind saying hello to her myself," the lieutenant said.

"After your date comes out of the can," Dave said.

He shoved the loafer's loop in the direction of Marian Singer and cut across to Amanda Vogel.

"You know Nan and Stanley Horowitz?" she said.

Dave put a forefinger to his temple, looked up at the ceiling in a burlesque of deep thought, and gave the sudden roaring in his chest a moment to settle down.

"Number Eight, Abraham Road," he said when his voice box was back in working order. "The ceramic tile in your rumpus room is buckling, and Mr. Palgrave swears the contractor will have his tile man there on Thursday to fix it. He will be there. Honest."

Nan Horowitz laughed. After a brief pause, during which he seemed to be considering whether he had anything more rewarding to do, Stanley joined her.

"You make us sound like a couple of *nudzhes*," Nan Horowitz said.

"You are, and you're entitled," Dave said. "You *nudzh*, we fix. I'd like you to meet Lieutenant Fortgang, but he seems to have headed back to Tokyo."

"No, I haven't," Lieutenant Fortgang said at Dave's elbow. "Mrs. Singer wouldn't allow me within striking distance of the sturgeon until I promised to come and get you."

"Related by any chance to the Fortgang Furniture Mart where we bought our love seat?" Nan Horowitz said.

"When I was in high school," Lieutenant Fortgang said, "I used to help out in the store on Saturdays, and when a customer proved to be in the market for a love seat it was my job to help try it on."

Through the laughter Dave tried to read Amanda Vogel's face. Nothing. Then he noticed she was wearing the shirt-waist dress with the red, black, and yellow stripes. She had been wearing it the day she first showed up at Beechwood. The same thing happened to Dave's chest.

"We're trying to find your handsome husband," he said. "Mrs. Singer is running interference, but we could use some hints."

"The rabbi?" Nan Horowitz said. "He's over there, by the fireplace. Talking to Judge Elphinstone. No, to the left. Just beyond Mrs. Marx? Her husband owns Beechwood Carpet?"

"In the dark brown dress?" Dave said.

"No, the beige," Nan Horowitz said. "With all that Mexican jewelry?"

"Oh, yes, I see him, thanks," Dave said. "Will you excuse us? The lieutenant and I have a message for the rabbi."

"Of course," Nan Horowitz said.

Her husband made not dissimilar sounds, but Dave did not catch the words. Moving with Lieutenant Fortgang away from Amanda Vogel toward her husband, Dave was watching her face. He could read nothing. She turned back into the conversation with the Horowitz couple. Dave's heart lurched with the pain.

"Where you been hiding?" Perry Vogel said.

"I feel like a salmon battling my way upstream to spawn," Dave said. "May I present Lieutenant Fortgang?"

"A pleasure," Perry Vogel said, taking the young man's hand. "This is Judge Elphinstone."

"We met a few weeks ago," His Honor said. "At a distance, of course."

"I'm delighted to get closer," Dave said. He shook hands with Elphinstone. "Lieutenant Fortgang is stationed in To-kyo. He's on General MacArthur's staff."

"John Hay wrote a remarkable series of letters to Henry

Adams from Tokyo," Judge Elphinstone said. "Have you ever read them?"

"I'm afraid not," Lieutenant Fortgang said. "We don't get much time for reading in Tokyo."

"The geisha girls, no doubt," Judge Elphinstone said with a manly chuckle.

"They're an improvement over the printed page, sir," Lieutenant Fortgang said.

"Not all printed pages," Perry Vogel said. "I can show you a few paragraphs in the Song of Solomon that are just waiting to get themselves banned in Boston. Dave, where are you going?"

"Remembered something I left in my office," Dave said across his shoulder. "If Your Honor will excuse me, I'll be right back."

He kept moving, through the crowded room, acknowledging with waves of his hand greetings only half heard. He came out into the foyer. Fanny was at the front door greeting Floyd Klenczewski. Her back was turned. It would not be turned for long. Floyd was a peripatetic type. There was no time to wait for the elevator. Dave cut swiftly across the foyer toward the men's room. At the far side, beyond the urinals, there was a door that opened into the kitchen area and the back stairs. These provided a quick short cut to Dave's apartment upstairs. Moving with his head averted to avoid being caught by Fanny's glance, he was caught by something else: a soft glow of colored lights up ahead.

Dave's mind, riveted on where he was heading, was jolted from its destination. His feet stopped moving. He didn't want them to, but they did. Immediately he grasped why. What had stopped him was a memory. Dave turned and moved toward it.

A long high tunnel. Not very clearly defined. A bit fuzzy at the edges. Waiting for him with a promise. A promise it had never failed to keep.

What was it doing here in Beechwood? On the night of

this party? When he had ordered the sanctuary doors kept shut? Because he did not want drunks making comments on what he had so carefully built.

When he reached the sanctuary doors Dave saw that he could stop worrying. There would be no drunken comments. The memory was brighter than the reality. The sanctuary doors were not really open. They had apparently blown or been pulled apart a couple of inches.

Dave started to push the doors shut. Then his hands stopped moving. The way his feet had stopped carrying him across the foyer. Dave peered through the narrow gap between the tall hand-carved doors. It was like looking back down a long tunnel to something he had not seen for many years. The synagogue on Westerlo Street.

Dave was seeing it now not because of what he had built. The builders of the synagogue on Westerlo Street could not have afforded what Dave Dehn had put together on Turkey Hill Road. But they had possessed something for which money was not needed. Something that brought the memory of long ago forward to meet the reality of today.

"Mr. Fortgang," Dave said.

The little old man did not move. Dave pulled the doors wider. He stepped through quickly. He pulled the doors shut behind him.

"Mr. Fortgang," he said again.

The little old man in the brown zipper jacket turned.

"I was just coming to find you," he said.

Dave made an effort. He dragged his mind back to the moment.

"What are you doing here?" Dave said.

"My grandson Marvin he brought me," the little old man said.

The bodiless statement had no weight. It hovered aimlessly, then settled into a recognizable framework.

"Oh," Dave said. "You're Marvin's date."

"His grandfather I know I am," Mr. Fortgang said. "His what you're now calling me?"

"When we invited Marvin to this party he said he'd like to bring someone," Dave said. "I didn't know he meant you."

"Neither did Marvin," the old man said.

He held up what looked like a paper towel. It must have come from the washroom at the other side of the foyer. The old man patted it across his knuckles.

"I always do what it says," he said.

"I don't understand," Dave said.

The statement, he realized, suddenly applied to his whole life. His existence had unexpectedly taken him by surprise.

"Out there," the old man said. He gestured toward the sanctuary doors behind David. "The other side the hall. In the toilet. The box with the paper towels. On the box it says pat, don't wipe, so me, I pat."

He patted the paper towel more vigorously across his knuckles.

"Well," Dave said, "I'd better be getting on."

"Where?" the old man said.

Dave tried to concentrate. What was he doing here in the sanctuary with Don Fortgang's father?

"I mean I was on my way to see somebody," Dave said.

"And me," the little old man said, "I was on my way to see you."

"About what?" Dave said.

"The behstits," the old man said. "They're doing something. My son won't tell me. He's afraid, like he's afraid all his life, but his father, me, I'm not afraid."

"Tell me," Dave said.

"Last month my son goes to have lunch with Colin Babington in the City Club," the old man said. "Can you imagine such a thing?"

"Not easily," Dave said.

"Sixty-one years he's old my son," Mr. Fortgang said. "Sixty-one years he knows this Colin Babington like he knows his own father. And for sixty-one years not once my son he's asked by his friend to put even half a foot in this place the City Club it's only for goyim God forbid a Jew should step inside. So one day, all of a sudden, he's asked to put in not only a foot, my son, one day my son he's asked to bring along also his stomach and come have there with Colin Babington the anti-Semite to come have lunch. This is something even a dumbbell he'd know right away it means something."

"What does it mean?" Dave said.

"It means the anti-Semites here, from top to bottom, starting with Colin Babington, I knew his father, he should rest in peace, a nice man, a gentleman, not like this *momzer* his son, they're making a scheme to throw you and the synagogue out of Beechwood."

Mr. Fortgang crumpled the paper towel and threw it on the sanctuary floor.

"Like that they're going to throw you out," he said.

"They've been trying to throw me out since I arrived," Dave said. "I'm not afraid of them."

"Now you better be," the old man said. "That's why I told my grandson Marvin, I said Marvin, your mother and father they're ashamed in front of their goyishe friends to go to a party in the Jewish Center for the new rabbi, but I'm not afraid. Marvin, I said, you take me to that party. I have to tell Mr. Dehn what the behstits they're doing."

Dave's heart was dragging him out of the sanctuary, but his head kept his feet anchored to the beautifully laid oak floor.

"I'm listening, Mr. Fortgang," he said.

"You got a wife," the old man said. "The *shikseh*. Her grandfather he left her all this land up here on Turkey Hill Road. This Colin Babington and his friends, the behstits, they made her a bargain. The land it's in her name. They'll pay everything for the lawyers, the behstits, they'll pay every penny to fight you in the courts. When she gets the land back, this Colin Babington and his friends, they'll buy it from her for a lot of money. A big price. She'll be rich, and you'll be out on your *tuchis*. That's what Colin Babington, the behstit, that's what he invited my son to lunch in the City Club to tell him."

"How does your son figure in this?" Dave said.

"My son his orders they are he goes to this Judge Elphinstone," the old man said. "His job it's to tell the judge he doesn't know you, he's not responsible for what you're doing here, the judge no matter what happens in the court with your wife and you, the judge he should know the Fortgang name it's not behind you. So when it comes in court the trial for your wife to get back her land from you, the judge he should know you're a liar you told him my son Donald Fortgang he's your friend here in Beechwood."

"How do you figure in this?" Dave said.

"Before it belonged to my son," the old man said, "the Fortgang name it belonged to me. It still belongs to me. I gave it to you in my house in front of my son. So my name belongs to you too. What happens in the court between you and your wife over the land, this I don't care. That's what I came here to tell Judge Elphinstone. In Beechwood here the name Fortgang it means something. And you have the Fortgang name to stand on."

Dave had something else. The knowledge came slowly, like a bubble surfacing through an oil slick. Something Dave had acquired during the innocent years on Westerlo Street, something he had lost on a savage afternoon in Germany. He looked at the little old man in the brown leather windbreaker. Mr. Fortgang was staring up at the sanctuary ceiling.

"All my life," the little old man said. "All the years I live here in Beechwood," he said. "Since Ellis Island sixty-three years," he said, "a *shul* like this, this is my dream."

Dave looked around with a feeling of surprised discovery. As though a suit for which he had suffered through many fittings had suddenly, now that all the basting stitches were removed, come to life for him in front of the tailor's triple mirror. He could see things he had not seen while the suit was being worked on.

Dave could see a boy of eight. Maybe nine. A boy whose mother had died in childbirth. A boy who had known only one parent: his father. A man who had made the long Saturday of every week a time of wonder and grace for the boy. Morning prayers in the synagogue. Home for the ritual meal that never varied and never failed to be more than the consumption of food. The silence during which the boy's father rested on the leather couch in the front room and the boy's mind ranged into areas that made his breath come in small gasps of awe. Then back to the place where the wonder was rooted. And after the synagogue, in the evening, the long, leisurely *meises*. The stories that were a part of Saturday, the way the synagogue was a part of Saturday, and Saturday was the part of life that mattered.

"Up there," Mr. Fortgang said. "The pictures."

The little old man gestured toward the stained-glass windows. They had come out of something inside Dave's head about which he had felt strongly but which he had remembered only vaguely. Mike Palgrave had provided the sharp outlines. With the help of a glass merchant in New York who dealt regularly with a firm in Venice. The panes of glass had been set in a long, sweeping semicircle, immediately below the molding of the hand-carved ceiling, at the western end of the sanctuary.

"To catch the early-evening light," Mike had said.

The multicolored glass panes were catching it now. Bringing into the high, domed room the soft golden glow that through the partially open doors had caught Dave's glance when a few minutes ago he was hurrying across the foyer.

"They were made in Italy," Dave said. "It's the story from the beginning. Over there, that one, that's Abraham. And then next—"

"I know," Mr. Fortgang said. "But that one, there."

The little old man pointed up toward the window at the bend of the semicircle.

"That's David," Dave Dehn said. "When he first came into the tent of King Saul carrying his harp."

The little old man studied the stained-glass window with a concentration that brought to his forehead knotty little ridges, like the old tin washboard on which Dave's father used to launder his sabbath shirt on Westerlo Street.

"That's you," Mr. Fortgang said finally. "I mean your name. David. No?"

"Yes," Dave said.

"So your father," the little old man said. "His name it must have been Saul."

"Yes," Dave said.

Without surprise. The words the little old man uttered seemed as inevitable as the signs on the walls of subway stations. He turned to face Dave.

"To have a son like you," Mr. Fortgang said. "To see a son build a *shul* like this," he said. "It's not right a man should not live to see it."

Surprised, Dave said, "How did you know my father is dead?"

Inside the brown leather windbreaker the small, thin shoulders moved in a shrug of inevitability.

"If he was alive," Mr. Fortgang said, "he would be standing here now."

Dave looked up into the early-evening light. The stained-glass king, facing the stained-glass boy with the harp, suddenly both seemed very much alive. Dave wanted to say something, but he couldn't get the words out. Then he heard them.

"Shmah Yisroel."

Dave turned. The little old man had mounted the three steps to the lectern. He stood at the slanted reading table, looking up at the ark. A couple of moments went by before Dave realized that out of the small, almost shrunken figure in the brown leather zipper jacket a musical sound was soaring up in a long, wailing chant, climbing toward the stained-glass windows.

Then, from behind him, Dave heard a long, wailing reply. He turned.

The sanctuary doors he had pulled shut behind him were now wide open. The guests were moving in slowly. They seemed confused. Hastily, as they crossed into the high, vaulted room, they stopped and set their cocktail glasses on the floor. Then Dave realized the long, wailing reply had not come from the people at the rear of the sanctuary. The sound Dave was hearing came out of a memory. It was inside his head. A memory of the synagogue on Westerlo Street in Albany. The memory was making of the people at the rear of the sanctuary an unwitting chorus. Like spectators in the bleachers of a ball park inadvertently joining in the national anthem as the visiting opera star sang it into the microphone behind home plate. This bothered Dave.

Before he could think his way more deeply into the puzzling worry, the little old man at the lectern took the sound of the chorus inside Dave's head as though it were a smear of paint on a palette and he wove it into a series of musical phrases. They made Dave's breath do what it used to do in the synagogue on Westerlo Street. He could feel his chest begin to pulse in and out in small gasps of awe.

The guests crowding into the sanctuary seemed to respond. Silently, without sound or movement, they seemed to soar, as though trying to reach something Dave could not see. But he could feel it. Feeling it made him turn again. Who was making this magic? This agonizing feeling by which he had been enthralled long ago, when he was a boy on Westerlo Street, and was now feeling again?

Astonished, he saw the mass of silent faces at the back of the sanctuary separate into individual outlines. They came out of the crowd. One by one they became the faces of human beings. Dave recognized them, but he was unable to credit the recognition.

Was this Mort Blumenfeld? The slob who a half hour earlier had been driving Dave nuts with his cheap efforts to promote the underwriting of his Beechwood Art Movie Theatre's overhead? Ray Schnur, the barrel-bellied owner of The Dress Box, gleefully smoking dollar cigars because the wives

Dave had brought to Beechwood were constantly pregnant and buying maternity clothes like crazy? Harry Honig, busily extending the Daitch Shopwell deli counter into the dry-cereals aisle? Larry Marx, licking his lips over the zooming sales of Beechwood Carpeting, Inc.?

Was it? Were they?

They were.

Dave could see the faces. He could hear the voices he had first heard in the synagogue on Westerlo Street. And Dave could feel the transformation. It was impossible not to. It was happening inside himself.

Dave turned back to Mr. Fortgang. The little old man in the brown zipper jacket was still chanting. Sending the eerily moving words up toward the boy in the stained-glass window carrying the harp into the tent of the king. The evening light poured down through the tent of the king on Mr. Fortgang, on Dave Dehn, on Mort Blumenfeld and Ray Schnur and Harry Honig and Larry Marx. Carrying them in its glow far away from Beechwood, to a place Dave could not see.

A place he could only feel.

An invisible, shining place, where nothing bad happened. Where nobody had to worry about the overhead of the Beechwood Art Movie Theatre. Or the markup on maternity dresses. Or the cost of pastrami. Or how to pay back a memory of joy on a street in Albany. Where savages functioned cheek by jowl with men whose way of life had been learned in the temple of Solomon.

There was something in the voices singing to him across the years that caused the small hairs on the side of Dave's jaw to tingle. The feeling he had not known since Westerlo Street swept through him.

The temple—building it, putting the pieces together, getting the job done—the daily drive had kept him going. Now he was suddenly aware of something more. The way Mort Blumenfeld and Ray Schnur were aware.

Dave turned back to Mr. Fortgang. The eyes of the little old man in the brown leather jacket were closed. As he sent his chanting voice up to the young David and the old king in the stained-glass window, the little old man swayed gently back and forth, like a child on a rocking horse.

The great, high room, the room with the hand-carved ceiling and the stained-glass windows, the room that had been for a year to Mike Palgrave a technical problem, to Sid Singer a fiscal headache, to Dave Dehn a passion he had not taken the time to understand, that room was suddenly more than a room. It was a single, orchestrated mass of sound and feeling that made the heart swell.

The swelling hurt.

Dave Dehn's throat grew tight. Slowly, his feet moving to the rhythm of the sound, his not-quite-focused eyes fixed on the boy with the harp in the tent of the king, Dave moved away from the pain.

Out in the foyer, he gently pulled shut the sanctuary doors. He waited a moment or two, motionless, sorting out the wonder of what had happened. It was the first time in his life that he had been trapped by something he had himself created.

Then Dave Dehn turned and moved out of glory into reality.

Pushing his way through the swinging door of the foyer washroom, he was assaulted abruptly by the certainty that in similar fashion, when he came out of the sanctuary, Ray Schnur would push his way into the office of The Dress Box on Main Street.

Dave moved across the washroom. Through the swinging door at the far end he punched his way out into the kitchen area. Somebody called to him from the big electric range at the deep end. Dave kept right on going, out into the service area. He dragged open the heavy iron fire door to the back stairs. He took the steps two at a time.

When he came into his living room she was standing at the window, looking out at the Sound. She turned, and Dave saw she had been crying. He crossed the room in four long strides, like a diver striding out to the end of the board for take-off, and he took her in his arms.

"What am I going to do?" she sobbed. "I didn't count on this. I didn't suspect I would fall in love. I don't know how it happened. What am I going to do?"

He didn't know. He had set out to hire a rabbi. It had not occurred to him that the act would change his life. He did not know how to handle it. He had never before been in love. So he just held her close. She was so thin it made his heart ache. It was like holding a child. After a few moments it got better. For him, anyway. Maybe for her too. He hoped so. She stopped crying. Then she stopped shaking.

They both turned toward the small sound of the opening door. Sid Singer came in.

"Mrs. Vogel," he said quietly. He held the door open. "I think you'd better go downstairs now."

She went without a word.

"Okay," Dave said. "I know what you're going to say."

"The hell you do," Sid said. "I just took a call from the New Rochelle police. Bella and Tony D'Alessandro were killed twenty minutes ago. A six-car pile-up on the Hutchinson. He was taking her home from the hospital. She gave birth to a girl there, four days ago."

"Was the kid in the car?"

"No, it's a preemie," Sid said. "The baby's still in an incubator in the hospital."

"I better get over there," Dave said.

"There's nothing you can do," Sid said. "She's dead."

"The baby isn't," Dave said.

He went to the closet and pulled out a coat. Sid came around in front of him.

"You can't go now," he said. "Everybody downstairs is waiting for you. You've got a speech to make."

"You make it," Dave said. "I'm going to the hospital."

"Dave, for God's sake, will you listen?" Sid said. "This is the best break you've had since we got to Beechwood. She died intestate. You're her husband. You're the next of kin. The title to the land is now legally in your name. You're out from under. You've got nothing to worry about any more. The Colin Babingtons of this town are off your back."

Dave's shove sent Sid skidding halfway across the room. He banged to a stop against the *Britannica*.

"You listen," Dave said. He could feel his voice begin to shred. "That kid in the incubator," Dave Dehn managed to say. "You stupid son of a bitch," he said. "She's my daughter."

27

The trouble with being a newspaperman in Beechwood, Oliver Stehli had found, was that the only stories worth printing were not the ones you ran into, but the ones that ran into you.

"Frankly, Mr. Dehn," he said, "I did not dig up this story. It dug me up."

"How?" Mr. Dehn said.

"There's a girl works in the admissions office of the New Rochelle Hospital," Stehli said. "Before the war she was what *Time* magazine would call my Great and Good Friend. That's all over now. We're both married to different people now, but we're still friends. Not so Great, you understand, but still pretty Good. When she runs into something she thinks is unusual she calls me. Last night, when the stories about your wife's death broke in the New York papers, my friend called me. Oh, say, Patsy!"

She came waddling over.

"Another round, Mr. Stehli?"

"Please," Oliver Stehli said.

Patsy pumped her massive buttocks toward the kitchen.

"By the way," Stehli said, "you don't mind my asking you to meet me here, do you?"

"Why should I?" Mr. Dehn said.

"Good," Stehli said. "I thought it would be less conspicuous than the Steak Pit or one of those other places on Main Street."

"Conspicuous for you?" Mr. Dehn said. "Or conspicuous for me?"

Oliver Stehli examined the man across the table. He had seen Mr. Dehn on the street a few times during the year and a half since the Biaggi property had changed hands. This, however, was the first time they had met.

Stehli knew all the external facts about Mr. Dehn. More accurately, he knew all the external facts that most people in Beechwood knew. Everything else Stehli knew about Mr. Dehn had come from Colin Babington. Oliver Stehli had learned long ago to take the opinions of his fellow member of the Board of Selectmen with a grain of salt. Rough translation of a grain of salt: the baskets in which Colin at the moment had placed some of his financial eggs.

Thus, when Babington had first mentioned Mr. Dehn to Oliver Stehli he had referred to the New Yorker as one of these snotty kikes. So Stehli knew one of Colin Babington's financial schemes had run into a snag for which he felt Mr. Dehn had been in some way responsible. One day, at their weekly lunch in the City Club, Colin had taken a third martini. For no reason that Oliver Stehli felt had flowed out of their preceding conversation, Colin had remarked that perhaps he'd been wrong about Mr. Dehn. He wasn't one of these pushy Jew boys. When you got to know Mr. Dehn he was actually a rather pleasant chap.

Oliver Stehli did not feel he had got to know Mr. Dehn. Not yet, anyway. They had been facing each other across Patsy's corner table only for the duration of one shot of Old Grand-Dad, slowly sipped. So Mr. Dehn might or might not prove to be a rather pleasant chap. From the shift in Colin Babington's opinion, however, Oliver Stehli knew that the snag in Colin's financial scheme, whatever it was, had disappeared. What had not disappeared was what Oliver Stehli knew the moment Mr. Dehn walked into the diner: the chip on the tall young man's shoulder was considerably larger than a chip.

"Conspicuous for both of us," Stehli said. "There are more Jews in Beechwood today than we ever had in all our history, thanks to you, but it's still an occasion for comment when an Old Settler lunches with a Jew in public. I didn't think either one of us wanted any comment about our meeting. Not yet, anyway. How's that?"

"Fair enough," Mr. Dehn said.

"I don't run the *Bugle* as a scandal sheet," Oliver Stehli said. "Partly because I don't like that sort of thing, but mainly because there's no money in it. Not in a town the size of Beechwood. There aren't enough toes around so a local paper can afford to step on any. Down in New York, if Winchell or one of those boys steps on a toe, there's maybe a threat of a libel suit, but rarely more than that. Up here in Beechwood, if I step on a toe, I get a subscription cancelled, and conceivably lose some advertising. A small-town newspaper publisher is like that princess who could feel a pea through seven mattresses. Every subscription, every ad, they're the peas I sleep on, Mr. Dehn."

"You look pretty well rested," Mr. Dehn said.

Oliver Stehli chuckled. He had come to know a few Jews in the Navy. They had been for him a pleasant surprise. Laughs were rare at meetings of the Beechwood Board of Selectmen. It occurred to him that Mr. Dehn might be worth cultivating.

"Don't be fooled by a sort of basic somnolence," Oliver Stehli said. "Low basal metabolism is endemic in the Stehli family. That's what brought me back to Beechwood after I got out of the Navy. It made me weary just to think of going back to Young and Rubicam. Not after what I'd seen."

"E.T.O.?" Dave said. "Or the Pacific?"

"I was in whichever one of those theaters they gave away free tickets to Iwo Jima," Oliver Stehli said. "It all became a great big blur to me, and I prefer to keep it that way. My father was a very nice man and he was very decent about it. With an Old World courtesy his son will never emulate, he had the decency and tact to die on the day MacArthur picked up all those Japanese autographs on the deck of the battleship *Missouri,* and he left all the Beechwood *Bugle* stock to me. I decided not to sell it. Instead, I stepped into what seems to have become a classic American postwar comedy role. The Madison Avenue Advertising Fireball Who Chucks It All to Become a Small-Town Newspaper Publisher."

"The role seems to agree with you," Mr. Dehn said.

"Anything you have to do only once a week is bound to leave very few wrinkles," Stehli said. "If the *Bugle* were a daily paper I wouldn't be able to hold up publication of a story to have this exploratory lunch with you before I decide whether or not I'm going to run it. I'd just have to rush it into print as is."

"If you had to print this story without this lunch," Mr. Dehn said, "what would come out in the *Bugle?*"

"I'll give you the facts I have to work with," Oliver Stehli said. "You be the judge."

Patsy arrived with the fresh drinks, set them down, and carried away the empty glasses. Oliver Stehli took a sip and said:

"Mrs. David Dehn, wife of a wealthy Beechwood real estate developer, gives birth to a baby girl in New Rochelle Hospital. Four days later, on their way home from the hospital, Mr. and Mrs. Dehn are killed in an automobile accident on the Hutchinson River Parkway. Except that the man who gets killed in the crash with Mrs. Dehn turns out to be not her husband. The dead man who checked her out of New Rochelle and was driving her home proves to be Anthony X. D'Alessandro, a well-known Beechwood building contractor. Mr. D'Alessandro and Mrs. Dehn were classmates at Beechwood High School, and for a long time before she married Mr. Dehn in 1946, Mrs. Dehn and Tony D'Alessandro were Great and Good Friends. Mr. Dehn could not be reached for comment, but his secretary at the Beechwood Jewish Center, where Mr. Dehn makes his home, said Mr. Dehn had been scheduled to make an important speech yesterday, so he could not go to the hospital, and he asked Mr. D'Alessandro, a family friend, to pick up Mrs. Dehn."

Oliver Stehli took a sip from his glass.

"Let's say you own the Beechwood *Bugle*," he said. "Would you print that story as is?"

"I would," Mr. Dehn said.

"Even if you knew Mr. and Mrs. Dehn had not been living together for many months?" Oliver Stehli said. "Even if you knew Mr. Dehn has been spending his time between his apartment in New York and his private suite in the Beechwood Jewish Center? Even if you knew Mrs. Dehn has been making her home at the Israel Putnam Motor Inn on the Post Road? Even if you knew Anthony X. D'Alessandro has been a daily visitor there, and her constant companion? Even if you knew that five days ago when Mrs. Dehn checked into New Rochelle Hospital she was accompanied not by her husband but by the deceased Mr. D'Alessandro?"

Oliver Stehli paused and took another sip. This one lowered the level of Old Grand-Dad in his glass to the tops of the almost completely melted ice cubes.

"Yes," Mr. Dehn said. "I would still print the story as you reported it before you got started on the *even ifs*."

"Why?" Oliver Stehli said.

"Because the Beechwood *Bugle* is not a scandal sheet," Mr. Dehn said. "And because I know that if I put the *even ifs* into the story I would lose not only Mr. Dehn's subscription but also the subscriptions of every one of the almost two hundred families now living on the old Biaggi property."

Oliver Stehli pursed his lips and stared at his glass through narrowed lids. It was as though he wanted the glass to know he was annoyed with it for allowing itself to be empty at this crucial moment.

"Mr. Dehn has that much power over the people living on the old Biaggi property?" Stehli said.

"He has, and their subscriptions are not the only things the Beechwood *Bugle* would lose," Mr. Dehn said. "The paper would also lose the considerable amount of institutional advertising the Beechwood Jewish Center has decided to start placing in the *Bugle*."

"When was this decision about the advertising made?" Oliver Stehli said.

"About ten seconds ago," Mr. Dehn said.

Patsy appeared with two more drinks.

"I didn't want to interrupt you by asking," she said. "It sounded like you were both going good so I thought you could use some fresh lubrication. If I'm wrong don't feel obligated. I'll drink them myself."

"If you do," Oliver Stehli said, "I'll put a nasty editorial in the *Bugle* about the excessive number of Board of Health violations tolerated by the slovenly owner of this eyesore."

"Don't be mean to your old friends," Patsy said. "This round is on the house."

After she went away Oliver Stehli played for a while with the Phi Beta Kappa key on his watch chain.

"I think the owner of the *Bugle* would be wise to print the story without the *even ifs*," he said finally. "Don't you?"

"He would be very wise," Mr. Dehn said.

"Would he be unwise if he asked for something in exchange?" Oliver Stehli said.

"Not for asking," Mr. Dehn said. "The owner of the *Bugle* is dealing with a sophisticated man. Generous. Outgoing. Wise in the ways of the world. Tolerant about people's foibles. Always on the alert for ways to improve his capacities for helping his fellow man."

"Then the owner of the *Bugle* will forge ahead," Oliver Stehli said. "Ready?"

"Ready," Dave said.

"I assume, Mr. Dehn, that you share with most businessmen the not unreasonable desire to make a profit from the ventures in which you invest your money."

"I've never lost money on an investment," Mr. Dehn said. "It would be a big disappointment to me to start now."

"What you've been doing up here in Beechwood has

caused a good deal of talk in business circles," Oliver Stehli said. "I hear as much of that talk as most people, perhaps more than many. It seems pretty clear that what you have already invested in this town could be described as a tidy sum?"

"Or a great big bundle," Mr. Dehn said.

"I think it would be very good for Beechwood, and therefore very good for the *Bugle*," Oliver Stehli said, "If you made a big fat profit on your great big bundle."

"You've taken the words out of my mouth," Mr. Dehn said.

"Now I would like you to take a few out of mine," Oliver Stehli said. "If it won't make you angry?"

"The last time I was angry was when the referee out in Chicago made Dempsey wait out that long count against Tunney," Mr. Dehn said.

"I'm going to give you some advice," Oliver Stehli said. "Advice that I think will help make your venture here in Beechwood a really big financial success."

"That kind of advice," Mr. Dehn said, "I always welcome."

"Okay, then," Oliver Stehli said. "I'll start by putting it in six words."

"And they are?" Mr. Dehn said.

"Stop being so God-damn Jewish," Oliver Stehli said.

"Are you suggesting plastic surgery?" Mr. Dehn said. "To restore what they took away at my circumcision?"

"Only if you're planning to add a nudist camp to your compound on Turkey Hill Road," Oliver Stehli said.

"I'm not," Mr. Dehn said. "I am susceptible to the common cold in some rather uncommon places."

"Good," Oliver Stehli said. "After Columbus Day this is a tough town to walk around naked in. It's also a town that I think you have misjudged."

"About what?" Mr. Dehn said.

"Beechwood's attitude toward Jews," Oliver Stehli said. "I've seen many examples of that piece of lumber known as a chip on the shoulder. You're the first man I've ever seen come into a town with a giant redwood balanced on his clavicle. It's true there never have been many Jews in Beechwood. It's true, until you came along, selling property to Jews has not been one of the town's more popular activities. It would seem to be true, therefore, that this is an anti-Semitic community."

"Isn't it?" Mr. Dehn said.

"Not at all," Oliver Stehli said. "What Beechwood is, it's a place where almost nobody knows anything about Jews except by hearsay. And what you learn by hearsay is always a bunch of clichés. I think I'm fairly typical. Except for Don Fortgang, I never really knew any Jews until I got into the Navy. I knew the shopkeepers on Main Street. I sat in the same classrooms with a few at Yale. That sort of thing. But until the war I never knew any Jews socially. The Jews I met in uniform were a pleasant surprise to me. I think you'll get further in this town, Mr. Dehn, if you allow yourself to be a pleasant surprise to the people of Beechwood."

"How do I do that?" Mr. Dehn said.

Oliver Stehli was disappointed. He had expected Mr. Dehn to be more than icily polite.

"Come out from behind your wall," Oliver Stehli said. "Invite a few Gentiles in. I don't mean for cocktails or a cookout or a poker party. I mean invite them in to live. That's pretty desirable property you've got over there on Turkey Hill Road. I happen to know the terms under which you've been selling pieces of it to Jewish vets. Sell a few pieces on the same terms to a few Gentile vets and you'll be astonished by the results."

"Anything else?" Mr. Dehn said.

Oliver Stehli had to admire the rudeness. It didn't show. It merely hit.

"Yes," Oliver Stehli said. "Do something for the town. I mean in addition to spending your money in our shops and introducing us to pastrami and corned beef and paying your taxes. Do something non-Jewish."

"Like convert to Catholicism?" Mr. Dehn said.

"No," Oliver Stehli said. He was grateful for the third Old Grand-Dad. "Like this drug-rehabilitation project you've started. Judge Elphinstone tells me you're expanding it to include the whole town. I applaud that. But I need hardly tell you it's not a Jewish problem exclusively. Yet that's the way you're handling it. You won't lose anything if you invite Father Boyle and the Very Episcopalian Very Reverend Very Touchy Dr. Hamish Flyte to join your board. Everybody likes a little credit."

"Then why don't they work for it?" Mr. Dehn said. "Why haven't they done anything about the drug problem up to now? Everybody knows it exists. The two cases that surfaced on Turkey Hill Road are not the first in town. You know that. Father Boyle and Dr. Flyte know that. They expect the Jews to put up the money and do the work. Then they send emissaries asking the Jews to tug their forelocks while they hand over the credit. That's a pretty tall order you're asking a Jew to fill."

"Not a Jew with imagination," Oliver Stehli said.

"Imagination?" Mr. Dehn said. "What's that?"

"What you just used in conning me into printing the story of your wife's death the way you want it printed," Oliver Stehli said. "I think it's known as *chutzpah*."

Mr. Dehn's cold face cracked. He grinned. Oliver Stehli felt better. He hated to misjudge people.

"Anything else?" Mr. Dehn said pleasantly.

"Two things," Oliver Stehli said.

"I'm listening," Mr. Dehn said.

"We have a long-standing custom in this town," Stehli said. "Our citizens have always abided by it. They still do. It would be a good thing for your investment, Mr. Dehn, if you as a new citizen followed their example."

"What custom is that?" Mr. Dehn said.

"When our homes are vandalized," Stehli said, "we appeal to our police force for redress. We do not dynamite the property of suspected culprits."

"The Jews of Germany tried calling the cops," Mr. Dehn said. "They ended up in Buchenwald. What's your second thing?"

287

"Beechwood's feeling about our past," Stehli said. "We're proud of it. From Lord Howe spending the night at the home of Aaron Coker two centuries ago to the Biaggi family growing onions on Turkey Hill Road for the better part of a more recent century."

"Beechwood is proud of the Biaggi family?" Dave said.

"Very," Oliver Stehli said.

"Then why did you try to tax the last surviving member of the Biaggi family out of existence?" Dave said.

"You say you are a sophisticated man," Stehli said. "You tell me you are quote wise in the ways of the world unquote. Surely as such a man you are aware of the difference between greed and tradition?"

"Not as aware as you seem to be," Mr. Dehn said.

"That property on Turkey Hill Road is extremely valuable," Stehli said. "Any red-blooded American with a healthy interest in the great American passion for acquiring money would lust after it. On the other hand, tradition is tax-free. That's why all Americans are so passionately devoted to it. Beechwood is no exception. Any ethnic group that threatens this passion will never become a part of Beechwood. I think you know the ethnic group I have in mind."

"I can guess," Mr. Dehn said.

"I ask you to stop guessing," Stehli said. "I ask you to listen."

"I'm listening," Mr. Dehn said.

"We here in Beechwood tried to tax Bella Biaggi out of existence, true," Oliver Stehli said. "Being human, however, for that greediness we find it in our hearts to forgive ourselves. But you are trying to erase the Biaggi name from what some Beechwood citizens think of as our glorious history. For that we cannot forgive you."

"Why not?" Dave said.

"It's what's known as taking over," Stehli said. "It's identified as pushing your way in and crowding us out. People think of it as coming into a community and making room for yourselves by shoving out what has existed there for a long time. Beechwood has always had room not only for founders like Aaron Coker but also for newcomers like the Biaggis and men like Don Fortgang's father. We're proud of that. Now you come along with a large flock of Jews and you jostle us into hostility by trying to erase the Biaggi name from our past, destroying a piece of our tradition that is admittedly distorted but is nonetheless precious to us perhaps because of its distortion. People don't like to be reminded that they're bastards. There's no need for you to do it. You can get what you want without getting our backs up. If you continue the way you're going you'll find in the end that your investment, instead of showing a profit, is dwindling away."

"What do you recommend?" Mr. Dehn said.

"Don't jostle our recollections of how we like to think we were," Stehli said. "Don't act like a threat. Act the way Don Fortgang's father acted when he came here sixty-odd years ago. Act like a beneficent settler, not a hostile replacement."

"How can I do that?" Mr. Dehn said.

"The center of your development down there." Oliver Stehli nodded toward the Post Road. "That thing that looks like someone started to put up a replica of the Statue of Liberty, then got tipped off France had changed its mind about sending over that statue. The big stone building you've put up at the entrance to Turkey Hill Road. You have a sign out front. It says Beechwood Jewish Center."

"Anything wrong with that?" Mr. Dehn said.

"From the standpoint of the profits you're looking for out of your investment it could be improved."

"How?" Mr. Dehn said.

"By making a small addition you could put the people of this town in your pocket," Oliver Stehli said.

"You want me to change the name?" Mr. Dehn said.

"Yes," Oliver Stehli said.

"Change it to what?" Mr. Dehn said.

"The Bella Biaggi – Beechwood Jewish Center," Oliver Stehli said.

28

"It seems to me Stehli's suggestion is a good one," Dave said at the staff meeting the next morning. "Mike, will it be difficult to make the change?"

Mike Palgrave looked up from his pad.

"I've sketched it out roughly," he said. "It means fourteen extra digits, plus two spaces. One for between the word *The* and the word *Bella,* another for between the word *Bella* and the word *Biaggi.* That's sixteen. Then, if you want a dash between the word *Biaggi* and the word *Beechwood,* that's three more. Space dash space. A grand total of nineteen additional digits. We can change the cornerstone, of course?"

"No," Dave said. "I don't want the cornerstone touched."

"I know you don't," Mike said. "I was merely presenting it as the first of three alternatives."

"Stick to the other two," Dave said.

"I can put a new facing on the cornerstone," Mike said. "It's a simple process. The old lettering is chipped away, and the surrounding area is leveled to the depth of the former lettering. Then you take a sheet of marble, with the new words already cut into it, and you cement it over the place where the old lettering used to be."

"What's the third alternative?" Dave said.

"Carve the new name into the frieze over the front entrance," Mike said.

"Sid?" Dave said.

"I like the frieze idea," Sid said. "Unless you think there might be some further change in the future?"

"I doubt it," Dave said. "When it comes to thinking up names for Jewish Centers one wife is enough. Fanny?"

"I don't like the idea of chipping away at the cornerstone," Fanny said. "The whole idea of a cornerstone, it seems to me, is not to disturb it. Couldn't we just cover the lettering that's on it now? And put the new name up over the entrance?"

"Mike?" Dave said.

"No problem," Mike said. He made a note on his pad. "Then it's cover the cornerstone now, and put the new name up on the frieze. Right?"

"Right," Dave said. "Anything else?"

"Chevra Bechrim B'nei Menasche Aharas Achim," Fanny read from her notebook.

"What's that?" Dave said.

"A synagogue up in Bridgeport," Fanny said. "The rabbi called yesterday. He's been hearing about what we're doing down here in Beechwood. He wants Mr. Dehn to come and address his congregation."

"I'm not a public speaker," Dave said.

"This rabbi didn't say they want a public speaker," Fanny said. "He told me they want ideas on moving out into the community in some of the directions we're taking."

"I'm sure they have enough pastrami purveyors in Bridgeport," Dave said. "Next."

"D.D., this rabbi sounded to me like a young man," Fanny said. "He also sounded serious."

"So am I," Dave said. "All they want is someone to come up and entertain them. Call him back and suggest bingo."

"If you say so," Fanny said.

No inflection.

"Don't make a thing about it," Dave said. "I don't want to waste time. I wouldn't know what to talk to people in Bridgeport about."

"I would," Mike said.

"Okay," Dave said. "You go up and talk to them."

Plenty of inflection.

"They don't know me," Mike said. "They know David Dehn. Anyway, they've heard of him. If what we're doing here in Beechwood is worth doing, it's worth spreading. What we just went through with Babington and his gang should convince us that it's a battle that never ends. The opposition hasn't quit for two thousand years. If there's anything we know for sure, we know the opposition will never quit. There will be other Babingtons. We can't trust to automobile accidents to come along at the right moment and pull us out of holes. It seems sensible to put our trust in some outside support. Spreading the word can't help but be healthy. I wish you'd go up to Bridgeport and talk to these people."

"About what?" Dave said.

The inflection took a noticeable drop in temperature. Mr. Palgrave, né Cohen, was getting to be something of a pain in the ass.

"What you once talked to me about," Mike said. "Masada."

Somewhere near the top of Dave's head a manhole cover seemed to lift away. Mike seemed to have the same feeling.

"A year and a half ago," he said. "Sitting out there on that log, facing the Sound. When you first talked to me. The things you told me then," Mike said. "Go up to Bridgeport and tell it to the Chevra Bechrim B'nei Menasche Aharas Achim."

Dave gave himself a moment. It helped.

"Okay, Fanny," he said quietly. "Call them back and make a date."

"Right," Fanny said.

She made a mark in her notebook.

"Anything else?" Dave said.

"Ernest Sternshus," Fanny read from her notebook.

"I know," Dave said. "I'm seeing him today."

"When?" Sid said.

Dave looked at his wrist watch.

"In a few minutes," he said. "I'm giving him a lift down into New York. We'll talk in the car."

Nothing happened. But the rhythm of the meeting had faltered. Dave was not surprised. Fanny picked up the beat. That didn't surprise him either. No matter what she was thinking, Fanny did her job. She kept things going.

"You're driving into New York today?" she said.

"I've got to," Dave said. "That kid can't spend her life in an incubator in New Rochelle Hospital. The doctors tell me she's picking up weight at a good pace. She'll be ready for discharge in a couple of weeks. I've got to find a place for her. I have a date with some nursery people in New York this morning."

Pause. The others didn't dare. So it had to be Fanny again.

"What about the funeral?" she said. "Unless you plan to get back to Beechwood by noon?"

"Not a chance," Dave said.

This time Sid.

"You're not going to Bella's funeral?" he said.

"No," Dave said.

Mike's turn.

"D.D.," he said. "If you don't mind my saying so—"

"I do mind," Dave said. "So don't say it. I'm not going to the funeral. Period. Any comment?"

"Yes," Sid said. "What are we going to tell Father Boyle?"

"Mr. Dehn is stricken," Dave said. "He is locked away with his grief. He won't be able to face people for some time."

29

He certainly was not able to face Ernie Sternshus.

They sat side by side on the front seat of the Cadillac. All Dave could see was the left side of the young man's face. Nothing came out of it while they put almost five miles of the Hutchinson River Parkway behind them.

"When we get to New York I've got a date," Dave said finally. "I'm not going to have time to sit in the car on Forty-seventh Street and have a chat. You told Miss Mintz you wanted to see me. You'd better start talking."

"He's the wrong guy for the job," Sternshus said.

The words emerged in a perfectly normal conversational tone. But Dave knew better. He'd just heard a small explosion. Or rather felt it. As though a cork had erupted from a bottle unaccompanied by the sound of a pop.

"Who?" Dave said.

"This rabbi you've got," Sternshus said.

"Vogel?" Dave said.

"Peretz Vogel," Sternshus said. "Call me Perry."

All at once Dave knew something without knowing what it was he knew.

"Do you?" he said.

"He's my spiritual adviser, isn't he?"

Dave's mind darted back to Rabbi Goldfarb on Westerlo Street. Aside from the horror of the rabbi's death Dave had never thought much about the short, square man with the plump face that seemed to hang like a sorrowful mask between the stained black fedora and the full black beard. There was nothing to think about. Rabbi Goldfarb was there. A solid, comforting presence. A man who knew everything there was to know, and everything he knew was at your disposal. A man you were glad to have in your corner. A man you didn't fool around with. Call me Perry? Never. My spiritual adviser? The words would have meant nothing to Rabbi Goldfarb. Even less to Dave.

"He's the official rabbi at the Center," Dave said. "In your case, you and the Metuchen kid, the relationship may be a little closer. It doesn't matter what you call him. What matters about the relationship is that it should be working. Is it?"

"I thought it was," Sternshus said. "Until the son of a bitch showed his hand."

"You better tell me more," Dave said.

"There's nothing more to tell," Sternshus said. "He's a shit, that guy."

All at once Dave knew what it was he had known he knew without understanding the nature of the knowledge.

"You're back on?" he said.

Sternshus shook his head at the ribbon of concrete pouring up toward them and disappearing under the front wheels.

"No," he said, "I'm clean. The Metuchen kid too, if you're worrying."

"What the hell do you think I'm doing?" Dave said. "Celebrating? If it's working, if you and the kid are both okay, who cares about Call Me Perry's character?"

"I do," Sternshus said. "So does the kid. You find out the guy is rotten, it throws you. You lose confidence in the guy. When that happens you're not walking good any more. You're back on eggshells. Any minute it could stop working."

"What do you want me to do about it?" Dave said.

"Get rid of the son of a bitch," Sternshus said. "Throw the bastard out while the kid and I are still ahead."

"And?" Dave said.

"Get us a real rabbi," Sternshus said.

"What's a real rabbi?" Dave said.

"A guy without shit," Sternshus said.

"I know what that means with ordinary people," Dave said. "With rabbis you better be more specific."

"God was never around much in our family," Sternshus said. "I mean, I wasn't raised with religion. I knew I was a Jew because every now and then I got dumped on for it, but that was about the size of it. When I got into trouble, after Guadalcanal, I broke my balls trying to think my way out of it. There are guys who like it or don't mind being hooked or don't give a fuck. I did. I hated it, but I couldn't get away from it. Then, up here in Beechwood, this guy came along. The word rabbi threw me at first. When you're in real trouble you learn soon enough to stay away from the come-to-Jesus boys. They don't know their ass from a hot rock what it's all about. They just get you in deeper with promises they can't keep. Then the cops came in and I knew I had to try anything, no matter what, so I tried Call Me Perry. It started to work before I knew it was working. When I caught on I tried to figure out why."

"Did you?" Dave said.

"With the kid's help," Sternshus said. "He's got brains, that kid. We talked about it, and he cut it out of the herd before I did. What made it work at the beginning was this guy was a come-to-Jesus boy without the crap. He was a rabbi, sure, but you could tell he was something else. He was a guy just like you and me and the kid and pretty near everybody else, a guy shitting green deep down inside him over something that was killing him. Whatever it was with him I don't know, but he was a damaged boy. You could feel it. Something was eating him. He was scared of something, the way we were, and it sort of made us buddies. He didn't hock us. He was just there."

"Now he's not?" Dave said.

"Not the same way," Sternshus said.

"What's the change?" Dave said.

"All of a sudden he's too much there," Sternshus said. "He's on top of us. He's hounding us. The kid and I, both of us, we both feel it."

"Feel what?" Dave said.

"The son of a bitch is using us," Sternshus said.

"How?" Dave said.

"Like, like, like, I don't know," Sternshus said. "Like he's starving and we're the first food he's seen in a hell of a long time."

"What's that got to do with your problem?" Dave said.

"We were depending on him," Sternshus said. "Now he's depending on us."

"In what way?" Dave said.

He had to push. He had to force him to the heart of the problem. Dave had to get it in words he understood.

"Whatever it was," Sternshus said, "that bug up his ass, the thing that was killing him, he found a way out of it. Us. Me and the kid. Now he's using us to save himself. From being just a guy it was safe to be around, all of a sudden, overnight, he's a come-to-Jesusnik in spades. He's clawing at us. Sucking us dry. Like he was drowning and we were a life preserver or something. He's trying to help himself, not us. It makes you sick. Me, anyway. The kid too. What I'm asking for both of us, what we want, get us a guy who is interested in helping us, not himself. We don't have anything to give other guys. We're fighting for our lives. Get this bastard off our backs. He stinks, this louse. We need someone who will fight for us, not for himself."

"How much time have I got?" Dave said.

"Not much," Ernie Sternshus said. "I'm slipping. The kid too. You gotta get us somebody, Mr. Dehn."

"How long can you hold out?"

"I don't know," Sternshus said.

"A few days?" Dave said.

"Not much longer," Sternshus said.

"It won't take me that long," Dave said. "When you come home from work tonight call me at the Center. I'll have someone."

30

Dave had someone before he got to his apartment. Not the actual man. Not his name. But the name was only a detail. What mattered was that he had it worked out in his head. He knew what he had to do.

"David?"

His heart stumbled. It always did when she spoke his name.

"It's me," he called toward the living room.

He pulled his key from the lock and turned to close the door. When he turned back, Amanda was coming toward him. He had a moment of disappointment. She was wearing a skirt and a sweater. All the way across town from the office building on Forty-seventh Street where he had dropped Ernie Sternshus, Dave had been seeing her in the shirtwaist dress.

"Oh," she said.

She rose on her toes. She reached up with a gesture of curious delicacy. He might have been something precious and fragile on a high shelf. She put her arms around him. He pulled her close. The bundle of delicate bones seemed to fold and disappear into his jacket, like the blade of a pocketknife slipping home into its slot.

"Oh," Amanda whispered again. "Oh, darling."

Later, in the bedroom, he lay back and watched her get dressed. She saw him watching and turned away.

"Don't do that," Amanda said.

"I like watching you," he said.

"You can't," she said. She skinned hastily into her underpants. "I look horrible."

"Not to me." He swung his legs over the side of the bed. "Show me what's horrible."

She straightened and turned swiftly, all in one motion. Her lovely breasts bounced with the thrust of energy, then settled slowly, bobbing up and down like—like what? He couldn't remember.

"I've been ashamed all my life," she said.

"Of what?" he said.

"Can't you see?" she said. "My left breast is lower than the right."

Dave kissed the nipple.

"Better?" he said.

"Much."

He skinned her out of the underpants. A couple of minutes later he remembered the *like what?* That morning at the Israel Putnam Motor Inn. When he had unfastened Bella's brassiere. The way her breasts had bounced. Bobbing up and down. Like the necks of geese hurrying down to a pond.

"Something wrong?" Amanda whispered.

"No, no," he said.

But the damage was done. He kept going until she came.

"I'll use the other bathroom," he said.

When he walked out of the room he turned away from her so she wouldn't see his erection—stiff as a chair rung, and just about as useful.

"I've got it all figured out," he said when he came out into the living room. She was pouring coffee. He took a cup and sat down facing her.

"You've got what figured out?" Amanda said.

"You and me," Dave said. "I've put all the pieces together. You want to hear?"

"Of course."

"One," Dave said. "You get a divorce from Perry. Two, you and I get married. Three, we fix up this place, or we put a nursery into my suite at the Center, maybe both. Four, we move in with Rachel and live happily ever after."

"Rachel?"

"My daughter," Dave said. "Remember?"

It was obvious, when she did, that it had required an effort.

"How do you like my scenario?" Dave said.

"The picture will never be shot," Amanda said.

"Why not?"

"I can't divorce Perry," she said.

Dave would not let the words come into his head. He held them at bay, outside, waiting.

"I'll show you how," he said.

Amanda shook her head.

"You can't, darling. Nobody can. I can't divorce Perry."

The holding action collapsed. The words came thundering in. Too fast, like a blast of wind. They made a mess. He needed a few moments to tidy up.

"Why not?" he said.

The mop-and-broom words. To scoop away the worst of the mess. When things were tidied up, the other words would arrive.

"Perry is going through a crisis of faith," Amanda said. "Being at Beechwood, working with those two men, Sternshus and the Metuchen boy, it may heal him. It's his only hope. He's like a drowning man at the moment, grasping at anything to save himself. Until he finds his way back to God, until Perry is a whole man again, I can't leave him."

Now the words came into their own. They hurt, but could not be disregarded. They had come for a purpose. Dave used them.

"Then you'd better leave with him," he said.

She blinked. Only once. She had more than any girl he had ever known. She did not need time. Not for what counted. She picked up the real things fast. First time around. More than that, she did not whine. She accepted the decision the way his father had accepted Westerlo Street. You didn't fuss about the inevitable. You lived with it. Watching the way she put down the coffee cup made his heart hurt like a punched bruise.

"Perry is fired?" she said.

"As of now," Dave said.

She stood up. The hard words, the words that had to be said, were shoved aside. Inside his head the stupid words took over.

Don't be a damn fool. You'll never have another chance like this. Fuck that God-damn temple up in Beechwood. It's eating you alive. It will kill you. She's your only hope. Don't let her go.

"I'll go home and pack," she said. "Will you give me a lift back to Beechwood?"

"Take the train," he said.

She came around the coffee table and started for the hall closet.

"Leave your key," Dave said. "I don't want you showing up here ever again."

31

"I can offer you an Upmann or a quotation from Churchill," Dr. Bieberman said. "Say which."

"Thanks, neither," Dave said. "What I would like is an explanation for why you sent for me."

"Your secretary called yesterday," Dr. Bieberman said. "She told me you fired Peretz Vogel and you wanted me to send you a new rabbi."

"That's right," Dave said.

"No, it's not," Dr. Bieberman said. "That's why I sent for you."

"I don't understand," Dave said.

"The Central Rabbinical Assembly is not Macy's," Dr. Bieberman said. "We don't fill telephone orders."

"I'm sorry," Dave said. "I've been up to my ears, and Miss Mintz is not exactly my secretary. She's my assistant. She does so many things for me that I didn't stop to think when I asked her to do this that I was being rude. I apologize."

"For rudeness I don't ask people to come down from a nice clean place like Westchester into this dirty city," Dr. Bieberman said. "I would ask a man to make such a trip only when it involves something serious."

"You're right, of course," Dave said. "Changing the rabbi for a congregation is a very serious matter. I can see that."

"In this area," Dr. Bieberman said, "I have a feeling, Mr. Dehn, your vision is not exactly twenty-twenty."

He chose this moment to embark on the complicated ritual of getting his Upmann properly lighted. Dave could not remember if Dr. Bieberman took longer this time than he had taken when Dave had first sat through the performance. Dave was aware, however, that so far as the head of the Central Rabbinical Assembly's Placement Committee was concerned the time was not being wasted.

"You're probably right," Dave said. "Choosing a rabbi is a new experience for me. The only yardstick I can go by is trial and error. I tried with what you sent me, and I failed. I'm sorry it happened. I'd like to try again."

"It would help if you told me just what did happen," Dr. Bieberman said.

Dave did. Sticking strictly to the facts. Just as strictly keeping himself and Amanda out of it.

"You say you tried and you failed," Dr. Bieberman said when Dave had finished. "You admit, then, that it was not Peretz Vogel who failed."

"I don't understand," said Dave, who all at once understood clearly. The Central Rabbinical Assembly might not have been Macy's, but to Dr. Bieberman the man sitting beside his desk was nonetheless a dissatisfied customer.

"I'm disappointed in you," Dr. Bieberman said.

"Why?" Dave said.

"You should meet some of the types that come through this office," Dr. Bieberman said. "Heads of pulpit committees trying to find rabbis for their congregations. When these people say they don't understand something, I believe them, and I explain. A good Jew always tries to shed light. When *you* say you don't understand something, I'm disappointed."

"Again why?" Dave said.

"Because the last thing I expected from you, Mr. Dehn, I did not expect a man of your intelligence would lie to a man of my intelligence."

Dr. Bieberman checked the ash at the end of his Upmann. Dave did not step into the pause. The ash passed the test. Dr. Bieberman put the Upmann back between his Mark Twain mustache and his Joseph Conrad Vandyke. He took a puff. Removed the cigar from his face. Blew out the smoke. Adjusted his *yarmulke*. Swiveled his desk chair a few inches to bring himself more directly face to face with his visitor. And let Dave have it.

"When a man of your intelligence lies to a man of my intelligence," Dr. Bieberman said, "I have to conclude you think you're talking to the average-type *shlemiel* you deal with in business. From my standpoint, Mr. Dehn, that's a personal disappointment. From your standpoint it's a mistake. When it comes to your various business activities, naturally you know more than I do. Things like your investment in that Wyoming cattle farm. Your piece of that wire-insulation company in Jersey City, the Noonan brothers. Your share in the Broward County Land Development Corporation in south Florida. Those grain elevators up in Saskatchewan you and your partner Mr. Singer, you bought into the Canadian company last March. Those things, naturally you know more than I do. It's your business. Placing rabbis in American congregations? That's my business. Nobody knows more about my business than I do. That's where you made your mistake, Mr. Dehn."

Dave thought fast. Not fast enough, however, to escape Dr. Bieberman's awareness that his opponent was assessing a position before making his next move.

"I'll add a footnote that might help you," said the head of the Central Rabbinical Assembly's Placement Committee. "A lot of people have sat in your chair, Mr. Dehn. In the tactic of pulling wool over Silas Bieberman's eyes, not one of them in twenty-six years has even bunted."

"In that case I'm not even going to try," Dave said. "But I'm going to ask a question."

"Maybe I'll answer," Dr. Bieberman said.

"How do you know so much about my business affairs?" Dave said.

"These pulpit committees that go out looking for rabbis," Dr. Bieberman said. "Who do you think serves on them? Filling-station attendants? Plumber's helpers? Clerks in grocery stores? No, Mr. Dehn. The members of pulpit committees are always substantial people in the community. Successful businessmen. Doctors. Lawyers. People with money. Movers and shakers, Mr. Dehn. All of them, all over the country, they have to come to me. I give them what they want. In exchange I get something I want. Something I need to do my job right. I get information.

"This office, it's the engine room of American Judaism, you could say. A man comes to me for a rabbi, I don't just give him a warm body the way I'd give him a pound of pastrami if I ran a delicatessen. A man who comes to me for a rabbi is coming to me for a link in the chain that holds American Judaism together. I can't afford to give him a link that could break. A link doesn't always break because it is weak. Sometimes a link breaks because the fastenings to the other links in the chain are weak. So I check the fastenings very carefully. I call on my information network. All over the country. When you came to me for a rabbi the first thing I did was check you out with my network. That's how I learned about your business interests. As a fastening in my chain you looked solid. So I gave you a link. And you let me down."

"Not at all," Dave said. "The link you gave me let me down. I explained it."

"What did you explain?" Dr. Bieberman said. "You fired Peretz Vogel because two young drug addicts complained he wasn't helping them the way they want to be helped to cure their addiction?"

"Isn't that enough?" Dave said.

"For you, maybe," Dr. Bieberman said. "For me, it's foolish. I made a marriage. You and Peretz Vogel. He hasn't even had time to send out his extra *tallis* to be dry-cleaned, and you kick him out. Why? For a reason that in a regular marriage it would make just as much sense as a husband kicking out his wife on the morning after the wedding night because he discovers she doesn't squeeze the toothpaste tube from the bottom."

"Dr. Bieberman, you're being frivolous."

"Mr. Dehn, you're being stupid."

"I don't see—"

"Watch the birdie, young man, and you will," Dr. Bieberman said. "In my work, in every case I handle, I have two objectives. One, satisfying the immediate needs of the person who comes to me. Two, holding intact the framework of the structure on which the strength of American Judaism rests. Ideally, I try to meet both objectives. Most of the time I do. When I don't, one objective has to lose out. There's never any question in my mind which one it is. You want to guess?"

"Number one, of course," Dave said.

"Of course, Mr. Dehn," Dr. Bieberman said. "Very much of course, and it's always of course. It has to be. If I gave in to your request, if I let you fire Peretz Vogel for the reason you gave me, I would damage the reputation of the Placement Committee of the Central Rabbinical Assembly. You think I would do such a thing to satisfy the whim of a rich young man who is playing games with forming a congregation and choosing a rabbi to give it spiritual guidance because he is bored with golf or making fast bucks or chasing *shiksehs* or whatever it is that has driven you to whatever it is you are doing up there in Westchester with all this money you've been all of a sudden making since the end of the war? Don't think that, Mr. Dehn. Any more than you should think Silas Bieberman is any more frivolous than Savonarola."

"You obviously want me to do something," Dave said.

"Of course," Dr. Bieberman said.

"What?" Dave said.

"Live up to your contract," Dr. Bieberman said. "I gave you what you wanted."

"You mean I'm stuck with Peretz Vogel," Dave said.

"If you want to continue whatever it is you're doing up there in Westchester, yes," Dr. Bieberman said.

"I could refuse," Dave said.

"You could also shoot yourself," Dr. Bieberman said. "You will find the consequences equally salubrious."

"I could go out and hire my own rabbi," Dave said.

"You could go out and hire your own Congressman," Dr. Bieberman said. "His vote won't be tallied on the floor of the House."

"These are the tactics Hitler used," Dave said.

"They worked," Dr. Bieberman said.

"So the method doesn't matter," Dave said.

"Only the objective," Dr. Bieberman said.

"I see what I did wrong," Dave said.

"We're making progress," Dr. Bieberman said.

"I got in your way," Dave said.

"The way Peretz Vogel got in your way," Dr. Bieberman said.

Dave nodded.

"I'm going to have to leave him there," Dave said. "Standing in my way."

Dr. Bieberman returned the nod.

"Too bad you're not a rabbi, Mr. Dehn," he said. "In a year, in eighteen months at most, I would have you in the pulpit of Emanu-El, and the two of us, working together, we would take over American Judaism. We would weld together all its warring factions. We would make of our great spiritual heritage what it should be. A powerful world force that could lift humanity out of the filthy puddle of oil in which it is being choked to death by a rabble of stinking camel merchants who were living in dung-filled desert caves when your ancestors and mine were priests in the temple of Solomon."

"You make me feel sorry I'm not a rabbi," Dave said.

He was only mildly surprised to discover in the echoes of his own voice a fleeting note that was almost truth.

"It's a regret I share," Dr. Bieberman said.

Dave stood up.

"Well," he said, "I guess that wraps it up."

"Not quite," Dr. Bieberman said. "There's one thing."

"What's that?" Dave said.

"I think you owe me a box of Upmanns," Dr. Bieberman said.

32

"Upmanns?" Fanny said. "What's that?"

"Cigars," Dave said. "You won't get them up here in Beechwood, I don't think. Try Dunhill's down in New York. Have them put in a card with my name. What else have we got?"

Fanny tapped the pencil on her notebook. Like a conductor alerting the orchestra by rapping a signal on the edge of his lectern with the baton.

"Oliver Stehli called," she said.

"What's on Horace Greeley's mind this morning?" Dave said.

"He's planning to run a front-page editorial hailing the new state," Fanny said. "He wondered if you'd like to add a statement. The paper doesn't go to press until nine o'clock tonight."

"Hailing the what?" Dave said.

He was looking at Fanny, but out of the corner of his eye he could see Sid catch it. Sid always caught things first.

"Israel," Sid said without any special where-the-hell-have-you-been emphasis. "President Truman's recognition of Israel as an independent state is what Stehli is hailing."

"Oh, that," Dave said. "Sure."

He didn't think he quite made it with the I-knew-it-all-the-time inflection, but he was sure he got by. This was his team. Here, no matter what, he always had a margin for error.

"My mind was on something else," Dave said.

"No wonder," Sid said. "The stuff you've had dumped on you these last few days."

Fanny performed the rite that was traditional with chestnuts. She pulled them out of the fire.

"Truman doing a thing like that," she said smoothly, "Stehli feels it's a or an historic event."

"Good for him," Dave said. The recovery was complete. "What are Stehli's other feelings?"

"He felt as the leader of the Beechwood Jewish community you'd probably want to make a statement," Fanny said. "In fact, he made no bones about it. Stehli very much wants you to do it, D.D. If you're too busy to do it yourself he's willing to write it for you. Right on the front page, D.D. Stehli said he's pretty sure he knows your thinking."

"See?" Dave said. "How times change? The editor of the Beechwood *Bugle* has come around to the belief that Jews on his front page sell copies of his paper."

Dave turned back to Fanny. He did it as though he were unfurling a pennant. What had slipped out of focus for a while because of Amanda and Bella's death and the birth of the baby had come back to him. Once again he had it all where it belonged. In his own hands. Once more, as always, Dave Dehn knew where he was going.

"Tell Mr. Stehli I'll write this myself," he said. "I'm the only one who knows Dave Dehn's thinking."

33

The platform of the bathroom scale was three inches high. Sally Palgrave came down from it to the tile floor like Marie Antoinette in an M.G.M. production descending the steps of her throne to mingle with the members of the court at a levee.

Sally felt her airy, gracious movements should be accompanied by music. Mike, however, was the only musician in the family. He had driven off to New York at dawn on another of his endless missions for Mr. Dehn. So Sally made her own music. As she crossed to the Formica counter in a twisting little dance step she whistled the opening bars of "Hail to the Chief."

Sally had always found time for everything. She was not surprised to find, therefore, that in her explosion of joy there was time for a moment of wonder. Where had that dance step come from? Since she was also a girl who never forgot anything, the filing system in Sally's efficient mind promptly disgorged the answer. It was the step she had perfected when she used to dribble her way across the court for Brearley, avoiding the clutching hands of the little Dalton creeps who played basketball as though it were a game of Pin the Tail on the Donkey.

The scrap of dance brought Sally to the ledger on the Formica counter. She snatched up the pencil like Arthur hauling

Excalibur from the stone. When she scrawled on the ledger sheet the numbers the bathroom scale had just registered, Sally added to her piercing rendition of "Hail to the Chief" a screech of delight that was straight out of the Tunnel of Love scene in any one of those movies set in an amusement park.

"One twenty-one and a half!" she screamed.

Sally Palgrave was back to what she had been when she was Sylvia Mersky.

"Hey, all you goys down there!"

She danced to the open window, enjoying the fact that looking down over her bouncing breasts she could no longer see her belly. It had vanished.

"Hear this!" Sally bellowed toward the boat docks emerging from the morning mists of Sequesta Pond. "You don't have to be Gentile to be thin!"

"How true."

Sally turned. Mr. Dehn was standing in the bathroom doorway.

"Oh, my God!"

Sally slapped her arms across her chest.

"Here," Mr. Dehn said. "Allow me."

He took down the terry-cloth robe from the hook on the door and held it wide. Sally came into it backward, then leaped away and whipped the folds around her body. She was pulling the belt tight when she turned.

"I'm sorry," Sally said.

If her face looked as hot as it felt she hoped she would sink into the floor.

"I'm not," Mr. Dehn said. "I've believed for some time I should be seeing more of you."

He released a small, pump-priming laugh. Sally caught up with the joke. So she laughed too. Then it was all right.

"I'm not a peeping Tom," he said. "I drove up with completely honorable intentions, rang the bell, and waited. Nothing happened. Then I heard screaming, so I thought I'd better investigate. Since we've had this influx of Jews in the area no woman in Beechwood is safe in her own home."

"I'm safer than most Jewish women in this town," Sally said. "I've got that name. Gentile prowlers don't rape Palgraves. It's part of the folklore dispensed on page three of the New York *Daily News*. If we get out of this bathroom and into the kitchen, I'll give you a cup of coffee. I'm sorry Mike isn't here. He drove off to New York at the crack of dawn."

"I know," Mr. Dehn said. "I sent him."

Pause. Sally was aware she was not the only one contributing to the small island of silence.

"Well," she said, defusing the moment. "If you'll step aside."

"Of course," he said. But he didn't. "As long as my honorable intentions brought me a dividend," he said, "I think it's only fair to say I think what you and Mike have done for yourselves in the year and a half since I met you is extraordinary. Your screams of triumph directed at the surrounding goyim are justified. Mrs. Palgrave, you've got the best figure in the Western Hemisphere since Betty Grable."

Sally wondered about a man who could say a thing like that and, while saying it, sound like Gregory Peck telling the assembled Elders of Zion about his vision of a promised land somewhere west of the Rockies.

"Please call me Sally," she said. "I don't like it any better than I like Palgrave, which Mike says we're stuck with until you release us back to Cohen, but Sally seems more appropriate under the circumstances."

"Okay, Sally," Mr. Dehn said. Stepping aside, he added, "My friends call me Dave."

She noted the remark but let it go. He followed her out into the kitchen.

"I was thinking about you," Sally said from the stove.

She nodded toward the Beechwood *Bugle*. It was spread out on the table under the picture window that looked down Cavalry Road toward Main Street.

"Mike and I were discussing at breakfast your statement about Truman's recognition of Israel." She snapped the switch on the burner under the kettle. "Mike and I are strictly saccharin, but I have sugar if you prefer that?"

"Just black, thanks," Mr. Dehn said.

She tried in her mind to use the privilege he had conferred on her, but she could not think of him as Dave. Not yet, anyway. There was something off-putting about him. The manner was relaxed and easy. But the impact was slightly forbidding. Mr. Dehn reminded Sally of the way she used to think about her father. He too had been a handsome man. With a heartbreaking sad smile and a gentle quality that invited you in. But Sally had never succeeded in accepting the invitation, although God knew she had tried. Underneath the warmth and friendliness she had felt her father carried a hard core of secret knowledge he could not share with ordinary people. Not even with a daughter who did not doubt for a moment that he loved her. She was not worthy. Not yet, anyway. Perhaps someday she would be. She had never doubted for a moment that it was worth waiting for. Mr. Dehn was like that.

"What did you think of my statement?" he said.

The kettle started to cough itself into a whistle.

"I didn't understand it," Sally said.

She snapped the switch, poured the cups full, and set the kettle on a cold burner.

"Four paragraphs?" Mr. Dehn said.

With both hands he smoothed the front page of the *Bugle* on the table in front of him.

"What can there be in these three hundred and forty-six words that a Bennington girl does not understand?" he said.

"The basic ambivalence," Sally said.

She set a cup in front of him, then came around to the other side of the table. With her cup in both hands she sat down facing him.

"Explain, please," Mr. Dehn said.

"You hail Truman's act," Sally said. "At long last the Jewish homeland is a legal reality. Never again will the Jews as a nation have to face the horror of Masada. But legality is merely a scrap of paper. To make it a reality the Jews of the world must never relax. Including the Jews of America. They must make themselves strong. So that never again will a Roman army trap them in a beleaguered fortress and force them to choose mass suicide rather than surrender. Unquote."

"What's ambivalent about that?" Dave said.

"You hail the establishment of Israel," Sally said. "And to make it a reality you call on the Jews of America to become strong. The people you are urging to become strong are six thousand miles away from the fortress that must never again be beleaguered. If you mean what you say, if you expect it to work, you've got to do something about that six-thousand-mile gap that separates you from them."

"How?" Mr. Dehn said.

"By cutting out the play acting over here," Sally said. "By going over there to do the job where the action will take place, when and if."

"You trying to say to be a good Jew a man must leave America and settle in Israel?" Mr. Dehn said.

"Is there any other way to say the obvious?" Sally said. "When the Arabs start shelling the King David Hotel in Jerusalem, what good will it do the State of Israel to have over here in the Bella Biaggi – Beechwood Jewish Center a troop of tough young Boy Scouts with big muscles working away on Turkey Hill Road tying sheepshanks and weaving raffia baskets?"

Mr. Dehn started to lift his coffee cup, then set it back on the table.

"That's not what I came here to discuss," he said.

Sally knew that tone of voice. Her father used to sound that way sometimes when she came too close to the thing he was guarding inside him. The iron door had closed.

"You write something for a newspaper," Sally said. "You get it printed on the front page. People will discuss it."

"Okay," Mr. Dehn said. "You've discussed it."

Sally suddenly wished she hadn't. There was something in his eyes. A look she remembered from the days when her father had meant a lot to her, the days when she was still trying very hard to understand him. A look that told her she had come too close to the hard core of secret knowledge he could not share with others. If she didn't back off, he might forget he loved her and become ugly.

"It's just one girl's opinion," Sally said. "Don't take it too seriously."

"I must," Mr. Dehn said. "I sent Mike into New York this morning so I could come over here and have an uninterrupted talk with you because I take you very seriously."

"Mr. Dehn," Sally said, "let's not start that."

"Start what?" he said.

Then he got it.

"Oh," Mr. Dehn said.

She could see the anger scoop him up like a wave roaring in to a beach.

"Mrs. Cohen," he said, "when I want to get laid I don't have to resort to the cheap trick of sending a subordinate out of town so his wife will be available to spread her legs."

It was not fake. The rage was real. Sally knew the difference.

"I'm sorry," she said. "A girl gets back to her schoolgirl weight, she also gets back to her schoolgirl ideas. I said I'm sorry. I'll say it again. I don't usually say that kind of stupid thing."

His smile was worth the humiliation of the apology. A girl could keep going quite a while on a smile like that.

"Neither do I," he said. "Let's both quit saying stupid things. I want to ask you about something that means a great deal to me. To do it I've got to ask you about something that means a great deal to you. You'll probably get sore. I know I'd get sore if you asked me. But I know I can't do it any other way. So I'm going to ask it. Okay?"

"Probably not," Sally said. "But one thing about Bennington. They teach you to Face Up to Life."

"You and Mike have been married for over six years," Mr. Dehn said. "You have no children. What I want to know is whether that's because of a decision you both reached, or whether nature screwed you up and you can't."

"You can hang that rap on nature," Sally said. "The doctors say we can't."

"Have you done anything about it?" Mr. Dehn said.

"What pretty much everybody gets around to doing," Sally said. "We've made inquiries about adoption."

"Just inquiries?" Mr. Dehn said.

"Not much more than that," Sally said. "You're the stumbling block."

"Me?" he said.

Genuine surprise, she was sure. But also a touch of pleasure, Sally noted. Mr. Dehn, like her father, had many qualities. Modesty was not one of them.

"You know how they dig into your background with questions," she said. "Mike and I stopped short of the one that was sure to come up. If your name is Cohen how come you want to go around behind a name like Palgrave?"

"I seem to have come to the right place," Mr. Dehn said.

"In what way?" Sally said.

"I can fix it so you and Mike can stop being Palgraves and go back to being Cohens," Mr. Dehn said.

"Mike's been saying for a year and a half you were saving that for the right moment," Sally said.

"I think it's arrived," Mr. Dehn said. "It's no secret to you that I've had a bum marriage. Since everybody else knows the circumstances of my wife's death, I'm sure you do too. She left me with about four and a half pounds' worth of daughter. Rachel is still in an incubator at New Rochelle Hospital."

"That's the only thing I didn't know," Sally said. "I didn't know you'd named her Rachel."

"It was my mother's name," Mr. Dehn said. "I never knew my mother, but I know her name."

"You want to get someone to take care of Rachel," Sally said.

"Yes," Mr. Dehn said.

"You'd like me and Mike to take her," Sally said.

"Very much," Mr. Dehn said.

"Why?" Sally said.

"The reasons are obvious," Mr. Dehn said. "But I wouldn't want you and Mike to think I'm taking advantage. I'm trying to sell you, but I don't want to con you. I want the child near me, but I don't want her growing up in a bachelor household."

"You might marry again," Sally said.

"No," Mr. Dehn said.

It was clear he intended to say no more. Not on that subject.

"So Mike and I would be ideal," Sally said.

"You've been thinking of adopting a child anyway," Mr. Dehn said.

"The key word, Mr. Dehn, is adopting."

His eyes narrowed. As though he wanted to get her into sharper focus.

"Have I missed something?" Mr. Dehn said.

"I'm sure Mike will feel the way I do," Sally said. "We'll be delighted to take Rachel. But not as foster parents. If we take her we must take her as Rachel Cohen."

Mr. Dehn looked startled, and then a startling thing happened. He turned his back on her and went to the door. He did it very carefully, with movements so precise that he might have been carrying a large jug full to the brim with a precious fluid he did not dare spill.

Sally's heart seemed to stop. It was as though she were seeing her own father turn from an unexpected blow, a blow he dared not let the world know he had received. The world never knew, but Sally always did. Just as she knew now. Sally had a moment of panic. What had she done to inflict the pain Mr. Dehn was so carefully concealing?

She had told him the truth. She had felt he deserved that. He had struck her as a man you could not fool with empty words. She had wanted him to know that she and Mike wanted a child. They did not want to settle for the role of paid caretakers. She had assumed Mr. Dehn would understand that.

It had not occurred to Sally that the child was anything more to him than an accident. A nuisance he had not expected to turn up in his path. An irritating obstacle he wanted to put behind him so he could get on with his work.

It was clear to Sally that she had misjudged him, as long ago when it was important to her she had misjudged her father. Mr. Dehn obviously had depths of feeling whose existence she had not suspected from his smooth, machine-tooled exterior. More things were piled up inside this man than the problem of what to do about his infant daughter. The problem of the child was clearly the end of some sort of line, a final burden added to an accumulation of burdens that had become unbearable.

Mr. Dehn reached the door. His tall frame seemed to grow taller. Sally remembered her father doing that. The shock of the blow had been weathered. Mr. Dehn was back in charge of Mr. Dehn. It was safe for him to turn around. He did.

"Thanks for the coffee," he said.

There was nothing in his face or voice to indicate that he had just come through something difficult. Nothing but the telltale shadow of the only man with whom Sally had failed: her father. The shadow told her she had failed again.

"Look," she said, "I didn't intend to make that sound as blunt as it obviously did. I'd like to explain what I mean."

"That won't be necessary," Mr. Dehn said. "I know what you mean."

Long after he was gone Sally was still standing in the doorway, seeing the long, strong strides that had carried him down Cavalry Road, away from the scene of injury, away from her. When she realized her cheeks were wet, Sally turned and went into the house and closed the door gently.

34

"Good afternoon, gentlemen," Colin Babington said from the head of the table. His gavel tapped the marble block. "The sixty-third meeting of Beechwood's Sixteenth Board of Selectmen will consider itself in session. Have I got the numbers right, Sig?"

Sig Wolton, the board secretary, poked the plate-glass-thick half moons up on his nose and dipped his bony bald skull down over his papers.

"Sixty-second, actually, Colin," he said. "We've been one number behind ever since we skipped that meeting last January because of the flu epidemic."

"Well, whatever the number," Colin Babington said, "the meeting is in session."

Sig Wolton made a note. He did it the way, on his early-morning prowls through the vast greenhouses of the Wolton Nurseries, Ltd., on the Post Road, he made a note on the temperature chart of a hybrid he was bringing along from some improbable cross-pollination. Sigismund Wolton had in his time, which was not short, created any number of spectacularly ugly flowers by which professional gardeners were awed into presenting him with gold medals but for which no woman interested in a corsage would give him a nickel.

"By the way," Colin Babington said. "Anybody feel cold in here?"

"I called Moses this morning and told him to lay a fire," Jim Martineau said.

The Wall Street brokerage firm that bore his name occasionally used Martineau's membership on the Beechwood Board of Selectmen as a jumping-off place for making a point in its weekly market letter:

Speaking of the current picture in U.S. Treasury Notes, it might be interesting to point out that Jim Martineau, our President, was remarking at the last meeting of the Board of Selectmen in Beechwood, N. Y., of which he is a member, that the SEC position in Washington is at considerable variance with the Federal Reserve Board's incursion into the Senate Banking Committee investigation of prime interest rates as they affect . . .

"Laying a fire is one thing," Colin Babington said. "Lighting it is what keeps you warm."

Jim Martineau pushed back his chair.

"I'll go get Moses," he said.

"Life is not long," Beverly Udall said, *"and too much of it must not pass in idle deliberation how it shall be spent."*

"What?" Jim Martineau said.

"Samuel Johnson," Beverly Udall said. "By the time you locate Moses and the old coon gets up here we could be halfway through the agenda. It's pretty short today, and if we put our backs into it we can finish before any of us freezes to death."

"Very sound," Colin Babington said.

Jim Martineau sank back into his chair.

"If Johnson said anything on the subject of people who can't make up their minds about fires," Oliver Stehli said, "don't quote it now, Bev."

Don Fortgang sent a furtive look toward the editor of the *Bugle.* He picked up nothing. Stehli was playing with his Phi Beta Kappa key as he studied the agenda.

"I'll entertain a motion that the minutes of the last meeting be accepted without being read," Colin Babington said.

"So moved," Sig Wolton said.

"Seconded," Jim Martineau said.

"All in favor?" Colin Babington said.

Don Fortgang joined the murmur of "Ayes" even though he was wrestling demons that threatened to strangle him.

"Carried," Colin Babington said. "Thank you, gentlemen. The only thing that troubles me about presiding at the meeting of this board is a recurring fear that some day somebody will want to hear the minutes of the last meeting read aloud."

He studied the papers in front of him.

"Gentlemen," Colin Babington said finally. "Since this meeting has been specially convened, we will omit the usual agenda and go at once to the one item I felt it unwise to list on an official agenda. I'm sure you all know to what I refer, but before any of us mentions any names I'm going to ask Sig Wolton to recap his fountain pen. With your permission, gentlemen, I would like to have today's discussion off the record."

"Agreed, agreed, agreed."

The jumble of voices flowed across the board table like spilled syrup.

"Any disagreement?" Colin Babington said.

Silence.

"Very well, then," Colin Babington said. "I refer, of course, to the statement on the front page of this morning's *Bugle* by Mr. David Dehn. I assume everybody at this table has read it?"

Heads nodding.

"Oliver," Babington said, "I assume you solicited the statement from Mr. Dehn?"

"I did," Oliver Stehli said. "The President of the United States does not recognize new independent nations every day in the week. When he does, it's news. In the case of Israel it is very special news in any community with a Jewish population. Until a little over a year ago we never had a Jewish population in Beechwood. Now we have, and it is growing. It seems to me a matter of not particularly brilliant but certainly elementary journalism to ask the leader of the Beechwood Jewish community for a statement."

"Did you suggest to Mr. Dehn what he should say in his statement?" Colin Babington said.

"Now, Colin, will you please cut the Oliver Wendell Holmes crap?" Stehli said. "You know as well as I do that there are certain things you don't suggest to a man. I've never been a Jew, but if I had been nobody would have to tell me what to say on an occasion like this."

"We have a Jew on our board," Colin Babington said. "Let's ask him what he would have said. Don?"

The years of practice came to Don Fortgang's rescue. Up from the confusion and fear with which he had been living since breakfast came the voice he had fashioned long ago for use at this table: civilized, calm, well modulated, bemused, affable, friendly, courteous, and full of shit. The voice of One of Them.

"Pretty much what Mr. Dehn said, I should think," Don Fortgang said to his fellow members of the Beechwood Board of Selectmen. "I would have welcomed the new country to the international family of nations. I would have saluted the brave men and dedicated women who had brought it into existence. I would have wished it a long, happy, and successful life."

"Anything else?" Colin Babington said.

Don Fortgang pursed his lips and looked up thoughtfully at the ceiling, displaying for the benefit of his fellow board members the intense sincerity of his quest for additional information they as well as he knew did not exist.

"Don't you think that would be adequate?" he said finally.

"I would," Colin Babington said. "But Mr. Dehn obviously didn't."

"I'm not Mr. Dehn," Don Fortgang said.

"If you were," Colin Babington said, "would you have added to your statement what Mr. Dehn added to his?"

You son of a bitch, Don Fortgang thought without losing

his small, civilized, bemused smile. There was only one way to handle this. He had been doing it in this room for eleven years.

"Let's look for a moment at what Mr. Dehn added," Don Fortgang said. "He added that every Jewish community in every part of the world, including the United States, is now responsible for the survival of Israel as an independent nation. Beechwood, Mr. Dehn added, is no exception. He doubted, however, that the Jewish community of Beechwood is capable under its present leadership of discharging its responsibility to Israel. The man who now represents the Beechwood Jewish community on our Board of Selectmen, Mr. Dehn said, is not representative of our Jewish community. He is, and I quote, a prop Jew. Meaning a toady to his Gentile neighbors. This man, Mr. Dehn said in print this morning, must go. And Mr. Dehn concluded his statement by announcing his intention to run at the next election for this man's post on the Board of Selectmen. Have I omitted anything?"

"Only what Mr. Dehn omitted," Colin Babington said. "The name of what he calls our prop Jew."

Don Fortgang had no trouble with that one either.

"He obviously felt it was unnecessary," Don said. "He obviously assumed the name is as well known to readers of the *Bugle* as it is to the men in this room."

"Okay, Don," Beverly Udall said. "*Clear your mind of cant.*"

"I don't have as much to clear out as Dr. Johnson had," Don Fortgang said.

How did the bastards like them apples? Penn State was not equipped with a Skull and Bones or a Porcellian, but it offered its sons the services of some damn good English profs.

"Perhaps not," Beverly Udall said. "But you've got as much as most men have, including me. You don't have to be a Jew to reach our age and discover your head is jam-packed with nonsense. We pick it up the way a blue serge suit picks up lint. What I meant by rid your mind of cant, Don, I meant

325

get rid of the idea that anybody in this room is out to get you. You're among friends."

"I'm sorry if I gave you the impression I thought otherwise," Don Fortgang said.

He could talk their double-talk better than they could. It was their native tongue, so they used it with the slovenly ease of familiarity. But he had been forced to learn their language in order to survive. He spoke it with the artificiality of textbook grammar.

"The fact is," Don said, "I'm on today's agenda but the First Selectman doesn't want me on the record. It gives a man pause."

Screw the bastards. Let them think he was quoting from one of the minor poems of John Milton.

"Don is quite right," Colin Babington said. "I assumed he would know why I wanted this discussion to go unrecorded, just as everybody else in this room knows it, but since I now learn that Don does not know, I think I should clear the air for him."

His idea of clearing the air, Don noticed it, was to fill it with great big clouds of smoldering "My Mixture" by lighting up his stinking straight-grain briar.

"If there's no extra charge," Oliver Stehli said, "you mind clearing it for me too, Colin?"

"Of course not," Colin Babington said. "It's no secret that the competition for seats on the Beechwood Board of Selectmen is hardly what can be described as spirited. There's no money in it, as we all know, and plenty of hard work. Once we get the seven slots filled, the general tendency is to heave a huge sigh of relief, which lasts for two years, until Election Day begins coming up over the horizon again. Every man at this table knows the pattern. Months before Election Day we start talking about getting new blood on the board, the same people can't be expected to do the work forever, it's time for others to take a crack at it, and so on. Six weeks before Election Day, because nobody else in town has come forward with an offer to serve, the seven of us wearily agree to take on another term, and work harder next time to get new members on the team. That's the pattern we went through this year. All of us have served for so long that we wanted out, but unfortunately we could find nobody who wanted in. We agreed that the present members of the board, the people at this table, would once again stand for re-election.

"This morning, on the front page of your newspaper, Oliver, I read that Mr. Dehn intends to contest the seat of one of our members. It seemed to me the matter should be discussed by us in confidence. In confidence means, I have always assumed, off the record. That's why I did not have the matter placed on the agenda, and that's why I asked Sig Wolton to put the cap back on his fountain pen. Does that satisfy you, Oliver?"

"Except for one point," Oliver Stehli said.

"Yes?" Colin Babington said.

"What's there to discuss?" Oliver Stehli said.

"Perhaps it would be more appropriate if Don answered that," Colin Babington said. "Do you mind, Don?"

Had Ruth Snyder minded discussing whether she would prefer to walk to the electric chair in her I. Miller spike heels or shuffle her way to the death chamber in her Bloomingdale bedroom scuffs?

"Not at all," Don Fortgang said. "Of the seven slots on the board, Mr. Dehn has announced that the one for which he is going to run is mine. He's not contesting Colin or Jim or Neil or Beverly or Sig or you, Oliver. The man Mr. Dehn has announced he intends to drive out of office is me."

"I'm not stupid, Don," Oliver Stehli said. "I read Mr. Dehn's announcement on the front page of my paper this morning. It may come as news to some people, but I read what I print. I'm aware, Don, that Mr. Dehn has set his cap for your seat on the board. All of Beechwood is now aware of it. My question is why, then, does the board have to arrange for an *in camera* discussion of something everybody in town knows?"

Don Fortgang looked toward Colin Babington. The First

Selectman took the pipe from his mouth and bobbed his head.

"The ball is still in your court, Don," he said.

That's not the place, Don Fortgang thought savagely, where I would like to shove it.

"Because what Mr. Dehn has done, Oliver, has never before happened in Beechwood," Don Fortgang said. "Mr. Dehn has set up a public scrap between two prominent Jews in a town that has never before had a Jewish problem."

"Do we have one now?" Oliver Stehli said.

Don Fortgang didn't have a pipe to pull out of his mouth, but he had a head that could be nodded. He nodded it toward Colin Babington.

"I think, Colin, the ball is now in your court," Don Fortgang said.

"I disagree," Colin Babington said. "We will have a public scrap only if Don stands for re-election. If he bows out before the ballots are printed the way will be clear for Mr. Dehn's name to be inserted. If Don does not bow out we will definitely have an ugly fight for the seat. What do you say, Don?"

You slimy slob, Don said, but he said it to himself, of course. And not without a touch of bitter admiration. Even when they wanted your balls cut off they made sure you wielded the knife. An ugly fight for his seat was a horror Don Fortgang did not want to face. The alternative, however, was worse. What he could never face was losing the badge of office that guaranteed his role as Beechwood's prop Jew.

"I will do what the board wants," Don said. "I have served on this board for eleven years. I have always assumed I was serving with friends, and I see no reason to change that assumption now. If the members of this board want me to fight for my seat I can guarantee Mr. Dehn a lively scrap."

"Speaking for myself, Don," Oliver Stehli said, "I would like to see you make a fight for your seat. Beechwood hasn't had a lively scrap since Lord Howe tried to sail the British fleet up the Bronx River to take West Point, and we know how much in the way of community fireworks this town got out of that."

"Thanks, Oliver," Don Fortgang said.

"We're the ones who should be thanking you," Oliver Stehli said. He turned to the others. "What sayeth the rest of this off-the-record board?"

They said "Hear, hear!" and "By all means!" and "Absolutely!"

"Okay, Don," Jim Martineau said. "Get in there and beat the ass off this Mr. Dehn. We're all behind you. Now I've got to go back to my office and do something about earning my living."

The scraping of chairs, the shaking of hands, the pats on the back, the hearty good wishes all formed a blur so pleasant that for Don Fortgang it was almost like all of the past eleven years. In the warmth by which he was now surrounded he realized it was better than the past eleven years. For the first time in his life Don Fortgang not only felt like a Gentile. For a few delicious moments he believed he was a Gentile.

Then the warmth eased away with the departure of the other members and he was alone in the room with the First Selectman.

"I'm glad you decided to fight," Colin Babington said. "You know that promise I made to put you up for membership in the City Club?"

"I'm sorry about the way I acted that day," Don Fortgang said. "I didn't mean to—you know—I mean, I'm afraid I sounded angry."

"Not at all," Colin Babington said. "I wanted you to do something for me. You had a perfect right to demand a *quid pro quo*."

"I didn't deliver," Don said.

"Neither did I," Colin Babington said. "But now we've both been given another chance. You beat the ass off Mr. Dehn and I'll put you up for membership in the City Club."

Don Fortgang shook his head with the skilled counterfeit

of admiration that eleven years of practice had honed to perfection.

"Colin," he said, "you're a very generous man."

"Not generous," Colin Babington said. "Patient. *The Jew has taught me how to wait.*"

If Don Fortgang had learned anything in his eleven years at the board table in the upstairs room of the Beechwood Town Hall, he had learned to recognize a quotation when he heard one.

"Shakespeare?" he said.

"Ibsen," Colin Babington said. "*Peer Gynt.*"

"Thanks," Don Fortgang said. "I won't disappoint the board."

"The one not to disappoint is me," Colin Babington said. "I don't give third chances."

35

The next morning, when the impending election came up on the staff agenda, Dave was ready.

"We've thrown our hat in the ring," Sid Singer said. "Or rather, you have. And it worries me."

"Why?" Dave said.

"Everything we've done up to now we've done under our own steam," Sid said. "When people got in our way, guys like Babington, those Catholic War Veterans, then Riordan, we just turned our own steam up a few notches and plowed through them. Winning an election, I don't know, Dave, that's a different kind of ball game."

"In what way?" Dave said.

"It doesn't depend on our own steam," Sid said. "It depends on the steam of all those people out there who do the voting. What I'm saying, or trying to say in my nervous, worried Jewish way, Dave, I'm saying it's dawned on me we're wading into something on which we have no track record."

"How much track record did we have on building synagogues?"

"We didn't need any," Sid said. "We had something better. We had something inside your head. We had Mike's talent. We had what we believed in. Plus we had the land and we had the money and we went ahead and did what we wanted to do with both."

"I know what Sid means," Mike said. "We had a conviction. That's what gave us the steam. We knew what we wanted and why we wanted it and nobody was going to stop us. This thing, Dave on the Board of Selectmen instead of this Fortgang character, I don't know why we want that. All I know is that if we win, what have we won? But if we lose it's our first public bloody nose in this town where an awful lot of anti-Semites would be very happy to sit around chortling while we bleed to death."

"We can't have that," Dave said. "Can we?"

"You bet your ass we can't," Sid said.

"Then we've got to win," Dave said.

"Is it worth the effort?" Mike said.

"You pour a fortune into building a ship," Dave said. "Is it worth the effort to build a life raft?"

"Ships sink," Mike Palgrave said. "We're one hundred and eighty acres of solidly anchored real estate."

"Anything will sink if somebody blows a hole in the bottom from inside," Dave said. "As long as Don Fortgang sits on that Board of Selectmen we've got a guy with a stick of dynamite and a lighted match prowling our basement. You want to be left out of this?"

"Of course not," Mike Palgrave said. "You know that."

"Okay, then," Dave said. "You've got your list. Sid's got his. Anything else, Fanny?"

"This congregation in Mt. Vernon," Fanny said. "They asked again. You can set your own date."

"Fanny, for God's sake," Dave said. "We've just taken on a political campaign. I don't have a minute to waste."

"It's your own fault," Fanny said. "You apparently wowed them in Bridgeport, and some of the ladies told some of their friends and *mishpocheh* down in Mt. Vernon, so they want you to come speak."

"Dave?"

"Yes, Sid?"

"I'd do it," Sid said. "You're worried about Don Fortgang prowling in our basement with a stick of dynamite and a

lighted match. It can't hurt to make friends outside our basement. You never know when you'll want an extra fire extin-
guisher. Fanny's right. You did impress them in Bridgeport.
Floyd Klenczewski told me he heard the same thing from the
guy who delivers his beer. He lives in Bridgeport."

"The guy who delivers the beer to Floyd Klenczewski's
Steak Pit is a Jew?" Dave said.

"Up in Bridgeport you spoke in a synagogue," Sid said.
"Right?"

"Not in the sanctuary," Dave said. "It's a Jewish center,
like here. They have an auditorium."

"Well, the guy who drives the truck that delivers Floyd
Klenczewski's beer heard you," Sid said. "I don't imagine
many harps on their way to Mass were dropping in off the
street to catch your act. So it seems reasonable to assume he's
a Jew."

"Then something else seems all of a sudden reasonable,"
Dave said. "There must be a lot of people around who are
Jews but you never think of them as Jews."

"Maybe you don't," Sid said. "But they do."

"That's my point," Dave said.

"That they're closet Jews?" Mike Palgrave said. "Hiding
out behind names like Palgrave?"

"Some of those, yes," Dave said. "But a lot of others, too.
People who don't think much about being Jews one way or
another. Because being a Jew has never affected their lives.
It never kept them from landing a job, or marrying the girl,
or renting an apartment, or checking into a hotel, or anything else. Part of that could be just dumb luck. Part of it
could be what these people do for a living. Part of it could
be stupidity or laziness or they're simply not interested in
what they are. Whatever it is, up to now I've been thinking of
self-conscious Jews. Like me, for example. It occurs to me
now there must be a hell of a lot more Jews around who are
not like me than there are Jews like me."

"You can say that again," Sid said dryly.

"I will," Dave said. "Because now I'm running for public

office I've got to talk like a politician. If I don't I won't get the votes, and if I don't get the votes I don't get Don Fortgang's seat on the Board of Selectmen. I won't get that seat if I count only on the votes he got."

"You can't count on those votes," Mike Palgrave said. "Not all of them, anyway. A lot of Don Fortgang's votes came from people like Colin Babington. People who think it's a good idea to have a prop Jew on the board. Most of those people are not going to switch their votes from a Jew on a leash to a Jew on the make."

"The closet Jews, though," Dave said. "The Jews who never thought much about being Jews, the people who never bother to vote for anything or anybody, the Jews like you, Mike. Those are the people I have to reach."

"You'll have to find an issue that will shake them out of their closets," Mike Palgrave said.

"Harry Truman found it for me," Dave said. "By recognizing Israel. Every closet Jew in the country is going to come out in the open now. As they do, there I am, waiting with what I said on the front page of the *Bugle*. All I have to do is say it over and over again. Not only here in Beechwood. I'm going to say it all over the map. Beginning with your friends down in Mt. Vernon, Fanny."

"They'll be pleased, D.D.," Fanny said.

"Let's please a lot of people," Dave said. "Look into the lecture circuit. Lay out a schedule. Let's get the silver-tongued orator of Westerlo Street out on the hustings. But lay off the make-up. I don't want to sweat streaks of Max Factor grease through the Jewish centers of Westchester County and Connecticut. Don Fortgang won't know what hit him."

"Perhaps not," Sid Singer said. "But let's us not be looking the other way when he starts swinging."

"I don't expect him to take the stump for me," Dave said. "What else, Fanny?"

"Only the Mort Blumenfeld thing," Fanny said.

"I'll take care of that personally," Dave said.

36

Dave did not himself realize how thoroughly he had taken care of the Blumenfeld thing until he came down from his apartment on the Saturday morning of Monroe Blumenfeld's bar mitzvah.

"My God," Fanny Mintz said in the lobby. "Do you think we'll be able to feed them all?"

"If not all at once," Dave said, "it will be done in shifts. Let Floyd Klenczewski handle it. He's always refused to admit Jews to his place in ones and twos. At eleven bucks a head he's willing to take them in carload lots. The ones he doesn't feed he doesn't get paid for. That's the deal I made with him. So don't worry. He'll feed them all if he has to carry orders of Matzoh Brei Ben-Gurion out to the sidewalk. You seen the bar mitzvah boy?"

"He's in my office with his father," Fanny said.

"I'd better go in and say a few words," Dave said.

"Don't say too many," Fanny said. "The natives in the sanctuary are getting restless."

On his way across the lobby Dave caught a glimpse of the sanctuary through the open double doors. People were coming in from the parking area, moving into the pews, filling up the large, high-ceilinged room. Dave moved on into Fanny's office.

"Dave," Mort Blumenfeld said.

He came up from the chair behind Fanny's desk with his cigar in one hand and his other aimed at Dave's navel.

"Hello, Mort," Dave said, taking Blumenfeld's outstretched hand. "How's the bar mitzvah boy?"

Monroe was sitting in the visitor's chair next to Fanny's desk. He came to his feet like a stunted West Point cadet wheeling on parade in the direction of the colors.

"Monroe has something to tell you," Mort Blumenfeld said.

The boy bobbed his head.

"Mr. Dehn," Monroe Blumenfeld said. "Today I stand on the threshold of manhood. This is the most important moment of my life. To remember it always will help make me a better Jew and a better man. Because of your kindness and generosity it will be easier for me to remember this moment as long as I live. I want to thank you from the bottom of my heart for providing me with this beautiful setting for my bar mitzvah. I will always try to justify the confidence you have shown in me."

The boy might have said more. Dave was not sure. Monroe's strained voice, his awkward stance, the frightened look on the thin, bony face had unexpectedly carried Dave back to the night before his own bar mitzvah. The night when his father had rehearsed him in the speech the old man had written for Dave to deliver privately to Rabbi Goldfarb. The speech that thanked the rabbi for the time and trouble he had taken in preparing Dave for this most important event in his life. Dave had never delivered that speech. Rabbi Goldfarb had burned to death on the sidewalk in front of the synagogue on Westerlo Street an hour before Dave entered man's estate. But Dave remembered the words. They had not been his own. The feelings, however, had been. Those feelings were suddenly very real to Dave.

"I thank you," Monroe Blumenfeld said.

Dave did not answer. The remembered feelings had betrayed him. They had carried him forward. They had lifted him across the mental barrier that for years had shielded him from the morning of the horror. The remembered feelings had thrust him into the hours beyond his terrifying recollection. Beyond Sid Singer's yelling. Beyond Dutch Stuermer laughing. Beyond Rabbi Goldfarb screaming. Beyond the police who had carried away the charred corpse and taken Dutch Stuermer into custody. Dave was suddenly back with his father in the tenement kitchen.

"The suit," the old man said. "We'll have to change."

He spoke calmly. Moving easily, as though it were the most commonplace activity of an ordinary day, he helped the boy out of the destroyed clothes that a half hour earlier had been brand new. Without comment Dave's father rolled up the burned jacket and the singed, kerosene-soaked longies. He wrapped the ruined finery in several pages of yesterday's *Jewish Daily Forward*. He stuffed the evil-smelling bundle into the garbage pail and set it out in the hall.

"Wash the face," Dave's father said.

The boy bent over the kitchen sink. His hands moved without help from his brain. The inside of his head was a dull, shapeless ache.

"Scrub the neck," his father called from the bedroom. "The new *tallis* must be kept clean."

The word stabbed into the lump of numbness between Dave's ears. What *tallis*? His father came out of the bedroom. The old man was carrying a towel and a bundle of clothes.

"It's a bar mitzvah," Mr. Dehn said. "For a bar mitzvah a boy must be clean so he can become a clean man."

The boy's brain seemed to turn over and stretch. It came awake. He remembered. Today was the day for which Rabbi Goldfarb had been preparing him for months. Then he remembered what had just happened to Rabbi Goldfarb.

"Pa," the boy said.

"The shirt is clean," Mr. Dehn said.

He held up one of Dave's old shirts. The boy remembered what had just happened to the new one.

"The pants are clean enough," his father said.

He held up the pair of knickers Dave had worn all week to school.

"It's not so warm today," the old man said.

He held up Dave's school sweater. The boy understood.

"Okay, Pa," he said.

The neatly pressed jacket, the first pair of long pants, the freshly laundered shirt no longer existed. The old man expected him to make do with what was left.

"I'll go get the rolls for breakfast," Mr. Dehn said.

The boy understood something else.

"No," he said, poking his leg into the old knickers. "No," Dave said again, pulling on the sweater.

What he understood was what the old man was telling him. Rabbi Goldfarb was gone. The bar mitzvah ceremony was waiting.

"I'll get the rolls," the boy said. He wanted his father to know he understood. So the boy said it again. "I'll get the rolls."

More than twenty years later, in Fanny Mintz's office, he could hear the words that had carried him across the invisible boundary line into manhood.

Before he was aware of what he was doing Dave dipped down. He put his arms around Monroe Blumenfeld's skinny shoulders and pulled the boy close. Dave held him for several moments. By the time the door opened Dave was all right again. Fanny Mintz stuck her head into the room.

"D.D.?" she said. "Now?"

Dave's memories slid back into the drawer in his mind out of which they had erupted.

"Okay, Fanny," he said.

She pulled her head out. The door clicked shut. Dave straightened the shoulder padding of the boy's blazer.

"Mort," Dave said. "You know where you're sitting?"

"Front bench, center," Mort Blumenfeld said. "Facing the steps up to the Torah."

"Right," Dave said. "You better go in now. I'll be another minute."

"Okay, Monroe," Mort Blumenfeld said.

He punched out his cigar in the smokador beside Fanny's desk. He took his son's hand and turned to Dave.

"That goes for me too," Mort Blumenfeld said.

"That's all right," Dave said.

It was. For the first time since they had met he liked Mort Blumenfeld. Father and son started for the door. Dave remembered something. "Monroe," he said.

The boy turned.

"I was scared too," Dave said. "Everybody is. You have to be. It's part of the deal. But the people out in front, nobody notices you're scared. They're waiting for the words. That's all they notice. You just say the words and you'll be okay. Say them good and loud."

The planes of the boy's face started to rearrange themselves.

"Yes, sir," he said.

"I'll be out there listening," Dave said. "Say the words to me, the way you've been saying them in rehearsal. Never mind the other people. Just say the words to me. That way you won't make any mistakes."

The shifting planes of the boy's face settled down. They had formed a shy smile.

"Yes, sir," Monroe Blumenfeld said again.

Holding his father's hand the boy walked out of the office. Dave gave them a couple of minutes. Then he followed. The foyer was empty. At the far end of the corridor the sanctuary doors were open. A low murmur of sound came rolling down toward Dave. He moved up to meet it. In the doorway he stopped. The service was under way.

"Thy house I enter constantly, through Thine abundant mercy."

Perry Vogel's voice rose from the raised platform on which he stood in the middle of the room.

"Still worship at Thy holy fane," Vogel sang up to the ark. *"In reverence of Thee."*

Dave looked around. The people directly in front of him could be identified only by the backs of their heads. The members of the community were no problem. The men all wore the black silk *yarmulkes* provided by the Center. The women had scarves knotted over their heads and under their chins. The rest were probably strangers from Mt. Vernon and Norwalk and Westport who had responded to Dave's ads in the local papers promising a free lunch at Floyd Klenczewski's Steak Pit to all who attended Monroe Blumenfeld's bar mitzvah. Most were bareheaded, men and women alike. Goyim, no doubt. The others were probably Jews. The men wore snap-brim felt hats, the women head scarves.

"*How goodly, Jacob, are thy tents,*" Perry Vogel chanted. "*Israel, thy abodes.*"

The pews to the left and right, Dave saw, were filled with pretty much the same mix. About half his own people, the other half strangers.

"*O Lord, I love Thy dwelling place, wherein Thy glory rests. There humbly bow and bend the knee, before the Lord, my Maker.*"

The words meant nothing to Dave. Perry Vogel was chanting them in Hebrew. The cadences, however, were as familiar to Dave as his own face in the shaving mirror.

"*And offer prayer in time of Grace, Eternal! unto Thee: O God! Thou ever merciful, respond with true salvation.*"

The rhythms carried him back. Back to the kitchen on Westerlo Street and his father's voice telling *meises*. Back to the synagogue and the enveloping sense of safety. The rhythms also carried him forward. To the good places and the bad. Allowing him to pause with the good. Hurrying him away from the bad. Bringing him to the best of all. The best of all, and the most troubling. Now. Rachel.

"*Extol the living God! His praises sound! Whose being unbegun no time can bound.*"

A tug on Dave's sleeve. He turned. Sally Palgrave had come up beside him.

"Don't worry," she whispered. "She's sleeping. Daisy Sternshus is with her. Where's Mike?"

Dave nodded down to the front.

"First row," he said. "Halfway over from Mort Blumenfeld and Monroe."

Sally lifted her one hundred and twenty pounds to her toes. She peered. Dave had never seen her body from this angle. He swallowed away the dry spot in the back of his throat. He moved his right thigh to accommodate the faint stir in his loins.

"A unity is He, beside Him none. By mortal unconceived, Eternal One."

Sally came back down on her heels.

"He'll be a while, won't he?" she whispered.

"Vogel?" Dave said.

"No, Mike," Sally said. "But I guess I mean both."

"Nobody will be getting up and going out for at least an hour," Dave said. "This is the opening part of the service." He paused, then said, "If that's what you mean?"

"Yes," Sally said. "I thought you'd like to come over and see her for a few minutes."

Then Sally seemed to understand what Dave meant. She giggled.

"You idiot," she whispered. "I mean Rachel."

The stirring in Dave's loins eased away. He was not sorry to feel it go. Not at the moment.

"I can't now," he said. "Could I come over later?"

"Of course," Sally said. "Any time."

She groped for his hand. They stood there, side by side, staring down toward the chanting rabbi.

"Without similitude, or corporeal frame, Man's lips His hallowed state can ne'er proclaim."

Sally's hand squeezed his.

"I better go," she whispered. "Daisy wants to come over. She's never been to a bar mitzvah."

"Okay," Dave whispered back. Then, "She's okay?"

"Of course she's okay," she said. "How can any daughter of yours not be okay?"

Dave squeezed her hand hard. He shot a quick glance to left and right. He started to step backward, through the open sanctuary doors, into the corridor. Sally's body resisted.

"No," she said. "Not here."

She worked her hand loose and stepped backward alone, out into the corridor. She hurried toward the foyer, stopped, and turned. Dave had turned to watch her. She blew him a kiss, then disappeared. His heart eased. Rachel was safe.

"Or ere creation rose, He stood sublime, Alone and sustained before all time."

Dave turned back to the congregation.

"Yield with my soul this frame of mine," the rabbi chanted. *"My God is near; I know not fear."*

He turned slowly from the ark to the congregation.

"And now," Vogel said in English, "we come to an event that is a regularly recurring part of our Jewish life. Nevertheless, no matter how frequently it occurs, this event makes of every sabbath an occasion of very special brightness. I refer to the bar mitzvah ceremony. Today it is our honor, our pleasure, and our treasured duty to perform this ceremony for Monroe Blumenfeld. Monroe?"

Dave saw Mort Blumenfeld give his son the small push the boy needed to make it smoothly to his feet. Once on them Monroe looked steady enough. He walked forward and climbed the three platform steps. Perry Vogel took the boy by both biceps and turned him gently to face the congregation. Then he put one arm across Monroe's shoulder as though to keep him steady.

"This is the first bar mitzvah ceremony to be performed in this sanctuary," Vogel said. "As such it has a dual significance. Today's ceremony marks not only the entrance of Monroe Blumenfeld into man's estate, but also the entrance of this congregation into the spiritual life of our community. To mark this unusual occasion we have decided to call upon a special sponsor for Monroe. Will Mr. Israel Fortgang please come forward?"

Dave watched Lieutenant Fortgang do for his grandfather what Mort Blumenfeld had just done for his son. The young man in blue uniform gave the old man in black broadcloth a gentle but firm shove upward. Don Fortgang's father came to his feet. The little old man tugged the black broadcloth jacket down straight over his nonexistent hips. He checked the arrangement of the *tallis* across his shoulders. It was an old *tallis*. Yellow with age. Like the *tallis* worn by Dave's father in the painting on the wall of his living room upstairs. The little old man touched the *yarmulke* to make sure it was sitting firmly on his head. Then he marched down the aisle to the platform. He climbed the three steps as though they were parts of a ladder. Bringing both feet together, side by side, on each step before he tackled the next-higher one.

"Ladies and gentlemen," Perry Vogel said. "Mr. Israel Fortgang is the first Jew who ever came to live in the town of Beechwood. That was sixty-three years ago. Today Mr. Fortgang is the oldest living Jew in this community, and a charter member of our congregation. Mr. Fortgang will conduct the bar mitzvah ceremony."

Vogel stepped aside. Mr. Fortgang went to the lectern. From the lower level, below the unrolled Torah, he took a blue velvet pouch. It was embroidered with strands of woven gold braid and with silk threads of red and blue and green. Mr. Fortgang drew from the pouch a flat packet of folded white silk. He brought it to the boy. The little old man shook out the folds of the *tallis*. He held it wide, as though he were proudly exhibiting a brand-new flag before running it up the pole. He spoke quietly but clearly. Dave at the rear of the sanctuary heard every syllable.

"*Blessed art Thou, the Eternal,*" the little old man said in Yiddish. "*Our God, King of the universe, Who hath sanctified us with His commandments.*"

He spread the prayer shawl across Monroe Blumenfeld's shoulders. He smoothed the wings down the front of the boy's blazer. Like a meticulous tailor, satisfied at last that the fit of his creation is perfect, the little old man lifted the tassels at the end of the right wing and placed them in Monroe's hand.

"Now you," the little old man said.

"Blessed art Thou, the Eternal," Monroe Blumenfeld said, but not very clearly. His voice was too high, and it wavered. *"Our God, King of the universe."* The voice came down and, like a bird, settled into place. *"Who hath sanctified us with His commandments."*

"Kiss," the old man said sternly.

Monroe kissed the tassels. For a few moments he held them in the air, mouth high, uneasy about his next move. Gently the old man moved the boy's hand down to his side and eased the clutching fingers away from the silken tassels. He whispered something in Monroe's ear. The boy's face flushed. He bobbed his head. He lifted his right arm. The little old man folded the wing of the *tallis* back across Monroe's shoulder and down his back. He opened the middle button of the boy's blazer. Carefully, as though he were removing the wrappings from a piece of fragile china, the little old man worked Monroe's arm out of the sleeve. He folded back the blazer so that the right side of the boy's white shirt was exposed. Then he opened the button of the cuff and folded the shirt sleeve back up above Monroe's elbow.

"Hold," the little old man said.

Monroe held the folded shirt sleeve in place while the little old man returned to the lectern. From the embroidered pouch he drew a package of neatly folded narrow leather straps. Mr. Fortgang wound one of the narrow leather straps around Monroe's bare right forearm as though he were decorating a barber pole. He left spaces of visible skin between the twists of the strap. Just below the boy's elbow the strap ended in a small black leather cube. It looked not unlike one half of an outsize pair of unmarked dice. The little old man anchored the black cube to Monroe's arm, then carried the lead strap around the boy's back and up over his head. The strap ended in another black cube. Mr. Fortgang set this on Monroe's forehead, and anchored it solidly by working the attached strap back up under the boy's *yarmulke.* Then the old man addressed the ark, speaking across the boy's head.

"Thou hast selected us from all peoples," Mr. Fortgang chanted. *"Loved and taken pleasure in us, and exalted us above all nations, sanctified us with Thy commandments, and brought us nigh, O our King! unto Thy service, and by Thy name, the great and holy, hast Thou called us."*

He paused and nodded to Monroe. The boy repeated the chant. When Monroe swung into *dyim in dyim ein mollach tzim onderrin,* Dave stepped from the shelter of the last row of seats and moved swiftly down the aisle. He stopped at the first row, just below the platform, and touched Mort Blumenfeld's shoulder. Blumenfeld looked up, nodded, and swung his knees aside. Dave slid into the pew and sat down in the space Monroe had vacated.

"How we doing?" Blumenfeld whispered.

"Great," Dave whispered back. "The kid's a winner."

Don Fortgang's father up on the platform clearly agreed. When Monroe came to the end of the passage the little old man thrust out his hand. Monroe took it. They shook like fighters meeting in the center of the ring before the bell for the first round. Perry Vogel stepped forward.

"Now we come to what through many centuries of our history has gradually evolved into a treasured tradition," the rabbi said to the congregation. "In the final exercise of the bar mitzvah ceremony the young man who has just assumed the duties and responsibilities of an adult in the Jewish community addresses himself to the members of that community. The subject of his address is a matter of the young man's own choice. In the old days the words he employed were, of course, Hebrew. Today in our homeland the young men of Israel still address their bar mitzvah congregations in the language of Abraham and Isaac. In this country, where Hebrew is not spoken generally, our young men usually address their bar mitzvah congregations in Yiddish. Sometimes, for obvious reasons, in English. Communication is sometimes more important than tradition. Which will it be, Monroe?"

345

"English, please," the boy said.

"Ladies and gentlemen," Perry Vogel said. "Monroe Blumenfeld."

The rabbi took two steps back, until he stood at the side of Mr. Fortgang. The two men, like an honor guard, watched the boy step forward.

"My dear father," Monroe Blumenfeld said. "Rabbi Vogel, Mr. Fortgang, and fellow members of the congregation. Today, as I assume the burdens and duties and the privileges of a Jew among my fellow Jews, I would like to thank those who have helped me reach this privileged state. First, I want to thank my dearly beloved departed mother, whom God in His wisdom saw fit to take from me before I knew her but without whom I would not be standing here today. Then I would like to thank my dearly beloved father, who has been an inspiration and comfort and support to me through all the years that have brought me to this moment. Then I want to thank Rabbi Vogel for the time and trouble he took in preparing me for these ceremonies. And last but not least I want to thank Mr. Israel Fortgang for his kindness in acting as my sponsor here today."

Monroe cleared his throat.

"I feel deeply privileged to have reached man's estate as a Jew in this fateful year," the boy continued. "After centuries of persecution my people have finally achieved their great goal. At long last we have our homeland. The fact that this is no longer a dream but a reality has been demonstrated by our beloved President of these United States, Mr. Harry S. Truman, who recently recognized Israel as a legal member of the international family of nations."

With his clenched fist Monroe caught two barks of a modest cough.

"We all know what the realization of our great dream has meant to the Jews of America," the boy said. "I feel it is fitting and proper that I tell you what it means to me. It means the dedication of my life to the strength and protection of our Jewish homeland. It is the hope of this congregation that as

346

our young boys grow into manhood they will pledge themselves to the course of action I now plan to undertake."

Another cough. A straightening of the narrow back. A circling lick of the tongue around the suddenly dry lips.

"I hereby pledge by the God who has today in His mercy
received me as a Jew," Monroe Blumenfeld said in a loud,
clear voice, "that as soon as I graduate from high school I will
go to live in Israel and devote my life to the flowering of our
Jewish homeland. I thank you."

Monroe bowed to the congregation. He turned and walked
back to the honor guard. Perry Vogel and Mr. Fortgang made
room for him. The boy stepped between the two men. The
man on the seat beside Dave stirred. Dave turned. Mort Blumenfeld was coming out of shock.

"Jesus!"

His voice choked.

"The little *shmuck*," Monroe Blumenfeld's father managed to say. "Where the hell did the stupid kid get that crap?"

37

"From me," Dave said.

But he did not say it to Mort Blumenfeld. Dave said it to Rocky Riordan in the washroom of Floyd Klenczewski's Steak Pit.

"Is that what you made Blumenfeld promise in exchange for this great big free bar mitzvah blowout?" the police chief said.

Dave rinsed the last of the soap from his hands and snapped two paper towels from the white enamel container on the wall over the basin.

"A man wants something?" Dave said. "He'd better be ready to give something. So now you tell me what you want."

"What makes you think I want something?" Rocky Riordan said.

"The speed with which you followed me in here," Dave said. "I didn't even have my pants unzipped."

"The joint is jumping," Rocky Riordan said. "I wanted to get with you before you got snowed under by your guests."

"Get with me for what?" Dave said.

"To get his fancy bar mitzvah for free Mort Blumenfeld had to get his kid to promise he'd go over and fight for Israel," Rocky Riordan said. "What do I have to promise to get you to sell my kid brother that lot on Saul Road?"

"Votes," Dave said.

"Votes?" Rocky Riordan said.

"I'm running for Don Fortgang's seat on the Board of Selectmen," Dave said.

"I know," Rocky Riordan said.

"Then you also ought to know what it takes to win," Dave said.

"Meaning what?" Rocky Riordan said.

"Meaning not just the two votes you control up on Spinning Wheel Lane," Dave said.

"What other votes do I control?" Rocky Riordan said.

"If your kid brother comes to live in this town," Dave said, "he'll probably join the Catholic War Veterans."

"I haven't given any thought to that," Rocky Riordan said.

"Give some thought to it now," Dave said.

Riordan looked at him in the mirror over the row of washbasins.

"Okay," he said finally. "I guess the kid will."

"If your brother joined before the election," Dave said, "you'd have some clout with those organized harps."

"What kind of clout?" Riordan said.

"You're the Chief of Police in this town," Dave said. "You're also a harp. They'd listen to you if you told them it would be to their advantage in the law-and-order department if they used their votes to throw Fortgang out and put me in."

Riordan hesitated. Not for long.

"How soon can my kid brother get title to that lot?" he said.

"How soon can he get to see Sid Singer?" Dave said as the door opened.

Sid poked his head into the washroom.

"Who wants to see me?" he said.

"Rocky's kid brother," Dave said.

"How about Monday?" Sid said to the police chief.

"Monday's fine," Riordan said.

He started for the door. Sid pulled it wide and held it for the police chief.

"Try some of the *tsimmes* à la Chaim Weizmann," Dave said.

"I sort of had my heart set on the Matzoh Brei Ben-Gurion," Riordan said. "See you both."

He stepped out. Sid stepped in. The door swung shut.

"How about seeing me for a minute?" Sid said.

"I have to get out there with the guests," Dave said.

"The guests can wait," Sid said. "What I'm sitting on can't."

"What are you sitting on?" Dave said.

"A man named Ludwig Leverson," Sid said.

"Who is he?" Dave said.

"I don't know," Sid said. "But he was in the synagogue. He heard Monroe Blumenfeld make his pledge to go live in Israel."

"So did everybody else in the sanctuary," Dave said.

"Everybody else in the sanctuary doesn't want what Mr. Leverson wants."

"What does he want?" Dave said.

"Jersey City," Sid said.

Dave's mind jumped. Jersey City meant only one thing.

"The Noonan people?" he said.

"That's all we've got in Jersey City," Sid said.

"What are the Noonans doing with this Levinson?" Dave said.

"Leverson," Sid said. "You really ought to get over the idea that when a Jew changes his name he always picks Belmont."

"We may have to change this bastard's name to mud," Dave said. "The Noonans are our babies."

"They seem to have developed a sudden interest in establishing a new paternity," Sid said.

"Can they?" Dave said.

"Given the right point of view," Sid said, "anybody can do anything. The law-abiding citizen looks for sunsets. The crook looks for loopholes."

"This one won't find any," Dave said. "I wrote the Noonan basic-rights contract myself."

"And I dotted the i's and crossed the t's," Sid said. "Just the same, the Noonan boys are playing footsie with Mr. Leverson."

"One of us better pay a visit to Jersey City," Dave said.

"I did," Sid said. "Yesterday. I've been trying to get you alone in a corner since I got back last night. The Noonan boys are no longer tugging their forelocks and digging their toes shyly into the hot sand. They've been talking to lawyers."

"I think maybe I'd better have a talk with this Leverson," Dave said.

"He wants to talk to you," Sid said.

"Is he out there with the *tsimmes* à la Chaim Weizmann?" Dave said.

"No," Sid said. "He told me he wants to meet you on neutral ground."

"What's neutral ground in this area?" Dave said.

"Lola Truscott's house," Sid said. "You're expected for lunch at twelve-thirty. On Magruder Crescent."

What Dave knew about Lola Truscott did not quite fit Fanny Mintz's definition of a *megillah*. The information could not have been engraved on the head of a pin. On the other hand, it would not have slopped over the head of a pin by very much. Dave knew only two facts.

One: Mrs. Truscott was the widow of Colin Babington's former law partner.

Two: Through Babington she had sewed up the Metuchen property on Beach Road before Dave had been able to make a bid.

When he pulled his Cadillac into the Truscott driveway Dave knew something else.

Three: Ludwig Leverson, Mrs. Truscott's guest, was not the kind of Jew who liked people to know he was meticulous about not contributing to Germany's dollar credits in American banks. The car with the Pennsylvania license plates parked in Mrs. Truscott's driveway was a custom-built Mercedes.

Mrs. Truscott, who opened the door for Dave, said, "Mr. Dehn, for heaven's sake."

"I seem to have done something wrong," he said.

"Howlingly so," Mrs. Truscott said.

"You mean you're not going to let me in?" Dave said.

"I shouldn't," Mrs. Truscott said. "But I will. Please do come in and give me your coat."

"What have I done that's so howlingly wrong?" Dave said.

"You've had the audacity to live up to your billing," Lola Truscott said. "Colin Babington told me you look like Gary Cooper in a Brooks Brothers navy blue blazer, and here you are, doing precisely that."

"Nobody told me you look like Madame Bovary," Dave said.

"It's this silly hostess gown," Mrs. Truscott said. "Colin gave it to me for Christmas. He doesn't really know why, but I do. Colin's awareness of women began and ended with an image created by Flaubert. It's a terrible thing they do to those nubile, antiseptic boys in places like Deerfield. If you're taught directly or indirectly to believe that Emma Bovary is the target to shoot at, what's the point of panting over Susan Hayward or Greer Garson?"

"I was taught the same thing," Dave said. "As between Susan Hayward or Greer Garson, however, and a girl wearing that thing, I know how my decision would go."

"Why don't you come in and meet Mr. Leverson?" Mrs. Truscott said. "After we get rid of him we can pursue your decision."

Mr. Leverson, waiting in Lola Truscott's living room, could have been Winston Churchill waiting in a Toronto photographer's studio to be recorded for posterity by the lens of Yusof Karsh. Mr. Leverson had been gifted by nature with the head of a pig. It looked at the moment as though it were about to have an apple inserted in its mouth. It was obvious that Mr. Leverson was rich enough to disregard his resemblance to a citizen of the barnyard. He had chosen a more aggressive image. The bulldog.

"I'm damned interested to meet you," he said to Dave. "I was in your synagogue this morning. I heard that boy make his pledge about going to live in Israel. I now understand why Lola has been telling me you've been setting this old-fashioned Westchester town on its ear."

Mr. Leverson said this without removing his right fist from his hip. It was planted inside the jacket. The stance thus revealed one of those double-breasted vests called on Savile Row a waistcoat. A gold watch chain, with links as large as quoits, looped its impressive way across his middle. This outlined for the waiting camera a belly that had been put together by a couple of decades of vacillation between prime cuts selected by Henri Soulé and pastrami sandwiches sneaked from the Stage Deli. Mr. Leverson was clearly what Dave Dehn's father used to call a *chazer*.

"I don't know much about setting old-fashioned Westchester towns on their ears," Dave said. "I'm a boy from Albany. When I set places on anything it's usually their ass."

He got the right reaction. Mr. Leverson stopped posing for Karsh. He looked sharply at the young snot-nose Lola Truscott had brought into the room. Dave made a mental note on his side of the scoreboard.

He knew how to handle these bloated *chazers*. Dave had learned the trick in the E.T.O. Weeks—no, days—after he and Sid had rolled their jeep through the north gates of Buchenwald in April of 1945. They had been waiting, these big-bellied slobs.

Wearing uniforms tailored by Dunhill on Fifty-seventh Street and authorized by the p.a. boys in the Pentagon. Carrying cards signed by the Adjutant General, United States Army, Washington, D.C. Identifying the card carrier as a "noncombatant attached to the Army of the United States in the European Theater of Operations and, as such, in the event of capture by the enemy, is entitled to be treated as a prisoner of war, and that he will be given the same treatment and afforded the same privileges as an officer in the Army of the United States of the grade of Lieutenant-Colonel, by order of the Theater Commander, Elmer F. Poelke, 1st Lt., A.G.D."

The *chazers* were never captured, of course. They were too fast on their feet. Nimbly making the deals with the laundered Nazis that later earned them the prime cuts of beef chosen by Henri Soulé. And the Savile Row waistcoats from behind which they gave the finger to the Dave Dehns who survived. Or tried to.

"I can tell when men are trembling on the verge of a discussion they would rather not have women hear," Lola Truscott said. "This is clearly the appropriate moment for me to disappear into the kitchen and make sexy noises to a cheese soufflé that I hope will be responsive. Mr. Leverson, Mr. Dehn, I leave you to your own devices. The Mercurochrome and the Band-Aids are in the cabinet over the basin in the powder room."

She walked out into what Dave assumed was the kitchen.

"Great gal, Lola," Mr. Leverson said.

A man to whom women were gals had obviously learned how to throw his fast one in the days of Warren Gamaliel Harding. Times had changed. Mr. Leverson was about to learn how much.

"First time I've met the lady," Dave said. "I take it you're old friends?"

"Her brother and I roomed together at law school," Mr. Leverson said.

"Mockies always work out their housing problems before they roll up their sleeves," Dave said.

Mr. Leverson's face did something for which a plastic surgeon's bill would have lifted things the doctor's scalpel had never been called upon to raise.

"Okay, wise guy," Mr. Leverson said. "Let's cut the shit."

In a voice that would have given Yusof Karsh trouble with his lens opening.

"It's your shit," Dave said. "You cut it."

"Okay," Mr. Leverson said. "Here's a pencil."

It was made of gold.

"Stick it up your ass," Dave said. "What I can't remember I don't write down."

Mr. Leverson looked at the gold pencil as though it were a thermometer that had been eased out of an orifice he had neglected to remember he did not admire.

"Okay," he said. "Here are the facts."

Mr. Leverson tossed the gold pencil over his shoulder as though it were a crumpled Kleenex into which he had just blown his nose. Dave could see the wisdom of the act. Mr. Leverson's nose was not something that could have been blown twice into a tarpaulin, much less a face tissue.

"You own forty-nine per cent of the stock of an outfit in Jersey City named Noonan Cable Coverings, Inc.," Mr. Leverson said. "They make insulation for electric wire. They sell about eighty-five per cent of their product to Westinghouse. This gives Noonan Cable Coverings a gross annual take of six million six, almost seven. Your share, Mr. Dehn, has been running about seven hundred thousand net, before taxes."

"Seven-fifty," Dave said. "After taxes."

"My accountant disagrees," Mr. Leverson said.

"I stay out of jail by paying taxes on the figures prepared for me by the accountants whose fees I pay," Dave said. "When you find yourself picking nits out of your scalp in the Federal pokey, Mr. Leverson, you might be interested in their services. My secretary will supply you grudgingly with their names and phone number."

"When I find myself in the pokey," Mr. Leverson said, "this country won't even be remembered as a contributor to the U.N.'s annual budget. You better listen to a man who is in a position to send you back to a three-room cold-water flat on Westerlo Street in Albany."

"By comparison with any room into which you happen to have come crawling out of the woodwork," Dave said, "Westerlo Street is the cocktail lounge of the Roney Plaza Hotel when Milton Berle is packing them in. I suggest you get to your point before you begin to sound as stupid as you look."

"I sound stupid only to *shmucks*," Mr. Leverson said. "Here's your last chance to stay out of that category. As of this morning your forty-nine per cent of the stock in Noonan Cable Coverings, Inc., is worth slightly less than half a dozen sheets of used toilet paper. I just bought the other fifty-one per cent from the Noonan boys. My first act as the new majority stockholder, I shifted the operations of the company from making cable coverings for Westinghouse to manufacturing violin bridges for Jascha Heifetz. I haven't had the time to check into all the activities you and your partner Mr. Singer are engaged in, but I'm sure what we've been able to do to your Noonan operation should give you a pretty clear picture of what my colleagues and I are in a position to do to you across the board, all the way from your cattle holdings in Wyoming to your grain-elevator interests in Saskatchewan and all the bases in between, not one of which we will fail to touch."

"Who are your colleagues?" Dave said.

"A group of patriotic American Jews who do not take orders from anybody," Mr. Leverson said. "Especially the stupid bastards who are telling us to turn our backs on our native land and go live in Israel."

"Okay," Dave said.

It was. What had been missing was the boundary lines of the threat. Now that they had come clear he could take care of the son of a bitch who had made it.

"Now I suggest you stop talking tough," Dave said. "And start talking sense."

With a sharp forward thrust of his right buttock, a hard downward shove of his left palm, and an openmouthed expulsion of breath, Mr. Leverson managed to heave his belly up out of Lola Truscott's chair. Hearing her guest get to his feet was obviously a signal for which she had been waiting. Mrs. Truscott came out of the kitchen.

"Oh, dear," she said. "I'm afraid I've ruined the soufflé. I hope you won't be annoyed if I give you each a nice bowl of hot soup for lunch?"

"Not for me, Lola, thanks," Mr. Leverson said. "I'm afraid I won't be able to stay for lunch."

"But it's Pepper Pot," she said.

"Lola, baby," Mr. Leverson said. "Next time you want to tempt a visitor from Philadelphia to break an important engagement and stay for lunch, make the soup anything but Pepper Pot."

"Oh, dear, and I've just opened a fresh tin," Lola Truscott said. "You'll stay, Mr. Dehn, won't you?"

"You bet he'll stay," Mr. Leverson said. "He says he's ready to listen to sense. You feed it to him, Lola."

He kissed her cheek.

"I'll go to the door with you," Lola Truscott said.

"I never have trouble finding doors," Mr. Leverson said. "Besides, don't waste your time. This boy has got a lot of listening to do. Thanks for taking him off my hands."

Dave waited until he heard the front door close behind Mr. Leverson before he said, "What's he so sore about?"

"The statement that boy apparently made in your synagogue this morning," Lola Truscott said. "Plus your statement about Israel on the front page of last week's Beechwood *Bugle*."

"You sent it to him?" Dave said.

"He got it from his clipping service," Lola Truscott said. "He called to ask if I could tell him something about you, and then he asked me to set up this appointment. He didn't tell me that on his way here he would be stopping off in your synagogue. After he called me his clipping service apparently sent him something else. Your advertisement about the Blumenfeld bar mitzvah in the *Bugle*."

"I thought clipping services were for actors and politicians and playwrights," Dave said. "People who like to see their names in print."

"Ludwig Leverson pays to have his name kept *out* of print," Lola Truscott said.

"He sounds pretty confused," Dave said.

"Since President Truman gave the new state of Israel that international pat on the back," Lola Truscott said, "there are very few rich Jews in this country who are not confused. The richer they are the greater their confusion. Ludwig Leverson is very rich indeed. By the way, since the death of my husband I no longer go out socially, so it's possible that customs have changed without my being aware of it. I do recall, however, that in my youth when a friend came to one's house for lunch one offered him a drink. May I?"

"If it means we're friends," Dave said.

"I don't see how we can avoid being," Lola Truscott said. "Trying to unconfuse Ludwig Leverson tends to bring people together."

She walked across to the bar.

"Can I help?" Dave said.

"Only by sitting down," Lola Truscott said. "What would you like?"

"Whatever you're having," Dave said.

"My husband refused to let me set our wedding date until I had learned to make a martini that met with his approval. When I learned that, he refused to let me learn how to make anything else. You cannot improve on one hundred per cent was the way he put it. I've never tried. Martini, then?"

"Please," Dave said.

"My husband also used to say the best place to begin is at the beginning. With that sample of his wit out of the way, I assure you, Mr. Dehn, you have heard the last quotation from my husband to which you will be subjected today. Besides, there are some things with which it is impossible to begin at the beginning because one doesn't know the beginning. That's my problem with Ludwig Leverson. Since his beginning he's done so much to himself that I suspect even Ludwig would be unable to find his way back to it.

"His father was a German immigrant. Ludwig was born either on the ship that brought the family to this country or a few months before the ship sailed for America. In any case, you can see where that small discrepancy leads to a large neurosis. Being regarded as a one hundred per cent native loyal patriotic American is a matter of great importance to Ludwig. It was not so important in the early years, when he was poor and hungry and clawing his way up out of the gutter. In those days Ludwig's sole concern was the almost universal concern of all poor boys from Julien Sorel to Billy Rose. How to make his fortune. While he was making it he shared with his parents all the conventional attitudes of a poor immigrant family that had been hounded out of its home in Europe. Among these the two most common attitudes were fear of anti-Semitism and distrust for the rich, who were more commonly identified as the exploiters. Then one day Ludwig, who surprised himself by proving to be not untalented at the exploiting game, discovered he was rich. He looked around at his fellow exploiters, and he liked what he saw. This was quite a country and, somewhat to his astonishment, Ludwig realized he owned a not inconsiderable piece of it."

Lola Truscott came across with two glasses and gave one to Dave.

"Here's to Ludwig Leverson's confusion," she said.

Dave took a sip.

"And to Mr. Truscott's sound good sense," Dave said. "As a martini-making teacher he was clearly of championship caliber."

"Thank you," Lola Truscott said.

She sat down facing him. Dave noticed she seemed to have a little trouble with her right foot. Casually but carefully Mrs. Truscott spread the skirt of the red velvet hostess gown across her ankle.

"While Ludwig had been poor," she said, "he parroted all the things his father and mother used to say about Jews

359

and Gentiles and anti-Semitism and Palestine and the dream of a Jewish homeland. Through his parents, therefore, Ludwig got involved with Zionist thinking. He didn't do anything about it, because he was too busy exploiting his way up to his private financial pinnacle. If you've accepted certain beliefs all your life, however, it can be quite a shock when you learn in your middle years where those beliefs have led you. Here was Ludwig Leverson, madly in love with the America that had showered on him the good rich life. What in God's name was he doing supporting the dream of getting out of America and going to live in a piece of godforsaken desert at the other side of the world? A place without custom-built Cadillacs or superbly trained servants, without private golf courses or French food prepared by your own imported chef? A place where everybody would be expected to do manual labor so the dream could be dug out of the desert sand?

"Well, not to put too fine a point on it, Mr. Dehn, in the circles frequented by Ludwig Leverson, Zionism became a dirty word. Ludwig and his friends made it plain that they believed anybody who was a loyal Zionist was a disloyal American. Since Ludwig and his friends have plenty of money, they rented offices, set up a staff, and hired press agents to trumpet their one hundred per cent Americanism under the banner of something they decided to call the Organization for American Judaism. When you hire press agents you sometimes get more than you expect. What Ludwig and his friends got was a slogan to hurl in the teeth of those disloyal Americans who wanted to leave the land of plenty for life on a scrap of godforsaken desert in the Middle East. Ludwig and his friends accused their coreligionists of something called dual loyalty. It sounded marvelous. It was marvelous indeed. It got Ludwig and his friends into more trouble than the Internal Revenue Service had ever managed to bring down on them.

"With two words they insulted every Jew in America who did not own his own golf course. People like Ludwig's parents, people who loved America and were proud of being

Americans, people who at the same time had lived for so many thousands of years with the dream of a Jewish homeland that they didn't know how to turn off the dream.

"While Ludwig and Company were floundering in the mess of their own creation, the President of their great and beloved adopted country pulled the rug out from under them. Truman recognized Israel as an independent state that the United States is proud to welcome to the international family of nations and call its friend. Another drink, Mr. Dehn?"

"Yes," Dave said. "If you'll tell me why this has made Mr. Leverson sore at me."

Lola Truscott stood up and moved to the bar with what Dave now saw was a small limp.

"President Truman has taken away the issue that was keeping alive Ludwig's Organization for American Judaism," she said. "While Zionism was something to hurl insults at, he could fight it because it was a threat. What Ludwig cannot fight is a three-dimensional reality. Israel is no longer a scrap of desert in the Middle East where only a fanatic would go to live. Israel is now a great and glorious dream come true. Without taking any insults from Ludwig and his friends in the Organization for American Judaism, American Jews can now pour their money and strength as well as their love into Israel. Why should the American Jew now be concerned if Ludwig dislikes him? The American Jew now has President Truman on his side. The American Jew can go to Israel without being called disloyal to America. In other words, the word Zionism may be dead but the spirit of Zionism is very much alive. Stronger than ever, taking a form Ludwig cannot fight, and he is sore at you because it's all your doing."

"Somebody should correct the sights on his rifle," Dave said. "Until a few minutes ago I never even heard of Leverson and the Organization for American Judaism."

"He's heard of you," Lola Truscott said. She came back with the refilled glasses. "No, don't, please," she said. "I can manage, and it's not painful. It merely looks awkward."

Dave sank back into his chair. She set the fresh drink beside him and went back to her own chair. She went through the same small performance with the skirt of the hostess gown and the ankle.

"He hasn't heard of me for very long," Dave said. "That statement in the *Bugle* appeared last week. It would take any clipping service at least three or four days to get the news to him."

"He called me day before yesterday," Lola Truscott said.

"He came out of Philadelphia awfully fast to see a man he hadn't even heard about forty-eight hours ago," Dave said.

"Ludwig Leverson didn't really come to see you," Lola Truscott said. "You're just a symbol."

"Of what?" Dave said.

"The young Turks about whom he is almost paranoid," Lola Truscott said. "Put yourself in Ludwig's place for a moment. He's invested a large part of his emotional capital in this anti-Zionist fight. It's been going on for years. Suddenly the fight is over. Ludwig has lost it. I'm not quite sure what he talked to you about while I was out in the kitchen ruining the soufflé, but I can imagine. Ludwig enjoys a fight. He's done it all his life. He doesn't really know how to do anything else. He hates to lose. He really doesn't know how to do that either. His first thought, therefore, is how to renew the battle. While he's thrashing around for an opening you come along with your statement in the *Bugle* about Masada."

"This makes me somebody he must destroy?" Dave said.

"Oh, dear," Lola Truscott said. "It sounds as though what Ludwig talked about while I was out in the kitchen was on the ugly side."

"Don't worry about that part of it," Dave said. "When it comes to handling ugliness I'm neither shy nor helpless. Please just stick to connecting up Leverson's paranoia with my statement in the *Bugle* that we must make Israel strong so the Jews will never have to face another Masada."

"It's one of those words," Lola Truscott said. "Like Pearl Harbor or Valley Forge or Dunkirk or Judas. Masada. It sets off a noise inside your head. If you're paranoid about killing

Zionism or even the most vestigial remnants of Zionism, the word Masada will bring all your raw nerves quiveringly alive. Not your nerves. Ludwig's. They will explode pictures in his feverish mind that would astonish you. They will scream at him. *There it is. There's how they will come at me. That's how they will try to destroy me. By rallying people around that God-damn word. Masada. What have we got to offer against that? Nothing. And we'll never find anything that comes even close. So I've got to destroy him before he gets a chance to rally my enemies around that word."*

"Were you ever on the stage, Mrs. Truscott?" Dave said.

"Before the accident in which my husband was killed and my foot was injured," she said, "I was on the board of the Beechwood Players. We did some rather nice things. I was in the managerial end mainly, but we all had to do a bit of acting now and then."

"If they had a part calling for an imitation of Ludwig Leverson," Dave said, "you'd have brought down the house."

"I'm afraid my acting days are over," Lola Truscott said.

"There's one performance you can still give," Dave said.

"What's that, Mr. Dehn?"

"I'd like to hear a convincing explanation," Dave said. "Why would a woman like you serve as intermediary for a man like Ludwig Leverson?"

Lola Truscott looked down into her drink. The movement of her head caused the silky hair, parted in the middle, to fall forward like a couple of small curtains that framed her patrician face. Dave's heart moved. The drink seemed to displease her. Mrs. Truscott scowled. Then she put aside the glass, stood up, and went to the piano at the other side of the room.

On it was a group of stand-up silver picture frames clustered around a bowl of zinnias. Lola Truscott chose one of the frames and brought it back to the chairs near the fire. She held out the picture frame to Dave. He took it as she had offered it, without a word.

The silver frame contained a snapshot of a young man's

head and shoulders. He wore some sort of crumpled army blouse and a beret. He was smiling shyly into the lens. There was no mistaking the resemblance.

"Your brother?" Dave said.

"My younger brother," Lola Truscott said.

She took back the silver frame and stared at the picture for a few moments.

"This was snapped by some other boy in the International Brigade," she said finally. "I never learned his name. They were both killed the next day. November 12, 1936, at Carabanchel. As soon as the news broke, Ludwig Leverson came up from New York to see me here in this house. A lot of people had asked if there was anything they could do, and I'm sure they meant it. But at times like that people always wait for you to ask them. One never does, of course. Ludwig Leverson didn't wait. We had known each other ever since he and my brother had been at law school together. Ludwig knew what I wanted. So without asking he went out and did it."

Lola Truscott carried the picture back to the piano. She replaced it with care in the cluster of other frames around the bowl of zinnias. She came back and sat down facing Dave. She took a sip from her glass.

"He flew to Madrid," Lola Truscott said. "The siege was at its height. It was difficult to get into the city, but Ludwig Leverson got in. He also got out. With my brother's body. And he brought it home to me. Any further questions?"

"One," Dave said. "How do I fit into the picture?"

"Through Colin Babington," Lola Truscott says. "He serves as my eyes and ears in Beechwood. Watching your activities through Colin, I got the picture of a bright, aggressive, no-nonsense man. All these qualities are probably common to many real estate developers, but you did not strike me as being a real estate developer. Certainly not a common one, at any rate. The pattern eluded me, as I said, until I read your Masada statement. Then I got it."

"Got what?" Dave said.

"The feel of the rebel," Lola Truscott said. "The man with the fixation. It runs in my family. That's why my younger brother was in Spain. That's why I did all those things like the Beechwood Players and the League of Women Voters. The things I stopped doing after my husband died. That's why I was so eager to act as intermediary for Ludwig Leverson."

"I still don't understand why," Dave said.

"Mr. Dehn," Lola Truscott said, "I want to stop cooking and go back to living."

"You think I can help you," Dave said.

"I know you can," Lola Truscott said.

"Okay," Dave said. "Maybe we can help each other."

38

At nine-thirty Monday morning Lola Truscott took the maybe out of Dave Dehn's statement. She appeared in Colin Babington's office. She was carrying a thermos jug.

"Lola," he said. "How did you get here?"

"I called Teddy's Taxi Service," Lola Truscott said. "The car wouldn't start."

"How could it possibly start?" Colin Babington said. "It's been up on blocks in your garage for six years."

"I forgot that," Lola Truscott said. "I hadn't been out in the garage for six years. That's why I went back into the house and called Teddy's Taxi Service."

"Lola," Colin Babington said. "You have not been out of your house since Hector died six years ago. Why did you come out of your house today?"

"There's something important I want to ask you to do for me," Lola Truscott said.

"You could have called me on the phone," Colin Babington said. "You call me constantly about all sorts of things. Or you could have waited until I came to your house on Wednesday."

"This is something special," Lola Truscott said. "If you decide to say no I didn't want you saying it in my house because if you say no I won't want you in my house ever again."

"I can't imagine you asking me to do anything I would refuse," Colin Babington said.

"Nor can I," Lola Truscott said. "But as Hector so frequently pointed out, one never can tell."

"What do you want me to do?" Colin Babington said.

"Two things," Lola Truscott said. "You know that piece of property you bought for me a couple of months ago down on Beach Road?"

"The Metuchen place," Colin Babington said. "What about it?"

"I want to give it to the Bella Biaggi – Beechwood Jewish Center," Lola Truscott said.

"Give?" Colin Babington said. "How do you mean, give?"

"A present," Lola Truscott said. "A gift. I want to give it to them."

"Legally?" Colin Babington said. "Deed it to them?"

"Yes," Lola Truscott said.

"Why?" Colin Babington said.

"Mr. Dehn has asked me to work with him on their drug-rehabilitation project," Lola Truscott said. "We've decided to house it on the Metuchen place."

"We?" Colin Babington said.

"Yes," Lola Truscott said.

"You sound like Lindbergh and *The Spirit of St. Louis,*" Colin Babington said.

"I hope Mr. Dehn and I will do as well," Lola Truscott said.

"What's the second thing you want me to do?" Colin Babington said.

"You know, of course, that Mr. Dehn is running for Mr. Fortgang's seat on the Board of Selectmen," Lola Truscott said.

"It's hardly a whispered rumor," Colin Babington said.

"I want to make the outcome a fact," Lola Truscott said.

"How can you do that?" Colin Babington said.

"I can't," Lola Truscott said. "You can."

"How?" Colin Babington said.

"By coming out publicly for Mr. Dehn," Lola Truscott said.

In the sudden silence Colin Babington noticed an odd thing. Both of them were on their feet, facing each other across the desk. He wondered if the bulge in his tweed crotch was noticeable.

"I can't do that," he said finally.

"I'll just leave the Pepper Pot here," Lola Truscott said. She set down the thermos jug on his desk. "Sip it slowly. It's the last meal I will ever cook for you."

She turned toward the door.

"Lola," Colin Babington said. "Wait."

"I can't," Lola Truscott said across her shoulder. "Teddy's taxi is waiting. I have a date on Turkey Hill Road in ten minutes."

"With whom?" Colin Babington said.

"Mr. Singer," Lola Truscott said.

"Dave Dehn's partner?" Colin Babington said.

"Yes," Lola Truscott said across her shoulder.

"Why?" Colin Babington called.

Limping to the door, Lola Truscott said, "I'm turning over to him the legal job of transferring title to the Metuchen place to the Bella Biaggi – Beechwood Jewish Center."

39

It was a piece of legal business that Sid Singer didn't yet know he had lost.

"Look at that," Marian said the morning of Election Day.

She set down on the breakfast table the copy of the Beechwood *Bugle* she had just brought in from the back porch. Sid's coffee cup was on its way to his mouth. The headline stopped his hand in the air.

BABINGTON DECLARES FOR DEHN

"Wow!" Sid said softly.

"Keep reading," Marian said.

Her slice of buttered toast touched the subhead like a schoolteacher's pointer touching a blackboard.

She read aloud:

"What this community needs is some fresh blood in the management of our affairs," the chairman of the Beechwood Board of Selectmen declared today in an exclusive interview with the editor of the *Bugle*. *"I urge my fellow citizens to do what I intend to do in the balloting booth tomorrow: vote for David Dehn."*

Sid reached his free hand across to the phone next to the toaster. He dialed the private number.

"Dave?"

"Yes, Sid."

"Did you see the front page of the *Bugle?*"

"Not yet," Dave said. "But Fanny just called and told me."

"How you ever swung it," Sid said, "I don't know, and I suspect I'd better not ask, but I think this puts the election in the bag. Congratulations."

"Thanks, Sid," Dave said. "I'll tell you all about it at the staff meeting. Right now I think I'd better get you off the blower and call Mrs. Truscott."

"Find out why she didn't show up on Monday," Sid said. "She called first thing in the morning and asked if she could come in to see me about the Metuchen place. I said by all means, and we made an appointment, but she never kept it."

"She found out later she didn't have to," Dave said.

"She's changed her mind about giving us the Metuchen place?" Sid said.

"Stop screaming," Dave said. "You haven't been hit. Mrs. Truscott has not changed her mind. We will definitely get the Metuchen place, as promised. When she called you she was not yet sure how to keep the promise, so she set you up as a backstop. Just using the information that you were waiting in the wings did the trick. She found she didn't need your help, so she didn't keep your date."

"She could have called," Sid said.

"No, she couldn't," Dave said. "Her hands were full."

After almost three decades of intimacy neither Sid nor Dave had to ask what the other meant. They spoke a shorthand instantaneously comprehensible to both.

"Mrs. Truscott told you that?" Sid said.

The incredulity in his voice made Dave laugh.

"Of course not," Dave said.

"Then how do you know?" Sid said.

"Remember back in Ethan Allen High?" Dave said. "That word Miss Marine used to be so fond of?"

"What word?" Sid said.

"Ratiocination," Dave said.

"You're pronouncing it incorrectly," Sid said.

"But doing it perfectly," Dave said. "Try it sometime. See you at the meeting, counselor."

After the polls closed that night, when word came over the radio that Don Fortgang had conceded, Dave Dehn waved to the cheers that erupted in the assembly hall and dipped down to Sid Singer's ear.

"Keep this going," Dave said. "I'll be right back."

He walked swiftly through the back-slappers, out into the foyer, and took the elevator up to his apartment. Dave locked the door behind him, went to the phone in his bathroom, and dialed the Fortgang home.

"Hello?"

Dave recognized the voice of Marvin.

"Lieutenant, this is Dave Dehn. I'd like to talk with your grandfather."

"You can't," Lieutenant Fortgang said. "He's sitting *shivah*."

For a moment the word did not register. When it did, Dave spoke before he had time to think.

"Somebody died?"

"My father," Lieutenant Fortgang said.

"What?" Dave said.

"He killed himself out in the pagoda," Lieutenant Fortgang said. "Right after he took a call from the Beechwood *Bugle* and conceded defeat."

Into Dave's head came a picture of the red tile walls. The matching red tile bar. The swaying red-and-green Japanese lantern. The smoking bronze incense burner. The avocado green and the cherry red chaise longues. The mobile of Hirohito twisting slowly over the sauna door. The bamboo *mezuzah*.

The center of the picture was dominated by something Dave did not want to see: a heavy-set figure, with enormous sunglasses, wrapped in a bright red kimono.

Because he did not know how to get off the phone Dave

said the last thing he would have wanted to say. The last thing he would have wanted to say was the first thing that came into his head.

"How did he do it?" Dave said.

"Hara-kiri," Lieutenant Fortgang said. "You fucking murderer."

40

The next morning, as Dave was on his way down from the apartment to the staff meeting, Lieutenant Fortgang's angry voice was still ringing in his head. Ringing in an odd way. Not until Fanny had guided them through the day's agenda did Dave realize what was odd about it. The young wearer of the loafer's loop had been sobbing.

"I'm sorry, Fanny," Dave said. "My mind was on something else."

"The last thing on the list for today," Fanny said. "Oliver Stehli called. If you want to issue a tribute to Fortgang he'll be glad to run it in the *Bugle.*"

"Yes," Dave said. "I do want to issue a tribute, but not to the Fortgang who killed himself. I want to issue a tribute to his father."

"Suggestion?" Sid said.

"Let's have it," Dave said.

"Why not make it a tribute to the whole Fortgang family?" Sid said. "The one who killed himself may have been a shit, granted. But people don't like to hear that sort of thing said out loud about a guy who has just cooled. In this case nobody has to hear it. The old man is still alive. So is the young son. The old man was in at the beginning of this town, you might say. The young man will be in on the future. It seems to me with that sort of bracketing you get an opportunity to say something more than the usual crap about a man who's just died. Paying a tribute to the Fortgang family, their role these last sixty years here in Beechwood, it's a setup for you. As the dead man's successor it gives you a chance to say out loud how you see your role in the future of Beechwood. What do you think?"

Dave made an effort. He knew what Sid wanted him to think. But his thoughts took him where they wanted. Dave thought of his father in the tenement on Westerlo Street. He thought of Don Fortgang's father in the pagoda on River Lane. He thought of Rabbi Goldfarb and the thirteen-year-old boy he had guided through the preparations for the bar mitzvah the old man had never attended. Dave thought of the evening light pouring through the stained-glass windows high up in the sanctuary. Dave could hear again, very clearly, the sorrowful joy in the voice of the little old man in the brown zipper jacket as it soared up toward the boy with the harp in the tent of the ancient king. Dave's chest tightened. He shivered slightly. His thoughts darted to the young lieutenant sobbing on the phone last night, and then thinking came into focus. Dave Dehn thought of his daughter.

"Yes, Sid, thanks," he said. "That's a good idea. I'll draft the statement right after this meeting."

"That does it, then, for today, D.D.," Fanny said. "Except for any extras not on the agenda?"

"Any extras?" Dave said.

"Yes, one," Mike Palgrave said.

"Shoot," Dave said.

"Sally and I have been talking," Mike said. "For a few months now, off and on, we've been doing some thinking about the future."

"Don't we all?" Dave said.

"Sure, of course," Mike said. "But Sally and I, we've been doing it in a sort of special way."

"Tell us," Dave said.

"I think I've done here just about as much as I can," Mike

said. "I want to move on to some place where I can do more."

Dave gave himself a moment for the thought to sink in. Beechwood always seemed to begin for him with a fat boy sitting beside him on a log facing Long Island Sound and talking about the Statue of Liberty. What Mike had said seemed to threaten the existence of that beginning.

"You have a place in mind?" Dave said.

"Yes," Mike said.

"Where?" Dave said.

"Israel," Mike said.

Dave's first reaction was amusement. It was funny to see the glare come up like an angry sunrise on Fanny's face. As though Mike had said something insulting to D.D. The amusement did not last long. In a couple of moments Dave grasped that Fanny's reaction was correct. What Mike had said was more than insulting. It was inadmissible.

"Why?" Dave said.

"I'd like to get back to work," Mike said.

"I thought you were working here," Dave said.

"I thought so too," Mike said. "At the beginning. But now —for a long time, actually, it hasn't really been work."

"What has it been?" Dave said.

"Talk," Mike said. "I want to get over there."

"Jews talk no matter where they are," Dave said. "You'll run into just as much over there as over here."

"They're talking about something," Mike said. "It's real. The talk is about survival. So is the work. If the work doesn't get done over here the worst that could happen, the Board of Selectmen could do something like, say, change a few zoning regulations and it might affect our property values up here on Turkey Hill Road. We're not surrounded by millions of armed Arabs with itchy trigger fingers. And even anything the Board of Selectmen could have thought up against us, that threat is gone as of this morning. You're now a member of the board. You're our nuclear deterrent. We've won this fight, whatever the fight was about. I sometimes have trouble remembering. So, well, anyway, Morris Cohen wants to go where there's a fight going on that he can recognize and get into."

"There's going to be plenty of action here," Dave said. "We're just beginning to get under way."

"Maybe," Mike said. "But I've made up my mind."

"Sally too?" Dave said.

"The whole Cohen family," Mike said.

41

"The whole Cohen family means more than Mike and you," Dave said. "Now it also means Rachel."

"You sound as though you're making a discovery," Sally said.

"I am," Dave said.

"But that was understood from the beginning," Sally said.

"Not by me," Dave said.

Sally hesitated. She started to say something, then stopped. "Here," she said. "Better let me take her."

Dave handed over the baby. Sally carried her across to the canvas-topped table near the crib. She embarked once more on what had become for Dave Dehn an endlessly fascinating process: changing a diaper.

"I don't understand what it is you don't understand," Sally said as she worked.

"I don't understand why you and Mike want to take my daughter away from me," Dave said.

"We're not," Sally said.

"You're going to the other side of the world," Dave said.

"And taking our daughter with us," Sally said.

"But she's not your daughter," Dave said. "Rachel is—"

His voice stopped. So did Sally's fingers. But she did not look up. After a few moments her fingers went back to work, more slowly. She put the last pin into place, checked the finished task, and picked up the baby.

"Here," Sally said. "Hold her while I turn on the coffee."

Dave took his daughter. He settled her in his arms. He leaned back in the chair that had become his. Sally went across to the stove and flipped the switch under the Silex. She turned, hesitated, then leaned back against the stove. It was as though she had decided it would be easier for both of them if she kept the distance of the room between them.

"What's the alternative?" she said finally.

"The alternative to what?" Dave said.

"Taking your daughter away from you," Sally said.

Dave got it. Sally saw him get it. Sally saw also that he could not say it. So Sally said it for both of them.

"If we don't take your daughter away from you," Sally said, "you'll take our daughter away from us."

"You're talking technicalities," Dave said. "You and Mike know that Rachel is my daughter."

"We know more than that," Sally said. "We knew it from the beginning."

"Knew what?" Dave said.

"That neither of us could have it both ways," Sally said. "As long as she remained your daughter technically, she could not be our daughter, and what we wanted was a daughter. Not a job as diaper changers. We were sure you understood that."

He had. But of course he hadn't. Not until now.

"What I didn't understand was that you would pick her up from Cavalry Road, where I can see her every day, and take her to some godforsaken scrap of desert at the other side of the world."

"Did you consider it a godforsaken scrap of desert at the other side of the world when you bribed Monroe Blumenfeld to pledge he'd go over and spend his life there?"

"Monroe Blumenfeld is not my son," Dave said.

Then he wished he hadn't said it.

"And Rachel Cohen is not your daughter," Sally said.

"Only because a legal document says so," Dave said.

"That's why Mike and I insisted on having it written and signed," Sally said.

Astonished, Dave said, "You knew when you adopted Rachel that you were going to do this?"

A slash of anger raced across Sally's face. Or so Dave thought. It was gone before he could be sure. It was possible that he'd been wrong. He hoped so.

"You know better than that," Sally said.

He did.

"Of course," Dave said. "I'm sorry."

"That's all right," Sally said.

"No, it isn't," Dave said. "It's all wrong."

"It wasn't all wrong yesterday," Sally said. "What's made it all wrong today?"

"Yesterday you hadn't told me you were taking Rachel with you to Israel," Dave said.

"Wouldn't you take her?" Sally said. "If you were going?"

"But I'm not," Dave said. "You and Mike, you're the ones who are going. I don't know why, and I don't care. What I care about is Rachel. If you and Mike want to indulge some damn-fool whim about changing your lives, okay. Go ahead. But why do you have to change mine?"

"*Whither thou goest,*" Sally said, "*I will go.*"

"That's not Rachel," Dave said. "That's Ruth."

"Rachel was not my choice," Sally said. "If she'd been mine and Mike's from the beginning we would have named her Ruth."

"What's wrong with Rachel?" Dave said.

"It's your mother's name," Sally said. "My mother's name was Ruth."

Dave looked down at the blanket-wrapped bundle in his arms. He knew he had lost. Because his only real argument would not come to him in words. It was something he was holding. He didn't know how to put that into words.

"Dave."

He lifted his head. Sally looked wiser than he felt.

"Dave," Sally said again.

"Yes?" he said.

"Why don't you come with us?" Sally said.

PART IV

PART IV

42

A quarter of a century later, on the morning of his sixtieth birthday, Dave Dehn still could not answer that question. He pushed it out of his mind. Hammering at the door inside his head for attention was what Fanny Mintz had just told him on the phone.

Fanny had said all she was going to say. This, as Dave knew, meant that Fanny knew she had said enough. So far as Renata Bazeloff of *Mitzvah* magazine was concerned, the ball was now in Dave's court. Since he would not get to the ball until Miss Bazeloff met him for lunch in the City Club at twelve-thirty, Dave was free to start his day all over again.

He went back to the basin. He picked up his razor and looked in the mirror. The lather had gone dry. He turned on the tap, squeezed a blob of Palmolive Brushless into his palm, and started it toward his cheek. The shaving cream did not reach its destination. Dave's hand stopped in mid-air.

It had happened. What Fanny had wanted. It had caught up with him. All at once Dave knew Miss Bazeloff's call was as important as Fanny felt it was.

Dave rinsed the Palmolive Brushless from his palm and went to the window. He moved slowly, as though he were picking his way through a mine field. He was trying to think. About what? He didn't know. Not that there was a scarcity of material to think about. Twenty-eight years' worth was kicking around inside his head. Too much for seven-fifteen in the morning on a man's sixtieth birthday. Where did you start?

At the bathroom window, of course. The way Dave started every day. With a leisurely survey of the Matto Grosso.

The view from Dave's bathroom window was as different from the Matto Grosso as Zsa Zsa Gabor was different from Fanny Mintz. On the surface, anyway. It would not have surprised Dave to learn, however, that if you could see into the engine rooms that kept them going, you would discover that the two women were not dissimilar.

Just as the Matto Grosso, which Dave knew only from recollected fragments of high school geography, was in appearance totally different from the town of Beechwood, in which Dave had lived for twenty-eight years.

Yet he knew things that a stranger, seeing Beechwood for the first time, would never suspect. Things that made the Matto Grosso seem by comparison—

The sentence came to a stop inside Dave's head as though it had slammed into a stone wall. He went quickly out into the living room. The *Britannica* was on the bottom shelf of the bookcase to the right of the TV set. Dave squatted down on the floor and pulled out one of the M volumes. He could not tell how long he had been studying it when he heard the phone.

It was the phone in the bathroom. So it had to be one of the three people who knew the number, and Dave was certain it would not be Fanny. Not again. She used that phone sparingly. So he would always know, when it rang, that picking it up would not be a waste of his time. Fanny had done her job on Renata Bazeloff. Fanny would not dilute the effect of her achievement with a follow-up call so soon.

Dave scrambled to his feet. He hurried back into the bathroom. His heart was suddenly going. Of the remaining two people who had that number he knew the one he wanted it to be.

"Dave?"

It wasn't. His heart throttled down.

"Happy birthday," Sid said.

"Thanks," Dave said.

"How does it feel to be sixty?" Sid said.

"You ought to know," Dave said. "You crossed the line two weeks ago."

"But I can't remember anything about how it felt," Sid said. "That's why I'm asking you."

Dave gave it a moment of thought. Sid's questions were always worth at least that.

"It's like when they were getting ready to take the shrapnel out of my thigh in the field hospital at Aachen," Dave said. "They didn't know how bad it was, and I was all tensed up, waiting for the anesthetic and the knife and what they might find, and Christ knows what else. Then a cute nurse clapped the ether cone on my nose, and the next thing I knew it was all in the past. The pain. The worry. Everything. The shrapnel was sitting in a water glass on the table by my bed, a souvenir from the surgeon, and the cute nurse was telling me everything was okay, and I tried to remember what I'd been all tensed up about, but I couldn't. The same with today. For a week, maybe more, I've been all tensed up about hitting sixty. A landmark. A significant date. A watershed. And a lot more crap like that. But when I woke up about an hour ago, it wasn't anything like that at all. It's just a number."

"I'll tell that to Marian," Sid said. "She's got a year and a half to go before she hits that number, but already she's parsing the sentences of her obituary. What are you doing?"

"You really want to know?" Dave said.

"Would I ask if I didn't?" Sid said.

He wouldn't. So Dave told him.

"I'm looking up Matto Grosso in the *Britannica*."

"On his sixtieth birthday," Sid said, "doesn't everybody?"

"You didn't," Dave said.

"I didn't have to," Sid said. "I've known all about the Matto Grosso since Ethan Allen High."

"Okay," Dave said. "Tell me."

"What's there to tell?" Sid said. "It's the worst and most

deadly jungle in the world, somewhere down there in South America, full of poisonous snakes that don't even have to bite you to kill you, wild animals that eat each other on sight, alligators with teeth like butcher knives, and a lot of other cheerful things like that, all designed for a Jewish boy to stay away from."

"Okay, Jewish boy," Dave said. "Now listen to the *Britannica.* Hold on."

He put down the phone, went out to the living room, and came back with the M volume.

"You ready?" Dave said into the phone.

"Wait till I sit down," Sid said. "Okay, go."

"*A state in southwestern Brazil,*" Dave read. "*Area over 530,000 square miles. Population about 350,000.* Then a lot of *shtuss* about boundaries and stuff like that, followed by— yes, here; quote: *Heavily forested, with extensive natural resources of gold, diamonds, silver, manganese, lead and platinum. Its agricultural regions produce coffee, sugar, tobacco, and maté,* whatever that is. *The railroads of the state cross the southern part from São Paulo to Paraguay.* What have I left out?"

"Not you," Sid said. "The *Britannica.*"

"Okay," Dave said. "What has the *Britannica* left out?"

"The stuff I've been carrying around in my head since Ethan Allen High," Sid said. "The poisonous snakes and the alligators and the wild animals. I guess I was wrong."

"So was I," Dave said.

But he knew better. He had not been wrong. Not twenty-eight years ago. Not when he first came to Beechwood.

"Besides the *Britannica,*" Sid said. "What else are you doing?"

"I'm about to take my third stab at a shave," Dave said. "Aside from my birthday, anything else on your mind?"

"This lunch you're having at the City Club at twelve-thirty with Miss Bazeloff," Sid said. "You want me to come along?"

Ordinarily the fact that Sid knew his schedule for the day before he and Dave had discussed it would have done nothing

386

to Dave's mind. Sid and Fanny checked each other constantly to see what bits and pieces of Dave's daily burden they could carry for him. This morning, however, was no longer ordinary. Fanny's phone call had made it special.

"Does Fanny think you should come along?" Dave said.

"No," Sid said. "I mean, it never occurred to me to ask her. It's just that after we went over the schedule for the day I had a delayed reaction to this Bazeloff thing."

"Why?"

"I've been reading her magazine," Sid said. "It strikes me as the sort of outfit to which you're probably better off not doing any talking without the presence of a third party."

Dave hesitated. He had leaned on Sid for so many years that the possibility of not leaning came as an arresting new concept. Arresting and disturbing. Like the day Artie Steinberg, on what must have been Dave's hundred-and-umpteenth routine checkup, had looked up from the needle descending slowly on the dial of his Baumanometer and said, "I'm afraid we're going to have to start medicating you for high blood pressure."

"Reporters are all alike," Dave said into the phone. "I've been talking to them since 1947."

"We were all young in 1947," Sid said. "We were just a hole in the ground on an old onion farm in a sleepy little Norman Rockwell town."

"Don't you listen to the TV laxative ads?" Dave said. "You're as young as you feel. If your bowels are open, anyway. So we're still young today. Sixty is just a number. Remember?"

"How can I forget?" Sid said.

"By sending a caretaker along to my lunch with a reporter," Dave said. "To make sure I don't dribble my food."

"You cut that out," Sid said.

"Okay," Dave said. "I didn't say it."

"Don't say it again," Sid said.

"All right, all right," Dave said. "Stop hollering on me. How many times do I have to say I'm sorry?"

"Never," Sid said. "Sixty is just a number. But it's also a lot of years. Like it or not, we're both entering the phase of life known to my son Ezra as Old Fartsville. It's no place to start kicking the shit out of something you've given your life to."

"Why would I do anything as dumb as that?" Dave said.

"Why would you begin thirty years ago smuggling into this country souvenirs of Buchenwald?" Sid said. "Why would you start this whole crazy thing up here in Beechwood in the first place? Because you've got a mind like your father. It ranges. You don't think the way other people think. And you don't always think at all before you start swinging. You don't take crap from anybody. Especially reporters. Remember that guy with the nose from *The Jewish Daily Forward* in 1947?"

"Does Gertrude Ederle remember the English Channel?" Dave said.

"In her day it was a different channel," Sid said. "Only real champs made it. Now anybody with a can of axle grease and a rowboat can swim the damn thing. Just as everybody with a little guts and some money is now doing all over this country what you did here thirty years ago."

"Twenty-eight," Dave said. "You helped."

"That's why I'm talking this way," Sid said. "This *Mitzvah* thing has me worried."

"Why?" Dave said.

"They're on to something," Sid said. "Anyway, they think they are."

"What the hell could they be on to?" Dave said.

"I've been thinking back," Sid said.

"How far?" Dave said.

"All the way to Germany," Sid said.

"The Army?" Dave said.

"What else?" Sid said.

"Stop knocking yourself out," Dave said. "That was almost thirty years ago. Nobody cares about a couple of obscure second lieutenants in the Army thirty years ago."

"Nobody except rags like *Mitzvah,*" Sid said. "That's all those bastards care about. Raking up smells is their stock in trade."

"Sid," Dave said. "You scared?"

"My gut is sending me a message," Sid said.

"Saying what?" Dave said.

"It's telling me at this particular point in our lives it's a good idea maybe to be a little scared," Sid said.

"Why?" Dave said.

"This Bazeloff lunch could explode," Sid said.

"Never," Dave said.

"It's safer to think around that word never," Sid said.

"Why?" Dave said.

"Because if this thing blows up," Sid said, "your life and my life blow with it. I haven't got another thirty years to give to anything. Neither have you. The best part of the race is run."

"What?" Dave said.

"Kipling," Sid said. "When you get your nose out of the *Britannica* stick it for a few minutes into *The Oxford Book of Modern English Verse.* I don't want to blow what we gave those thirty years to. That's why I offered to go along with you to this lunch with Miss Bazeloff. I withdraw the offer."

"Thanks, Sid," Dave said. "I won't blow it."

"Who knows that better than yours truly?" Sid said. "Marian expects you for breakfast."

Dave hung up. Immediately the phone rang again. For a moment Dave couldn't believe it. Then his heart started to go. Of the three people who had the unlisted number, Fanny had already checked in and Sid had called. This time it had to be.

"Pop?"

It was.

"Hello, chicken."

"Happy birthday, Pop."

Everything got better.

"Where you calling from?" he said. "This is a lousy connection."

"They don't have any other kind in Elat," Rachel said. "Happy birthday, Pop. Did you hear me? I said happy birthday!"

"Years ago I told that damn fool Alexander Graham Bell there's no future in this foolish invention," Dave said. "Why don't you grab a plane and come on over and tell me happy birthday in person?"

"It's too late, Pop," Rachel said. "Your birthday is happening this minute."

"I can fix that," Dave said. "You tell me when you can get here and I'll hold my birthday for your arrival."

"You'll throw the whole town of Beechwood into a panic," Rachel said. "Fanny wrote me they've got a banquet laid on for you tonight in the Town Hall and the school kids pooled their bubble-gum money to have Tiffany make you a solid-gold key to the city."

"That's just for starters," Dave said. "In addition, the Board of Selectmen is doing something real classy."

"Like what, Pop?"

"They're voting me the town's Honorary Gentile," Dave said.

He waited for the laugh.

"That's great," Rachel said. No laugh. "From now on, Pop, you'll be able to meet your daughter halfway."

Things stopped getting better. He tried to hold on to a scrap of what her voice had brought into his morning. Too late. The day had already started to go brown.

"You remember Fiorello LaGuardia?" Dave said.

"He was before my time, Pop. I was born in 1948. Remember?"

My God, he thought. The things kids can do to you with a word.

"Here's something I want you to remember," Dave said. "A rival politician once attacked LaGuardia for always bragging about his Italian ancestry. The guy wanted to know how come LaGuardia never bragged about the fact that his mother was Jewish. You know what he said?"

"Tell me, Pop."

"LaGuardia said he always figured being half Jewish is not enough to brag about."

"It's not," Rachel said. "I've kept it a secret from the rest of the people on the kibbutz."

Dave had learned long ago that when you have nothing to say, the best thing to do is keep your trap shut. Even at transatlantic toll rates.

"Pop?"

"I'm on, chicken."

"That was a shitty thing to say," Rachel said.

"It was that," Dave said.

"I've loused up your birthday."

"Not quite," Dave said. "Without putting your back into it, chicken, you couldn't really louse up any day for me."

"I'm sure you'll give me credit for trying," Rachel said. "Pop, I'm sorry. I didn't mean that."

What made him sorry was that the second half of her one-two punch should be a lie.

"When are you coming home, chicken?"

"Pop," Rachel said. "I *am* home."

For a couple of moments he thought the roaring sounds were inside his head. Then he realized the phone had gone dead. Dave jiggled the hook. The operator came on.

"Can I help you?"

"I was talking on an overseas call," Dave said. "We were cut off."

"I'm sorry, sir," the operator said. "If you'll give me the information I'll try to get your party back."

What could a telephone operator do in a few moments that he had fallen flat on his face trying to do for more than twenty-six years?

"On second thought, operator," Dave said, "never mind, thank you."

He hung up. He stood there, his hand resting on the phone.

A few moments went by before he realized he was trying to remember his morning schedule. What came next? It was, he realized, one of the penalties of touching the sixty mark.

Until 59 plus 364/365, the balls came in across the plate without pause. The action from the mound kept the batter going. There were always too many things that had to be done, and too little time in which to do them. So you did them all by making the time.

Then the needle on the gauge jumped to sixty, and you realized the time was no longer yours to make. Others were doing it for you. Others were standing at the plate, swinging at what came over. You no longer had to worry about whether any of the pitches would be missed. You had put together a good team. You had sent only the best hitters to the plate. You could watch them doing it. You had built yourself the vantage point from which to do the watching. For you it was bench-warming time.

"Up yours," Dave said.

Then asked himself: was this a way to talk to God?

Why not? Why should He do all the talking? Dave Dehn knew the answer to that. He had learned it on an April day in Germany almost thirty years ago. God did all the talking because that was the limit of His responsibility. Answers were your job.

As he wondered all at once how well he had done the job, Dave's mind was suddenly invaded by his wedding day. And the man who had married him. Judge Martelli. Dave could see again the little old man who had looked like a rhesus monkey. Patting Bella's thigh on the couch beside him. While his white-haired wife, in the dress decorated with beaded calla lilies, pattered about with a tray of small glasses. Urging on her visitors the rum she and His Honor had brought back from Haiti. The real voodoo.

All at once Dave was not standing at the window of his bathroom up in Beechwood. All at once he was standing beside Judge Martelli at the window of the apartment high over upper Broadway. Looking down toward the Paramount Building.

"Long ago, when I was a kid from Mulberry Street with a shoeshine box," Judge Martelli had said. "I made up my mind someday I was going to live where from my window I could look out and see the face of the Paramount clock."

He had made it. Judge Martelli had certainly sounded as though he believed he had made it.

Twenty-eight years later, seeing the little old man again inside his head, Dave could hear Judge Martelli's voice. Dave had heard it originally as a sound of quiet triumph. He realized now that he had missed something. The first time around Dave had missed in the little old man's voice what he could hear now on the replay: the tremor of terror.

Judge Martelli had expected the satisfaction of achievement. He had not expected to get, along with it, an astonishing question from left field: Could he have spent all those years in a better way? What was so great about seeing from your easy chair the face of the Paramount clock?

Dave looked at his own Paramount clock. It sat on the tower of the Beechwood Town Hall down on Main Street. Beyond the checkerboard of neatly laid-out lawns and tree-shaded houses and the Jews who lived in them. Jews who had been brought to Beechwood by Dave Dehn. Jews who had bred more Jews. They had changed the town. No. Dave Dehn had changed the town. Why?

For a moment he couldn't remember, and then like a physical blow the sense of urgency came back to him.

He remembered it now.

He stood there shaking with the savage recollection. The grim knowledge that, in the beginning, had not been grim. The knowledge that he had to live long enough to do it. The welcome belief that he had to do it in order to survive. The exhilarating awareness that with his bare hands, if nothing more efficient was available, he wanted to kill every fucking German on God's green earth.

The feeling was suddenly as alive now, on his sixtieth birthday, as it had been when he was thirty. Rachel's words had brought the banked fire back to roaring life. The intensity of the flame hurt.

When had it gone underground? Why had it come out of hiding?

Dave turned, as in moments of stress he always turned, to the only man he had ever been able to respect without qualification. What would his father have said to help him now?

"Never sire a daughter five minutes before you break her mother's nose."

The line between wisdom and smart-aleckry suddenly seemed as thin as a John Held, Jr., flapper. Dave's father had been too wise to say anything so witless. And if his father's son had any of that wit left he would pretend it was yesterday. When he had not yet touched the sixty mark. When Dave Dehn, at 59 plus 364/365, had still known what he had known every day of his life since he had come home from Germany twenty-nine years ago: what to do next.

He crossed to the closet, pulled out his sweat shirt, and went downstairs to the gym.

Artie Steinberg had set the routine of Dave's morning workout soon after the young doctor had come to live in the compound. Artie's work in the Army had been mainly with heart cases. He had brought to Beechwood his discharge money, which went into the down payment on his house, and a number of theories about how to make people live longer. These went into ears that were rarely attentive.

"The toughest kind to deal with are people like you," he said to Dave when Artie checked him out for the first time. "People who believe they are going to live forever."

"Where did you get that idea?" Dave said. "It never crossed my mind I'm going to live forever."

"It doesn't have to," Artie said. "You believe it. Any trained observer can see that."

"What can you see?" Dave said.

"A great big healthy human machine," Artie said. "The

kind about whom people say he never had a sick day in his life."

"I never have," Dave said.

"That's not going to prevent you from someday having just one," Artie said. "And that one may be enough. Chronic invalids and hypochondriacs don't die suddenly. Their bodies and their psyches are conditioned to take an endless series of aches, pains, disturbances, blows, all kinds of symptoms real and fancied. When something really real hits them, every cell in their bodies is geared to ride with what seems just another punch. So they ride with it, and survive for the next punch. The guys who never had a sick day in their lives, however, guys like you, they get a sprained ankle or a hangnail and the experience is so new and unexpected that what you could say is no more than the shock of surprise, it kills them."

"You telling me I'm going to die from a hangnail?" Dave said.

"You might," Artie said. "Unless you start doing something now, when anybody but a doctor would say you don't need it."

"Need what?" Dave said.

"Some regular exercise," Artie said.

"Don't start with the golf and the tennis," Dave said. "Just the sound of the words bores the ass off me."

"That's one way to lose weight," Artie said. "Regular physical exercise is a better way."

"I'm fat?" Dave said.

"Not yet," Artie said. "But sure as God made little green apples you're going to be before long unless you do something about it."

"Do what?" Dave said.

Artie told him. That had been in 1949. For the next quarter century, every morning, it had been fifteen minutes of calisthenics, including knee bends and push-ups; a mile in the gym on the overhead track; and twenty laps in the pool. What had started as a chore he sought to avoid had become for Dave a pleasure to which he looked forward.

At that hour of the morning, except for Mr. Zwilling, the custodian engineer, Dave had the building all to himself. The knowledge soothed him as he jogged around the track.

On this morning, during his third lap, Dave became aware that he was not alone. Before he could break stride for a look behind him, a voice rapped out a warning.

"Track!"

Dave pulled toward the rail. A figure in running pants and a sweat shirt came up beside him.

"Happy birthday," Artie Steinberg said.

"Thanks," Dave said. "If you do this for all your patients on their birthdays you'll be the one who will soon develop the impression you're going to live forever."

"There are mornings when I feel I already have," Artie said. "How does it feel to be sixty?"

"You know what would be a nice refreshing question on a morning like this?" Dave said.

"What?" Artie said.

"If someone asked me how it feels to be sixty-one."

"I'm saving that question for next year," Artie said.

"If I make it," Dave said.

"You'll make it," Artie said. "I just told a girl named Renata Bazeloff you would."

Dave did not exactly falter. Jogging had become so much a routine that he was able to maintain his pace without thought. But Dave was aware that he had to take a longer stride to catch up with the few inches Artie's remark had caused him to lose. Half an hour ago Fanny had planted in his mind the uneasiness about *Mitzvah*'s interest in him. Sid had nourished the uneasiness into fear with his offer to accompany Dave to his lunch with Miss Bazeloff at the City Club. Now Artie Steinberg, merely by mentioning her name, had exploded the twelve-thirty meeting into something Dave felt as terror.

"You know our rules," he said. "It is forbidden to talk with girl reporters in the men's locker room."

"Actually," Artie said, "I talked with Miss Bazeloff in my bedroom."

"Was Betty there?" Dave said.

"Of course," Artie said. "She always answers the phone in our house. How did you know Miss Bazeloff is a reporter?"

"She told Fanny, and Fanny told me, and then Fanny told Sid, and then Sid told me, and now it seems that nobody in this place has been telling me anything else for several, no for dozens, of long, long, long weeks," Dave said. "To hold my interest, Artie, you'd better come up with something newer than the fact that Miss Bazeloff works for a magazine called *Mitzvah*."

"I haven't talked with Fanny or Sid this morning," Artie said. "So if I repeat some stuff they told you, you will forgive an old Jewish country doctor. Miss Bazeloff, however, did not sound like the sort of girl who asks the same questions twice."

Dave wondered what she would ask David Dehn, and if he would be able to answer.

"She must have asked you some pretty hot ones," Dave said. "To get you off your ass and out of the house and into a pair of running pants at this hour of the morning."

"Actually, she asked only one question," Artie said.

"What was that?" Dave said.

"She wanted to know how you're feeling," Artie said.

"I wonder how she broke out of the rut of asking how it feels to be sixty," Dave said. "What did you tell her about how I feel?"

"I said as your doctor I couldn't tell her anything specific," Artie said. "She'd have to get that information from you. But I did tell her I thought you're in great shape."

"Thanks," Dave said.

"Did I tell her the truth?" Artie said.

"You ought to know," Dave said.

"I ought to, but I don't always," Artie said. "There are things go on inside people that don't always show up on thermometers and X-rays and blood-pressure gauges. I remember in medical school, the man who taught us gynecology, he said it's not enough for a doctor to know the human anatomy. It was also important, he said, for a gynecologist to know and take into consideration the fact that people fall in love."

Dave wondered what Artie's professor would have said about people who fell in love not with another person but with an obsession.

"Yes," Dave said. "I think you told Miss Bazeloff the truth."

"Let's check it out," Artie said.

He slowed to a walk. So did Dave. They moved up the incline to the locker room. Artie went to the south wall, opened his locker, and pulled out the little black bag.

"Sit here," he said.

Dave straddled the bench. Artie sat down facing him and wrapped the flat gray sleeve around Dave's biceps. Artie pumped it full of air. He kept his eyes on the gauge as he eased out the air. Artie did it three times, then leaned back on the bench.

"Dave," he said. "What are you worrying about?"

He was a small man. Smaller than Sid Singer. With a face that in repose must have been very appealing. Dave's uncertainty was due to the fact that he had never seen Artie Steinberg's face in repose. He was always worrying about his patients. They became his patients with the first visit. Even if they moved away to distant climes, or went on to some other doctor who sang a more soothing siren song. Artie Steinberg could never get out of his head what he took in with his eyes. His life was an endless worry about human beings who were on their way out of life.

"Yesterday you were one eighty over ninety," Artie said. "Today you're one eighty-five over ninety-five."

"Is that bad?" Dave said.

"With your history," Artie said, "it's not good." He hesitated. Then: "Dave, what are you scared of?"

It was Dave's turn to hesitate. Then he realized it was Artie

Steinberg facing him on the bench. It was all right to say it out loud.

"What I've done with my life," Dave said.

"I don't know any man who's done more with the years he's had," Artie said.

"It's not what I've done," Dave said. "It's what I've left out."

"The way I read history," Artie said, "nobody gets it all done."

"Probably not," Dave said. "But it would annoy me to die before I finish the job."

43

What job?

As he eased the Cadillac out of the parking lot behind the Center into the early-morning stillness of Turkey Hill Road, the unexpected question caused Dave's toe to come down hard on the brake. The car shuddered to a stop.

For a few moments he was hopelessly lost. He did not know which way to turn. Left toward Saul Street for Marian Singer's breakfast blintzes? Or right toward Beach Road for Lola Truscott's common sense?

The choice didn't seem to offer much hope. He wasn't hungry: he didn't want food. He wasn't riding a flight of fancy: he didn't need common sense.

What Dave wanted was an answer. To the question his mind had flashed in his path like an unexpected red light at an intersection. What job?

The job that had brought him to Beechwood, of course. Twenty-eight years ago. With rage in his heart. And a vision in his head. Knowing exactly how he intended to spend the remaining years of his life.

What had brought Dave's foot down on the brake, however, was not the question. What had stopped him cold was the arithmetic in which the answer was embedded.

The remaining years of his life?

"They're behind you, stupid," Dave said aloud.

Whatever years he'd had ahead of him when he came to Beechwood, those years had been spent. All of them. All the good ones, anyway. Give or take the few that might still remain to a man on 750 milligrams of Aldomet daily, with a blood-pressure reading of one eighty-five over ninety-five. For the second time that morning Dave's father's words came back to him.

"You're young and you're young and you're young. Then one day you look in the mirror and you realize you're not young any more."

This second time around, the words cast a different light. As though the mirror had been jostled in Dave's hand. Now it showed him more than the crow's-feet gathered at the corners of his eyes, more than the crepe sack in the sag of skin at the throat. It showed Dave Dehn something about which he once would never have believed he'd have to be reminded. It showed him what it had been like in the beginning.

At thirty-one, when he had come to Beechwood, he had been coming to the Matto Grosso. Now he was sixty, standing in the same place onto which twenty-eight years ago he had parachuted. The place where with savage confidence he had started to swing his machete at the jungle growth.

Dave looked to his left and then to his right. Up Turkey Hill Road and down. The jungle growth had become a vast lattice of TV antennas and a forest of outdoor clotheslines. The ominous shadows that had once darted threateningly through the fetid gloom had become a Disney world of diapers flapping in the sunlit breezes from Long Island Sound.

Dave waited for the feeling of revulsion. It did not come. So he knew the nature of his trouble.

He had come here as a young man. Carrying in his heart something hard and bright and good. Fixed like a diamond in a sense of purpose as inflexible as a platinum setting. Dave remembered the sweet tang of the inner fury, the excitement the secret rage had brought to every waking moment. He remembered being so alive it had hurt.

The pain was gone. What hurt now was its absence.

Dave took his toe from the brake and moved it to the accelerator. To hell with the blintzes. He turned the car down toward Beach Road.

Reaching it had once been an irritating, time-consuming, roundabout business. All the way down to Main Street; east to the blinker beyond Fowler's Funeral Home; sharp right going south toward the Sound; around the statue of the Minuteman into Beach Road; then back west to the Metuchen gateposts. Dave had corrected all that.

Soon after Lola Truscott had deeded the Metuchen place to the Center, and she took over active management of the drug-rehabilitation program, Dave had fixed it. He had cut a two-lane black-top driveway down the hill from the western end of the Center compound to what had then still been the service entrance to the Metuchen property. He had walked that road many times. Eight to ten minutes, depending on the weather. This morning, however, he was not in the mood for what Lola insisted her husband had always identified as shank's mare.

Dave's life had not been spent exclusively with the Ludwig Leversons of the world. Lola Truscott was not the first honest person Dave Dehn had ever known. She was merely the first honest person Dave Dehn had known who was honest the way decently made fudge ripple ice cream is honest. Good goods layer after layer all the way down the line. Lola Truscott was honest in small as well as large things.

She had refused, for instance, to have her name placed on the signs at the front and rear entrances to the Metuchen property.

"This whole enterprise is the Bella Biaggi – Beechwood Jewish Center," she said when Dave had brought her Mike's sketch for the bronze plaques Dave wanted to put up on the gateposts. "My contribution is an old house and a few acres of older land. I bought them for very little and I did not really want them until you came along. In exchange I have been given more than I deserve. The right to stop opening tins of Campbell's Pepper Pot that never get eaten and the opportunity to do something nature never gave me a chance to do. Raise some children. Not out of the cradle, of course, but out of the gutter is just as satisfying. Maybe more so. Keep bringing the children who need help and keep my name off the plaques."

Dave had respected her wishes. Every time he brought the Cadillac into the turnaround behind what had been the Metuchen green house, however, he saw her signature all around him the way the visitor to St. Paul's saw the signature of Sir Christopher Wren.

This morning it took the form of two of Father Boyle's young priests. They were supervising the gravel-raking detail. Being what Father Boyle called good young men, they set a good example. Their cassocks were tucked up to their knees to avoid the dust. They wielded their green metal leaf rakes with more vigor than most of the boys they were supervising.

"Good morning, Mr. Dehn," one of the priests called. "Happy birthday to you, sir."

"Thanks," Dave said.

He wished he could remember the young man's name, but Dave knew there was no point in trying. Years ago, soon after Lola had brought Father Boyle into the project, Dave had learned that to him all young men in cassocks were like all Chinese. He couldn't tell them apart.

"Really your birthday today?"

Getting out of the car Dave saw the speaker.

"Really is," Dave said to the wiry little black boy.

"What number?" the boy said.

"Sixty," Dave said.

"Man!" the boy said.

"What's your number?" Dave said.

"Dunno," the boy said.

"Yes, you do, Gregory," the other young priest said. He stepped across the small hill of gravel he had been raking out of the edges of the pachysandra bed. "We had a birthday party for you yesterday," he said. "Mrs. Truscott baked the cake herself."

"That my party?" the boy said.

"Of course it was your party," the priest said.

The boy shook his head in wonder.

"Man!" he said.

"Tell Mr. Dehn what number," the priest said.

"Dunno," the black boy said.

"Yes, you do," the priest said. "How many candles did Mrs. Truscott have on the cake?"

"Dunno," the boy said.

"Close your eyes and count them," the priest said.

The boy folded both hands on top of the rake, rested his chin on his laced knuckles, and closed his eyes.

"One, two, three, four, five," he said aloud. Then his voice died away, but the boy's lips continued to move. Finally, opening his eyes, the boy said with a giggle of delight, "Fawteen!"

"No;" the priest said. "Thirteen."

"They wuz fawteen candles," the boy said. "Ah see them in mah haid. Ah see them right now."

"That's true, Gregory," the priest said. "But you were thirteen years old yesterday. The fourteenth candle, Mrs. Truscott put that in the middle of the cake for the one to grow on."

"Man!" the boy said.

"How was the cake?" Dave said.

"Man!" the boy said.

"Think there's a piece left over for my birthday?" Dave said.

"Certainly not."

Dave turned with the priest and the black boy toward the kitchen window.

"That cake was for Gregory," Lola Truscott said. "It was his birthday, not yours. Now you come around to the front door and stop interfering with the gravel detail."

She pulled her head in the window.

"Got to go, Gregory," Dave said. "Boss's orders. Happy birthday."

"Thank you, suh," Gregory said.

The priest leaned over and whispered in the boy's ear.

"Yes, suh," Gregory said. He raised his voice and called after Dave, "Happy birthday, Mistuh Dehn!"

It wasn't, of course. Not any more. But Lola didn't have to know that. Dave shifted facial gears.

He was smiling when he came clumping up the steps of the front porch. She was waiting for him in the open doorway. She limped out onto the porch and took his hand. Her own smile sank back into the lean, strong face that the years had made leaner and stronger, and more beautiful.

"Something's happened," Lola Truscott said.

"No," Dave said.

Then he remembered the lesson she had taught him long ago without ever making him sit down and fold his hands on a desk in a classroom. If there was one person with whom you were always honest, the lies you had to tell other people sounded more convincing.

"Yes," Dave said.

"Don't tell me," Lola said. "Not for a moment."

She led him into the house and closed the door. They walked through the hall, past the bulletin boards and posters, into the small room on the right. It had been the Metuchen butler's pantry. With a desk, a chair, a typewriter, and a green metal filing cabinet, she had converted it into Mrs. Truscott's office. With the black-marble-topped Empire table and the cluster of silver-framed pictures from the house on Magruder Crescent she had made it Lola Truscott's place.

"I wanted you to see this first," she said.

On the table, in front of the picture frames, a small cake sat in one of the Center's thick crockery soup plates. The cake was shaped to resemble a can of Campbell's soup. It was a good resemblance. What made it almost a replica was the lettering in chocolate around the red and white icing: "Pepper Pot." On top, in a circle, around the single candle, the lettering read, "Happy Birthday Dave." Lola Truscott struck a match and touched it to the candle.

"Blow," she said.

Dave blew.

"Did you make a wish?" Lola said.

"Of course," he said.

"Then it will come true," she said.

"It can't," Dave said.

"Why not?" Lola said.

"It already happened," he said.

"When?" Lola said.

"Twenty minutes ago," Dave said.

"Rachel called," Lola said.

He didn't bother to ask how she knew. Why waste time? After twenty-six years Lola Truscott knew as much about him as his father had known. No. Lola knew more. Dave's father had died before Buchenwald. Before the bad things had started to happen to his son.

"She called from Elat," Dave said.

"What was your wish?" Lola said.

"That she hadn't," Dave said.

Lola Truscott turned to the coffee percolator behind the desk. She poured two cups.

"My husband Hector used to say never drink anything standing up," she said. "Your feet are not the place you want the stuff to reach."

Dave laughed. She smiled. He felt better. Sitting down in the chair beside her desk, Dave wondered what he always wondered when he was in her presence. What could a woman of this caliber have seen in a horse's ass like Hector Truscott?

"I'm not going to ask you something I'm sure you've been asked quite a few times already this morning," she said.

"You're the only person I wouldn't mind telling how it feels to be sixty," Dave said.

"You don't have to," Lola said. "Eleven years ago, when I

was sixty, I remember all the answers I gave to friends who asked."

"You were never sixty," Dave said.

"Ask Fanny Mintz," Lola Truscott said. "We're exactly the same age."

"I don't want to do any more talking to Fanny today," Dave said. "She'll start telling me all over again about a girl named Renata Bazeloff."

"Fanny doesn't know the things I know about Renata Bazeloff," Lola Truscott said. "So what I tell you won't be repetitious."

"My God, you too?" Dave said. "Does this Miss Bazeloff make a career of haunting people on their sixtieth birthdays?"

"Only if they're Rachel's father," Lola Truscott said.

Dave stopped slouching back in the chair. He sat up straight. He took a sip and set his cup on Lola's desk.

"Okay," he said. "Tell me."

"You don't know Miss Bazeloff," Lola said. "But you once met her father."

"Mordecai J. Bazeloff," Dave said. "J for Judah. That time when you and I met. Ludwig Leverson and his Organization for American Judaism. After you got old Ludwig off my back the Lessing Rosenwald bunch got into the act and they sent a committee up here to Beechwood to see me. As your husband Hector would undoubtedly have said, this Bazeloff was a boy who would never set the Thames on fire."

Lola Truscott laughed.

"Since this is your birthday," she said, "I'm going to give you a little present. It's disloyal of me, but after all these years I feel you've earned the right to know that Hector was really quite a dim bulb, modeled after Mr. Toots in *Dombey and Son,* who never could have said anything as witty as that."

"Neither could I," Dave said. "I remember it from something we had to read in school. *Pendennis,* I think."

"Anyway," Lola said, "I'm sure you can see how, out of that background, when Mr. Bazeloff's daughter grew up the one thing she wanted to do was go to Israel and work on a kibbutz. What better way to make her father squirm? Mr. Bazeloff screamed as well as squirmed, but Renata went to Israel and that's how she met Rachel. They've been living on the same kibbutz for almost two years."

"She's home on a visit?" Dave said.

"No," Lola Truscott said. "Miss Bazeloff is home for good."

"Fed up?" Dave said.

"I don't think so," Lola said. "I get the impression of a very strong, very ambitious girl. I think she went to Israel the way Lady Mary Wortley Montagu went to Persia. As an experience, to pick up something she could later peddle, and now she's come home to peddle it."

"Why can't Rachel do that?" Dave said.

"Rachel's experience has been somewhat different from Miss Bazeloff's."

"I take it you and Miss Bazeloff have talked?" Dave said.

"A few minutes ago," Lola Truscott said. "She called to tell me she was coming over from Greenwich to have lunch with you at the City Club. Ludwig Leverson had told her I knew you quite well, so she wondered if I could tell her anything about you that might help her."

Dave's curiosity took an odd turn. Once, during the war, his C.O. had asked him to choose six men for a job that required the usual amount of muscle but also a certain amount of intelligence. Dave had been given a batch of personnel files from which to make his selections. By mistake the clerk had included in the bundle of files Dave's own biographical sketch. He remembered the funny feeling it gave him to read the blunt sentences never intended for his eyes.

"What did you tell Miss Bazeloff?" he said.

"I told her the only thing that could help her in an interview with you is not to be ugly," Lola Truscott said.

Surprised, Dave said, "Is that true about me?"

"The only ugly woman I've ever known you to like is Fanny Mintz."

"Oh, well, Fanny," Dave said.

"Exactly," Lola Truscott said.

"Did Miss Bazeloff say why she wants to see me?" Dave said.

"She's got a job with this new magazine *Mitzvah*," Lola Truscott said. "Or rather, she's got the promise of a job. Her father is one of the magazine's financial backers, and he got the editor to give her a chance. She was quite honest about confessing she's totally inexperienced. She's never worked on a magazine before. In fact, she's never written anything professionally. To put it bluntly, and Miss Bazeloff did not hesitate to put it bluntly, she is a rank amateur, which is why this assignment is so important to her. She suggested it herself. For obvious reasons, of course—her friendship with Rachel.

"The editor, she informed me, snapped at the suggestion. He told her not to worry about her inexperience. To let herself go was the way she put it, because being an amateur, she says the editor said, would enable her to come up with things a professional writer might dismiss just because of their obvious amateurishness. This struck me as being not unlike calling in a professional hockey player to look at your toothache because his approach to the complexities of the human mouth are bound to be different from that of a trained dentist. Nevertheless, the lady apparently has carte blanche to do anything she wants in the way she wants to do it. If the editor likes what she does he will put her on the staff in a permanent post.

"I have no way of knowing what Miss Bazeloff will come up with, but from the way she sounded on the phone I have a feeling her manuscript will be unlike any her editor has ever seen, conceivably unlike anything the world of journalism has hitherto ever seen. Which is another way of saying the editor may feel his obligation to Miss Bazeloff's father will have been discharged by giving her this chance and he will feel free, if the stuff is awful, to chuck it in the waste-basket. So I don't think your lunch with Miss Bazeloff at twelve-thirty is anything for you to worry about."

"I'm not," said Dave. Which was an odd thing to say, since he had been worrying his head off about it since Fanny had called him an hour ago. "What I meant was about Rachel," he said. "You said Rachel's experience on the kibbutz was somewhat different from Miss Bazeloff's. That's the real reason she called you, isn't it?"

"Yes," Lola Truscott said.

"That means she's got news to break to me," Dave said.

"Yes," Lola Truscott said.

She knew what he knew: good news reached its destination unaided. Bad news had to be broken.

"Tell me," Dave said.

"Rachel has just had a baby," Lola Truscott said.

"When is just?" Dave said.

"Six weeks ago," Lola Truscott said.

"Son of a bitch," Dave said. "She was on the phone twenty minutes ago. Why the hell didn't she tell me? Happy birth-day she tells me. Some happy. She's sitting on a piece of news like this and instead of telling me she kicks me in the teeth. What the Christ did I ever do to deserve that kind of—?"

The ugly sounds coming out of his mouth shuddered to a stop the way the Cadillac had ground to a halt on his way out of the Center parking lot. Pause. Then the enraged thumping of his heart seemed to shift gears. The thing hesitated, hung motionless in his chest, then walloped off in a new direction.

"Oh," Dave said.

He touched the brake gently. His heart slowed down.

Then, quietly: "There's trouble?"

"Only if you make it," Lola Truscott said.

Another pause.

"Does Rachel know who the father is?" Dave said.

"Good Lord, yes," Lola Truscott said. "They've been liv-ing together for a year and a half."

Dave gave himself a moment. Then it was all right. That

part of it didn't matter. That part of it was okay. He eased his toe toward the accelerator. He let his heart go.

"Boy or girl?" he said.

"Boy," Lola Truscott said.

The laugh came out of him in a roar. Lola Truscott smiled.

"I had a feeling Rachel's display of intelligent common sense in having a boy as her first child rather than a girl would please you and make up for a lot of other things in the past," she said.

"It sure does," Dave said. "I struck out with a daughter. Maybe I'll get me a hit with a grandson."

Lola Truscott's laugh matched his own.

"I take it it's all right, then?" she said.

"If I may quote your husband Hector," Dave said cheerfully, "it's the cat's pajamas."

44

The City Club was one of the few structures on Main Street that had not changed since Dave Dehn first arrived in Beechwood. Only someone who had known the club twenty-eight years ago, however, would have been aware of this. Dave was intensely aware of it. He had a very clear recollection of Main Street on the day he first saw it.

The Club had towered impressively between a one-story Bohack's on the west and a Texaco filling station beyond the Club parking lot on the east. As the community Dave had started on Turkey Hill Road spread out from the original Biaggi property into all parts of Beechwood, and the population of the town doubled and trebled, property fronting on Main Street had gradually become too expensive to be used for parking space. The City Club had sold off its two hundred feet of Main Street soon after Bohack's had sold out to a New York developer with whom Sid Singer had worked out a profitable participation deal for himself and Dave.

As a result, visitors to the City Club now had to drive through a lane that cut in from Main Street to a new parking lot behind the Club. The Club itself no longer towered. It sat like a neat little white clapboard sugar cube between the huge Sequesta Shopping Center on the west and the eight-story Babington-Dehn Office Tower on the east. Aaron Coker's old home had not changed since General Howe had spent an uneasy night in it in 1776. It had merely been sandwiched in between a couple of million dollars' worth of progress.

"Counting your rents?"

Slamming the Cadillac door, Dave turned toward the voice. Colin Babington was coming out into the parking lot from the side entrance of the Babington-Dehn Office Tower. At ninety, he seemed smaller than when Dave had first met him, but his step was still firm and his voice was still irritating to the ear.

"Hi, Colin," Dave said. "No, I let Sid Singer do all my counting. He doesn't have to use his fingers. What I was looking at, that thing up there."

Dave pointed to something that resembled an enormous asparagus spear on the edge of the cornice.

"What are they doing to our building?" he said.

Colin Babington turned to follow Dave's finger, then laughed and turned back.

"I shouldn't tell you," Babington said. "It's a surprise. But you and your insatiable curiosity, you'll keep asking everybody you run into, and somebody is bound to let the cat out of the bag, so I might as well tell you. It's an anchor for a banner. At five o'clock, when the crowd starts to gather at Town Hall for the banquet, a banner will be stretched across Main Street between that anchor on top of our building and another one like it across the street on top of the Equitable Life Building, and guess what it will say?"

"Keep Cool with Coolidge!" Dave said.

"You aren't old enough to remember that," Colin Babington said.

"I'm sixty," Dave said.

"That's what the banner will say," Colin Babington said. *"Happy Sixtieth Dave."*

"If you ask me what it feels like to be sixty," Dave said, "I won't come to your banquet."

"I remember distinctly what it feels like to be sixty," Colin Babington said. "So come on in and let me buy you a birthday drink. There's something much more important I want to ask you."

He took Dave's arm and started steering him across the parking lot.

"I can't have a drink with you," Dave said. "I'm meeting a reporter inside for lunch. But I'll answer anything except how you and I got to own an office building together. I haven't figured that out yet."

"Neither have I," Colin Babington said. "That's why I asked Lola."

"About this eight-story slab of reinforced concrete behind us?" Dave said.

"Not directly, no," Babington said. "What I wanted to ask you was do you remember that day you and Sid first came to see me? When my office was down the street? In the old Paternoster wheelwright shop?"

"Nineteen forty-six," Dave said. "Sid had made the deal with you to buy the Biaggi property, and I'd come up with him from New York for what we thought was going to be the closing. You hit us with that stuff about Bella's grandfather had just died, and she was his sole heir, so she could no longer sign for him, but she'd have to sign for herself, and she couldn't do that until the estate was probated. That about it?"

"Except for one thing," Colin Babington said.

"What's that?" Dave said.

"You accused me of refusing to close the deal because you said I didn't want a Jew buying property in Beechwood," Colin Babington said.

"Was I wrong?" Dave said.

"No," Colin Babington said.

"Then what's your question?" Dave said.

"That was 1946," Colin Babington said. "Today, twenty-eight years later, we own an office building together, and I'm stretching banners across Main Street congratulating you on your birthday. How come?"

Dave stopped at the foot of the wooden steps that led up to

414

the Club entrance. How come he had once wanted to kill every fucking German on the face of God's green earth?

"You asked Lola the same question?" Dave said finally.

"Word for word," Colin Babington said.

"What was her answer?" Dave said.

"Lola said you came to Beechwood to take something out of this town," Colin Babington said. "Instead, you stayed and put something in."

"Most Jews do," Dave said.

Babington gave him a funny look.

"I'm going to tell that to Lola," he said.

"She probably knows it," Dave said.

"I daresay," Colin Babington said. "She knows everything else there is to know."

At the top of the steps the doorman tipped his forefinger to the visor of his cap.

"Mr. Babington," he said. "Mr. Dehn."

He held the door for them. Dave and Babington went through.

"I notice," Dave said, "whenever we come here together he always greets you first."

"Seems only fair," Colin Babington said. "After all, I was the one who put you up for membership."

He took the pipe from his mouth, touched the stem to Dave's shoulder, and walked off to the men's room. Babington had told Dave a month ago that Artie Steinberg had put him on a diuretic.

"Mr. Dehn, sir. Happy birthday."

"Thanks, Paul," Dave said.

"Your table is ready, sir," the headwaiter said.

Dave followed him across to the booth in the corner. Dave didn't like that booth. Sitting in it cut off part of his view of the bar. In a restaurant, Dave had learned long ago, the thing to keep your eye on was the bar. That was where the action started. But the corner booth was in Paul's opinion the most desirable table in the Club. He always held it for Dave. His feelings would have been hurt if Mr. Dehn had asked to sit anywhere else. As he pulled out the table, and dipped over it to make sure Dave slid in properly, Paul's head came close to Dave's ear.

"Miss Mintz is very anxious to reach you, sir," he said quietly.

"When did she call?" Dave said.

"An hour ago, sir."

Dave glanced at the mahogany grandfather's clock near the door. It showed exactly twelve-thirty. Fanny had told him she would make the reservation for twelve-thirty. She knew he was punctual. It was not like Fanny to waste time leaving a message a full hour ahead of his arrival when she knew that by calling at twelve-thirty sharp she could talk to Dave directly.

"I'll bring you a phone, sir," Paul said.

"Not right now," Dave said. He pushed the table back. "I'll just go along to the men's room first."

"Very good, sir," Paul said, holding aside the table he had just pushed into place.

"I'm expecting a lady," Dave said. "I won't be long. Give her a drink."

"Yes, Mr. Dehn."

Dave walked back across the room. Someone tugged his sleeve. He stopped and turned.

"When I achieved the sixty marker, my boy," Father Boyle said, "I abandoned the youthful practice of walking swiftly. At sixty, David, you will find people are willing to wait for you. A gloriously happy birthday to you, my boy."

"May I echo that with all my heart," said the Very Reverend Hamish Flyte.

"Thanks, gentlemen," Dave said. "You shouldn't be seen lunching together like this in a public place. If Rabbi Vogel hears about it he'll demand equal time."

"I did, and I got it."

Dave turned. Perry Vogel had appeared at the table.

"Hey, what is this?" he said. "A *minyan*? Happy birthday, Dave."

"Thanks, Perry," Dave said. He shook hands with the three men while the waiter pulled out Rabbi Vogel's chair. "Is this the proper setting for an ecumenical congress?"

"It is if you want to get the proceedings under way with a decent lubricating draught of Irish whiskey," Father Boyle said. "What we're plotting and planning is the order of speakers at the banquet in your honor tonight. So make yourself scarce, my boy."

Dave laughed and waved and moved on to the foyer. Coming around the mahogany gate he bumped into Colin Babington coming out of the men's room.

"David," he said, "by the time I rise to say a few words in your honor tonight I will be tired of your face."

"I promise to stay out of your way until then," Dave said.

He moved across the foyer, past the men's-room door, and stepped into the phone booth. The headwaiter came out into the foyer.

"Your table is ready, Mr. Babington."

Colin Babington came up to Paul Zwingli and looked into the dining room.

"I think I'll skip lunch today," Colin Babington said.

"Anything wrong, sir?" the headwaiter said.

"Too many God-damn Jews in there today," Colin Babington said. He turned and walked out of the Club.

Inside the phone booth Dave dialed his switchboard.

"Biaggi – Beechwood Jewish Center, good morning."

"Shirley, it's me," Dave said. "Give me Miss Mintz, please."

"She's not in her office, Mr. Dehn."

Until five years ago Dave's next question would have been "Something wrong at home?"

The question was no longer available to Dave. Fanny's parents had died on the day of Nixon's first inauguration. Both went within an hour. As though they had made a pact. A decision that the time had come to deal their final blow to the humpbacked little creature whose life had consisted of the constant absorption of their endless blows. Poor Fanny. To the world at large hers had been a dreary life.

Poor Fanny my ass, Dave thought. He knew that in the place where it mattered most, the place the world could not see and did not suspect existed, Fanny's life had glowed with a beauty of which the people who pitied her, or were revolted by her, or never thought about her, had been deprived. The poor slobs were not even aware of their deprivation. They would spend their days carrying around their lovely profiles and sexy figures, showing off to the world the outward trappings of what, in the arena of conspicuous consumption, passed for happiness.

For so many years Fanny had constantly rushed back from the room outside Dave's office to the house in Saul Street to give her father the spoonful of medicine he refused to take from any other hand, or adjust the wheelchair pillow behind her mother's head because the old lady felt the housekeeper had decided that day to hate her. Then, with the death of her parents, the inner fire had gone out. Fanny still had the office, but she no longer had a place to which she could go from the office. At night Dave or Mrs. Spiegelberg, the librarian, had to hound her out of the Center to go home.

Dave could understand why Fanny now worked almost around the clock. What was waiting for her in the house on Saul Street? Peace? Quiet? Rest? Fanny Mintz had lived her life on the edge of a volcano called love. What was she to do with the empty pain of peace?

"When she left the office, Shirley, did she say where she was going?" Dave said.

"No, she didn't, Mr. Dehn."

"Try her at home."

"All right, Mr. Dehn, but please don't hang up."

A short time later Shirley came back on the wire.

"No answer," she said. "But Mr. Dehn?"

"Yes, Shirley?"

"I hope you don't think I'm, well, I'm not like you'd say squealing?"

Shirley Sternshus was the youngest daughter of the first successful graduate of the Center's drug-rehabilitation pro-

418

gram. Ernie Sternshus had made it. As a result, his devotion to the Center and its programs would have put Abélard's feelings for Héloïse in the category of a Hallmark greeting card. Each of Ernie's three daughters, on her graduation from Beechwood High, spent a year as a volunteer on the Center's switchboard before she went on to college. The word squealing in relation to Shirley Sternshus struck the ear like the word embezzlement in connection with St. Francis of Assisi.

"Shirley," Dave said, "cut it out. If you've got anything to tell me, please tell me."

"Yes, Mr. Dehn. I'm sorry. It's just you know how Miss Mintz is. She doesn't like people gossiping."

"If what you've got to tell me is gossip," Dave said, "skip it. I'm trying to find Miss Mintz."

"Yes, sir," Shirley said. He could see her drawing a deep breath for the plunge. "Right after the staff meeting this morning, Mr. Dehn, around about a quarter to ten, she went out. I happened to be coming in to work, so I saw her driving out of the parking lot in her Chevy."

What else would she drive out in? It was the only car Fanny owned. But Dave did not give voice to the irritated observation.

"Probably going back to Saul Street for breakfast," Dave said.

Although he didn't believe it. Fanny always had her breakfast before she arrived for the nine-o'clock staff meeting.

"That's what I thought," Shirley said. "So I didn't think any more about it. Then later, about an hour and a half later, it was about a quarter after eleven, she came back. I saw her go past the switchboard into her office. She was in there about fifteen minutes. Around eleven-thirty she came out and she gave me a message for you and she went out again."

"Where?" Dave said.

"She didn't say, Mr. Dehn."

"What's the message?"

"I don't know," Shirley said. "It's in a sealed envelope. Should I open it and read it to you?"

Dave did not hesitate.

"No," he said. "I'm coming right over to get it."

He hung up and stepped out of the phone booth, into the arms of Rocky Riordan.

"I was across the street, up on the Equitable Life Building," the police chief said, "watching them put up the anchor for that birthday banner they're hanging for you across Main Street, when I saw you and Mr. Babington go up the steps into the Club. So I told the boys not to drop the anchor on any taxpayers, and I came over to wish you a happy birthday."

"Thanks, Rocky." They shook hands. Dave said, "How's Mariacruz?"

"Fat but happy," Rocky said.

"That's the way to be," Dave said.

"Not necessarily," Rocky said. "You're about the happiest man I know and you look the way you looked when I first met you in 1948. Like Gary Cooper, Mariacruz says."

"Mariacruz never saw Gary Cooper after he lost his hair," Dave said. "You tell her if she wants me to start wearing a rug, for her I'll do it."

"She said if I run into you," Rocky said, "to say happy birthday for her too."

"Tell her thanks."

"Anything I can do for you on your Number Sixty?" Rocky said.

"As a matter of fact there is," Dave said. "I'm expecting a girl reporter for lunch, but I've just discovered I have to run over to the bank for a few minutes. You mind going in there and telling Paul when the girl comes to tell her I'll be back in a few minutes?"

"My pleasure," Rocky said.

He went through the wooden gate into the restaurant. Dave went out to the porch, down the steps, and around through the lane to the parking lot. The Center clock showed twelve forty-five when he came into the main hall. He crossed to the switchboard.

"Here it is," Shirley said.

She poked an envelope through the square hole in the sheet of glass that shielded the switchboard operator from drafts.

"Thanks," Dave said. "I'll be in my office."

He turned away as he ran his thumb under the pasted-down flap of the envelope and tugged it open. He pulled out a sheet of Center memo paper. On it, in Fanny's handwriting, were two words: "Matto Grosso."

Dave's mind stopped, then jumped. He turned back to Shirley.

"I'd better go upstairs first," he said. "I don't suppose Miss Mintz has come back yet?"

"No, Mr. Dehn."

"Well, give her another try at home, and ring me."

"Yes, sir."

The phone was ringing when he came into the apartment.

"No answer at Miss Mintz's home," Shirley said.

"Okay, thanks," Dave said. "If she comes in, or if you hear from her, let me know, will you?"

"Yes, sir."

Dave hung up. Carrying the sheet of paper, he crossed the living room to the *Britannica*. He dipped down and pulled out the same M volume. He didn't have to turn to "Matto Grosso." The heavy book fell open at the proper place. On the page with the Matto Grosso entry lay a legal-size Center envelope. The pasted-down flap bulged crookedly. There was more in the envelope than it had been built to carry. Dave tore it open and pulled out a fat batch of Xeroxed sheets. Clipped to the top of the batch was a page of Center memo stationery, like the page on which Fanny had written the words "Matto Grosso." On this second sheet she had typed:

To: D.D.
From: F.M.

After the staff meeting this morning, when I couldn't get you on the car phone, I decided to drive over to Greenwich and see

Miss Bazeloff in her friends' house. We had a talk. I told her you had asked me to see her before your lunch so that if there were any papers she wanted you to bring along I could dig them out of the file. Miss Bazeloff said she had a first draft of the piece about you that she plans to submit to her editor at *Mitzvah*. I asked her if I could read it. She said yes, and she gave me the attached Xerox. I read it in her presence, then asked her if I could take it back to Beechwood with me, since I was sure you would not only want to read it before you met her for lunch but I felt equally sure there were some things you'd want me to dig out of the file for you to take along and show her. Miss Bazeloff thought this was a good idea, so I brought her Xerox back, and here it is.

Fanny

P.S. I don't think you should go to lunch until you read this carefully. Even if it makes you late for lunch. The lunch is secondary. Besides, Miss Bazeloff will wait.   *F.*

Dave stood up. He slipped out of his coat and dropped it on the couch. Carrying the batch of Xeroxed pages, he walked out into the bathroom. He sat down on the edge of the tub, so that he had a clear view of the Sound, and he started to read.

45

TO: Milton Magid, Managing Editor
FROM: Renata Bazeloff
RE: First Draft, David Dehn piece

MR. AMBASSADOR?
By
Renata Bazeloff
(MITZVAH Staff Writer)

*WILL THE MAN FROM BEECHWOOD BE OUR NEXT
MAN IN JERUSALEM?*

Asked this question last week at his Tuesday press conference,
the Secretary of State smiled owlishly and said, "The answer to
that inquiry is not yet operative."
So this reporter decided to try for an answer on her own. I
was impelled by more than the journalist's lust for truth. My cre-
dentials for the quest are unique.
I have been hearing about David Dehn ever since I was a child
in Philadelphia, where my father helped Ludwig Leverson to establish the Organization for American Judaism.
After I graduated from Radcliffe I went to Israel as a volun-   ⸱
teer. I worked for two years on the kibbutz Ichud Givat Haim,
north of Elat, where I came to know an American-born girl
named Rachel Cohen. We became good friends, and exchanged
a great many confidences about our backgrounds. Originally, I

learned, she had been Rachel Dehn, but Rachel rarely spoke about her real father.

Ordinarily, this would not have been surprising. After all, I don't go around speaking about my father. The reason is simple. Nobody asks me. My father is not a famous man. David Dehn's fame, while very special, since it is pretty much limited to Jewish circles, is nonetheless very real.

It is an underground fame, the way the fame of Christiaan Barnard was for many years underground. In medical circles it was known for a long time that something significant was happening in South Africa, but the public remained unaware of it until heart-transplant operations hit the front page.

Similarly, in Jewish circles it has been known for a long time that something significant is happening in Beechwood, N.Y., but the general public is still unaware.

If the answer to the question asked of the Secretary of State last Tuesday becomes operative, David Dehn will hit the front page. The public will want to know about him. It is the hope of providing some enlightenment that caused *Mitzvah* to send me on this quest.

It seemed sensible to start with the subject himself. It did not occur to me that it would be difficult to arrange an appointment. After all, David Dehn is not exactly besieged by requests for interviews in national magazines. Aside from pieces in Beechwood's local paper, the *Bugle*, almost nothing about him or his activities has ever appeared in print. So I put in a call to his headquarters, the Bella Biaggi – Beechwood Jewish Center in Beechwood, N.Y.

I won't say I got a runaround. But I didn't get Mr. Dehn, either. I got his confidential assistant, Miss Fanny Mintz, who has sat outside his door, fending off the curious, since 1947, when Dehn's operation in Beechwood got under way. She asked why I wanted to see her boss. I told her. Miss Mintz said she would call me back.

She did. Three days later. She was sorry for the delay but Mr. Dehn was off on a speaking tour and she'd had difficulty tracking him down. I know something about speaking tours. When I was a child my father was constantly going off on them, talking it up all over the country on behalf of the Organization for American

Judaism. It never took my mother three days to track him down. Not since the long-distance telephone call was invented.

"Now that you've located Mr. Dehn," I said, "When can I see him?"

"I'm not sure," Miss Mintz said.

"Why not?" your reporter said.

"He's going up to Toronto in the morning," she said. "He has to give a speech on drug rehabilitation to a group of Canadian businessmen at the Empire Club of Canada, and then he's flying to Brussels for a zoning conference. He'll be back in Beechwood on Thursday, but only for a few hours because he's due in Dallas for a U.J.A. dinner that night, and the next day he speaks in Mexico City before the Pan-American Union. On his way back he'll be stopping overnight in Washington, possibly for two nights. The President wants him to sit in on a trade discussion with the Israeli Purchasing Commission. It will be at least a week, probably eight days, before Mr. Dehn will be back in Beechwood. May I call you then?"

"No," your reporter said. "I've decided to do a bit of traveling myself, and I'm not sure just where I'll be from day to day. I'll call you a week from tomorrow."

Your reporter has not made that call yet. I am saving it for the end of this article. It occurred to me that as long as I could not see Mr. Dehn for eight or nine days it might be a good idea for me to see some people who know him and find out what they think of him and his work. It seemed to me this would give my actual interview with Mr. Dehn a sense of culmination, a feeling that the man I finally face has been photographed for me from many different angles, and my job will take on for the reader some of the excitement of fitting a real man into a number of rough sketches. With luck I could come up with a rounded portrait. I checked out this plan with my editor.

"Go to it," he said. "That's what *Mitzvah* is all about."

The first person your reporter went to see was Miss Merle S. Marine, who taught English at Ethan Allen High School in Albany, N.Y., when Dave Dehn was a student there from 1929 to 1933. Needless to say, Miss Marine is not a youngster. Seventy-seven her last birthday, she said, although she does not look it, and retired from teaching for more than a decade. Miss Marine is a spinster. She lives with her spinster sister in a large, comfortable, old-fashioned apartment on upper Broadway in New York City, three blocks from the statue of Alma Mater in front of Columbia University.

"Come to tea," she said.

And tea it was. In delightful old Wedgwood cups, with slices of the sort of seed cake spinster ladies are always serving to the vicar in Trollope novels. Miss Marine had baked it herself.

"Of course I remember David," she said in response to your reporter's query. "I was very young when I first started to teach. Not quite twenty-one. I worried terribly about the fact that I would forget all the boys who passed through my classes. It seemed shamefully wrong to spend six months or a year with a group of boys and then have them move out of your life forever. So I started to choose one boy out of every class to put in my memory book, so to speak. I didn't have to choose David. He chose himself. You couldn't forget a boy like David."

"Because he was so bright?" your reporter said.

"No," Miss Marine said, "although he was bright enough. What made David memorable for me was that he was bright in so many different areas, but nothing held him for very long. I remember, for instance, in English Four, when we were studying the drama. I used to assign plays to the class. The boys would read them at home and then we would discuss them as a group in class. David became interested in Bernard Shaw. He read every one of Shaw's plays, including the prefaces, and he used to talk to us about them in an absolutely fascinating way, but then he abandoned Shaw."

"For some other playwright?" your reporter asked.

"No, for photography," Miss Marine said. "The most important thing about David was that he had a short attention span. He could learn anything overnight, but he couldn't stay with it. He learned all there was to know about Shaw, and then he lost interest. I always had the feeling that if David ever found a subject he could not exhaust, something that held his attention because he could dig into it deeper and deeper, he would make a great name for himself in that field. As I said, I've never forgotten him, but I've never heard about him, either. What line of work did he finally settle on?"

Your reporter told her. Miss Marine looked surprised.

"That's odd," she said. "I don't remember that he was ever interested in religion."

"Neither was Saul of Tarsus," your reporter said. "In his early years, I mean. It's the sort of thing that takes people at different times in their lives."

Miss Marine looked thoughtful. She seemed to be considering something in her mind.

"No," she said finally. "I don't see it."

"See what?" your reporter said.

"David Dehn and religion," Miss Marine said. "A person can come to God late. I'll grant you that. But there must be something in the person that makes him receptive to taking God into his heart when the appropriate time comes. It's been many years, of course, but David has remained sharp in outline to me. I can still see him very clearly. I see the intelligence, I see the impatience. But I don't see the warmth. Or rather, I don't feel the warmth, and it seems to me that's essential to a religious vocation. A feeling for the other human being. For people in general. A sense of compassion. In fact, now that we're talking about it, I think I see what drew David to Bernard Shaw. He was obviously attracted by Shaw's brilliance, but I see now that David must have been drawn also by Shaw's total lack of sentimentality. I think Shaw would have liked David," Miss Marine said. "The David I knew, anyway."

Morris Cohen is not so sure.

Mr. Cohen now lives in Tel Aviv. He is a native New Yorker who came to Beechwood shortly before Pearl Harbor and set up shop as an architect under the name Michael Palgrave. In 1946 he was chosen by David Dehn for the job of building the structure that later became known as the Bella Biaggi – Beechwood Jewish Center. He also laid out the housing development to which Dehn converted the old Biaggi onion farm. What was originally a purely business relationship developed into a warm friendship. So warm, in fact, that when Mrs. Dehn was killed in an automobile accident shortly after the Dehn's only child was born, Mr. and Mrs. Cohen legally adopted the infant girl, with Dehn's consent, and raised her in their own home.

"Dave has done a wonderful job over there in Beechwood, of course," Morris Cohen said to your reporter in his Tel Aviv office. "But I don't think it's a job he set out to do."

"Could you explain that?" your reporter said.

"When Dave arrived in Beechwood in 1946," Morris Cohen said, "he was a pretty terrifying guy."

"You mean terrifying as in terror?" your reporter said.

"Not in the Dracula–Bela Lugosi sense," Morris Cohen said. "I mean in the real sense. Dave Dehn when I first met him was a man with a furious vision. He had been with the Third Army when Buchenwald was liberated. The experience gave a direction to his life. You could say it turned him from a technical Jew into an aware Jew. He decided to build a community that would be a training ground for a new breed of Jew. A Jew who is not afraid was the way Dave put it. A Jew who would never have committed suicide at Masada but would have fought to the death with his bare hands, killing Romans until he was himself killed. Dave didn't talk about it. He just went ahead with his plans. Soon after he retained me, and I began to spend real time with him, I realized this was not a run-of-the-mill, smart-ass, bing-bing real estate developer. Before long I grasped the general direction in which he was moving. When we became friendly he laid it out for me. At first it was scary. I mean, it was an unusual passion to encounter in a sunny little Westchester commuting town. Like discovering a kindergarten kid crossbreeding the family poodle with a cobra in the rumpus room. But Dave has a tremendous gift for conviction. He's not an orator. He's a doer. And what he does has hair on it. You become aware of him not the way you become aware of someone through a spray of cocktail-party chatter. You become aware of Dave Dehn the way you become aware of the internal-combustion engine when you get hit by a truck. What Dave believes he makes you believe. It didn't take me long to come aboard."

"You are no longer aboard," your reporter said.

"No," Morris Cohen said.

"Why did you abandon ship?" your reporter said.

"Because it's no longer the same ship," Mr. Cohen said. "Dave has fallen for the same thing most American Jews have fallen for."

"What's that?" your reporter asked.

"The belief that the battle is won," Morris Cohen said. "It's an easy thing to fall into. We've got Israel. We own these lovely air-conditioned homes up there in Westchester with kidney-shaped swimming pools and garages with electronic-eye doors. The Dow-Jones index has broken a thousand. We get invited to the Babingtons' annual Fourth of July party. Nelson Rockefeller eats blintzes on Grand Street. It says in Leonard Lyons' column Jennie Grossinger twice a month air-mails kosher salamis to Buckingham Palace. Our sons have no trouble getting into American medical schools. Our daughters work in the Paris Office of *Vogue*. A Jew from Westerlo Street in Albany can get into the City Club on Main Street. What's there left to fight for?"

"You tell me," your reporter said.

"A vision," Morris Cohen said. "Once Dave Dehn had it in his heart. Now he's got a birthday banquet coming up in the Beechwood Town Hall."

"Isn't that better than anti-Semitism?" your reporter said.

"The two are not mutually exclusive," Morris Cohen said. "American Jews believe anti-Semitism has disappeared because that's what they want to believe. They've lost what Dave Dehn has lost."

"What's that?" your reporter said.

"The character it takes to stick to a strict diet of spiritual weight watching," Morris Cohen said.

"What do you believe?" your reporter said.

"The bastards are waiting," Morris Cohen said. "The way they've always waited."

"For what?" your reporter said.

"For the Dave Dehns to grow fat," Morris Cohen said. "When the Dave Dehns can't get it up any more the bastards will jump us again."

Rocky Riordan doesn't put it that way.

Mr. Riordan came to Beechwood in 1944, a sixteen-year veteran of the Los Angeles police force. Today, at sixty-seven, he has been Beechwood's Chief of Police for thirty years. He looks the part. Tall, broad-shouldered, flat-bellied, a two-hundred-and-seventy-five pounder with crew-cut white hair and a pleasant but guarded smile who looks as though he had been poured into his olive gabardine tunic. His wife, Mariacruz, a California girl whose parents were born in Guadalajara, is a Mexican beauty four years younger and two pounds heavier than her husband.

"I have no complaints," Rocky Riordan told your reporter. "This town has been good to me."

"It hasn't been bad to me either," Mariacruz said. "As you can tell from my shape. When we got here from Los Angeles and we moved into this house here on Spinning Wheel Lane, two of our kids were in nursery school and the third was just beginning to walk. Now we're building an extra wing so nobody will be crowded when the kids bring the grandchildren for Christmas. I attribute it all to Mr. Dehn."

"My wife believes civilization is moved forward only by good-looking men," Rocky Riordan said. "This guy who invented penicillin? You know who I mean. Fleming his name is? Right. Well, if it should turn out he didn't have a profile like John Barrymore and muscles like Maxie Baer, Mariacruz would never touch the stuff again. She'd go back to iodine."

"Why not?" Mariacruz said. "Mr. Dehn took this town when it was a village and the police chief earned fifteen thousand a year, gross. Today Beechwood is a city and my husband's take-home pay is almost thirty thousand, net. Mr. Dehn did that. He did it all. That Mr. Dehn, he has *cojones*, if you know what I mean."

"All *Mitzvah* staff writers worship at the shrine of Hemingway," your reporter said.

"I'm not knocking him," Rocky Riordan said. "But Mariacruz has what you might call an oversimplified view of how things work. Sure, Beechwood was once a village and now it's a pretty busy little city, junior grade. And it's true the growth of Beechwood has all taken place during the twenty-seven years David Dehn has been throwing his weight around in it. But who knows? Suppose he'd never come to Beechwood? Does that mean the place would have remained a sleepy little village full of New York commuters?"

"I came to you, Mr. Riordan, with questions," your reporter said. "Not answers."

"Okay," Rocky Riordan said, "here's an answer. I think without David Dehn this town would be just about where it is now. Places are like kids. You treat them right, the chances are they'll grow. These last thirty years, you couldn't treat a place like Beechwood wrong. The country growing fast. Everybody making money even faster. The cities like New York stuck with their stupid boundaries and those cockamamie streets you can't expand and make wider. It was inevitable the crowding would force people into the suburbs. When you start looking for suburbs, naturally you look for the good ones before you settle for the bad ones, and there's nothing forty minutes from Madison Avenue that can touch Beechwood. It was bound to prosper no matter who did the wheeling and dealing. In Dave Dehn this town has been lucky. His wheeling and dealing has been different from most I've known, like out in Los Angeles, say, where you start off by assuming everybody you meet is a crook, and most of the time that's a very sound assumption. The thing that makes Dave Dehn different is that it wasn't money he wanted. What he wanted was a place that's good for the Jews. By working for what he wanted, and by getting it, a lot of other people got it too. That's the plain and simple a, b, c of it."

"Here's the d, e, and f," Mariacruz said. "Other Westchester towns have prospered. Never mind the rest of the country. Let's just stick to us and our neighbors. They've got the nice homes too, and the good schools, and no ghettos or beggars. But they haven't got what we've got here in Beechwood, and you know it, Rocky. Let's take a couple of for instances. They've all got a drug problem. Beechwood hasn't. Why not? Mr. Dehn. He zeroed in on that when it first showed its head, and he licked it. Another thing, Beechwood is still the only place in this area, maybe even in the whole country, where people don't have to lock their doors at night. I'll grant you this is probably due to the fact we have a good police chief."

"Probably she says," Rocky Riordan said.

"Okay, let's say undoubtedly," Mariacruz said. "But why is it undoubtedly due to the fact we have a good police chief? Because the prosperity Mr. Dehn brought to this town made it possible for Beechwood to pay its Chief of Police thirty thousand a year, take-home."

"All right, all right," Rocky Riordan said. "Let's not knock ourselves out going down the whole list, including the Bella Biaggi – Beechwood Jewish Center scholarships, available to all kids, regardless of race, color, creed, or previous condition of servitude. We know all that, and it's all good. But basically what it is, Miss Bazeloff, is this. Mr. Dehn came to Beechwood to do something for the Jews. He was all set to take on a bunch of tough anti-Semites. When he found they weren't so tough, Mr. Dehn was surprised, but he didn't stop. He's that kind of guy. Once he sets himself in motion he keeps going. He kept on working for what he wanted for the Jews, and in the process what he wanted for the Jews slopped over on the Catholics and the Protestants and the cigar-store Indians. I say hooray to all that, but I also say that doesn't mean Mr. Dehn is a happy man."

"How can he be unhappy?" Mariacruz said.

"Honey baby, you give any man a chance to work at it for a while and he'll figure out a way," Rocky Riordan said. "You're the chief cop in a place, you get to know things other people don't know."

"What things?" your reporter said.

"This off the record?" Rocky Riordan said.

"Completely," your reporter said.

With crossed fingers.

"Mr. Dehn is a prick," Rocky Riordan said.

"Now, look, Rocky," Mariacruz said.

"You look," Rocky Riordan said. "This is something I know about. I learned it walking a beat in L.A. and working a patrol car in places like Watts. For thirty years I've applied what I learned out there in that lousy jungle to what I've seen here in this sunny, healthy, happy town where you look at the pictures in the *Bugle* there's not a disease ever happens in Beechwood you can't cure it with a Band-Aid. People are the same the whole world over. A prick is a prick, in Watts or in Beechwood. David Dehn is a prick. A defused prick, at the moment, but a prick just the same."

"Defused?" your reporter said.

"You remember in the Bible this guy Samson?" Rocky Riordan said.

"His strength was in his hair?" your reporter said.

"That's the boy," Rocky Riordan said. "David Dehn reminds me of Samson. He was once the most powerful son of a bitch I ever met. Now he's just a guy taking bows."

"What happened?" your reporter said.

"His girl friend gave him a haircut," Rocky Riordan said.

"In the Bible," your reporter said, "Samson's girl friend was Delilah."

"In Beechwood her name is Public Citizen Number One,"

Rocky Riordan said. "That's what I meant when I said David Dehn is a defused prick. They cut his hair."

"If I get your drift," your reporter said, "you're saying he's basically a bad person?"

"You got it," Rocky Riordan said. "David Dehn is a bad person who for purely selfish reasons decided to do good. He did it, and up here in Beechwood we all benefited, but that doesn't change what he is. A bad person."

"Does it matter?" your reporter said.

"At the moment, no," Rocky Riordan said. "But moments go like they come. Fast, when nobody's looking. If things change up here in Beechwood, if it's no longer in his selfish interests to do good, David Dehn will go back to doing what he was doing before he came to Beechwood. You can take it from an expert, what he was doing before he came to Beechwood was not good."

"Are you advancing a theory?" your reporter said. "Or do you have any proof?"

"I don't have any proof personally, but there are plenty of people who have," Rocky Riordan said. "You can bet your ass on that."

Fortunately, your reporter had no time to adopt Mr. Riordan's suggestion. Your reporter had an appointment with Miss Helen Drake in apartment 2-B at 163-24 Seventy-third Avenue, Kew Gardens Hills, Flushing, N.Y. 10067.

Your reporter's first impression of Miss Helen Drake was puzzling. She seemed relaxed to the point of torpor, but one could hear something ticking inside the lady.

"It's very good of you to see me," your reporter said.

"Tell me what you want," Miss Drake said.

So much for the amenities. Your reporter was not surprised. When Miss Drake had been approached for this appointment her first reaction was a flat refusal. The day before the appointment was requested, however, your reporter had spent the morning at the Immigration and Naturalization Service in Washington. When this fact was conveyed to Miss Drake on the phone she changed her mind about the appointment. Not, however, about her attitude toward it. She received your reporter in her Kew Gardens Hills apartment with nothing that could be described as enthusiasm. It seemed sensible to warm her up a bit.

"Miss Drake," your reporter said, "I think it would be a good idea if I tell you what I know before I start asking you to tell me what you know."

"If you like," she said coldly, "but I have nothing to tell."

"You might take yourself by surprise," your reporter said. "To begin with, I learned in Washington your real name is not Helen Drake. Your real name is Hella Drachenfels. You were born in Bremen, Germany. During the war you were employed as a member of the secretarial staff to the commandant at Buchenwald. According to the file at the Immigration and Naturalization Service, your duties included more than typing and stenography. Just before the Allied armies liberated Buchenwald you disappeared underground. The word underground, according to your Washington file, is a figure of speech. In actual fact you were for seven months a prostitute in Bremen. Through British Army connections made in your new line of work you succeeded in getting to London, where you worked as a manicurist in the barbershop at Selfridge's and became a naturalized British subject. Your contacts widened and before long you were working in the hairdressing salon on the *Queen Elizabeth*. Am I going too fast for you?"

"When I want you to slow down," Hella Drachenfels said, "I will so state."

"To continue, then," your reporter said. "One of your London contacts introduced you by mail to a man in New York named David Dehn. You went to see him and entered into a business relationship with him. Mr. Dehn was interested in collecting souvenirs of Buchenwald. Because of your job on the *Queen Elizabeth*, which carried you back and forth regularly from Europe to New York, you were able to bring these things to him. Before long, and again I quote from the Washington file, the relationship between you and Mr. Dehn became more personal. In fact, he was directly responsible for your success in obtaining a permanent resident's visa in this country. In 1950 you moved into this apartment here in Queens. When you signed the lease you used the name Helen Drake. Correct thus far?"

"Do not interrupt yourself," Hella Drachenfels said. "If any interruptions are necessary I will make them."

"In 1953 the German War Crimes Commission asked the U.S. State Department for your extradition," your reporter said.

434

"They wanted you to stand trial in Germany along with other Buchenwald employees for atrocities committed while you were working at the concentration camp. Mr. Dehn intervened. The immigration authorities are not quite sure how he did it, but he had contacts on upper levels in the U.S. Government, and one fact is a matter of record. At just about this time you and Mr. Dehn were married in secret. This fact apparently was conclusive so far as the Washington people with whom he had intervened were concerned. The German request for extradition was refused. A year later you became an American citizen. You have lived here in Queens ever since as Helen Drake, but in fact you are still Mrs. David Dehn. Have I left anything out?"

"Not enough to matter," said Hella Drachenfels that was.

The silence that followed provided your reporter with an opportunity to note that Miss Drachenfels must have been a great beauty. In her fifties she is still very handsome in a Gabor sort of way. This is not a bad way for a woman to be handsome.

"You are going to print this in your magazine?" Hella Drachenfels said finally.

"Yes," your correspondent said.

"It will hurt Mr. Dehn," she said. "It cannot hurt me. Not now. It all happened many years ago."

"I would not advise you to count on it," your reporter said. "Your Washington file is not closed. It is marked Pending. What we print in the magazine will change that. We will see to it that our information is placed before the proper authorities. We will also make sure that our story is passed on to our correspondent publication in Germany. The renewal of the request for your extradition to face a war-crimes trial is a certainty. It has happened before. You would be a fool to assume it will not happen again."

"I am not a fool," Hella Drachenfels said.

"I did not think so," your correspondent said.

"What do you want?" Hella Drachenfels said.

"Information," your correspondent said.

"About what?"

"David Dehn."

"What kind of information?" Hella Drachenfels said.

"Mr. Dehn's background," your reporter said.

"You know so much about me, a foreigner," Hella Drachenfels said. "Surely you know all there is to know about one of your own compatriots."

"I know a good deal," your reporter said. "There is one point, however, on which I need your help."

"And if I provide it?" Hella Drachenfels said.

"Then you will receive my help," your reporter said.

"How can I be sure of this?" Hella Drachenfels said.

"You can't be," your reporter said. "All you can be is sensible."

There was a pause. This middle-aged Gabor-type German beauty examined your reporter as though she were trying to guess my weight. It is, by the way, an unfluctuating 106 pounds.

"All right," she said finally.

"Good," your reporter said.

"State, please, what it is you want to know," Hella Drachenfels said.

"Where Dave Dehn got his front money," your reporter said.

"What is front money?" Hella Drachenfels said.

"When David Dehn was drafted into the United States Army in 1941," your reporter said, "he was twenty-seven years old. He was working as a piece-goods clerk in a large Seventh Avenue dress-manufacturing firm. He was doing fine, just beginning to make it, but in a very modest way. Four years later, in the fall of 1945, Mr. Dehn was discharged from the Army. He rented a business office on Madison Avenue with a lawyer who was his old friend and classmate, Mr. Sidney Singer. It has never been quite clear just what business or businesses Mr. Dehn and his partner Mr. Singer were engaged in. The only things that are clear are on the record. In 1946, one year after he got out of the Army, Mr. Dehn, through his partner and lawyer Mr. Singer, offered three hundred and thirty-five thousand dollars for an onion farm up in Westchester. The money was never paid because before the offer could be accepted Mr. Dehn married the owner. He thus had the use of the property without paying out the three hundred and thirty-five thousand dollars. In the next three years, however, from the fall of 1946 to the end of 1949, Mr. Dehn spent approximately three million dollars converting that onion farm to a housing development. Some of this money has been traced to a variety of business ventures, speculations, and stock-market transactions in which Mr. Dehn and Mr. Singer were involved during this period. Nobody, however, has ever been able to trace the initial amount with which Mr. Dehn and Mr. Singer went into business soon after they got out of the Army. They were penniless young men when they went into the U.S. armed forces. They came back from Europe with more money than most people ever earn or even see in a lifetime."

"They did not come back with it," Hella Drachenfels said.

"Would you clarify that?" your reporter said.

"Mr. Dehn and Mr. Singer left their money in Switzerland," Hella Drachenfels said.

"You are talking about their Army pay?" your reporter said.

"Do not be foolish," Hella Drachenfels said. "I am talking about money."

"How did Mr. Dehn and Mr. Singer earn that money?" your reporter said.

"Sums of that magnitude," Hella Drachenfels said, "one does not earn."

"How does one get such sums?" your reporter said.

"One steals," Hella Drachenfels said.

"From whom?" your reporter said.

"The German army," Hella Drachenfels said.

"When Mr. Dehn and Mr. Singer entered Buchenwald with the U.S. Third Army in April of 1945," your reporter said, "the German army no longer existed."

"Not as a unified command, no," Hella Drachenfels said. "But there were still fragments, and each fragment was no longer fighting for the Fatherland but for whatever it could preserve for itself. No fragment fought harder than the S.S. They knew they were finished for the moment, but there was always tomorrow. It was for tomorrow, for after the war, that they tried to get the money out of Germany."

"What money?" your reporter said.

"Free funds," Hella Drachenfels said. "Large sums were fed regularly to the S.S. for what was known as morale operations. Nobody except the S.S. knew what that meant. But everybody knew the sums involved were vast. American intelligence knew it. So did the British and the French and the Russians. They all tried to track down those funds, to prevent the S.S. from moving the money secretly into Swiss banks. Among the people who helped in the tracking were Mr. Dehn and Mr. Singer."

437

"There is no record in their Army files that they were assigned to this work," your reporter said.

"Because they were not assigned to it," Hella Drachenfels said. "Mr. Dehn and Mr. Singer stumbled into it."

"How?" your reporter said.

Hella Drachenfels shrugged.

"The number of ways is limited only by the ingenuity of the men involved," she said. "I knew several British officers who stumbled into the same flow of outgoing money. Once they stumbled into it, the money stopped flowing into the S.S. bank accounts in Switzerland."

"Where did it go?" your reporter said.

"Into private bank accounts in Switzerland," Hella Drachenfels said.

"Mr. Dehn's account?" your reporter said.

"And Mr. Singer's," Hella Drachenfels said. "Among many others."

"Then Mr. Dehn and Mr. Singer were banking stolen money," your reporter said.

Hella Drachenfels shrugged again.

"Can you prove this?" your reporter said.

"I can document it," Hella Drachenfels said.

"How?" your reporter said.

"The number of people involved was not small," Hella Drachenfels said. "Many of them were high-ranking officers in the American and British armies. S.S. free funds were considered fair game. Mr. Dehn and Mr. Singer played the game better than most. Some of the other players were friends of mine. A few of them are still alive, British as well as American. Some of them are still my friends. If I were convinced it was worth my while I could direct you to them."

—30—

Dear Boss:

This is as far as I've taken the assignment. Tomorrow I am taking it a little further: a face-to-face meeting with David Dehn. I am going to let him read this piece as it now stands. I have worked out a closing section that should raise some eyebrows and land us more than a few readers. It is possible, however, that by his reaction to what I have already written Mr. Dehn may invent

438

a better closing section for us than the one I have planned. That depends, of course, on how he reacts to what I have uncovered. I imagine his defense will be that he used Nazi money to establish a haven for Jews in Beechwood. As I say, I imagine this will be his defense, but it is possible that my imagination is not active enough. Mr. Dehn may have other ideas. Men at bay do surprising things. At this stage, as I see it, only one thing is certain. Mr. David Dehn may well be the B'nai B'rith's next man in Leavenworth, but he sure as hell ain't gonna be our next man in Jerusalem.

Renata Bazeloff

There was, Dave noticed, a final page. He flipped to it. Another sheet of Center memo paper stared up at him. From it, in Fanny's handwriting, a short paragraph invaded the room like an order cut by the C.O. at h.q.

D.D.

Don't worry. Stick to your schedule for today as planned. Skip nothing, especially the banquet at the Town Hall tonight. You must be seen by everybody who expects to see you today. I will take care of the rest. *Don't, repeat don't, repeat again: DON'T WORRY.*

F.

Several moments went by before Dave realized the phone was ringing. Rachel would not be calling again from Israel. It had to be Fanny.

"Dave?"

It wasn't.

"Yes, Sid?"

"I just had a call from Rocky Riordan," Sid said. "He just had a call from the New York cops."

"All right," Dave said. "Tell me."

"Hella," Sid said. "She was shot and killed sometime this morning in her apartment in Queens."

Dave could feel it happen. Everything inside him coming together. Like iron filings slithering across a table to a magnet. Forming a barrier. A shield to hold off what the shield, which could not think, was unaware could not be kept away. But Dave was intensely aware. He could see the horror descending. But that was all he could do. He could not turn from the horror. He could not run. He could not even cower. He was immobilized in his own defeat. He could not move. All he could do was make his voice work. Just barely.

"No, not this morning," he heard himself saying. "I was not with her this morning."

"That's what the Queens doorman told the cops," Sid said. "Which is why I'm calling."

"Okay," Dave said. He sucked in air. "Sid," he said.

"Yes?"

"I didn't do it."

"I didn't think so," Sid said. "Who did?"

"You can figure that," Dave said.

"Not as well as you can," Sid said. "What's my next move?"

"Find Fanny," Dave said.

He hung up slowly. As though the telephone were an apple he had cracked into halves with a twist of his clenched hands. The problem now was to fit the two pieces together so carefully that the crack would not show.

He never made it.

Just before the phone reached its cradle, all sixty years of Dave Dehn's life came crashing down on him like a rockslide.

46

"You all right, sir?"

Dave moved his head. The source of the troubled question came into focus: a sight that brought with it a flicker of astonishment. He had not seen Rabbi Goldfarb since the day the old man had burned to death in front of the synagogue on Westerlo Street an hour before Dave's bar mitzvah. Thirteen from sixty. Forty-seven years ago.

"I'm fine," Dave said.

Except for Rabbi Goldfarb calling him "sir." Dave turned to push his body up on one elbow. The thrust of pain hurled him back like a blow.

Dave gave himself a couple of moments. He assembled the loose pieces darting about inside his head like sight cards in a quiz game. The pattern that emerged was more surprising than the pain.

"You're not Rabbi Goldfarb," Dave said.

"No, sir. I'm Abe Zwilling. The custodian engineer."

"What are you doing here?"

"You're not feeling good, sir."

"So I gather," Dave said. "Tell me why."

"Dr. Steinberg said it's your heart," Mr. Zwilling said. "He's gone over to Larchmont to get an oxygen tent."

"What's the matter with the telephone?"

"Dr. Steinberg felt it would be better to do it in person,"

Mr. Zwilling said. "A lot of things have happened, Mr. Dehn."

Yes, indeed. Yes, indeed. Dave's mind began to settle down. He turned it in the direction of the things that had happened.

"Did they find Miss Mintz?" he said.

"Yes, sir," Mr. Zwilling said.

Pause.

"Dead?" Dave said.

Mr. Zwilling cleared his throat.

"Okay," Dave said. "How did she do it?"

"Gas, sir," Mr. Zwilling said.

For years Dave had urged on her the advantages of a completely electrified kitchen. Fanny's parents, however, would eat nothing unless it was cooked on an open flame. Good for them, Dave thought. Gas was less painful. In the end they had found a way to repay her for something on which the tax gatherers had never been able to set a price: a lifetime of love.

"Where did Miss Mintz do it?" Dave said.

"The kitchen," Mr. Zwilling said.

"Here at the Center?"

"No, sir," Mr. Zwilling said. "Her own house, Mr. Dehn. On Saul Street."

Full circle. Why not? Neatness was her hallmark. She had never been untidy with her love.

"You know Mr. Singer's number?"

"Yes, sir," Mr. Zwilling said. "But he's not there, sir."

"How do you know?"

"He told me."

"Where is he?"

"The Town Hall," Mr. Zwilling said. "They've got this birthday banquet for you, Mr. Dehn."

"Don't ask me how it feels to be sixty."

"No, sir," Mr. Zwilling said.

"Mr. Singer told you what to do?"

"Yes, sir," the custodian engineer said. "Keep you quiet until he or Dr. Steinberg gets back."

"Either of them say how long that would be?"

"Dr. Steinberg thought about an hour," Mr. Zwilling said.

"Mr. Singer figured maybe a little longer. He's got to make a speech. Mr. Singer said the guests will be expecting you so he has to explain what happened without causing any, you know, any fuss."

Dave was sorry he would not hear that speech. Maybe Sid Singer would tell them something Dave now realized with astonishment he did not know: what had happened during the past twenty-eight years.

"You know Mrs. Truscott's number?" he said.

"No, sir," Mr. Zwilling said. "But it's in the Center directory."

It was in a more readily accessible place. Dave's head. He gave Lola's number to the custodian engineer.

"Get me Mrs. Truscott," he said.

It was never too late. If you knew what you wanted to do. Once he had known. Only once. In Germany. On that April day in 1945. But the knowledge had not worked out. What he had known had gone away from him.

Because he had taken on too much?

Maybe.

Because he had not been faithful?

Probably.

Only one thing was certain now: he could not take on too much any more. There was still enough time, however, for the one task that remained. There had to be. He would make the time.

He took the phone from Mr. Zwilling.

"David?"

"Yes," he said.

"I won't ask questions," she said. "I know all the answers. Sid called and told me."

"He didn't tell you what I want you to do."

"Tell me," Lola Truscott said.

Dave Dehn told her.

"I'll be there," she said.

He hung up.

"Anything I can do?" Mr. Zwilling said.

"Yes," Dave said.

"What?" Mr. Zwilling said.

"Get a sledge hammer."

"A what?"

"Don't ask stupid questions," Dave said. "Listen and get it right the first time. I haven't got any to waste. You're the custodian engineer of this place. You've got tools. You've got to own a sledge hammer. Go get it."

"Yes, sir," Mr. Zwilling said. He started for the door, then stopped. "Bring it here?"

"No," Dave said. "Take it to the northeast side of the building. The side that faces down Turkey Hill Road toward Main Street. Where we put the cornerstone."

"Yes, sir," Mr. Zwilling said. "What should I do when I get there?"

"Wait," Dave said.

"Wait?" Mr. Zwilling said.

"Wait," Dave said.

How he himself managed to get there Dave did not know. Nor did he care. He blacked out at least once. Maybe twice. It didn't matter. He got there. Mr. Zwilling was waiting.

"Jesus," the custodian engineer said. "You all right?"

"Of course not," Dave said. "Get going."

"Where?"

"The cornerstone," Dave said.

"What about it?" Mr. Zwilling said.

"Break it open," Dave said.

Mr. Zwilling had a few more questions. Dave did not remember them. What he remembered was the sound of the smashing blows. Mr. Zwilling swinging the sledge. And Mike Palgrave's double marble sheets cracking like glass. No. Morris Cohen's double marble sheets cracking like glass.

"Okay," Dave said. "That's enough. There are a lot of things in there. I want one of them."

The custodian engineer, on his knees, clawed about inside the hole. When he finished there was blood on his hands.

Scratches from the edges of the splintered marble. But Mr. Zwilling had found what Dave wanted.

"Now what?" he said.

"Carry it into the sanctuary," Dave said.

"What about you, sir?"

"Come back for me."

When Mr. Zwilling did, Dave's chest felt tight.

"Mrs. Truscott get here?" he said.

"She's waiting in the sanctuary," Mr. Zwilling said.

"Give me a hand," Dave said.

He seemed to gather strength as he moved. When they reached the sanctuary he was able to stand up straight in front of Lola Truscott. Mr. Zwilling moved to help him. Dave brushed him back. Nobody was going to help Dave Dehn put on his father's *tallis*.

"Light the candles," he told Lola.

She moved down the sanctuary to the raised platform. Dave could see the foot was bothering her. He was sorry about that. There was no time, however, to do more than record the sorrow. She snapped the switch. The electric candles came on.

"What do you want from me?" Lola Truscott said.

"An answer," Dave said.

"If I have it," she said, "you'll get it."

"What I did here in Beechwood," Dave said. "All these years. What I tried to do. Did I do the right thing?"

She hesitated. But not for long. She could not say what he wanted to hear. She had given him his groundwork in basic honesty. The teacher was trapped by her own lesson.

"I don't know," she said.

Having said it, she was free to add what the pupil was entitled to hear.

"Nobody knows."

"Nobody?" he said.

"Nobody," she said.

He drew a deep breath. She heard it whistle gently in his throat.

"You'll have to step down," Dave said. "Women are not permitted in the presence of the Torah."

Lola Truscott stepped down.

"Shmah Yisroel," Dave said to the ark.

He was pleased by the way he managed to get the words out. All of them. The words Rabbi Goldfarb had put together forty-seven years ago, for use in another synagogue.

For the final words Dave Dehn gathered himself and looked directly into the bulbs of the seven-branched candlestick. His eyes blurred. But his mind and his heart were suddenly clear.

All at once he knew the answers. There they were. In front of him. Alive with blazing clarity. Telling him what Rabbi Goldfarb's fiery death had meant on the sidewalk in front of the Westerlo Street synagogue. How the meaning had come alive in 1945 on an April day in Germany. What had happened during the twenty-nine years since that day. What he had left out. What still had to be done. How it would be done. Everything.

Dave felt it all. Even what he could not see. The answers of a lifetime were safely in his grasp. At long last he understood himself. He knew who Dave Dehn was. He saw clearly the importance of what Dave Dehn had done. And most important of all, he understood that the knowledge had to be passed on.

If it wasn't, what he had gone through, what he had been, all of it would be wasted. He could not let that happen. He had enough strength left to see that it did not happen. All he needed was a little more time.

Not years. Not months. No. Weeks would be enough. Or days. All right, then. Just a handful of hours. Or even minutes. Was that too much to ask? A few more minutes? Of course not. He had a right to ask. It was a right he had earned. He demanded it. His eyes lifted to the boy with the harp in the tent of the ancient king.

You hear? Dave Dehn demands the right to finish what he started. By passing on what he has learned. He is the only one who can pass it on. Please give Dave Dehn the scrap of time he needs to finish his work. Please.

The desperate words stopped struggling to break free. The tent of the ancient king was dark. Nobody was listening.

With his last breath Dave Dehn fell back on the words Rabbi Goldfarb had taught him. The words around which his father had built his life. They were all he had left.

"*Shmah Yisroel,*" Dave Dehn said to the ark. "*Ahdonoy Elohaynu Ahdonoy Echod.*"

Lola Truscott could see that he wanted to say more. She saw something else, however. He would not have time. Dave Dehn would never have any more time for anything. His luck had run out.

As she limped down the aisle toward him it occurred to Lola Truscott that the luck of Dave Dehn's neighbors was in somewhat better shape. Beechwood's time had not run out. Not yet. Used properly, the remaining time might still do the trick that the stranger in their midst had not quite managed. But the town could no longer count on help from Dave Dehn.

As of this moment Beechwood was on its own.